DEADLY
ALLIANCE

OTHER BOOKS AND AUDIO BOOKS
BY A. L. SOWARDS

Espionage

Sworn Enemy

DEADLY ALLIANCE

A WORLD WAR II NOVEL

A. L. Sowards

Covenant Communications, Inc.

Published by Covenant Communications, Inc.
American Fork, Utah

Printed in the United States of America
First Printing: April 2014

20 19 18 17 16 15 14   10 9 8 7 6 5 4 3 2 1

ISBN 978-1-62108-690-1

For Mom and Dad

May you always be blessed with friendship, love, and hope

ACKNOWLEDGMENTS

As with all my projects, this book involved more than just my efforts. I'm grateful for friends and family members who expressed their confidence in me when I wasn't sure I could write a book set in the Balkans during WWII.

I would like to mention a few people by name: Joseph, Melanie, Laurie, and Teresa, as well as writers Stephanie Fowers, Linda White, Terri Ferran, and Daron Fraley. Their help tightening the story structure and polishing the prose have made this a better manuscript.

I'd also like to thank Bradley and Lela for their help in acquiring some hard-to-find research books and the Goodreads World War Two Readers group for pointing me in the right direction when I was having a hard time finding the information I needed.

I'm grateful to my publisher, Covenant Communications, especially my editor, Sam. I'm hoping we'll work together on many additional projects. Thank you to Briana Shawcroft for creating a beautiful map of a complicated time and place.

I'd also like to thank my readers. Hearing from them (or finding reviews they've written) always makes my day.

USEFUL TERMS

Chetnik—Originally a general term for Balkan guerillas, but during WWII and for the purposes of this novel, the name refers to the Serb group led by Draza Mihailovich, which was loyal to the Yugoslav king and was usually at war with German, Partisan, and Ustaše forces

Feldwebel—Noncommissioned officer in the German Army; rank similar to a sergeant in the US Army

Gefreiter—Soldier in the German Army; rank similar to a private in the US Army

General-potpukovnik—Partisan officer; rank similar to a Lieutenant General in the US Army

Kapetan—Partisan officer; rank similar to a captain in the US Army

Kriegsmarine—German Navy

Luftwaffe—German Air Force

MI5—British Security Service; responsible for counterintelligence

MI6—British Secret Intelligence Service; responsible for foreign intelligence

NKVD—Soviet Secret Police from 1934–1953; responsible for foreign and domestic espionage

OSS—Office of Strategic Services; US intelligence and sabotage agency that operated from June 1942–January 1946

OVRA—Organization for Vigilance and Repression of Anti-Fascism; Italian Secret Police under Mussolini that operated from 1927–1945

Partisans—During WWII, there were irregular partisan forces fighting against Nazi armies in most occupied countries, but for the purpose of this novel, the Partisans were Yugoslavs following the Communist leader Josip Tito

Pukovnik—Partisan or Chetnik officer; rank similar to a colonel in the US Army

SOE—Special Operations Executive; British intelligence and sabotage agency that operated from July 1940–January 1946

Ustaše—A WWII group in Yugoslavia aligned with Nazi Germany and comprised of Fascists, anti-Communists, and Croatian Nationalists

reb

A RIVER

Hungary

Banat

DANUBE RIVER

dependent State
of
Croatia

Belgrade

DRINA RIVER

Serbia

BOSNIA

Sarajevo

ATIA

Split

Višegrad

Kragujevac

Kraljevo

HERZEGOVINA

Montenegro

Albania

ENLARGEMENT OF
VIS AND BISEVO ISLANDS

i

Brindisi

Vis

Komiža

VIS ISLAND

BISEVO ISLAND

CHAPTER ONE
HOW LEAVE WAS CANCELLED

Sunday, September 3, 1944
Bari, Italy

THE ADRIATIC SUN WARMED THE inside of the canvas tent to a temperature just shy of stifling. As Major Baker ended the debriefing, Peter Eddy fought back a yawn.

"Good job, men. Enjoy your leave."

Peter stood and stretched. He had enlisted almost three years ago but still loved hearing those words. The thought of leave was especially appealing since his girlfriend had somehow managed to show up at the same Italian base he'd been flown to earlier that morning. *Leave with Genevieve*—the anticipation was enough to distract him, for a moment, from the knowledge that Nazi Germany was not yet defeated, the war not yet ended.

Peter paused on his way out of the tent when Jamie Nelson's hand dug into his arm.

"Was that man sitting in the tent the entire debriefing?"

Peter glanced at the man Jamie was staring at, a British major with dark hair slicked back from his square face. "I think so. Why?" Peter hadn't paid much attention to the men on the back row, assuming they were present with Baker's permission.

"'By the pricking of my thumbs, something wicked this way comes,'" Jamie muttered under his breath as the major walked toward them. Jamie smiled and met the man halfway across the tent. "Phillip, old boy, delightful to see you again."

Peter suspected Jamie's friendliness was a show, but he shrugged off his curiosity, planning to ask Jamie about it later.

He followed Sergeant Moretti out of the stuffy tent and into the bright midday sun. A group of children were playing beyond a nearby fence. Moretti grabbed a handful of candy from his pocket and chucked it in their direction. "I swear these Italian kids can smell candy a mile away."

Peter checked his pockets, but they didn't contain anything edible. "Yeah, the Arab kids were like that too. Then their dads would act surprised when I didn't have any cigarettes."

Moretti pulled a Lucky Strike from his pocket and lit it. "Did you tell 'em why?"

"Naw, I don't speak Arabic." And Peter didn't think any of the English- or French-speaking Arabs had been interested in his religious beliefs.

"So how'd your girlfriend end up in Bari, sir?" Moretti asked.

"I'm not sure. I haven't heard the whole story yet."

Moretti raised an eyebrow. He had dark eyes and curly, dark hair. "You had over an hour to talk about it."

Peter held back a grin. "I guess our mouths were too busy for much conversation." They'd had seven weeks' worth of missed kisses to catch up on.

Moretti laughed as he found gum to toss to the clamoring children. He was muscular and agile, and like most American troops, he had a soft spot for kids.

"Do you know how long the paperwork takes for getting married over here?" Peter asked.

"Couple months, probably. Enough time to come to your senses."

Peter frowned at the answer but not because of Moretti's joke. "I was hoping it was more along the lines of a couple hours."

"Well, congrats on your engagement, sir."

The simple statement made Peter stop. They'd talked about marriage, but he hadn't actually *asked* Genevieve to marry him, had he? "You know, I don't think I got around to proposing."

Moretti laughed again, his deep rumble drawing glances from a few nearby soldiers. "All right, lover boy, our gear's in there." He pointed to a nearby tent, one of dozens along a dirt road. "Take your loyal sergeant's advice, and at least put on a clean uniform before you propose."

Peter glanced at his clothing—threadbare civilian articles meant to blend in with the population in war-torn Romania. His clothes still had bloodstains on them from the mission he and his team had completed the day before.

"You might wanna consider a bath too."

Peter followed Moretti's counsel and bathed, shaved, and put on a fresh uniform. He was thorough but quick, eager to see Genevieve again. When he emerged from the tent and saw Colonel Gibson waiting for him, his mood fell.

"Follow me, Lieutenant."

Peter obeyed, and Gibson led him into yet another tent. In the dim light, Peter recognized the man Jamie had spoken with earlier.

"Ah, Lieutenant Eddy. Good of you to join me." He held his hand out, and Peter shook it. The man's grip was damp and firm. "I am Major Kimby, SOE. Have a seat."

Peter sat in the chair Kimby gestured to, wary after Jamie's warning. It wasn't unusual for Jamie to quote Shakespeare, nor was it unusual for Jamie to pretend to like someone he despised, but Peter wished he could ask him what he'd meant before sitting down across from Kimby.

Gibson nodded to both of them, then left.

"Well done on your last assignment," Kimby said.

"Thank you, sir."

The man leafed through some paperwork. "Major Baker is flying to England, along with Privates Fisher and Quill. We thought it best to send them to hospital there."

Peter wanted to ask why the team's other injured members weren't headed for Great Britain too. Luke didn't have any family there—he was American. But Krzysztof's parents and younger sister had lived in England since 1939. Peter remembered Jamie's quote, and rather than asking why the injured Pole wasn't heading home with the other wounded, he kept his mouth shut.

"Baker left behind several papers: leave requests, immigration forms, a recommendation that you be promoted." Kimby shuffled through the forms and put them face down on the metal desk between them. He was about thirty years old, and his speech and carriage hinted at an extensive education and a high social status. "I am afraid we won't be able to process all of Baker's requests."

Peter nodded, assuming Kimby was about to turn down his promotion. He could even guess the reasons: Gibson, Baker's superior, hadn't liked Peter since one of his teammates had launched a practical joke and made Peter late to Gibson's briefing a month before, and Peter had evacuated two civilians without permission when the team had left Romania. It was a disappointment, but only a small one; Peter was more eager to end the interview and find Genevieve.

"I am putting together a team and would like you to lead it. I could send you off as a captain."

"With all due respect, sir, I would prefer leave over promotion."

Kimby stared at him, perplexed, but Peter was serious. He was due for leave, and he wanted to spend time with Genevieve—he'd only seen her for an hour and a half that morning, and though she'd seemed happy during most of their time together, he'd sensed her inner turmoil. Something was bothering her, something big, and he wanted to help her work through it.

"Well, if that is how you feel, Lieutenant."

"Yes, sir."

Peter hoped Kimby would dismiss him, but instead, he picked up another file from his desk. "I am also looking for an agent to go undercover in Berlin. I understand your girlfriend works for OSS and that she speaks German. She might be just the person I need."

Peter felt a sudden chill as he met Kimby's cold, hard eyes. "She wouldn't pass for a native German. Find someone else."

"We can form a cover story to explain her French accent." Kimby smiled.

"She'd be suspect the moment she opened her mouth—"

"I doubt that. She seems to have done an excellent job on her last mission." Kimby looked through the file as he spoke. "She can write in code, defuse a bomb, she's a decent shot, a talented seductress—"

"What?" *Seductress?* Peter reached for the file, but Kimby held it just out of reach.

"She gathered her information in a restaurant rather than a bedroom, but still, she shows promise. Plenty of German officers would take a French mistress. I'll suggest that tactic."

Peter's jaw clenched, and his hands balled into fists. With considerable effort, he kept his temper in check. He was willing to pummel Kimby, despite the muscular, six-and-a-half-foot-tall military policeman posted outside the tent, but that would just make things worse. "Sir, I don't know all the details about Genevieve's last assignment, but you can't send her out again. Whatever happened left her a little fragile. She needs rest. If you put her under too much pressure again, she won't make it."

Kimby's brown eyes studied Peter for a long moment. "I am also in need of a courier here in Bari. Light duty with a senior OSS agent."

"You need to release her completely. I think she's done her fair share and then some to end the war."

"I am not much interested in what you think, Lieutenant Eddy. But I will give you a choice. Accept my assignment. You and your team should be back within three days. Your girlfriend will be in Bari when you return. Or you can reject my request, and Genevieve Olivier goes to Berlin."

"She'll turn you down."

"I doubt that." Kimby picked through the file and read out loud. "*Agent feels obligated to oppose the Nazis. Duty stems from family history and strong idealism. Unlikely to refuse an assignment if convinced her actions will shorten the war and end the suffering of innocent people."*

Peter felt his options disappear, knowing a persistent intelligence officer could guilt Genevieve into accepting another mission. He didn't think she'd agree to pose as someone's mistress, but the result would be the same: Genevieve would go to Berlin, and it would be her death sentence. *Jamie was right*, Peter thought. *Kimby is something wicked*. "When do I leave, sir?"

"This evening."

Peter was shocked. The plane bringing him back from his last mission had landed only hours ago. He'd come awfully close to dying to be sent back out so soon, but he thought of Genevieve going to Berlin and squared his shoulders. "You said something about a team, sir?" Working with men he didn't know was unappealing, and it seemed there wouldn't be much time for introductions, let alone training.

"You can meet them at the briefing. Stay here, and I will round them up."

"Sir, I'd like to tell her good-bye."

Kimby looked amused. "After the briefing, I'll see that you have a few minutes."

A few minutes? Peter needed a few days or, better yet, a few lifetimes. "Can I at least have some paper, sir?" He felt like a condemned prisoner making his last requests.

Kimby gave him a few pages and left. Peter heard him tell the guard outside that Peter wasn't to leave under any circumstances. Peter shook his head. He'd had more freedom in Nazi territory.

He tried to use his time wisely, writing three letters: two for his family, one for his almost-fiancée.

As an officer, Peter could censor his own outgoing mail but suspected Kimby would go through it, so he hid two of the letters in his pocket and carefully chose the words for the third letter, the one he planned to send his family that day. He spent the remainder of his time trying to form a plan that could get him and Genevieve back to the States, but all of his ideas ended with him dead or in jail and Genevieve in Germany.

Peter looked up when Jamie and Moretti walked into the tent. "What are you two doing here?"

Jamie frowned. "It seems we are about to receive our next assignment."

If Jamie and Moretti were going with him, Peter felt better about the mission. But they deserved a break too. "Didn't you get run over by a fanatical Nazi in a car yesterday?"

"No," Jamie said. "I wasn't run over; I was merely hit. And yes, my back is still misery itself."

"Then why are you coming?"

"If Kimby is dragging you and Moretti into this, I can't very well sit it out, can I?"

Peter glanced at the MP's shadow falling across the tent and lowered his voice. "Tell me about Kimby."

Jamie sat in the chair across from Peter and motioned for Moretti to pull another chair over. "You remember what happened when I was in Italy with Wesley?"

"Yeah," Peter said. Major Wesley Baker, the man who'd led their previous mission, had worked with Jamie for almost a year before the team had completed their assignment in Romania. "Your cover got blown when you didn't want to work with a British Communist. An OSS agent warned you, and you slipped out in time, right?"

Jamie nodded. "Kimby is the Communist. And I suspect the reason for this assignment is less that something needs to be done and more that Kimby wants me out of Italy. So both of you should withdraw before the briefing so he won't have any excuse to force you along."

Peter felt his mouth go dry. He was being dragged away from Genevieve because James Nelson and Phillip Kimby didn't get along? He was furious with Jamie for about two seconds before remembering Jamie had saved his life yesterday and Jamie had just told him *not* to go on the mission. But Jamie didn't know about Kimby's search for an agent to infiltrate Berlin. "I can't back out."

"Why not?" Jamie asked.

Peter shook his head when he heard footsteps outside the tent. "Moretti, maybe you should transfer back to the 82nd Airborne."

"That wouldn't be much safer than following you around, would it, sir? Besides, I wouldn't wanna get bored."

Kimby returned with two strangers. One was a British lieutenant with a thin brown mustache and a nervous smile. The other was clean-shaven and wore civilian clothing, with the exception of a cap with a red five-point star emblazoned in its center.

Jamie glanced at the cap and turned back to Peter and Moretti, lowering his voice to a whisper. "That star is the symbol for the Yugoslav Partisans. You don't want to come on this mission."

"No, I don't," Peter said. "But I have to."

"Sergeant?" Jamie motioned toward the door. "This is likely your last chance to withdraw."

"Now I'm too curious to leave." Moretti leaned back in his chair, crossing his arms and his ankles.

By then, Kimby was too close for them to say anything else. At his direction, they pulled their chairs around, forming a row facing Kimby.

"Gentlemen, the future of the war depends on your upcoming mission." Jamie snorted derisively, but Kimby ignored it. "We have an urgent need for your skills, thus we intend to incorporate elements of an existing team into a new unit that can leave this evening."

Moretti inhaled sharply. Apparently, no one had told him they were leaving so soon.

Kimby continued. "Your assignment is to destroy a railroad bridge between Višegrad and Sarajevo. You will parachute in, demolish the bridge, and then return home."

"Phillip, old boy," Jamie said. "You may not have noticed, but all of our demolitions experts were killed or wounded during our last mission. Perhaps we aren't the right men after all."

Kimby smiled and motioned toward the mustached officer. "Lieutenant Chesterfield is a former sapper. He can direct your efforts and ensure they are adequate. He will lead this mission, since the other lieutenant in the room is less than enthusiastic about the assignment."

Peter clenched his jaw, thinking perhaps he should have fought for that promotion. He knew nothing about Chesterfield, and the prospect of being under a stranger's command was disheartening. Then Peter met Kimby's eyes and suspected the major would have denied the promotion anyway and put Chesterfield in charge regardless of what Peter had said.

"We are also missing a radio operator," Jamie said.

"Your radio operator will meet you at the airplane. I can assure you he is completely competent. Since our time is short, we shall have only a brief discussion of the target. It lies in territory held by the German Army, but it is in a mountainous zone, so you should meet only scattered patrols. The area is heavily occupied by Chetniks."

"Then why don't you ask the Chetniks to destroy this rail line?" Jamie asked.

"Don't be ridiculous, Nelson. The Chetniks are more likely to collaborate with the Third Reich than oppose it. If we were to give them the necessary equipment, they would probably use it against the Partisans."

"Excuse me, sir," Moretti broke in. "Who are the Chetniks? And who are the Partisans?"

Kimby stopped glaring at Jamie long enough to explain. "The Chetniks are mostly Serbs. Their leader is a man named Draza Mihailovich. They claim to be fighting against the Nazis in an effort to bring the Serbian king back to power, but all their recent activities have been against the Partisans rather than the Nazis. The Partisans are led by Josip Tito."

"The Partisans are the Communists," Jamie said.

Kimby narrowed his eyes again. "The Communists are the only forces in Yugoslavia seriously opposing the Nazis."

"That is because the Communists are the only people receiving British and American arms." Jamie seemed not to notice the way Kimby's face was turning red. "It is difficult to fight the German Army with nothing but pitchforks."

Kimby ignored Jamie's comments and motioned toward the man with a red star on his cap. "Mr. Raspolic is a member of Tito's Partisans. He will be your guide. He speaks limited English, which is why it is so important for you to accompany the team, Nelson."

Jamie didn't say anything, not in English, not in any other language he knew.

As Kimby continued the briefing, Peter's sense of foreboding grew worse and worse.

CHAPTER TWO
ANOTHER GOOD-BYE

GENEVIEVE HAD GONE AN ENTIRE hour without thinking about her recurring nightmares, but as she picked up a pile of used hospital bandages, she caught a scent that reminded her of the Marseilles prison she'd escaped from the week before. She shuddered at the memory and dumped the bandages into a fifty-gallon GI can so she could sterilize them. *Focus on the laundry.* But images of her thirteen dead prison-mates, all of them shot in the back of the head by a Gestapo agent, kept haunting her. She still couldn't tell if their faces, staring at her from her dreams, showed anger for their fate or condemnation because she'd survived and they hadn't.

She pushed her hair away from her face and stirred the bandages, forcing herself to concentrate on the wash instead of her recent OSS mission. But her mind kept wandering back either to those victims or the murderous Gestapo man she'd killed when he tracked her down after her escape. *It was self-defense, wasn't it?* But that didn't stop Weiss's face from appearing in her nightmares several times each night. She sighed, wondering when Peter would be done with his debriefing. *He'll make everything better again.* She hadn't been ready to talk about her mission when she'd seen him earlier, but she was ready now. She needed to tell him what had happened, and she needed to hear Peter reassure her that she didn't have to feel guilty for surviving, just grateful.

She looked up from the wash, and there he was, ten meters away, climbing out of the passenger's side of a jeep. She found that odd—he liked to drive—but shrugged it off. As he approached, she knew something was wrong. There was no smile on his lips, no mischief in his eyes. "What's wrong, Peter?" She looked from him to the parked jeep, where an enormous military policeman waited in the driver's seat.

Peter gave her a smile, but it seemed forced.

"Are you in trouble?" She couldn't imagine Peter doing anything that would anger the Allied authorities, but the way the MP watched Peter was disconcerting.

"I'm not under arrest or anything; I just came to say good-bye."

"What? You just got here." He still had a fresh scab from where someone had tried to slit his throat the day before.

"I know, but I have to leave again . . . in a couple hours."

She squeezed her eyes shut. "Please tell me you're leaving for England or the United States." *Someplace where no one will try to kill you.*

Peter wrapped his arms around her and pulled her to his chest. "I'm sorry."

"Where are you going?"

He glanced at the MP and lowered his voice to a whisper. "Yugoslavia."

"But, Peter, you'll be dropped in the middle of a civil war. And there are Nazis there, and you don't speak Serbo-Croat—" She broke off, knowing her emotions were about to choke her voice. She caught her breath and looked up at his face. "Can't you say no?"

He shook his head.

"Please, Peter," she whispered. "Haven't you done your share?"

"I tried, and I can't get out of it, but I should be back in a few days." The MP honked the horn. Peter turned to glare at him, then faced Genevieve again. "Can you do three things for me?"

"Yes." She pressed her face into his neck, smelling his shaving cream. "You know I'll do anything for you."

Peter pulled her closer. "I'm slipping two letters into your pocket because I don't want the MP to see them. One's for you. The other one's for my family. If something happens to me, can you mail it to them?"

Genevieve nodded, feeling nervous and dizzy and desperate.

"Next, I want you to promise me you'll stay out of Germany. Doesn't matter who asks you, doesn't matter how important they say it is—you turn them down. Promise?"

"Why would I go to Germany, Peter?" As long as Hitler was in charge, she had no desire to visit.

"Just promise me you won't." His hands clasped her shoulders, gently pushing her back so he could study her face with his dark brown eyes. The MP honked the horn again.

"I promise," she said, confused.

"Last, always remember I love you."

She nodded, blinking away tears. He wiped one of the tears with his thumb, and she closed her eyes and leaned into the gentle strength of his hand. She felt his lips brush against hers for an instant, then his lips and his hand were gone. She opened her eyes to see the MP towering over Peter's five-foot ten-inch frame, one of his hands digging into Peter's shoulder.

"Sir, it's time to leave," the MP said.

Peter glanced at the huge MP, clenching his jaw like he always did when he was trying to control his temper. He turned back to Genevieve. "I guess I have to go."

"But I need you, Peter," she whispered. She hadn't meant to let those words slip out because she knew she should be stronger, but she did need him, especially now. Couldn't he see that?

"I'm sorry. If there was any way for me to stay, I would."

"Sir, I've got to get you back." The MP motioned toward the road. "Now."

Peter reached for Genevieve's face, and she felt his fingers run along her cheek and into her hair. She caught her breath at the tenderness she felt in his touch, but like his return, his caress was over almost before it began.

"I love you," he said. Then, with a nudge from the MP, Peter turned and walked to the jeep. He looked back as the MP drove them away, watching her until he was out of sight.

She stood in shock, not knowing what to think. Why did he have to leave again so soon? She hoped it was all a mistake, that Peter would be waiting for her when she finished her shift at the hospital, but she knew it wasn't. His eyes, his voice—they both said the same thing: he was leaving, and he might never return. Then she felt a different emotion, something she rarely felt: anger. Would she ever be first priority in Peter's life, before his next mission, before his sense of duty? She cursed her tears, cursed the ache in her heart, and cursed the day she'd fallen in love with a spy.

CHAPTER THREE
RIPCORDS

PETER TRIED TO PAY ATTENTION to the maps in front of him, but a permeating gloom made it difficult for him to focus.

"You okay, sir?"

Peter answered Moretti without looking up. "I'll be better when we're finished and on our way back."

"How'd your girl take the news?"

Peter shifted his gaze from the maps to the airfield. They were in a tent next to a runway, with the front flaps open to let a breeze in. Jamie was a few yards away, translating for Chesterfield and Raspolic. "You've seen battle fatigue cases?"

Moretti nodded. He'd been with the US 82nd Airborne in Sicily, Salerno, and Normandy. He'd seen his share of combat and the physical and mental casualties that came with it.

"You know how they'd act before they got really bad? Like the sound of one more explosion would send them over the edge?" Peter tapped his pencil on the map. "I don't know what happened to her, but she did something for OSS, and she needs . . . I don't know, she needs something. Time. A break. On the front, you can pull a man back, give him a shower, a hot meal, dry socks, and a full night's sleep, and he usually feels a lot better. I guess I was hoping I could be Genevieve's equivalent of dry socks, but I think showing up and leaving again just made it worse." Peter tapped the pencil a little harder, unintentionally snapping it. "It's like she's drowning and asking for my help, and I'm swimming in the opposite direction."

Moretti was quiet for a while. "Sir, maybe you should stay."

Peter shook his head. "I can't."

"Why not? Go AWOL. Or let me accidentally shoot your foot while I'm polishing my pistol."

Peter shook his head again. "If I don't go, Kimby will send Genevieve on assignment to Germany. She wouldn't make it back, not in her current state."

Moretti flicked the broken end of the pencil off the map. "I think Major Kimby better make sure he's not alone in any dark alleys, or I might accidentally break his lousy neck."

Peter had similar thoughts, but before he could mention them, a jeep pulled to a stop outside their tent. The giant MP who'd pulled Peter away from Genevieve drove, and Kimby and Krzysztof sat in the backseat. "What's Krzysztof doing out of the hospital?"

Kimby smiled as he entered the tent. "I promised you a competent radio man. Here he is."

"Ain't you supposed to be taking it easy?" Moretti asked Krzysztof as he followed Kimby inside.

"I'm fine. It's a shallow wound."

Krzysztof's face was pale, and Peter could make out beads of sweat lining his forehead. Peter had been the one to hold Krzysztof's shoulder still the day before so a Romanian doctor could extract the bullet without anesthesia. It wasn't a shallow wound—the bullet had lodged itself deep in the muscle.

Krzysztof was doing his best to maintain good posture, but he was slowly tilting to the side. Jamie noticed, pulled the chair out from under Chesterfield's rear, and placed it behind the Polish radio man.

"Sit," Jamie ordered. "Phillip, take him back to hospital."

"I'm fine," Krzysztof repeated, but he sank into the offered chair immediately.

"Kapral Zielinski has assured me he is healthy enough for this mission." Kimby put a hand out to silence a protest Chesterfield seemed ready to make about his stolen chair. "Do you know any better radio operators, Nelson?"

"It doesn't matter how brilliant Krzysztof is if he develops gangrene while we are away."

"Leave it alone, Jamie," Krzysztof said quietly. "I have penicillin packed with my radio. I'm coming."

It took Peter only a moment to figure it out. Krzysztof was brave, but he wasn't suicidal. He was also loyal to his teammates, but he'd know joining them in his current condition would put all of them at greater risk. Krzysztof had fallen in love during their most recent mission—and

Peter was sure Krzysztof would have been more interested in staying with Iuliana Ionescu and her son than joining his teammates on a last-minute assignment.

Peter remembered the pile of papers Kimby had rummaged through—leave requests, Peter's promotion, and immigration papers. The immigration papers had to be for Iuliana and Anatolie, both of them Romanian civilians. Baker had been willing to pull a few strings to ensure the Ionescus weren't deported, but Kimby had conveniently arranged for Baker to be on his way to England.

Peter was trapped. Krzysztof was trapped. Moretti would come because he was an obedient soldier and because he wouldn't back down if his teammates were in jeopardy. Jamie too. He was a civilian, not a soldier, and obedience wasn't his strongest trait, but Jamie wouldn't leave his friends to battle Kimby's mischief alone.

Jamie met Peter's eyes. "Peter, will you talk some sense into him?"

Peter faced Krzysztof, seeing the familiar determination in the man's dark blue eyes. "Where's Iuliana?" It wasn't what anyone expected him to ask. Peter saw a look of confusion cross Jamie's face and noticed the muscles around Krzysztof's eyes twitch in panic.

Krzysztof shook his head, glanced at Kimby, and refused to answer. That was enough of a confirmation for Peter. Moretti glared at Kimby, making Peter think Moretti too knew why Krzysztof was coming.

Jamie shook his head in bewilderment and turned to Kimby. "I hope you have jumped through all the necessary hoops for this assignment. Wesley might not be able to prevent this mission because you put him on an airplane, but if you haven't followed protocol, I guarantee it will cost you your commission."

Kimby seemed amused. "I have my connections, same as you. And I am sorry to be the bearer of bad news, but your grandfather is ill. Of course, that might not be entirely bad news for you. But in any case, he won't be able to do much for you, other than make you extremely wealthy."

Jamie's face darkened. His grandfather had played a key role in shaping British Intelligence, and Jamie had followed in his footsteps. When his grandfather died, Jamie would inherit a vast estate and a title to go with it, but Jamie didn't seem eager for his grandfather, friend, and mentor to die. Nor did Peter. If Jamie's grandfather was dead, he wouldn't be able to convince his former colleagues that Kimby was up to no good.

"On the plane, all of you," Kimby ordered.

Peter grabbed Krzysztof's radio from the jeep and carried it with his own gear. He looked behind him and saw Moretti assist Krzysztof to his feet. They were the same height, just over six feet, and both had dark hair. As they walked to the plane, Moretti seemed angry. Krzysztof just seemed like he was in pain. Jamie gave Kimby a final glare before following the others, looking like a cranky movie star. Raspolic and Chesterfield received a few final instructions from Kimby and then grabbed their gear. Raspolic gave the British major a nod of determination, but Chesterfield seemed nervous as he glanced at the men and played with his mustache.

Peter looked around the airfield, hoping to catch of glimpse of Genevieve. But the airfield was more than a mile from the hospital where she worked, and Peter hadn't known which field they would leave from—not that he'd had time to give her directions. As he strapped on his parachute, he said a silent prayer. *Please help her, Lord. Don't let her get hurt. Don't let her hate me for abandoning her. And keep an eye on the Ionescus too.*

The men settled into the twin-engine Whitley night bomber, and Peter felt the familiar sensation of his stomach flipping as they sped down the runway and left the ground. Peter and the others from Baker's team congregated in the back, away from Chesterfield and Raspolic, who were up front near the Partisan jump master.

Jamie turned to Peter. "All right, no secrets between us this time. Why are you on this mission?"

"Kimby threatened to send Genevieve on assignment to Germany if I refused."

"And you?" Jamie asked Krzysztof.

"If I accepted the mission, Kimby said he'd send Iuliana and Anatolie to England. If not, he'd send them back to Romania."

"Women." Jamie cursed and shook his head. "'Fools are as like husbands as pilchards are to herrings—the husband's the bigger.' Genevieve and Iuliana are pleasant enough on the eyes, but I guarantee I could find dozens of women just as pretty. Are you really willing to risk your lives for them?"

"I would think my answer is obvious, Jamie," Peter said.

Krzysztof nodded. "As is mine."

"And you?" Jamie motioned toward Moretti. "Are you also in love with someone and, therefore, susceptible to Kimby's blackmail?"

Moretti grinned. "I've got about five women chasing me, spread from New York to Salerno, but I ain't willing to die for any of 'em. I'm just coming along to keep you three outta trouble."

"Jamie, you seem to be the reason behind this whole mission. What's going on?" Peter asked.

Jamie stared at his hands. "All I can think is Kimby is planning something with the Communists, or he's trying to hide something he has already done. Either way, he fears I will uncover it if I stay in Bari. I am sorry, chaps. I didn't mean for you to get dragged along with me."

"All right," Peter said. "Here's the plan. We're just going to get in there, blow the bridge, and get back to Bari. In, out, back. No heroics, no distractions, just business."

His friends nodded.

Peter, Jamie, and Moretti divided Krzysztof's equipment so he'd have a lighter burden. Jumping with an injured shoulder was going to be bad enough. Krzysztof didn't protest when they divvied out his load, which Peter took as a sign of just how bad the wound was. As they neared the drop zone, a red light turned on inside the airplane; it was time to prepare for the jump.

"Don't forget, these 'chutes ain't the type we normally use," Moretti said as they checked each other's packs. On all of Peter's previous jumps, he'd used a paratrooper parachute, with a line attaching his parachute to an anchor line on the plane. This time, he'd need to pull his own ripcord.

Chesterfield and their jump master had been studying maps for most of the flight. Peter hoped they knew what they were doing because the bridge they were assigned to destroy was over a ravine. They were supposed to land in the mountains, which was a little dangerous, but he preferred the hazardous terrain to the risk of running into German patrols down in the valley or of landing in the swift river at the bottom of the canyon.

The jump master uncovered a hole in the bottom of the fuselage.

Chesterfield pointed to Moretti. "Sergeant, you have the most jump experience. I'd like you to lead."

Moretti nodded and let his feet dangle through the hole, and Peter got in line behind him. Chesterfield positioned himself last. A sudden updraft of turbulence made the plane bounce, and Peter almost lost his footing as the light turned green. He held his breath as Moretti left, then he followed, knowing Krzysztof and Jamie were right behind him.

It was nearly a full moon, but he couldn't see much below. Everything was a textured field gray, the color of a German Army uniform.

Peter counted to three, just as he'd been trained, and pulled his ripcord.

Nothing happened.

He pulled it again, harder, and felt the ripcord detach from his pack. He stared at it, unconnected to anything, lying in his hand, then glanced down and fought back panic. He realized what his only chance was and reached behind his head, digging into the pack until he could feel the smooth fabric. He pulled it from the pack as quickly as he could, hoping the silk would catch the air and open before it was too late. It took six desperate pulls, but it finally caught, and Peter felt the harness yank him to a slower speed. He sighed with relief, hoping he still had enough altitude for the parachute to slow him sufficiently before he reached the ground.

A quick prayer of gratitude had just passed Peter's lips when his feet ran into something not completely firm. He felt the branches of a tree engulf him, and then his entire body smacked into something solid, and the world turned black.

CHAPTER FOUR
BROKEN PROMISES

Bari, Italy

IULIANA IONESCU HELD HER SLEEPING son and waited. *Where did Krzysztof go? He should be resting.* She'd spent most of the day with him until a British major asked for a few moments alone. The men had stepped outside, and minutes had stretched into hours. She was concerned for Krzysztof—she'd been worried about him since yesterday morning when he'd been shot in the shoulder while pushing her out of the bullet's path.

She'd first seen him a month ago but hadn't really met him until a few weeks later. Yet somehow, in the last two weeks, the logical, gentle Pole had entrenched himself in her heart. In many ways, Krzysztof was Iuliana's late husband's opposite, but they were both men firmly rooted in their ideals. When Anatolie's father was killed, Iuliana had thought she would never fall in love again—it was too painful. But Krzysztof was proving her wrong.

The British major who'd spoken with Krzysztof walked into the room and stopped in front of her. "Mrs. Ionescu?"

"Yes?"

"Come with me, please."

Anatolie woke, and though it was past his bedtime, she didn't try to make him sleep again. She put him on his feet and took his hand. He was getting heavy to carry around, and he'd been extra clingy the past day.

The major escorted her to a jeep and motioned her inside.

She hesitated. "Where are we going? And where is Krzysztof?"

"I have a letter from Kapral Zielinski." He took it from his pocket and pointed to the jeep's rear seat. Iuliana reached for her letter, but the major held it out of reach. "I am on a strict timeline."

Feeling uneasy, Iuliana stepped into the car. The major handed her the letter, then sat in the passenger seat, waving over a man from the shadows, who climbed behind the steering wheel. Iuliana opened the letter but couldn't read the words in the dark. When the driver stopped several minutes later, she could hear the ocean.

The British major led her past two men in caps with red stars to a small building and told her to wait inside. A dim oil lamp sat on a desk in the room's center, its light just sufficient to show her the furniture and the blacked-out windows. After laying Anatolie on a bench, Iuliana turned up the lamp and read her letter.

Dear Iuliana,

Major Kimby has promised to arrange transport to England for you and Anatolie. I wish I could travel with you, but there are a few things I have to do first. When you get settled in, please leave word with my parents (address below). I know you've had mixed luck with men, but I hope you'll let me call on you when I return to England. I look forward to spending more time with you and getting to know Anatolie better.

Krzysztof

Iuliana finished the letter as the officer came into the room, accompanied by the driver. "Are you Major Kimby?" she asked.

He nodded.

"Where's Krzysztof?" She hoped Kimby would tell her he was on a hospital ship headed for England.

"On assignment."

"What? He should be in a hospital!"

Kimby walked across the room and sat behind the desk. He motioned for her to sit across from him. "This was more important."

"More important than recovering from his wounds?"

Kimby nodded. "It seems Kapral Zielinski and his teammates were involved in some unpleasant contact with our Soviet allies during their last mission."

Iuliana inhaled sharply. *Unpleasant contact* was an understatement. But Major Baker had told everyone on the team *not* to mention anything about their conflict with the NKVD. Iuliana followed Baker's advice and feigned ignorance. "What happened between Krzysztof's team and the Communists?"

Kimby let out a short, mocking laugh. "I was hoping you could enlighten me on that very subject. You were there, after all, weren't you?"

When she didn't speak, he continued. "Lieutenant Eddy, Kapral Zielinski, and James Nelson ran into three NKVD agents. They killed one of our Soviet allies, and the other two disappeared after using Zielinski's radio to contact their associates. Can you explain what happened to the two missing agents?"

Iuliana shook her head, lying. Peter had taken out the first NKVD man as he was about to stab Iuliana, then shot the other two when they attacked Peter later.

Kimby frowned. He didn't seem fooled. "Giving Kapral Zielinski and the others a new mission was my only choice. I can't let them get away with killing Soviet soldiers—it could ruin our Alliance and lose us the war. But I can't punish them. There would be a public outcry if word leaked that we imprisoned our own commandos after what could be described as self-defense. I had no choice but to send them off again. Now when the Soviet government demands that we turn them over or punish them, we can honestly say they are away on assignment. You know the men, Iuliana. They'd prefer to be in the field rather than in a Moscow prison, wouldn't they?"

"Who is Krzysztof with?"

"Lieutenant Eddy, Sergeant Moretti, and James Nelson."

Iuliana felt a little relief. The four of them would look after each other. "And what about Daniel Fisher?" Fisher had nearly died during the debacle with the NKVD.

"Private Fisher was not mentioned by name in the radio report, so he can slip under the radar, so to speak. But you were mentioned, and you are a more serious complication, since I can't very well send you off on a mission."

Iuliana glanced at the letter in her lap.

"And I can't very well send you to England either."

"But you promised Krzysztof," she said as panic filled her chest.

"I lied." Kimby's face showed no sign of regret or shame.

"Please don't send me back to Romania," she begged. She had both Nazi and Communist enemies there. If one didn't find her and her son, the other would. She wouldn't last a week.

"That was never my plan."

"Then what is your plan?"

"I'm afraid I'm going to have to turn you over to the Communists. I apologize, but it is vital that I maintain our relationship with Stalin. We won't defeat Hitler without his help. I don't have a direct channel to the Soviet Union, but Tito's men have offered to take you."

Iuliana looked behind her at the driver, noticing the red star on his cap and realizing he and the two guards outside were Yugoslav Communists. She turned back to Kimby. "When Krzysztof returns, he'll come looking for me, and so will his friends."

Kimby glanced at his fingernails, then at her face. "I'm not too concerned about Krzysztof or his friends returning. I imagine at least half of them are dead already."

"What?" Iuliana forced herself to take a few deep breaths. "I know those men. They'll find a way back."

"You understand my position—if they complete their mission and return, I'll have to turn them over to the Soviet Union. But between the difficulty of finding the exact drop zone and the fickle nature of parachutes, I don't think that will be necessary."

Iuliana jumped to her feet, horrified. Kimby's words sounded like a confession of sabotage. "Radio the plane and have it turn around! No one on Baker's team will ever talk about what happened in Bucharest, and I won't either. You don't have to do this!"

Kimby grinned. "Perhaps not, but I'm going to do it anyway."

The Partisan behind Iuliana stepped closer and slapped a damp cloth over her mouth and nose. She grabbed at his wrist and tugged but moved his arm only an inch before he overpowered her. Her vision blurred. She saw Anatolie lying on the bench, asleep, and worked up enough strength to kick the desk into Kimby before she slipped into unconsciousness.

CHAPTER FIVE
OFF TARGET

Independent State of Croatia

PETER FELT SOMEONE TUG AT his boot.

"Peter?"

He swayed as his foot was released. His face and neck ached, and he had to fight back a wave of nausea. He opened his eyes and saw only dark leaves—he couldn't see Jamie, though he'd recognized his whisper. It took him a few moments to realize he was still in his parachute harness suspended from a tree. "Jamie?"

"I told ya he wasn't dead." Moretti's voice came from below.

"How high am I?" Peter pulled out a knife to cut himself down.

"Approximately seven feet, so cut slowly. And bring your parachute with you. We have already run into one German patrol. If the next patrol sees your parachute, our mission will no longer be secret."

"That's easier said than done, Jamie." Peter cut a strap and yanked. He hoped to feel the parachute loosen, but it stayed in exactly the same position. He sliced through another strap. "How big was the patrol?"

"Nothing we couldn't handle, sir. Three men," Moretti said.

"Where's Krzysztof?"

"With our gear," Moretti said. "I think that sudden tug when his chute opened was more painful than he's letting on. He looked kinda beat."

"What about Chesterfield and Raspolic?"

"They are also with the gear," Jamie said. "Chesterfield gave us a half hour to find you. He seemed certain you would be dead—so certain I wondered if he had somehow shot you on the way down."

Peter cut another line and yanked, finally getting the parachute to move. "I almost was dead. The ripcord pulled off in my hand. Had to dig the chute out of the pack with my hands. Only got it deployed a few seconds before I hit the tree."

Moretti and Jamie were silent. Peter kept working on his parachute. When he was within a few feet of the dirt, he unbuckled his harness and lowered himself to firm ground. The parachute was still caught, but he'd have better leverage pulling it from below.

"That is strange," Jamie said.

"Yeah," Moretti agreed.

"What?" Peter asked.

"Moretti's ripcord also detached when he pulled it. I assume things like that happen from time to time, but the odds are against it happening twice to a six-man team."

Peter thought back to when he'd boarded the plane. Kimby had handed parachutes to Chesterfield and Raspolic. The rest of them had taken some from a nearby pile. "I didn't trust Kimby before, but now I really don't trust him. And if Chesterfield was sure I'd be dead, I'm not ready to put much faith in our new teammates."

"Nor am I," Jamie said.

With Moretti's help, Peter finally freed the parachute. "Let's get back to Krzysztof before Chesterfield and Raspolic decide he's too injured to keep up and leave him for the Nazis."

When they got back to the rest of the group, Chesterfield ordered Peter to lead, and the team marched the rest of the night. But no one knew where they'd landed. Even Moretti, a former pathfinder for the US 82nd Airborne, couldn't figure it out, and Moretti had the best sense of direction Peter had ever seen. All the same, Peter thought it was a good idea to put some distance between them and their landing zone. He hadn't studied the tree he'd fallen into but guessed he'd broken enough branches that a clever patrolman would suspect something.

When dawn came, they could see mountains to the south—Peter assumed that was where they were supposed to have landed—outside the German sphere of power. Now they'd have to hike into the hills, increasing their risk and lengthening their assignment.

"Let's find somewhere to camp. We'll continue when it's dark again," Chesterfield said.

Peter agreed with Chesterfield's plan to rest by day and travel by night, but before they slept, he thought they should determine their location. "Sir, do you think we should figure out where we are first?"

Jamie nodded his agreement.

Chesterfield looked flustered. "Nelson, Moretti, go figure it out. Eddy, you and Zielinski find a place for us to sleep. Raspolic and I will wait here."

"Sir, are you sure you want to stay here?" They were between two hills, with a poor field of vision. "You'd be able to keep a better lookout from up there." Peter pointed to the top of the hill.

Chesterfield narrowed his eyes, glaring at Peter. "Lieutenant Eddy, you are not in charge of this team, and you will stop trying to order me around."

Peter didn't want to be in charge, but he also didn't want the team to make stupid mistakes. He considered arguing but gritted his teeth and saluted instead. "Yes, sir."

The four of them brought their rifles and maps but left most of their equipment with Chesterfield.

Moretti shook his head when they were out of sight. "Some officers lead, and some officers order. I guess Chesterfield's the ordering type."

Peter nodded his agreement. "How are you feeling, Krzysztof?"

Krzysztof didn't answer except to shake his head. They'd put his arm in a sling hours ago and found him a walking stick, but he still looked like a candidate for a long hospital stay.

"Why don't you rest for a while? Since we're talking about bossy officers, I'll even make it an order."

A smile crept across Krzysztof's face. "Giving orders, Peter? Chesterfield wouldn't like that."

Peter ran his hand through his hair. It needed a trim. "Yeah, I guess I don't care what he thinks, as long as he doesn't get us all killed. And as long as Kimby keeps his promises."

"Kimby is a snake," Jamie said. "'I will no more trust him when he leers than I will a serpent when he hisses.'"

Peter felt suddenly uneasy, but Genevieve would keep her promise to stay out of Germany, wouldn't she?

As they were about to separate for their assigned tasks, the four of them heard footfalls and dropped to the ground. A peasant girl, her head covered in a kerchief, walked along a dirt path, a basket full of roots hanging from her arms. It was like something from a fairy tale—or would have been if the young woman hadn't looked as though she was starving to death.

Jamie stood and brushed himself off. "I believe I shall go determine our location, gentlemen." Like everyone on the team, Jamie wore civilian clothing, and he knew the local language, so he was unlikely to cause alarm.

Peter watched the approach with amusement. Jamie could be absolutely charming when he wanted to be, and soon the girl was smiling, showing him what was in her basket, and laughing with him. Jamie walked along the path with her for a while before saying good-bye and rejoining the rest of them.

He held his hand out, and Moretti gave him a map. He studied it for a few seconds before speaking. "Our Communist jump master dropped us seventy kilometers from our target."

Despite his resolution to stop, Peter swore. An extra seventy kilometers through Nazi-occupied territory with an idiotic lieutenant in command and an injured radio man to care for would drag out their mission significantly.

"And Kimby seemed in such a hurry for us to get to that bridge," Moretti said as he folded the map.

Peter was about to ask if the Yugoslav girl had mentioned possible places to sleep when a rifle shot sounded from the north, where they'd left their gear and the remnant of their team.

"I care little about what happens to Chesterfield and Raspolic, but we will need our equipment if we want to survive and our radio if we want a lift home." Jamie checked his weapon's clip as the sound of small arms increased. "I suppose we should go relieve our teammates."

When they reached the hill just south of where they'd left Chesterfield and Raspolic, Peter could see exactly what had happened. A German patrol had spotted the two of them from the hill north of the little valley. If the British lieutenant had taken Peter's advice and kept to the high ground, he would have avoided his current fiasco of being shot at from above.

"Moretti, Jamie, circle around to the left," Peter said. "I'll circle around to the right. Krzysztof, stay here and cover us."

Peter took off quickly, hoping the firefight would mask any sound he made as he looped around to attack the German patrol from the side rather than head-on. He slowed as he neared the patrol, trying to determine how many there were. He counted five but assumed more were hidden.

Peter crept to within fifty yards of their position and knelt behind a fallen log. He took careful aim and squeezed the trigger. One of the German soldiers fell. When Peter hit his second target, the patrol leader ordered his men into better cover.

A feminine scream pierced the air, and a series of rifle shots sounded from the far side of the German patrol. It was the direction Jamie and Moretti had taken, but Jamie carried a Sten gun, and Moretti, like Peter, used an M1. Peter heard their weapons, but he also heard what sounded like multiple MP 44s,

German assault rifles, and knew his teammates needed assistance. But the remnants of the first patrol were blocking him. One of the nearby Germans lifted his helmeted head over the rock he hid behind, and Peter took him out and ran closer, drawing a few shots before ducking into a ditch.

Peter edged through the underbrush until he could see Chesterfield and Raspolic sheltering behind a cut of rocks. He caught their attention and motioned for them to join him. As a group of three, they'd be better able to break through to the others, but Chesterfield didn't seem interested in coming up the hill. That, or he couldn't make sense of Peter's hand signals. They were the ones Peter had learned in basic training, so he'd assumed they were almost universal, but maybe not for former British sappers.

Peter blew out a sharp breath of frustration, wishing Chesterfield and Raspolic would dig out the grenades they'd parachuted in with or, better yet, load the Bren machine gun. Peter crept closer to the patrol he hunted, his efforts bolder than he preferred, but most of the German patrolmen weren't aiming at him. They seemed more focused on the new skirmish with Moretti and Jamie or with driving Chesterfield and Raspolic into the open.

Peter took a few more shots, killing two additional German soldiers. He tried not to think about how many lives he was ending—he had to focus on survival—but he knew his conscience would remind him later, if he lived that long.

Through a patch of weeds, Peter could make out two more patrolmen, one of them firing at him, the other at Chesterfield. The second one shifted his position so Peter could get a clear shot. He squeezed the trigger but heard only the click of an empty clip. He still had his pistol and a trench knife, but to be effective with those, he'd need to move closer.

A cry that sounded like Moretti spurred Peter into action. He removed his Colt M1911 from its holster and shot off several rounds at the nearest patrolman, then zigzagged forward and dove to the ground near a dead soldier. Peter took the man's rifle and aimed at the patrolman who was trying to blow his head off, felling him with one shot. The last patrolman was still concentrating on Chesterfield when Peter got into position and shot him. Peter didn't want the German to follow him when he went to help Jamie and Moretti.

Once the patrol was taken care of, Peter ran toward the other skirmish, not bothering to ask for Chesterfield's and Raspolic's help—he'd already done that, with poor results. As he ran down the hill, he felt something grip his left ankle, and he tumbled to the ground.

CHAPTER SIX
COURAGE AND COWARDICE

PETER'S FOREHEAD CRASHED INTO A rock, and he dropped the German rifle as someone grunted and pounced on his back. Peter twisted underneath the man's weight, feeling a punch to the side of his already tender face and blinking away bright flashes of light that clouded his vision. His assailant was a large German soldier, his face twisted in rage and stained with streams of blood. He rammed his elbow into Peter's throat, and Peter's peripheral vision faded. *Stay awake!* he told himself, knowing he'd die if he lost consciousness. He gripped the knife attached to his belt and forced his hand free of his attacker, ramming the blade into the man's neck. The patrolman gasped and gurgled his last breath as Peter pushed the corpse away.

He staggered to his feet, dizzy, in pain, angry at the situation, and worried about his friends. It was quiet—the skirmishes were over. Peter winced when he tried to put weight on his ankle. Something was wrong with it. He limped down the hill anyway, determined to see if Jamie and Moretti needed his help. He'd hobbled about twenty-five yards when they came into view. Krzysztof had joined them sometime during the fight.

Moretti let out a low whistle. "All that blood yours, sir?"

Peter glanced at his shirt—one of his shoulders was solid red, and the rest of his shirt was splattered with blood. He put a hand to his face. It was sticky, and he had a cut where his forehead had struck the rock. Still, he thought most of the blood was the patrolman's. He shook his head, which only made him dizzy. He put a hand on a tree to steady himself and shut his eyes so the world would stop spinning. "How many did you run into?"

"Twelve," Jamie said. "You?"

"Seven, but one of them wasn't as dead as I thought he was." Peter lurched closer to them, stumbling as he put weight on his left foot.

"Let me help ya, sir." Moretti slung Peter's arm over his shoulder, helping him toward their gear and the rest of the team.

A few steps later, Peter noticed the bloody gash along Moretti's forearm. "What happened to your arm?"

"Grazed by a bullet. Stings like something else."

"Did anyone else get hit?" Peter asked, noticing the grim expressions Jamie and Krzysztof wore. "Jamie?"

He shook his head. "Not us—the peasant girl. One of the Nazis shot her. She is dead."

Peter felt sick. Less than ten minutes ago, the young woman had been laughing as Jamie flirted with her. What would have happened if they'd left her alone?

"Chesterfield and Raspolic dead or just wounded?" Moretti asked.

"As far as I know, neither."

"Then where are they?"

Peter grunted as he put too much weight on his ankle. "Probably still huddled behind some rocks, like they were the entire engagement."

"What?" The surprise and anger in Moretti's voice echoed on Krzysztof's and Jamie's faces.

"I think they fired a few shots in the beginning, but they didn't even bother to unpack the grenades, let alone reinforce me."

Jamie stomped ahead of the group and stopped when he reached Chesterfield and Raspolic. He crossed his arms and glared as the final two members of the team came out from behind their shelter.

"Jolly good show, men," Chesterfield said. "Although that last bit was rather sloppy, Lieutenant Eddy. I saw the whole thing. I don't know why you didn't check where you were going more carefully. Running past a body without checking to see if it's dead—you ought to know better."

"If you saw the whole thing, why didn't you shoot the Kraut?" Moretti asked, his dark eyes and eyebrows conveying fierce disapproval.

Chesterfield looked startled. "Me? My marksmanship isn't quite good enough for that distance."

"Then why didn't you close the distance?"

"We were protecting our supplies."

"Why you—"

Peter grabbed Moretti's arm before he swung at Chesterfield. "Let it go," Peter whispered. "Let's get your arm taken care of."

Moretti obeyed, forcing his clenched fists open as he walked past Chesterfield and dug out the aid kit. Jamie helped him with the bandages.

Peter sat down. He was angry at Chesterfield and frustrated to be in Yugoslavia, but most of all, he was exhausted. His face throbbed, and his neck ached, and his ankle felt awful. Jamie threw him a fresh shirt, and Peter used his handkerchief and canteen to wash the blood off his face.

"We need to move on," Chesterfield said, stroking his mustache.

He had a good point—the nineteen German corpses would be missed, and if the team was still around when the next patrol came, they'd be in trouble again.

"We can leave after I wrap Lieutenant Eddy's ankle." Moretti knelt next to Peter.

Chesterfield's eyes narrowed, but he didn't object. "Nelson, up the hill and keep watch. Zielinski, pack our gear."

"Guess he finally learned the benefit of keeping a lookout," Moretti mumbled under his breath.

"Better late than never," Peter said.

Chesterfield stepped closer, straining to hear them. "What was that, Sergeant?"

"I was just telling Lieutenant Eddy how many ankles I've wrapped since Sicily. Paratrooping can be rough on the joints." Moretti lied easily as he examined Peter's ankle and wrapped it tightly before replacing Peter's boot.

"Finally ready?" Chesterfield asked as Peter got to his feet. Peter clenched his teeth to keep from lashing out. *Finally ready? If you had listened to my advice, we wouldn't have gotten into this mess in the first place.*

"Should we bury that civilian?" Moretti asked.

Chesterfield rolled his eyes. "Serbian scum. She shouldn't have been there in the first place. We can't wait."

"She was Croatian, actually," Jamie said. "And this is her country. Why shouldn't she be out in the woods? Civilians have to eat the same as you and me. Not much food left in most villages."

"Are you questioning my orders?" Chesterfield said.

Jamie gave Chesterfield his most charming smile. "In this case, I happen to agree with you. I think it best her family finds her. If we bury her, they will never know what happened."

"Then move out," Chesterfield said. "Sergeant, you take point."

Peter slung his gear onto his back. Moretti's wrappings helped, but his ankle still hurt as he limped forward.

Chesterfield eyed him. "If you fail to keep up, Lieutenant, you will be left behind. The same holds true for you, Kapral."

Jamie stood only a few feet from Chesterfield. He dropped his gear, grabbed Chesterfield by his collar, and slammed his back into a nearby tree trunk. Raspolic brought out his pistol, but Moretti disarmed him in two seconds flat. Raspolic said something in protest, but it was in Serbo-Croat, and Jamie didn't bother to translate.

"Let me make a few things perfectly clear." Jamie's voice was calm, his face inches from Chesterfield's. "The only reason we are in this mess is because you failed to heed Peter's advice to take the high ground, where you would have been able to see what was happening. And the only reason Sergeant Moretti and Lieutenant Eddy are injured is because we came to rescue you after you got yourself into an untenable position. So if we are to leave anyone behind, it will be you because you are useless in a fight, useless when it comes to protecting us, and useless when it comes to leading us. You are both incompetent and cowardly, and I'll not obey your orders unless I agree with them. Nor will Sergeant Moretti or Kapral Zielinski or Lieutenant Eddy."

Chesterfield opened his mouth as if to protest. Jamie slammed him into the trunk again, and not even Raspolic moved to stop him. "Here is how the rest of the mission will proceed, you 'foul-spoken coward, that thund'rest with thy tongue, and with thy weapon nothing dar'st perform.' Should you wish us to do anything at all, you will say, 'Lieutenant Eddy, sir, would it be all right if we set out now,' or 'Lieutenant Eddy, sir, would it be all right if we camped now.' Furthermore, if you see or hear any of us in danger, you will come to our aid, even if it involves risking your pitiful neck. And should anything happen to Lieutenant Eddy, you will defer to Sergeant Moretti, then Kapral Zielinski. And should anything happen to all of them, I will either shoot you or abandon you. Do you understand, Lieutenant Chesterfield?"

Chesterfield was pale when Jamie released his collar, but he nodded.

"Then let's have a practice run, shall we?"

Chesterfield pushed himself from the tree, cowed into submission as Jamie, Krzysztof, and Moretti all glared at him. "Lieutenant Eddy, sir, is it permissible for us to move out now?"

Peter nodded, then trudged along for the next two hours. He was tired, his face hurt, and the pain in his ankle kept getting worse. He hated hospitals, but right then, he'd give just about anything to be in the one in

Bari, where he could put his foot up and Genevieve could run her fingers through his hair and hum a song until he fell asleep. He stifled a yawn. She wouldn't even get through a verse before he'd drift off.

CHAPTER SEVEN
BAKER'S INVESTIGATION

Monday, September 11
Bari, Italy

AFTER PUTTING CLEAN SHEETS ON another hospital bed, Genevieve slipped her hand into her pocket to feel the Purple Heart Peter had received after being wounded in Sicily. He'd given it to her a few months ago while he was on leave in London, then sent a letter telling her how he'd slept through General Patton's pinning it to his hospital pillow.

She'd been devastated when Peter had left. He'd seemed like the exact antidote she'd needed—someone to help her leave the past behind and focus instead on the future, a future with him. She was still angry that the war had dragged him away again when she needed him so badly, and she was frustrated with herself for being so feeble. Now that Peter had been gone a week—twice as long as predicted—worry that he might never return overshadowed her other emotions, making her feel constantly on the verge of tears, barely able to get out of bed each morning to complete her assignments at the hospital. She offered sincere prayers on his behalf several times each day, trying to bargain with the Lord to ensure his safe return. But how many times could Peter cheat death?

Genevieve forced herself through the rest of her shift. She made small talk with the patients and nurses, but her mind always came back to Peter, the man she loved, or to Weiss, the man she'd killed.

She was about to leave for the night when Dr. Lombardelli came in for his shift. "Miss Olivier?" Most of the hospital workers were American, but Lombardelli, like Genevieve, was an exception. He was Italian but spoke excellent English.

"Yes, sir?"

The gray-haired doctor motioned toward his office, and she followed him down the hall, worried. She hoped he wasn't going to chastise her for being so gloomy. She usually managed to smile for the patients but didn't bother pretending to be happy while she did laundry or washed scalpels. Or had she done something wrong with one of the patients? When the nurses were overworked, she assisted patients with their baths and checked their injuries for signs of infection. She couldn't remember doing anything incorrectly, but she wasn't a real nurse. She and the OSS officer who'd assigned her to work here had felt she knew enough to pose as a nurse's aide, but what if she'd made some horrible mistake?

Inside Lombardelli's office was a tall, muscular soldier in the uniform of a British major. He turned from the window as Lombardelli closed the door. His green eyes studied her for a moment. "Genevieve Olivier?" the major asked with a soft voice, extending his hand. "I'm Major Baker."

Genevieve took his hand as a knot formed in her stomach. Baker was Peter's most recent commanding officer, and she was terrified he had bad news for her.

"I was hoping you could help me with an investigation I'm conducting. It involves Lieutenant Eddy."

The knot in her stomach tripled in size, but Genevieve forced herself to speak. "Is Peter all right?"

Baker was quiet for several long moments. "I have absolutely no idea."

Genevieve felt her breath catch. No news was better than bad news, but not by much.

Baker motioned toward a chair. "As an OSS agent, I assume you can maintain silence regarding all I'm about to say?"

"Yes, sir."

"I'll start with some background. My team arrived in Bari last week, early on a Sunday morning. I was injured and eager to get some rest, so after the debriefing, when Colonel Gibson offered to fly me back to England, I took him up on it. It allowed me to escort two of my wounded men home and gave me the chance to see my wife again."

Baker pulled at his chin. "I'm afraid in my haste to see the wounded home, I neglected the needs of the rest of my men. I planned to give them all leave, promote some of them. We evacuated two civilians during our last assignment, and I began the paperwork to get them into England, then handed everything over to Gibson as I left. He told me he'd take care of it, but it's really something I should have done myself. I apologize."

Why is he apologizing to me? she wondered.

As if reading her expression, Baker continued. "I saw two of my men back to England, and one is still a patient in this hospital. The rest of my men, including Peter, and the civilians we evacuated, have all disappeared."

"What?"

"I've been looking for days. Gibson turned everything over to another officer at the debriefing, Major Kimby, but he's not talking. Something's up, and it hasn't gone through the normal SOE channels. OSS knows nothing. There is no record of assignment or transfer. My men are officially listed as *absent without leave.*"

"Peter wouldn't go AWOL."

"Nor would the other men," Baker said. "I feel I've run into a dead end, so I'm grasping at straws. You saw Peter before the debriefing, correct?"

"Yes." She fought back tears as she remembered how sweet it had been in contrast to the hurried good-bye later that day. "I also saw him that afternoon, briefly, before he left."

"Did he say where he was going?"

"Yugoslavia."

Baker dropped his hand from his jaw in surprise.

"That fits," Lombardelli cut in. "Kimby's on the Yugoslav section, and he's the one switching Miss Olivier's assignment."

"My assignment?" What was Lombardelli talking about? An American colonel in Marseilles had arranged for her to come to Bari, but he'd said nothing about an OSS assignment.

Lombardelli fiddled with the pen he held. He was short and a little overweight but still spry for someone in his sixties. "We share an employer."

She tilted her head to the side. They worked at the same hospital, but that didn't seem to be what he meant. "OSS?"

He nodded. "I knew when you arrived. I need a courier, but I was told your stay would be short, so I'd planned to find someone else. Only now Kimby's given me notice that he's sending you elsewhere."

"To Germany?"

Both men stared at her, surprised. Lombardelli recovered first. "How did you know that?"

"When Peter said good-bye, he made me promise I wouldn't go to Germany. How would he have known?"

Baker's hand went to his chin again. "Did Peter tell you anything else about his mission? Who he was going with, for example?"

Genevieve shook her head. "Just that he was leaving that afternoon and expected to return in a few days." Then Genevieve remembered Peter's letter. "He wrote that he had a bad feeling about his new mission."

"A letter? Did it say anything else?" Baker asked.

"The rest dealt with personal matters."

"May I see it?" Baker looked out the window, but when she hesitated, he turned back to face her. "If it contains any clues about his mission, it might allow me to help him."

"It's in my tent. I'll go get it."

She read the letter again on her way back to Lombardelli's office.

Dearest Genevieve,

I'm sorry I have to leave again. I can tell something bad happened on your last assignment, and there's nothing I want more than to stay and help you work through it. You are the most wonderful, most amazing, and most beautiful person I've ever met. And you're strong, so I know you'll make it through whatever it is you're struggling with. If all goes well, I'll be back soon, and then I'll do my best to help you.

If anyone asks you to go to Germany, turn them down. They can find someone else, so don't let them talk you into it. Please, please, keep yourself safe.

Stay strong in your newfound faith. Turn to the Lord for support. He'll never be forced away on a mission, so He'll always be there for you.

I promise not a single day will pass that I won't think of you, pray for you, and hope to one day marry you, but I have a bad feeling about my upcoming assignment. I hope it's just my concern about leaving you and not a premonition of disaster. If something happens to me, and I never return, please know in your heart that I loved you and that my leaving was better than the alternative.

All my love,
Peter

She'd read the letter more than a dozen times, and the words still evoked bittersweet emotions. If Peter loved her as much as he said he did, why hadn't he found a way to stay?

As Genevieve returned, she overheard part of the conversation between Baker and Lombardelli. "They could have been inserted by ship, but I think by air more likely," Baker said.

"Parachute or small plane?" Lombardelli asked. He noticed Genevieve and waved her in.

Baker shook his head. "I suppose there are airstrips in Yugoslavia not controlled by the Nazis, but the terrain isn't ideal for a quick landing and takeoff. I'd guess they went by parachute, but I don't suppose it matters."

Baker reached for her letter and read it with a look of concentration on his face. When he looked up, she saw compassion in his eyes.

"Any clues?" Lombardelli asked.

"Just what Miss Olivier already told us. He felt uneasy about his mission and seemed to think someone might ask her to go to Germany."

"And someone has—Kimby." Lombardelli tapped his pen against the desk.

Baker returned her letter. "I think it best if you refuse an assignment to Germany."

Genevieve nodded. She didn't want another mission, and she'd given Peter her word.

"Kimby won't ask. He'll order," Lombardelli said.

"You still need a courier, don't you, doctor?"

Lombardelli looked at Genevieve and nodded.

"Then she is your courier, and you won't let Kimby take her because she's indispensable to your work."

"Kimby has powerful friends."

"I have an English lord who helped form MI6, and he's extremely upset that his heir has gone missing. I think Kimby has the information we need—I just have to find someone ranked higher than me to put the correct pressure on him."

"A military policeman escorted Peter when he came to say good-bye. Do you think he would know anything?" Genevieve asked.

"Worth a try," Baker said. "Do you know his name?"

"No, but I'd recognize him."

Baker stood. "I have a patient to visit, then I'll talk to one of the MP officers. I'll need your help identifying the right man. Meet me here in an hour?"

Genevieve nodded, and Baker left, easing the door shut behind him.

Lombardelli sat quietly for a moment, letting Genevieve think. She looked at the pictures on his desk, focusing on the portrait of a young couple with two children. Lombardelli met her eyes. "I really do need a courier. Can I ask for your help? It should at least keep you out of Germany."

Genevieve didn't want to get involved in something new, but if it would help her keep her promise to Peter, she wouldn't say no. "What do you have in mind?"

He handed her an envelope. "I'm working with a local man. He's pretending to be a Fascist, and he's done a good job infiltrating the local organization. They don't suspect him—not that we know of—but it's a safe assumption he's being watched. I've been in touch with him several times, and I don't want any of his friends to get suspicious if they see us together again. I want you to take this to him."

Chapter Eight
A RELUCTANT SPY

Genevieve was glad Lombardelli hadn't asked her to do anything more than a courier run. Though she suspected espionage was a little like riding a horse—best to get right back on when you take a fall—she didn't feel like going at it again. She just wanted to be done. Her previous assignment had given the Allies useful information but nothing that changed the overall course of the war. And the cost had been high for her and for those she'd worked with.

She recognized the bistro and her contact from Lombardelli's descriptions. *Twenty-six years old, thin spectacles, short brown hair, broad shoulders.* He had a pleasant face, and he wore a shirt with a patched collar and pants with threadbare knees. His jacket hung over the back of the chair. He sat chatting with three other men at their table outside the bistro. None of them had any food in front of them, which didn't surprise her. Food was difficult for civilians to come by, and money seemed even more elusive.

Genevieve sat for a moment in a chair backing her contact and reached down to adjust her shoe, out of view of the other men. She slid the envelope into the man's jacket pocket and caught the man's eye as she stood to leave.

Lombardelli was in the ward when Genevieve returned, so she waited in his empty office, thinking of Peter. *I thought we were finally due for a break—one long enough to include a wedding.* She'd suspected something was wrong when Peter hadn't returned as scheduled, but hearing he was lost made elation and hope disappear, smothered by worry and depression. If no one would tell Major Baker where Peter was, she assumed whatever he was involved in was very secret, very important, and very dangerous. Perhaps Major Kimby or the giant MP would give them more information—but what if they didn't?

Baker returned with an American MP, a polite, businesslike sergeant with a distinctive drawl.

"Can you describe the man in question?" the MP asked her.

"He was tall," Genevieve said. "Well over six feet. Muscular. Blue eyes."

"Hair?"

Genevieve tried to remember. "He wore a helmet, but his eyebrows were blond."

"Sounds like Gliswell. I'll go find him."

He returned not long after with the correct MP. When Gliswell entered Lombardelli's office and recognized Genevieve, he took a step back. "Look, Sarge, I don't know what this is all about, but I haven't done anything wrong—I was just following orders."

Baker offered Gliswell his hand. "We aren't here to accuse you of any wrongdoing. But I would like to hear more about your orders, the ones from a Major Kimby." Baker made a signal through the open door, and Lombardelli joined them, closing the door behind him.

Gliswell looked at his sergeant for instructions.

"Answer their questions."

"How long were you working with Kimby?" Baker asked.

"Two days, sir."

"And what did he have you do?"

Gliswell glanced at Genevieve before answering. "I was guarding a tent. Making sure that lieutenant didn't run off."

"Just the lieutenant?" Baker asked.

"At first. Then a few men joined him—a US sergeant, a civilian, a British lieutenant, and a Yugoslav Partisan."

"Do you remember any names?"

"The first guy—Lieutenant Eddy. And the guy with the mustache— Lieutenant Chesterfield."

"Any others?" Baker asked.

Gliswell shook his head.

"Describe them, please."

"The sergeant—he was about six feet tall. Muscular. Dark hair, curly. Wore an 82nd Airborne patch and bloused his pants like paratroopers do. The civilian had blond hair, blue eyes. A little shorter than the sergeant but not by much. Carried himself well, had the type of face women fall for—ya know, like something from a movie poster. The Partisan had one of those caps with a red star. Thin build, brown hair."

"Did you hear anything about their assignment?"

"No, sir, I couldn't hear inside the tent. After the meeting, I took them all to the airfield, then drove Lieutenant Eddy to say good-bye to his girlfriend." Gliswell nodded toward Genevieve. "Major Kimby said he could have two minutes, so that's what I gave him, then took him back to the airfield. Kimby had me drive him here to the hospital, where I picked up the last man. I'd guess he was a patient—didn't look too healthy, ya know. Tall and skinny, blue eyes, black hair, narrow face. Probably in his twenties. He wore civilian clothing."

"And then?" Baker asked.

"They didn't seem to be getting along too well, Kimby and the others. But they got on the plane."

"Were the men in uniform when they boarded?"

Gliswell thought for a moment. "No, civilian clothes, except for the Partisan's hat."

"Did you see two civilians? A woman in her midtwenties, tall, black hair, brown eyes, feminine figure. And a little boy—her son—about three years old?"

"No, sir."

"Anything else you remember about your time with Major Kimby, anything odd or out of place?"

Gliswell shook his head, then paused. "The next day was warm, ya know. Kimby's work tent had one of those Sibley stoves with a chimney through the tent's corner. It was lit the next day. I could see the smoke coming out."

"It was warm enough that you wouldn't expect the stove to be needed for heat?" Baker asked.

"No, sir. I went swimming when I got off duty."

"Thank you for your time." Baker opened the door, and the two MPs left.

Lombardelli sighed as their boots echoed down the hallway. "I guess it wouldn't do us any good to go through Kimby's files. Sounds like he burned the evidence."

Baker nodded. "I'd bet the men Gliswell described are Moretti, Jamie, and Zielinski. So at least the missing men are together. But what happened to Iuliana and her son?"

"We could follow Kimby, see if it leads anywhere," Lombardelli said.

"Yes, but not you. Nor you, Miss Olivier," Baker said. "Doctor, find some Italian civilians, have them tail him. I don't want anyone with OSS or SOE connections on this."

"Does that mean you'd prefer they don't receive any OSS cash?"

"Jamie's grandfather is ill, but I went to visit him a few days ago. He might not be able to march off to London and demand answers just yet, but he'll fund us. I'll see that you get the money within a week." Baker turned to Genevieve. "Lieutenant Eddy is still missing, but it seems he is with friends. I will dig up what I can on Chesterfield and see if I can find someone to put pressure on Kimby. I'll let you know if I hear anything. Can I ask you to do the same?"

"Of course, sir. Anything to bring back Peter and his friends."

CHAPTER NINE
CHETNIKS

Tuesday, September 12
Independent State of Croatia

PETER EASED THE WEIGHT OFF his left foot. After a week of walking south through the increasingly steep terrain, his ankle still hurt most of the time. When it didn't ache, it was numb, and when he unwrapped it each morning, it was blue and swollen. Raspolic had made a crutch for him to use, and that helped, but it also made his hand blister. Jamie and Moretti were hauling most of his gear for him, but he still couldn't match their speed.

In the dark, Peter saw Moretti smile as he looked at the map. "We're getting close. 'Bout a mile away."

Peter sighed with relief. They'd made poor time the last week—largely due to Peter's ankle—and not a day had passed without running into a Nazi patrol. Most of the patrols had been small, and since Moretti or Jamie usually led the way and detected them early, the team was able to avoid them or quickly overwhelm them. Chesterfield was cooperating, but his irritation at Peter's pace was starting to surface again.

"I suppose I ought to start looking the part of a daring commando now." Chesterfield took off his boots and tossed them to Krzysztof. His shoulder wasn't getting any worse, but Krzysztof still looked exhausted at the end of each march. "Kapral, polish my boots."

"You can polish your own boots." Moretti grabbed the footwear and threw it back to Chesterfield.

"Officers don't polish their own boots."

"Then I guess you should of brought a batman," Moretti said.

"Our radio man can double as both. It's not as if he's keeping in touch with headquarters anyhow."

Krzysztof had kept quiet during the shoe debate, a slight frown his only sign of irritation, but he spoke up when Chesterfield questioned his competence. "We were told to maintain radio silence until the bridge is destroyed."

Peter cut Chesterfield off before he could argue. "You know, I'm an officer, and I always polish my own boots. But only for the parade ground and dates with my girl. Shiny boots might draw more attention than anyone with half a brain would want out here. We're supposed to be invisible while we destroy that rail line."

Jamie returned from the scouting trip he'd taken with Raspolic. "The road ahead is clear, for now." Jamie looked at the map and nodded as Moretti pointed out their current location. "We could push past this village before dawn, hit the bridge tonight."

As they approached the village, Peter expected to hear the same sounds they'd heard the other times that week when they'd drawn near populated areas: villagers foraging for food or chopping wood, sheepdogs barking at an unfamiliar noise. But as they walked along the north end of the village, it was silent, and it smelled like smoke.

"Go see what's wrong," Chesterfield said to Jamie.

Jamie motioned for Moretti to join him.

Moretti returned a few minutes later, alone. "Someone burned most of the village. It's deserted."

The fires no longer smoldered as they walked through the ruins of the village, but the smell of smoke still hung in the air. Near the town center, Jamie knelt on the ground, fingering a bullet casing. As Peter drew closer, he saw that casings covered the ground. "I would guess these came from an MG 42." Jamie pointed out two small holes in the dirt in front of him. "From the bi-pod."

"Why set up a machine gun in the middle of the road?" Peter asked. There were cottages on either side of the street that would have provided a more sheltered and secure position. As Peter limped past Jamie to where he guessed the machine gun had pointed, he noticed the freshly overturned dirt and suspected he was about to step on a mass grave. He turned back to his friends.

Jamie translated for Raspolic. "He says it is standard German reprisal. They shoot one hundred Serbs for every German soldier killed, fifty for every German soldier wounded."

Peter felt sick. An entire village had been destroyed and some of its inhabitants killed as punishment for someone else's actions. He looked back at the grave, not sure he wanted to know how many civilians were buried there.

The crack of a rifle sounded, and Moretti cursed and fell to the ground. As the incoming fire escalated, Jamie and Krzysztof grabbed Moretti's arms and dragged him into one of the half-destroyed homes. Peter ran to join them, stepping too aggressively with his injured ankle and falling when it refused to support his weight. He crawled the rest of the way to his teammates, who were sheltered behind the two-foot-high remnants of a charred wall. He untangled himself from his gear and peered over the ruin, looking along the top of his rifle to spot his opponents. Jamie and Krzysztof were next to him, doing the same thing.

Chesterfield and Raspolic were flat on the ground. "Load the Bren," Peter said. Neither of them budged. Jamie repeated the instructions in Serbo-Croat, and Raspolic started moving.

They were in a bad position—the wall was thick enough but short, and they were silhouetted against the coming daybreak while their attackers had the advantage of shadow. Peter could barely make out the German troops, about twenty of them. He and his teammates all found targets and aimed, but at that distance, it was too dark for accurate shots.

"There is a detachment coming around on our left." Jamie grabbed a few grenades and moved out to stop them. Peter covered him, hoping Jamie wasn't about to get killed.

As Jamie disappeared, Peter noticed another group of German soldiers and an armored personnel carrier. They were going to need more firepower.

Raspolic emptied the Bren and loaded another clip. Its firing rate of 500 rounds per minute would help, but it wouldn't solve their problems. Peter and Krzysztof were aiming for the closest troops, and Raspolic was slowing the German advance with the Bren when the carrier exploded. The flash was bright, and Peter had to blink a few times before he could focus on the remaining enemy.

How did Jamie do that? Jamie was capable of making things explode, but he hadn't had any of the right tools on him when he left.

Some of the remaining German soldiers turned as if to fight someone behind them. Grenades burst around Peter's opponents, and he could see another group fighting the Germans. They first appeared in pairs, and more advanced as the German troops steadily fell, overwhelmed by superior numbers and the surprise shot to their armored carrier.

It was over in five minutes. As the newcomers shot the wounded Germans, Peter turned to check on Moretti. He had a handkerchief over his wound, and the bleeding seemed under control. "How bad is it?"

"Unpleasant but not fatal." Moretti shook his head. "This country doesn't like me much. First that shot in the arm, now one in the butt."

Peter glanced at the faces of their rescuers as they approached, wondering who they were. They were male, military-aged, most of them with thick beards. Some of them wore what looked like military jackets, others what looked like military caps or pants, but it would be a stretch to say they were in uniform. Half of them wore rags over their feet instead of shoes, and they carried a variety of weapons.

Jamie reappeared and nodded to the man Peter guessed was in charge. He was medium height, with a dark beard and the most complete uniform of the group—though Peter still couldn't pinpoint what army he was part of.

As Raspolic put away the Bren gun and stood, one of the bearded men shouted something in a foreign language, raised his rifle, and shot Raspolic in the forehead.

Peter gripped his M1 and felt his throat go dry as Raspolic fell dead. He'd thought the battle was over. Had the men rescued his team from the Nazis only to kill them now? Peter swallowed, assuming he could take out a few of the irregular soldiers if he had to, but the odds were against his team's survival if the newcomers planned to ambush them. Jamie and Krzysztof looked tense, but none of the bearded men seemed like they were about to attack the team's remaining members.

"What is the meaning of this?" Chesterfield shouted, brandishing his rifle.

"He was a Partisan, wasn't he?" The man who spoke was the shortest of the group and the only one without a beard. His English had a slight accent.

The answer was obvious: Raspolic's cap emblazoned with a red star was still on his head. Chesterfield stammered. "He . . . he's one of my men. He traveled with a British officer and should have been granted the same respect you would grant me."

"The rest of you—you're British?"

"They're American." Chesterfield gestured toward Peter and Moretti. "He's Polish." He finished with a finger pointed at Krzysztof.

The short Yugoslav man smiled. "We like Americans. Welcome."

"Then why did you shoot their ally?" Chesterfield's face was red with rage.

The man who spoke English wasn't the one who'd shot Raspolic, but he didn't seem bothered by his comrade's behavior. "Phst, if you were in the middle of a battle with the Germans, and a Japanese soldier showed up, you'd shoot him, wouldn't you? It's not so different for us. We're Chetniks, so we try to kill Nazi, Ustaše, and Partisan troops before they kill us. I'm sorry that upsets you." The man turned around and spoke to the others.

Peter wasn't sure what to think, especially when he found himself being embraced by most of the Chetniks as they called out *Americanski* and kissed him on the cheeks. They'd helped finish off the Nazi patrol, undoubtedly saving all of their lives, but they'd shot Raspolic without warning. The Partisans and the Chetniks were in the middle of a fierce civil war, but couldn't they have taken Raspolic prisoner? Peter tried to shake off the shock of Raspolic's death, knowing it would be foolish to protest while he and his teammates were outnumbered. One of the Chetniks took the boots from Raspolic's feet and tried them on. They were too small, so he passed them to one of his shoeless companions.

The English-speaking Chetnik knelt next to Moretti. "Let me have a look."

"You a doctor?"

"Almost." He took out a small bag of tools and removed the handkerchief.

Moretti looked alarmed. "What's *almost* supposed to mean?"

"I was a medical student, in my last year, when the Germans bombed Belgrade in 1941. Graduation was canceled, along with the remainder of my classes. Trust me, I've dug out more bullets than most doctors have."

"You gotta name, doc?" Moretti asked.

"Miloš Colić."

"I'm Sergeant Moretti. This is Lieutenant Eddy. That's Lieutenant Chesterfield, Kapral Zielinski, James Nelson—ahhh!" Moretti screamed as Miloš extracted the bullet.

"We don't have much in the way of medical supplies. No anesthesia, no antibiotics. I don't suppose you have any?"

Peter dug through a pack and pulled out some sulfa powder. He'd been taught to pour a generous amount over an injury, but Miloš sprinkled it on, carefully conserving the remainder of the packet. "Do you want morphine?" Peter asked as Miloš started stitching Moretti's wound.

"Just one of these." Moretti lit himself a cigarette, then handed the pack to a nearby Chetnik, who took one and passed it along until it was empty.

"Thanks for the help," Peter said. "You guys just wandering around shooting Nazi patrols when you see them?"

"Wandering around without a purpose would be reckless," Miloš said. "We're on our way back from destroying a bridge. It was south of here."

"How far south?" Peter asked, waving Jamie over.

"Part of the railroad line between Višegrad and Sarajevo, two kilometers away."

That sounded a lot like their target. Jamie got out the map and had Miloš confirm it. Sure enough, if Miloš was telling the truth, their stretch of railroad was already destroyed.

CHAPTER TEN
MISPLACED TRUST

CHESTERFIELD CAME OVER TO SEE but seemed unconvinced. "I'll need to give Major Kimby visual confirmation." He lowered his voice. "Besides, you don't really trust that Chetnik, do you? He's probably lying—paid by the Nazis to prevent sabotage."

Peter glanced at the dead soldiers surrounding them, the ones Miloš and his men had shot. He doubted these Chetniks were taking Nazi pay, but if the bridge was really that close, it wouldn't take long to confirm it was destroyed. "What do you suggest?"

Chesterfield pointed to the map. "Take Zielinski and check the bridge. Nelson and I will move Moretti to the extraction point and meet you there."

Peter glanced at Krzysztof, who didn't look like he was up for a hike through the mountains: a mile and a quarter to the rail line, then almost a mile back to the extraction point. Nor did Krzysztof look up to carrying a litter—not that they had a litter, but maybe they could improvise. Peter wasn't looking forward to the assignment either; his ankle was throbbing worse than usual, thanks to his mad dash to shelter when the Germans surprised them.

Miloš cleared his throat. "We're always happy to show our work. And assist our wounded allies." He turned and spoke to one of his men.

Chesterfield's hands tensed on his rifle. "What did he say?"

Jamie rolled his eyes. "He sent some of his men back to their camp to retrieve a stretcher. Based on their assistance with the Germans, I think we can assume they aren't planning to kill us."

A smile crept across Miloš's face. "You speak Serbo-Croat?"

Jamie nodded.

"How?"

"My father sailed a yacht up and down the Danube. I accompanied him the first sixteen years of my life and somewhat more sporadically the next sixteen. We spent a fair amount of time in Serbia."

"Doing what?" Miloš asked.

"Smuggling things and people."

Chesterfield looked horrified. Miloš looked amused. Peter waited to see if Jamie would redeem himself in Chesterfield's eyes by explaining how many anti-Nazis he'd helped in their escape from Germany, but Jamie only glanced at Chesterfield and smiled, content to seem a rogue.

Miloš introduced them to their group's leader, Bogdan Brajović, and Bogdan offered to lead Jamie and Chesterfield to the destroyed bridge with a few of his men, then take them to the extraction point. Chesterfield scrounged a few German weapons, and the group headed off. Peter felt a little uneasy as he saw them go. He was grateful for the change in plan, that he and Krzysztof would no longer have to hike to the bridge, but he didn't completely trust their new allies.

The Chetniks Miloš had sent to camp returned with two litters, but Peter refused to ride. He let the Chetniks carry his gear when they offered, and he accepted their help burying Raspolic. It felt strange to him, working with the men who'd shot the Partisan so casually. Peter hadn't known Raspolic well—the language barrier and Raspolic's unflinching loyalty to Chesterfield had never been overcome enough to form a friendship—but he'd seemed like a decent man. He'd also been a good cook and a good volunteer crutch maker.

Peter walked next to Krzysztof, just behind Moretti's litter, as the two dozen Chetniks assisted them to the road that would double as an airstrip when their flight home arrived. Peter fell a few steps behind as they climbed a steep hill, then got behind Krzysztof as the path narrowed.

"Krzysztof? Did you check your gear back at that village?" A diagonal line of bullet holes extended from the upper left to the bottom right of his pack.

Krzysztof stepped from the trail and slipped his gear off. He checked the radio first. It had been punctured three times.

Miloš walked back to them. "Is everything all right?"

"You don't happen to have a radio, do you?" Peter asked.

Miloš shook his head.

"I might be able to fix it." Krzysztof packed it away. "I'll check it more thoroughly when we stop." Peter helped Krzysztof get his gear situated, but the depressed look on his friend's face had Peter worried.

"Have you been here long?" Miloš asked.

"A week and a few days." Peter stepped over a log and stumbled when he put weight on his injured ankle.

"And you're just here to destroy the rail line?"

"Yeah."

Miloš frowned. "We keep hoping the Americans will supply us like they do the other resistance groups. You saw how we put that panzerfaust to use?"

Peter nodded, remembering the way the personnel carrier had turned into a fireball.

"We took it from a German supply depot but lost a few men in the process. If we didn't have to waste time finding our own weapons, we could be more effective driving the Nazis out. I've heard on the radio how the Americans supply the British, the Russians, and the French Resistance. The stories are true, aren't they?"

"Yeah," Peter said.

"Then where are our supplies?"

Peter hesitated but decided to be honest, even if the answer was blunt. "I heard someone say they were worried you'd use the weapons against the Partisans instead of against the Germans."

"Phst, that doesn't stop you from supplying the Partisans. You know the Communists wouldn't lift a finger against the Germans when they first invaded? As long as Germany and the Soviet Union were allies, they sat on the sidelines."

Peter tried to remember his history. Hitler hadn't waited long to attack the Soviet Union after he invaded Yugoslavia—maybe two months. Not wanting to get into a political debate, Peter attempted to switch the subject. "Do you know what happened to that village?"

"Last week the Partisans came through and declared it liberated. They staged a few raids, made the Germans mad, then took off when the Germans got too close. Some of the villagers followed them, but most weren't quick enough and had to suffer the reprisals. Last night we helped an old woman who escaped. She said they killed over a hundred men there yesterday. And the Partisans don't care. Unless they're armed and fighting by their side, the villagers are useless to them. That's why Tito's numbers are growing so quickly. They come through and cause mischief, then move on and leave the villagers no choice but to join them or face death."

"You and your men are Serbs?" Peter asked.

Miloš nodded. "Bogdan and most of the men grew up in Serbia. I grew up in a village in Herzegovina."

"Who told you to destroy the railroad bridge?"

Miloš looked up at Peter with a smile. "General Mihailovich. He ordered mobilization the beginning of this month and requested attacks along a few stretches of rail. Perhaps if the Americans weren't ignoring us, you could have avoided your entire mission."

Yeah, that would have been nice. Peter had been exhausted all week. With the redundant nature of their mission, he was also frustrated.

"You should be hidden all day if you stay here," Miloš said when they arrived at a hill overlooking the evacuation point. "We can watch the roads for you—block them off so no one interferes with your plane."

But an hour later, when Chesterfield returned from checking the bridge, he didn't want any additional aid from the Chetniks. "You can move along," he told Bogdan and Miloš.

Peter was chagrined by Chesterfield's rudeness but not surprised. "Was the bridge destroyed?" he asked Jamie.

"Completely." Jamie gave Peter a wry smile.

"How was the trip?"

"I had a delightful conversation with our Serb friends in Serbo-Croat. I don't think Chesterfield enjoyed not being able to understand any of it."

Peter shook hands with the Chetniks as they left.

"When you get back, tell them we're on your side, eh?" Miloš grinned as he said good-bye.

Peter smiled back, glad Chesterfield's abrupt send-off hadn't angered Miloš. The Chetniks disappeared into the trees. They were merciless with their enemies and rivals, but they were a competent guerrilla force.

"Any progress with the repairs?" Chesterfield asked.

Krzysztof had been working on the radio continuously since they'd stopped walking. He frowned. "I might be able to make something work, but I'll need new parts. Do you suppose that armored personnel carrier in the village would have useful scraps?"

"If it did, they're burnt to a crisp now," Moretti said.

Peter sat next to Jamie, depressed. His ankle throbbed, and now they had no way to contact their ride home. Their mission was complete—not because of them, but that didn't matter. There wasn't any reason for them not to be in Italy the next day, but no pilot would land to pick them up unless he knew the team was waiting. "I think we're in for a long walk," he said to Jamie. "We could make for the Dalmatian Coast. It's liberated, isn't it?"

"So the Partisans say. But the Germans can take it back whenever they want to," Jamie said as he watched Chesterfield walk away from the group, seeming to contemplate their next move. "It looks as though we are indeed up for a long trek, with a destination that may or may not be safe." Jamie lowered his voice. "And Moretti can't walk, and you and Krzysztof aren't exactly in top form either." Moretti lay on his stretcher, playing with an unlit cigarette, and Krzysztof fiddled with the radio, both of them on the far side of a dying oak tree.

"Which means you get to carry the litter more than a hundred miles through Nazi territory and try to convince Chesterfield to help you."

"Convince him I shall as long as—" Jamie stopped midsentence as he glanced toward the British lieutenant. "Get down!"

Peter caught movement in his peripheral vision, and then the world around him exploded. The blast sucked the air from his lungs and shoved him to the ground. A crack followed the initial roar, and the oak tree fell, pinning Peter's arms and chest to the ground. Peter knew what he'd seen: a German Stielhandgranate 24, usually called the potato-masher grenade by Allied troops. What he couldn't figure out was why Chesterfield had thrown one at his teammates.

Peter lay flat on his back, fighting to fill his lungs with air again, his breath coming in short, uneven gasps. His ears rang, and pain screamed at him from every appendage, yet at the same time, his head felt disconnected from his body. He tried to move but couldn't. Eventually, he forced his head to the right. Krzysztof lay flat on the ground, one arm stretched above his head, his eyes closed, cuts on his cheek and forehead. The tree blocked Peter's view, so he couldn't tell if his friend's chest was still rising or not. Moretti was out of his sight entirely. With effort, Peter turned his head the other direction.

Jamie was conscious, the tree trunk across his thighs. His pistol was inches out of reach—probably knocked away during the explosion. As Jamie struggled to get out from under the log, Peter tried to help shift the wood, but his hands wouldn't do what his brain told them to. Jamie managed to scoot a few inches forward, but before his fingers could grip the pistol, they were crushed by a boot.

Chesterfield stood over them, stepping on Jamie's hand, his pistol pointed at Jamie's forehead.

"Why?" Jamie was only two feet away, but Peter felt like his voice was coming through a tunnel.

"Major Kimby told me the four of you weren't to return alive. I thought most of you would be dead by now so I wouldn't have to finish you off." Chesterfield was calm, his pistol never moving from its target. "I didn't do it earlier because the four of you were an asset to survival. But when Sergeant Moretti was injured and the radio destroyed, you became a liability. I might have kept you around, given your language abilities, if I thought there was any chance you'd leave the others."

Peter tried to force his hand to his weapon. He had to save Jamie and make it back to Genevieve, but his hand wouldn't move. Chesterfield's finger tightened on the trigger, and then a crack sounded, and a bullet pierced Chesterfield's forehead, spinning the British lieutenant around and dropping him to the ground.

"Liability, huh?" Moretti said.

Jamie reached for his weapon and stared at Chesterfield's corpse. "Excellent shot, Sergeant. I believe I owe you my life."

"Don't want it. But I've got some damage from that blast and wouldn't mind some help getting patched up. Krzysztof could use a little help too."

"Is he alive?" Peter asked, his voice a raspy whisper.

"How bad is Krzysztof?" Jamie asked, his voice carrying more volume than Peter's.

"Not sure," Moretti said. "Breathing and bloody. How's Peter?"

"Stuck under the log with me. Conscious. I only see a little blood."

Peter wondered where he was bleeding—everything hurt, but he couldn't pinpoint any wet sensations. Jamie was having difficulty getting the log off his legs but finally managed to slide out. As he moved, the log shifted, and the confining pressure on Peter became crushing. The steady pain suddenly intensified, and Peter could barely breathe. "Jamie," he gasped.

Jamie tried to stand, but his legs wouldn't support his weight. He crawled back to the log and pushed, but it wouldn't budge. Every breath Peter took was more labored, and the pain threatened to consume him. His hearing was already off, and as Jamie struggled unsuccessfully with the log, Peter's vision grew fuzzy too. Despite his efforts, he could move neither his arms nor his legs. He felt himself slipping away and could do nothing to stop it.

The next few hours were snatches of foggy memory. Peter could remember the Chetniks returning to lift the tree trunk, remember the sight of Moretti's chest, bloody and burned, remember being carried on a litter through the forest and put on a truck with the others. Overshadowing everything was the pain—constant and severe.

CHAPTER ELEVEN
CASUALTIES

German-occupied Serbia

MARIJA BRAJOVIĆ LOOKED UP FROM her laundry as her cousin Bogdan returned to the village. His team was with him, smaller than it had been when they left, and they carried four men on stretchers.

Bogdan came over to her. "Is my father here?"

Marija shook her head. Her uncle, Pukovnik Stoyan Brajović, had left the day before. "He said he'd be gone a few weeks."

"We came across two Americans, a Pole, and an Englishman."

"Wounded?"

"They are now." Bogdan shifted the rifle strap on his shoulder. "Another Englishman, someone on their team, tried to kill them."

British soldiers trying to kill each other? Now she'd heard everything.

Bogdan went back to help the foreigners into a village home across the street from where Miloš Colić lived. Marija continued to scrub her laundry in the fading light. She normally did wash when she could see better, but the day's earlier chores had taken longer than usual.

Everything had since General Mihailovic ordered mobilization a week and a half ago and all the men had gone off to fight. She was glad Bogdan and Miloš were back. She felt less vulnerable when they were around, though she knew a German platoon or an Ustaše or Partisan group could still wipe them out in minutes. *It won't be long. Maybe a few days, maybe a few months and then we'll all be dead anyway.* Death itself didn't scare her, but there were many ways to die, and some of the possibilities were terrifying.

Miloš came out of the house and walked toward her. "Hello, Marija."

"Hello, Miloš."

"I was thinking, Marija, that we should get married."

Marija's hands didn't pause as they scrubbed out a shirt. "We can't get married."

"Why not?"

Marija wrung out the shirt, not bothering to look at him. "I'm taller than you."

"Phst. Only by an inch. I will wear tall shoes and forget to comb my hair. No one will notice I'm so short."

"I don't love you, Miloš."

Miloš stayed where he was for a few minutes. She knew he was there, but she didn't meet his gaze. Then Miloš spoke again. "Perhaps tomorrow you will love me."

She watched him walk away, glad he wasn't dead. The people needed a doctor, and perhaps even more, they needed someone who could look on the bright side the way Miloš always did.

She turned back to her wash, trying to remember how many times Miloš had proposed to her. *Probably a hundred by now.* She was surprised he hadn't given up. Bogdan had commented more than once that maybe she should give in, but that was poor advice. If Miloš knew the truth about her past, he wouldn't want to marry her anyway.

Marija finished her laundry and moved on to her next chore. Later that night, she saw Miloš again on her way back from gathering kindling. For the first time she could remember, he looked unhappy. He walked from the home the foreigners were in and kicked a stump, then hopped away, obviously in pain. Bogdan came out a minute later, looking equally distraught. She moved closer to them, wondering what was wrong.

"Someone must have put pressure on him. Or it's a feign. He wouldn't turn on us—we're his most loyal subjects," Bogdan said.

"You heard him. He just did." Miloš noticed Marija. "Did you hear the broadcast, Marija?"

"No."

"Our king told us to join the Partisans." Miloš kicked a rock across the dirt road.

"He can't have meant it." Bogdan's voice wavered as he spoke.

"You heard his speech!" Miloš yelled. "He told all loyal Yugoslavs to join Tito." Miloš kicked another rock. "Perhaps he's been away too long—under too much English influence."

"But we can't join the Partisans," Marija said. "They'd kill us."

* * *

When Peter woke, he felt as if he'd been hit by a panzer. Every breath was agony, like a knife in his lungs. His chest, ankle, and head all ached, and though his hands now followed the commands his brain gave them, movement made the pain worse.

The walls surrounding his teammates and him were made of stone and mortar and were topped with a thatched roof. The home was sparsely furnished with a table near the fireplace, two chairs, and a few wooden shelves and cupboards. The remnants of their gear were piled in a corner.

Peter lay on a low bed with a thin straw mattress. Krzysztof and Moretti were asleep. Jamie sat on his cot with his back against the wall, reading something. Peter didn't dare try the same thing—if breathing was painful, sitting was bound to be excruciating. He could see daylight through the window over Jamie's bed and cottages that looked similar to the one they were in. The village was in the mountains, surrounded by a forest.

"What are you reading?" Peter's voice was raspy and slurred.

"Serbian poetry. All about choosing a heavenly kingdom over an earthly one and being slaughtered by the Turks. I suppose this time they are fighting different foes, but some things stay constant in the Balkans. The Serbs have a long association with martyrdom." Jamie put the book down. "You don't look as awful as you sound."

"Good. Every time I come back from a mission, Genevieve's gotten prettier, and I've just collected more scars." Peter breathed in too deeply and winced. "I told her I'd be back in a few days." He squeezed his eyes against the physical pain and the disappointment at how their mission had turned out. "Is it Wednesday? Or was I out awhile?"

"Yes, it is Wednesday. And were any bookmakers nearby, I would bet in favor of her waiting for you."

Peter doubted Genevieve would fall for someone else, but he was worried she'd be manipulated into something dangerous during his absence.

Miloš walked through the front door, carrying a loaf of bread. His smile wasn't as broad as Peter remembered it, but he looked cheerful. "Good morning."

"You seem to be taking last night's broadcast rather well," Jamie said.

Miloš frowned. "We're used to bad news."

"What broadcast?" Peter asked.

"The Yugoslav king, Peter Karadjordjević, spoke to his country over the BBC last night. He said all his loyal subjects should join the Partisans."

As Jamie spoke, Miloš's face showed increasing gloom. "'Though those that are betrayed do feel the treason sharply, yet the traitor stands in worse case of woe.' What will you do?"

"I'm not sure. I feel like the king's given up on us, but he's my king—I can't turn against him. I have to hope he'll change his mind." Miloš was quiet for a moment, staring out the window. "I was there, in Belgrade, during the coup. March 1941. We were all so angry when his uncle, the regent, signed the pact with Hitler. But then a few air force officers put Peter on the throne and refused Axis demands, and we felt like men again. We knew we weren't strong enough to defeat the Nazis if they attacked, but we had spat in Hitler's eye, and for the moment, we were free."

Miloš drummed his fingers along the windowsill. "I saw the king driving to the palace the day after the coup—not yet eighteen, waving to the people, willing to lead them in their resistance. I've never felt more alive than I did that day. Then came April and the Luftwaffe. They destroyed Belgrade, killed seventeen thousand people in four days. The king escaped to London, and I escaped into the mountains with part of the military. And we've waited and starved and fought . . . and now I don't know what we'll do."

Miloš looked around the room. Krzysztof and Moretti had woken, and Miloš smiled. "I'm sorry. I'm talking politics, and I should be looking after my patients. I'll start with you, Sergeant." Miloš checked the bandages wrapped around Moretti's chest and side.

"How bad are those burns?" Peter asked.

Moretti made a noise somewhere between a grunt and a growl.

"They cover a large area, but for the most part, they're shallow," Miloš answered. "The skin should heal itself, but it might scar. The main concerns are infection and pain. Same with the bullet wound. It shouldn't cause permanent damage if we keep it clean."

"We've got some stuff in our kits," Peter said. "Morphine for the pain and sulfa powder for infection."

"Yes, I've been using the sulfa powder. We don't have anything like that available here, so I'm trying to make it last."

"Did you use all the penicillin?" Peter asked Krzysztof.

"What was left got destroyed with our radio." Krzysztof's voice was weak and gloomy.

"Are you okay, Krzysztof?" Peter tried to sit so he could see his men better, but the pain in his chest forced him to stay put. He gritted his teeth to keep from crying out.

Miloš walked over to him. "You might want to stay immobile most of the day, Lieutenant. I don't have an X-ray machine, but I'll wager you have a few broken ribs. That, deep bruising in your chest, a cut on the back of your head, and an ankle I'd also like to X-ray."

"And Jamie and Krzysztof?"

"I suspect Mr. Nelson's left femur is broken. Kapral Zielinski has a concussion and several cuts I've had to stitch up. His shoulder is stable."

Peter felt sick to his stomach, and it wasn't just the increased pain as Miloš checked the bump on his head and unwrapped his ribs to make sure the bruising hadn't changed overnight.

Krzysztof might be up for a hike to the Dalmatian Coast in a week or so, but Jamie and Moretti couldn't walk, and Peter could only hobble. By the time they were healed, they'd be out of shape, and it would be winter. Unless they fixed the shot-up radio and convinced someone to fly them out, they were going to be in the little village on the Croatian-Serbian border for a long time.

* * *

It was a miserable day. Jamie translated some of the poetry, but tales of epic battles between Serbs and Turks didn't lessen the pain in Peter's chest or his worry about Genevieve.

Miloš returned that evening carrying bread again. A young woman followed with goat milk. The bread was rough and dense, but Peter assumed it was fresh because it was still warm, as was the milk. The woman was thin, with the slouched shoulders of someone who wanted to blend in with her surroundings. A pale kerchief covered her light brown hair, and it, like her clothes, was frayed at the ends but clean. She didn't speak to Miloš or the men but nodded when they thanked her, whether they used English, as Peter, Moretti, and Krzysztof did, or Serbo-Croat, as Jamie did.

Miloš watched her leave and finished checking Moretti's bandages. "Will you excuse me for a few moments? I need to propose to the woman I've been in love with most of my life."

Peter followed Miloš's progress through the window above Jamie's cot. The skinny woman helped an equally skinny child wrap a scrap of cloth around a doll. Miloš caught up to her and waited until the child skipped away, her doll swaddled.

Peter studied their faces as they spoke. The woman wore a perpetual frown, but Miloš didn't seem discouraged by her lack of warmth. He smiled and looked into her face; she stared at the ground and kept her face reserved. It wasn't until Miloš walked back to the house that her expression changed. She watched him leave, and for a second, her face softened and her eyes sparkled—a glint of life in a face of stone.

"How did it go?" Jamie asked when Miloš returned.

Miloš shrugged. "Eventually, she will run out of excuses."

"This is not the first time you have proposed marriage to her?" Jamie was more amused than sympathetic.

Miloš smiled, neither discouraged nor embarrassed. "I propose every day I see her. Today she said we can't get married because we'll all be dead in a few weeks. I told her that means we should act quickly. But today is not right. One day, she will say yes."

"Are you sure?" Jamie asked.

"Yes. It's not me she's rejecting."

"If it isn't you, what is it?"

Through the window, Miloš watched the woman disappear farther into the village. "Hope."

* * *

Dearest Genevieve,

I've been lying in bed with an injury for a week. Several of them, actually. Krzysztof found a few sheets of paper to help with the boredom, but I think I could fill them up in an hour if I'm not careful, so I'll ration them and make them into a letter for you while we're apart. Things haven't gone as planned. I still hope for a miracle, one that will let me see you again soon, but I'm afraid I may be forced to make these scraps of paper last a long time.

I miss you, and I love you,

Peter

* * *

"Hello, Marija."

She looked up from the goat she was milking, then back to her work. "Hello, Miloš." He was up early. The other men were still sleeping; Bogdan had led them on another raid the night before.

"I was thinking, Marija, that we should get married."

"We can't get married."

"Why not?"

"I have no dowry." She had only one change of clothes and two spare socks. Everything else—the bucket she used to milk the goat, the dishes she used for cooking, the thin blanket she slept with—belonged to her uncle. She had no money, she depended on her uncle's family for food, and she doubted any of those facts would change in the near future.

"Phst. There's a war on. No one has dowries nowadays. The only people who might care are my parents, and they're dead. You don't need a dowry to get married."

"You have no job, Miloš."

"Phst. I've picked up a thing or two about farming. And the villagers have no real doctor, so I get work here. I set a broken arm and get a basket of eggs. I deliver a baby and get a few pounds of pork. I help someone with influenza and get a pair of wool socks. We wouldn't starve any more than we're already starving. And when the war is over, I will finish my training and live in Belgrade or Sarajevo, and I will be busy all the time, and some of my patients will pay me with money. Until then, being poor and married is better than being poor and unmarried, isn't it?"

"I don't love you, Miloš."

Miloš petted the goat until Marija finished milking it. "Perhaps tomorrow you will love me."

CHAPTER TWELVE
DARK RENDEZVOUS

Thursday, October 5
Bari, Italy

WEEKS PASSED WITH NO WORD of Peter. Genevieve ached for him, prayed for him, and carefully analyzed every word when Dr. Lombardelli shared updates from Major Baker. Money for the agents tailing Kimby hadn't been a problem, but they'd found nothing. Whatever Kimby was up to, he had hidden it well. He also had powerful friends. A brigadier general had warned Baker to leave the matter alone. Then Baker had been sent on another assignment. He promised to continue the investigation if he returned, but he would have to be discreet.

Lombardelli often had small assignments for Genevieve, courier work to several agents in Bari. One of the agents uncovered an assassination plot, so his contacts were all arrested. One blew his cover and had to flee, and another moved back to Rome. But the man Genevieve had delivered a letter to the day Lombardelli recruited her continued his work, preventing several Fascist agents from infiltrating OSS headquarters and learning the names of dozens of committed Fascists, skilled men and women loyal to Mussolini and his government in northern Italy.

Genevieve was to meet the man with glasses before work the first Thursday in October. The rendezvous was a dark apartment with a single window not covered by blackout curtains. The sun hadn't risen, but light from the eastern horizon spilled into the suite's front room and left the rest of the rooms in shadows. She searched the small apartment, finding no one. She heard a sound and froze, wondering if it was her contact. A rat scurried across the floor, and Genevieve shuddered, stepping to the side of the room opposite the pest.

She watched the sky change colors and waited, hoping there weren't any more rodents. A man walked through the door and glanced around the room until he found her shadow. She hadn't seen him since the night at the bistro—most of his communication was through dead drops—but she recognized him. He was dressed in dark clothing, his hat pulled low on his brow.

"You're Lombardelli's messenger?" he asked in Italian.

Genevieve nodded. She spoke poor Italian, but she could understand a few things. "Do you speak French? Or English? Or German?"

"*Ja.*"

Genevieve switched to German. "Dr. Lombardelli wanted me to give you these." She held out a pistol and several spare clips, a bundle of cash, and a sealed envelope with Lombardelli's requests. The man moved closer to take them. "He also asked me to pass on his thanks and a warning. He heard from another source that someone in the Fascist leadership suspects there's a mole in Bari."

The man nodded. "You're the girl from the bistro, aren't you?"

"Yes." She was disappointed he'd recognized her. She'd worn her hair differently and put on a hat and coat, but what she really needed was a disguise kit like the one her brother had always kept.

"It's your eyes."

"I should purchase glasses, then."

He pushed his own glasses farther up his nose. "Or avoid eye contact. Tell me, are you as good at picking pockets as you are at stuffing them?"

"I've never tried."

He smiled. "My name is Giacomo."

"I'm Genevieve."

He held up a finger. "I've been trying to place your accent. I suppose you're French?"

"Yes."

"How did a French girl end up in Bari?" He examined the pistol and put it in his pocket.

Genevieve shrugged. "I fell in love with an American. I was supposed to meet him here, but he's gone missing."

"I'm sorry."

"He'll turn up," she said, forcing her voice to stay even. She knew the odds were against it, but she still clung to the hope that Peter was alive, somewhere.

"I hope my wife has your faith. I haven't seen her in two years. When the armistice came, I was down south. There wasn't a way for me to get back to my village in the Alps before the Germans took over. I haven't even been able to get a letter through." He shook his head in frustration. "I hope she's waiting for me. And I hope she's safe. I have a daughter too. She was just a baby when I left."

"Were you a soldier?"

He looked at the floor. "Yes, drafted."

"There's no shame in fighting if your government forces you into the army."

"Maybe. But someday my daughter will find out I fought under Mussolini, and I dread that day." He held up the envelope from Lombardelli. "But at least I'll be able to tell her I did this for her, for a better future. I have a message for Lombardelli. I've been introduced to a leader—Basileo Ercolani. He's higher up than any of my other contacts. He's planning something, and it involves explosives."

"In Bari?"

Giacomo straightened his glasses again. "I'm not sure. He's a smart one—cautious. He'll work by himself unless he needs something. I just hope he'll need assistance soon and that I'll have what he needs. I'll keep an eye on him, but like I said, he's cautious."

"Be careful."

"You as well." He shook her hand and led her out the door.

They turned opposite directions as they left.

Genevieve glanced back a block later. There were several people behind her, walking the same direction. An older woman and a schoolboy were ten meters back. Beyond them was a civilian man, and trailing behind was a young couple, their arms entwined and their heads nearly touching. Genevieve smiled as she turned away, wondering if the couple had gotten up early or been out all night. Her smile was bittersweet because when she saw the couple, she also felt a pang of longing. She wanted Peter's arms wrapped around her, his fingers tracing her face, his lips caressing hers.

A few minutes later, Genevieve pulled herself out of her memories and checked behind her again. She saw a woman carrying a toddler on her hip and the man who'd been there earlier. She studied him for a few moments. She'd never seen him before that morning, but his walk hinted at a military background. That wasn't unusual, but she decided against going directly to the hospital, even though an indirect route would make her late for work. *And I still need to change clothes.* Lombardelli would be finishing up, and he'd make sure she wasn't disciplined. He usually worked the night shift and had her work the day shift so one of them was always available to check dead drops or meet with contacts. Genevieve hated to disappoint Dr. Bolliger, the doctor she normally worked with, but she would hate it even more if she didn't take her customary precautions and led someone to her work. It was no secret that most of the hospital staff lived in a tent city near the hospital, so she'd also be leading the man to her home.

She took three left turns in succession, then paused in front of a shop window, watching the reflections in the glass and sneaking a glance in the man's direction. He was farther back, behind a dozen other pedestrians, but the man was still there, a tall figure in a dark suit. *Who is he, and why is he following me?*

She turned right onto a busier road and headed briskly to the first alley she saw. She ducked into the side street and crouched in the shadow of a doorway until the man walked past her on the main road. His pace was unhurried, but she caught hints of frustration in his tightly clenched jaw as his eyes searched for her.

Genevieve sighed when he walked past the lane, relieved he hadn't seen her. She hurried to the other end of the alley and took off her hat. She removed a few hairpins and used her fingers to brush her hair out, then shoved her hat and pins into a coat pocket, hoping she'd be harder to recognize. She draped her coat over her arm and walked onto the road, looking around and seeing only unfamiliar faces.

Lombardelli was waiting when she rushed into the hospital. He took her arm and led her to his office. "What happened?"

"I was followed." Genevieve twisted her hair into a knot and secured it with her hairpins. "After the meeting. I've never seen the man before, but I'll recognize him if I see him again."

"Did he follow you here?"

She shook her head. "No, but it took some time to lose him. I gave Giacomo your warning. He said he's been introduced to someone, a leader named Basileo Ercolani. He's not sure what Ercolani's up to, but he thinks it involves explosives."

"Ercolani." Lombardelli repeated the name, then was quiet for a few moments, staring out the window. "So do I pull Giacomo out now that he's attracted enough attention for his accomplices to be tailed, or do I leave him in because I need his information and don't think I can get it from anyone else?" He sighed. "First I'll tell Dr. Bolliger I've severely reprimanded you for your tardiness. Go change into your uniform and wash up."

Genevieve spent the morning helping injured airmen take sponge baths. She gave them her time and her sympathy, but more than once, her mind wandered to Giacomo. Had the man following her been following him initially? Was Giacomo playing a double game, or did his Fascist contacts doubt his loyalty?

Dr. Bolliger pulled her aside midmorning, his young face showing exhaustion after a complicated surgery. "I'm sorry if Dr. Lombardelli was too hard on you. Don't let it bother you. Keep up the good work." Bolliger gave her a warm smile and continued his rounds.

"Thank you, sir."

He turned back toward her, giving her another smile and a quick wink with his vibrant blue eyes.

* * *

A week later, Lombardelli found Genevieve at the end of her shift. "Meet Giacomo in the alley by the scrap market at 2200 hours. I think he's got more information about that sabotage project."

Genevieve arrived a few minutes early and strolled along the nearby buildings, expecting Giacomo to arrive any moment. As she walked down the alley, she saw a dark heap on the ground, and as she got closer, the hairs on the back of her neck began to prick. A body with a knife in its back lay in the alley. She bent and turned the victim over, recognizing Giacomo, searching for signs of life but finding none. She looked around, but the alley was deserted. With shaky hands, she opened Giacomo's messenger bag. It was empty, as were all of his pockets. Whoever had killed him had also taken his papers.

Genevieve felt sick. Her fingers trembled as she pushed the man's glasses up so she could close his lifeless eyes. Then she searched for help, finding an American military policeman and telling him she'd seen a dead body. She kept her connection to the man secret, and when the MP found out she worked at the American hospital, he let her leave.

It was a slow night, so when she walked into the ward, it wasn't difficult for her to motion Lombardelli aside for a report.

"He was dead. Someone stabbed him in the back."

Lombardelli's face fell. "And the papers?"

"Gone."

He led her to his office. "I should have pulled him last week. Are you all right?"

She sank into a chair. "Whoever killed him was gone when I arrived. No one attacked me. I don't think anyone even saw me, and I wasn't tailed."

"But are you all right?"

She looked away. "It's not the first time I've seen a dead man. But I can't help thinking of his wife and daughter."

Lombardelli nodded. "I don't even know her name to tell her when the war's over. If it ever ends." She caught him looking at his pictures. He picked up the one nearest him. "My son, Lorenzo."

She took the picture of a young man in an Italian naval uniform and noted the family resemblance. "He's handsome."

Lombardelli nodded. "He was."

Genevieve looked up with dread. "He's dead?"

"1943, right after the armistice. The German Navy wasn't too happy about the sudden shift in alliances."

"I'm so sorry, Dr. Lombardelli."

He took the picture from her and put it back on the desk. "He left behind a devastated father and a heartbroken fiancée. Giacomo leaves behind a wife and child." He shook his head. "They don't know it yet, but one day they'll realize he's not coming back, and it will be my fault."

Genevieve wasn't sure what she would have done had she been in Lombardelli's place. He could have pulled Giacomo from his assignment, but trailing Ercolani had seemed important. "You did the best you could." Her eyes focused on another picture. She reached for it and examined the two couples. The first was a tall man and his pregnant wife. The woman seemed happy, a contented smile on her lips as she leaned on her husband and supported her pregnant belly with both hands. She had the same eyes and same nose as Lombardelli and Lorenzo, only feminine. Lorenzo was also in the photo, his arm wrapped around their hospital's head nurse. "Vittoria was Lorenzo's fiancée?"

Lombardelli nodded.

That explains why Vittoria never smiles, Genevieve thought. "And the other woman, she's your daughter?"

"Yes. She lives with her in-laws near Trieste. There are two grandchildren now, last I heard. My son-in-law is a POW, captured by the Germans."

Genevieve studied the picture a few seconds longer. The Germans had killed Lombardelli's son and taken his son-in-law prisoner. She'd never questioned why Lombardelli was so motivated to work with OSS, but now she knew.

CHAPTER THIRTEEN
UP IN FLAMES

Friday, October 13

THE NEXT DAY BEGAN QUIETLY, but that changed midmorning when a pair of litter bearers rushed into the hospital, their load a wounded Air Corp officer.

Dr. Bolliger motioned the men into the operating room. "Genevieve, Vittoria, I'll need your help."

"What happened?" Dorothy, another nurse, asked.

"There was an explosion at the airfield," one litter bearer said. "A big tank of gasoline blew, lit up one of the B-24s, and killed a few men. We've got more wounded coming in right behind us."

Two more stretchers came in as the man spoke, with an additional thirteen men admitted over the next hour. Genevieve followed orders from Bolliger, Vittoria, and Dorothy, fetching bandages and hauling away clipped-off burnt skin and pieces of metal dug from flesh. Most of the sixteen new patients had burns, and some of them had shrapnel wounds as well. Two corpses lay in a nearby room, men who hadn't survived the journey from the airstrip to the hospital.

One of the ambulance drivers sent for Lombardelli, and he arrived within the hour, bringing two additional nurses. By late afternoon, Genevieve was exhausted, but things had calmed down enough that she could stop running. She glanced at her skirt, noticing the blood smears for the first time. One of the patients in a nearby bed reached out and grasped her hand. Bandages covered burns on his face, and blood covered his hand. Bolliger had removed three pieces of shrapnel from the man's body, and Genevieve could tell he was still in pain.

"Did they bring in Albert?" he gasped.

Genevieve was touched by the man's concern for his friend. "I'll look for him."

She checked all the patients, asking them their names if they were conscious and pulling out their dog tags if they weren't. She wrote the names on existing charts or began new ones. Albert was four beds from his friend, burned and unconscious but stable and alive.

She went back to Albert's friend and washed his bloody hands. "Albert is alive, just a few beds over." She gave the man a smile and finished gathering names for the remaining patients.

Genevieve took a break to eat that evening, glad to be off her feet for a few minutes.

Bolliger returned from a smoking break, rubbing the back of his neck with his hand. He was a handsome man, and Genevieve knew of at least two nurses who were secretly in love with him.

"What a day. I feel like I'm back in a field hospital." The tall doctor from Chicago looked older than his thirty years as he sat next to her and stretched his long legs. "You have a good bedside manner. On days like this, it's easy to forget we're treating individuals, not just cases."

"I'm not doing anything special, just trying to remember how important they are to someone."

"One of your smiles goes a long way."

Genevieve turned her head, surprised. "All the nurses are friendly with the patients when they have time."

Bolliger shrugged as he stood and returned to the ward.

As Genevieve was leaving that night, Lombardelli pulled her aside. "That explosion wasn't an accident."

She inhaled sharply, not sure she wanted to hear more. "It wasn't?"

"I spoke with someone from the airfield. Sabotage. It's a bit of an assumption, but I'll bet Giacomo's contact was behind it. He was planning something. I wonder what else Ercolani has in the works."

Genevieve was weary and discouraged as she trudged to her tent. The latest war news was dismal. A daring paratroop raid into the Netherlands had ended badly, and now the liberating armies from Britain and the United States were bogged down in the thick forests along the French and Belgian borders with Germany. Progress in Italy was painfully slow, and in the east, the Nazis had crushed the Polish Home Army. Things had seemed so different that summer, when it had been possible to believe the war might end in just another month or so. Now it seemed like it would take much, much longer.

Nightmares of Weiss and the prisoners he'd executed still haunted her sleep. She made it through with prayer, Peter's Purple Heart, the book of scripture he'd given her, and his letters. Genevieve reread all of Peter's letters often, except one. The tent was cold, and she shivered as she knelt at the foot of her cot, in front of a chest. She'd never read the letter Peter had written to his family and left in her care, afraid reading it would be admitting he wasn't coming back.

As she pulled the envelope from the chest and stared at it, she wondered if Peter's family worried about him like she did. They would have already received a telegram telling them Peter was missing in action—Baker had changed his status from AWOL. *Of course they worry about him.* She wondered if their concern was worse, knowing no details, or easier, ignorant of the mystery surrounding his disappearance.

He'd been missing for more than a month, and she knew it was time to mail his letter to his family, but first, she was going to read it.

September 3, 1944
Dear family,

If you are reading this letter, you have no doubt already received a telegram telling you I'm missing or dead. I apologize that I let you believe I was still working in an office far from any danger when I was really carrying out other activities. It wasn't my intention to be misleading, but it was my duty to be quiet about my assignments.

I hope receiving this letter won't shock you too much. I had a friend keep it with the promise that she would mail it should I disappear. The thing is, I've written letters similar to this one several times, but I have a feeling this one might actually be sent.

I don't regret volunteering to fight. I've seen how bad things can be when liberty is in chains and people live in fear. And I've remembered how good things can be when there is freedom and family and love. If I could go back, I would repeat my efforts to oppose tyranny. I only hope they will not have been in vain and that the war will end soon and that good will prevail.

I love you all. I also love the Lord, and I've come to realize He never leaves us alone—even in a war zone. I pray He will help and bless you all. If each of you stays close to Him, everything will be all right in the end.

Love,
Peter

* * *

Basileo Ercolani glanced over his shoulder, making sure no one was behind him. He turned and crossed the street, entering the apartment complex through the back entrance. He knocked on the door three times before entering and smiled when he saw her. *The best part of my job.* She had black hair, wide, brown eyes, playful lips, and a curvy, feminine figure. *No, not the best part of my job*, he corrected himself. *The best part of my life.*

"How was your day, Belina?"

She smiled. "Not as exciting as yours. Congratulations. All the rumors say the explosion at the airfield was sabotage, but no one knows who's responsible. Except me."

Basileo loosened his tie and removed his coat, placing it on a hanger in the closet near the front door. "Good thing I trust you; otherwise, I'd have to kill you. What exactly did you hear today?" Belina worked as a telephone operator and was sometimes privy to useful conversations.

She sat on the sofa and waited for him to join her. He lowered himself to the floor in front of her and sighed with pleasure as she rubbed out the knots in his shoulders. "Just the normal—a few stores placing orders, a few neighbors calling one another . . . and rumors about the explosion."

"Mmm. I wonder why every man doesn't marry someone who gives good back rubs."

"Because not every man is as smart as you. I'll expect repayment though—after dinner."

Basileo took her hand and kissed it. "Gladly."

She bent and brushed his ear with her lips. "Such a good soldier, Basileo, taking orders from Il Duce and from your wife."

"We're still on our honeymoon. Wait six months, and I won't be so malleable."

"I doubt that."

He smiled, shaking his head. She was right; she had him wrapped around her finger, and he doubted that would change. Other things would but not the way he felt about Belina. He thought of his country and of his leader. Italy had suffered a setback, but he had faith that Il Duce would return Italy to greatness, the way it was supposed to be.

Basileo hadn't begun life as a Fascist. He'd originally found Mussolini appealing for his firm stance against the Mafia—the very entity that had ruined his family's life. Basileo's father had refused to pay for protection when the Mafia had insisted. The next day, Basileo's father had disappeared, until young Basileo found his mutilated body a week later.

He had seen enough of human avarice. Fascism promised something different from the corrupt struggle of greedy capitalists concerned only with themselves. He could still remember his favorite uncle telling him how Mussolini would lead the country to glory. Under Fascism, everyone worked together as a unified whole. No more did individual greed determine the future and act as the primary motivator. Everyone devoted themselves to the greatness of Italy, and under the leadership of Il Duce, Italy went from a kingdom to an empire, and Basileo's heart had soared.

Much had happened since those days when Basileo had sat at the scratched-up table across from his uncle, wearing the black-and-olive uniform of the Italian Fascist Youth and eagerly absorbing all his uncle promised. Now his uncle was dead, Il Duce in exile, and southern Italy in the hands of the British and Americans. *Perhaps if everyone had been truly devoted to Italy*, Basileo thought, *then things might not be so dire.* But at least he had Belina, and she shared his beliefs. He stood and helped her from the sofa, pulling her into an embrace.

She kissed him on the cheek. "I should go make supper."

He nodded, then kissed her mouth, delaying their meal for a few minutes. There was a sweetness and hunger in her kisses that increased the longer they were together. He would never grow tired of kissing her. "I love you."

"I know." She smiled as he followed her into the kitchen and watched her work. "There was one odd call today, placed from the air base to the hospital where the survivors were taken."

"That doesn't seem so odd."

"No, it wasn't the connection that was strange. It was the conversation— nothing about the casualties, just information about the explosion itself and all the evidence they'd gathered to suggest sabotage. It seemed more like a report they'd make to the police or someone in charge of security. Why would they make a report like that to the hospital?"

Basileo didn't know, but he'd find out. His work in Bari had just begun— he had men to assassinate, buildings to destroy. And he needed to find that woman, the one he'd seen with Giacomo last week. He doubted it was coincidence—she had to have been helping the traitor. He didn't know who she was, and he hadn't seen enough of her face to recognize her if he saw her again. All the same, she was now on his hit list.

Chapter Fourteen
WOUNDS MADE AND MENDED

Monday, October 16

Basileo pulled the collar of his jacket up to protect his neck from the wind. He shivered as he watched the night doctor leave the hospital. He followed him, staying half a block away, doing his best to blend with the other pedestrians. When the doctor entered his small apartment, Basileo waited awhile longer, then concluded the man would spend the morning sleeping. Lombardelli had, after all, just finished a twelve-hour shift.

Basileo had begun monitoring the hospital after Belina's comment about the telephone report, and on his first day, he'd recognized Lombardelli. The man had been in Venice that summer, working for the Americans. And he'd successfully warned two British agents to flee minutes before Basileo could arrest them. The incident had been a black mark on an otherwise impeccable career with OVRA, the Italian Secret Police. Yet Basileo owed Lombardelli his gratitude—if it hadn't been for him, Basileo never would have met Belina.

Basileo wandered through the Bari alleys, avoiding the military policemen who'd become as common as rats in this city. *Someday,* he thought, *Italy will drive out the invaders and, together with our German allies, achieve all that was promised.* Then he and Belina would have normal lives devoted to Italy and to each other.

He returned to the small apartment he shared with his wife and knocked three times before letting himself in. "Good morning, Belina. How are you?"

She planted a soft kiss on his lips. "I was a little lonely, but not anymore."

"I think I found him, Belina."

"Who?"

"Maybe I should make you guess." Basileo took off his coat and helped himself to some bread.

Belina raised one eyebrow and placed a hand on her hip. "I waited breakfast for you, and now you're dangling shadows in front of my eyes and wanting me to guess who they are?"

Basileo reached out and found her hand. "Remember last June? The pair of British agents who set up a spy ring in Venice?"

She clamped down on his hand, holding it with such force he almost winced. "Which one?"

He looked at her, watching her blush as she guessed what he was thinking. One of the agents had successfully romanced Belina, gaining more information from her than she'd like to admit before breaking her heart. Basileo had been there to pick up the pieces, but he suspected she still had a soft spot in her heart for the blue-eyed, blond-haired agent from England. "Not him." He watched her reaction, not sure if she was relieved or disappointed. "But I think I've found Lombardelli." And Basileo planned to take care of him that week.

* * *

Five days had passed since the explosion at the airfield. Genevieve yawned as she finished her hospital shift. She'd forgotten how hard it was to work through the night. Maybe she could adjust if it happened all the time, but the occasional shifts threw her off for a few days. She breathed in the sea air, smiling. It would be a beautiful day, but she would sleep through most of it. She felt a sudden yearning for Peter, wishing he was there to share the sunrise with her. They'd watched nearly a dozen sunrises in Normandy that summer. The rising sun had meant a reprieve from their nightly marches as they'd fled the Gestapo.

"I miss you, Peter," she whispered. She'd dreamed about him a few nights ago, a pleasant change from her nightmares, but it had only made her feel more alone when she woke.

She glanced after Lombardelli as he left the hospital and headed to his apartment. The years and the constant night shifts were wearing him down—he'd developed several new wrinkles around his eyes in the mere two months she'd known him. The war was taking its toll on him. On her. On everyone. Lombardelli had taken Giacomo's death and the subsequent sabotage at the airfield particularly hard. She watched the doctor and the people behind him, wondering how the war had affected each of them. She was about to look away when her eyes riveted on a man ten meters behind Lombardelli, recognizing his military bearing and stylish suit as he stayed a steady distance from his quarry.

She followed, hoping it wasn't the same man who'd tailed her after she gave Giacomo his final instructions, but she suspected it was. *And he's probably the man who killed Giacomo and blew up the fuel tank at the air base.* Lombardelli thought Basileo Ercolani was behind both crimes, and Genevieve suspected he wasn't out for an innocent stroll: he was tailing Lombardelli. She didn't know how Ercolani knew of Lombardelli's connection to Giacomo, but she doubted he had good intentions.

She closed the gap to within a few meters of the man and confirmed his identity. *What is Ercolani planning now?* She slowed her pace until she'd slipped farther back, looking for someone in uniform but seeing only civilians. *I wish I had a weapon.* When Lombardelli took a shortcut through an empty alley, Ercolani quickened his pace and followed, and a knot developed in Genevieve's stomach.

She entered the alley and saw Ercolani push back his jacket to reveal a knife. He wielded it with ease, as if it was an extension of his hand. The blade reflected the sunlight as he lifted it to shoulder height.

"Dr. Lombardelli, watch out!"

Both men turned toward her, and Lombardelli drew his pistol. Ercolani glared at Genevieve, then looked back at the doctor's weapon. Ercolani hesitated an instant, then threw his knife at Lombardelli. The pistol went off a moment later, but Genevieve didn't notice where the shot hit because Ercolani pivoted and ran toward her. He caught her before she could flee the alley, shoved her down against a brick wall, then muscled his way past several pedestrians who'd been attracted to the alley's entrance by the gunshot.

Genevieve's shoulder caught the worst of it. She pulled herself to her feet and considered chasing Ercolani, but she was more concerned about Lombardelli. She wouldn't be able to catch Ercolani anyway and didn't know if she'd get any help from the civilians gawking at her from the street. None of them looked like athletes. "Are you all right, sir?" she asked.

Lombardelli leaned against a doorway, breathing hard, with Ercolani's knife protruding from his shoulder. "I'll need a few stitches. Better that than a casket."

"Come on, I'll help you back to the hospital."

When they reached the street, another man offered to help Lombardelli, so Genevieve followed, her eyes darting to everything that moved as they walked to the hospital, but the tall Italian didn't come back for a second try.

"What in heaven's name?" Dr. Bolliger was the first to notice Lombardelli's return. He rushed over and had him lie on one of the beds. "What in the world are you doing in your spare time?"

Lombardelli didn't answer his associate, turning instead to the head nurse. "Vittoria, will you retrieve Dr. Bolliger's suture supplies?"

"Are you going to tell me how you ended up with a knife in your shoulder?" Dr. Bolliger asked.

Lombardelli raised one eyebrow. "Yes. It was supposed to end up in my back or across my throat, but Genevieve called out a warning before that could happen. I suppose this was the man's backup plan."

"So Genevieve saved your life?" Bolliger took his supplies from Vittoria when she arrived, but his eyes focused on Genevieve.

"Luck. I was in the right place at the right time," Genevieve said. "And Dr. Lombardelli shot him before he could try more than once."

"And this man, what did he want?" Bolliger pulled the knife out and cleaned the wound.

"Probably just a thief," Lombardelli said.

Bolliger didn't seem convinced as he started stitching. "How fortunate that you happened to be carrying a pistol."

"I normally carry a pistol."

"Yes, I know. You put it in your top right drawer while you're working, then put it on before you leave. And despite my frequent inquiries, you never tell me why."

"To scare off cutthroats and thieves."

Bolliger shook his head and finished the stitches, then turned to Genevieve and stared at her arm. "And what happened to you?"

Genevieve followed his gaze to a large bloodstain on her jacket's right sleeve. "The man shoved me into the wall as he passed, but it didn't break the skin, and I hit the wall with my left side."

"I imagine his hands were bloody. I shot him in the shoulder, so he would have been putting pressure on his wound before he reached out to push you as he ran off. I would have shot him somewhere fatal, but I was afraid I'd hit you instead," Lombardelli said.

Bolliger frowned. "Are you going to tell me what you're up to?"

"No. And you can tell that MP waiting to question me that I'll talk to his commander but not to him." Lombardelli waved Bolliger away. "Shoo. I'd like to thank Genevieve for saving my life without an audience."

Bolliger didn't look pleased, but he walked over to the military policeman.

"I'm sorry I got in the way of your shot," Genevieve said.

Lombardelli half laughed, half snorted. "If you hadn't been there, I wouldn't have been alive to take the shot in the first place. The least I could do was avoid shooting you while aiming for him. I should probably go practice a bit more when my arm mends."

"It was the same man who followed me after I met Giacomo."

"Yes, Ercolani. I've seen him before in Venice. He's Italian Secret Police. And he's seen your face now, so you'll need to be careful. I was afraid he was going to kill you in that alley."

Genevieve had feared the same thing. It wouldn't have taken much—a different angle on his push, propelling her head into the wall and smashing her skull. Ercolani certainly had the strength.

Bolliger came back with the military policeman, one Genevieve hadn't seen before. He left the MP with Lombardelli and gently took Genevieve's uninjured arm to lead her away. "I'll let Dr. Lombardelli tell the MP to call his commander. Now where exactly did you hit the wall?"

"My left shoulder."

"Let me have a look."

Genevieve took her jacket off. Her uniform underneath had short sleeves, so Bolliger pushed the left one up to examine the damage. He had her move her arm and came to the same conclusion she'd reached: nothing was broken or dislocated, just bruised.

"I'll get you some ice."

"Dr. Bolliger, I know where the ice is. I can get it myself."

He smiled, his blue eyes meeting hers. "Yes, I know you know where it is, but you are going to sit right here and let me fetch it for you." He returned a few minutes later and gently placed an icepack on her shoulder. "There, keep that on for twenty minutes. And if it bothers you at all when you come to work tomorrow, tell me, and I'll make sure we give you an assignment that won't irritate it."

"Thank you, sir."

"You can call me Nathan when you aren't working." He brushed his hand along her forehead. "I'm glad it was your shoulder that plowed into the wall and not your head."

* * *

Basileo had known it would take awhile for Belina to find a doctor they could trust, but he hadn't known how miserable the wait would be. He'd been able to run after Lombardelli's bullet struck, adrenaline helping him move past the woman, past the people on the streets, but now the adrenaline was gone, replaced with pain. He'd been so close to accomplishing his goal—so close.

His thoughts turned to the woman in the alley. Was she the same one he'd seen with Giacomo? He wasn't sure, but he hoped she was. That would make it so much more satisfying when he caught up with her again. She'd been wearing what looked like a nurse's uniform, so he knew where to begin his search when the time came.

When the door opened, Basileo lifted his head from the sofa, making sure it was Belina and not someone from the American Army. He winced with pain as he strained to see her face. He'd never seen her this worried before—not even when she'd discovered her boyfriend was a British agent and another member of OVRA had wanted to arrest her. Basileo's perfect record and high position had saved her then and saved him when the agent and his accomplices slipped away before he could reach them.

She knelt by his side and took his hand. "I was worried you'd be dead by the time I found anyone."

He squeezed her hand. "I'll be fine. It's not a mortal wound, just an inconvenience, a setback of a few months."

The doctor was a good Fascist, and he went to work at once removing Basileo's shirt and cleaning the skin surrounding the wound. Basileo could tell the next half hour or so was going to be excruciating.

"Belina, would you go buy me some cigarettes?"

She looked at him with her mouth slightly open. He didn't smoke more than a cigarette or two a day, and he had several packs in the kitchen. "But you have some already."

"Please?" He bit his lip to hold back a groan.

She looked hurt, but she left. Basileo sighed as she shut the door behind her, relieved she wouldn't be in earshot should the next cry of pain make it past his lips.

Chapter Fifteen
FALLEN FIGHTERS

Tuesday, December 5
German-occupied Serbia

Miloš checked that the sweater he'd washed the day before was dry. He pressed it to his nose, glad it smelled like the fireplace where it had dried. There wasn't anything offensive about a fireplace scent, was there?

He found Marija alone in her uncle's cottage. "Hello, Marija."

"Hello, Miloš." She glanced up from the bread she kneaded. "How are the foreigners?"

Miloš didn't think a day had passed since their arrival that Marija hadn't done something for the foreigners—baked bread, brought milk, knitted scarves or socks. "Jamie is upset that I won't let him put much weight on his leg yet, but I don't want him to reinjure it. He seems to be adjusting to his crutches, even if he hates them."

"And Peter?"

Miloš sighed. Peter's ribs and ankle were better, but a month ago, he'd developed a persistent cough that had steadily grown worse. The last few days had been the most dangerous—he was barely able to breathe. "Delirious."

"Still?"

Miloš nodded.

Marija added some flour to her dough. "Do you think he'll get better?"

"If he was in a real hospital, yes. Here, I'm not sure." Miloš was frustrated, knowing there were better treatments available for Peter's pneumonia but unable to offer them because he didn't have the correct supplies. "Right now, I don't think he'd survive evacuation."

Bogdan had passed on credible rumors of other Chetniks evacuating shot-down American airmen. Miloš was sure it was an exaggeration, but Bogdan claimed hundreds had been flown to Italy and that the airfields were still operating. But that was to the east, toward the Red Army. Miloš wasn't sure why, but the foreigners all seemed wary of Soviet troops. Moretti and Krzysztof were in good enough shape to make it, even if they had to carry Jamie, but none of them wanted to leave Peter behind.

"I brought you something." Miloš pulled the sweater from behind his back. "It's not new, and it's not the right size, but it's getting cold. Just don't ask me where I got it."

"From a body?"

"Phst. He won't need it anymore, but you will." He watched for a reaction but couldn't tell what she thought of the gift. "I washed it. You will wear it, won't you?"

"Yes, thank you."

"I was thinking, Marija, that we should get married."

She continued her kneading. "We can't get married."

"Why not?"

"Because you're very educated, and I'm not."

"Phst. When the war ends, you can take classes if you like. Or I can teach you. You're clever, and you'll catch up to me. Besides, you like to read. You can learn a lot if you read the right books."

"I don't love you, Miloš."

Miloš stayed where he was for a few minutes, watching her knead her dough, her eyes never meeting his. "Perhaps tomorrow you will love me."

* * *

Peter turned in his bed and coughed again, almost vomiting as he expelled the blood-tinged mucus. He could hear himself wheezing as he tried to catch his breath. His ribs had stopped hurting for about a week. Then he'd got the flux. Then the cough had set in, and now his whole body ached. At least he could think today—the last week had been an incoherent, painful blur.

Movement was painful, and he was too weak to sit. Shivering, Peter pulled the blanket around his shoulders. He opened his eyes when he felt a hand on his forehead.

"You cold, sir?" Moretti asked.

"Yeah," Peter whispered.

"You feel hot to me." Moretti grabbed another blanket and put it on Peter's legs.

Peter was still cold. "You're staring at me like I'm a corpse."

Moretti smiled. "To be honest, sir, I've seen corpses that look better than you do."

Peter tried to force a laugh, but it didn't come. "That bad, huh?"

"Blue lips, blue fingernails. I hear ya coughing all night long, and it sounds like you're struggling for every breath." Moretti threw another log into the fireplace. "And you say you're cold when ya feel like the end of my rifle after target practice."

"What did Miloš say?"

"Just that pneumonia is common after chest injuries. Penicillin's supposed to help, but our quartermasters ain't dropping medical supplies to the Chetniks. Keep coughing that stuff up—that's supposed to be good."

"Coughing hurts." Peter watched the fire. "So does breathing. Did Miloš send you to give me my deathbed talk?"

"Naw, you're gonna get better, sir, but Miloš thought somebody should stick around while you slept. He's out with Krzysztof. A plane crashed not too far away, and they're gonna try and scavenge some parts—maybe get that radio fixed. Jamie's trying out his new crutches. Marija's making you some soup."

Peter looked out the window at the quiet village. There were a few elderly residents and a handful of young mothers with children, but most of the men had left with Bogdan again. Miloš probably would have gone with them if Peter hadn't been so sick. "Maybe Miloš should get pneumonia; then Marija could feed him her soup. She actually smiled at me last week."

Peter coughed up phlegm again, and the effort left him trembling. He hated being so sick, especially in front of someone as tough as Moretti. He should be somewhere with Genevieve, not stuck in an obscure Serbian village dying of pneumonia, but he was so sick and exhausted he couldn't even maintain much anger for Major Kimby or Adolf Hitler or any of the other people he normally blamed his problems on.

Marija came in with a steaming pot. She rarely smiled, she rarely spoke, but she was always busy, and lately, Peter had been a frequent recipient of her service.

"How is he?" she asked Moretti. She spoke English with a noticeable accent but seemed to have a large vocabulary.

"He's making lame jokes, so he must be on the mend," Moretti said.

Peter didn't feel like he was getting better, but he hoped Moretti was right.

* * *

Miloš stopped when Krzysztof raised his hand. The airplane had just come into view, and the Polish man checked all directions to ensure the clearing was as deserted as it appeared.

"Did anyone see a parachute?" Krzysztof asked.

"No." It was a small plane, some type of American fighter.

Krzysztof watched for several minutes before he nodded, and the two approached the plane. It was partially burned, and one of the wings lay several yards from the rest of the wreck.

"What type of plane is it?" The shape of the fuselage reminded Miloš of a German fighter, but the tail was still in good enough condition that he could see the white star identifying the aircraft as American.

"A P-51 Mustang. They're fast but not invincible."

Nothing was, especially in Yugoslavia. The pilot was still in the plane. They could follow the trail of bullets across the cockpit and into the man's chest. Miloš assumed he'd been dead before the plane had crashed. They took him out, planning to bury him later. The village priest liked to give dead Americans a good Serbian Orthodox funeral. Miloš looked at the dog tags and saw the letter *C* listed for the man's religion. He'd have to tell the priest the man was Catholic. There were plenty of Catholic priests in Bosnia and Herzegovina, but Miloš only knew one of them from the village where he'd grown up. It was several days' journey away, and he didn't trust the priest. If he ever ran into him again, Miloš would be tempted to shoot him. The dead American would have to be content with an Orthodox Christian funeral.

Krzysztof pried off and unscrewed some of the electronics and handed them out. Miloš wiped off the bloodstains and put the equipment in a sack.

"Do you want the guns?" Krzysztof asked.

Miloš looked at the machine guns in the wing still attached to the plane. They would be hard to remove, and they looked damaged, so he shook his head. The Chetniks often reused .50-caliber machine guns from crashed bombers, but with the corpse and the electronics, he and Krzysztof already had enough to carry.

They didn't linger. Krzysztof slung the electronics over his shoulder and picked up the pilot's legs. Miloš followed behind, supporting the body by the shoulders. They were halfway back to the village when the sound of small arms erupted to their left. Miloš was impressed with how quickly and gently Krzysztof put the pilot down and crouched to the ground. He pulled his pistol out, put the sack down, and moved toward the sound all within seconds. Miloš followed him, wincing as he snapped a few twigs buried under the snow. He wasn't sure how Krzysztof could move so silently, but Miloš too wanted to see who was fighting whom. If one or both sides in the skirmish were their enemies, they'd have an easy time following Krzysztof and Miloš's footprints in the snow.

As they reached the edge of the clearing, Miloš recognized Bogdan and Bogdan's father, Pukovnik Stoyan Brajović. They'd both been gone for weeks and were now being ambushed on their way back to the village. With them were a dozen men spread sparsely throughout the trees, fighting a detachment of Ustaše troops.

Miloš didn't like the Germans, he looked down on the people who worked with the puppet government in Serbia, and he hated the Communists. But more than anything, he despised the Fascist Ustaše. It looked like the Ustaše had already killed several of his friends, and Miloš was furious that he had no weapon to shoot at them.

"The pilot might have a sidearm," Krzysztof whispered as he aimed for the nearest Ustaše.

With Krzysztof's successful shot, he and Miloš lost the element of surprise, so Miloš ran back to the dead pilot without bothering to be stealthy. He found a loaded pistol still strapped to the man's waist. When he returned, the battle had turned in favor of the Chetniks. Normally Miloš would have felt relief that the battle was nearly finished because he didn't enjoy war and didn't enjoy shooting other humans, but in his mind, the Ustaše weren't really human. He wished he could have shot one or two himself.

The Ustaše still standing tried to surrender, but the pukovnik's men shot them anyway. When the shooting stopped, the Chetniks examined the fallen men. They helped their wounded comrades to their feet and shot their injured enemies in the head. Krzysztof found one Ustaše with a leg wound and tied the man's hands behind his back using a belt taken from one of his dead comrades.

"We don't usually take prisoners," Miloš said.

"Prisoners are a good source of information. Don't you want to know where they came from and how they knew to hit the pukovnik's men here? And don't you want to know if they planned to attack the village?"

Miloš shrugged. He supposed those were useful things to know, so he explained Krzysztof's reasoning to Pukovnik Brajović, and the pukovnik agreed. The Chetniks took their wounded, their dead, and their single prisoner back to the village. Miloš and Krzysztof retrieved the airman's corpse and the electronics and followed.

Chapter Sixteen
MARIJA'S PAST

A few days after the skirmish, Miloš found Marija sitting on a log outside, where the sun provided sufficient light for mending the frayed bottom edge of her apron. She was shortening it and repairing a torn tie. "Hello, Marija."

She glanced at him before returning her gaze to the needle. "Hello, Miloš."

"I was thinking, Marija, that we should get married."

"We can't get married."

"Why not?"

Marija was quiet for a long time. As Miloš watched, he realized sewing wasn't one of her talents. The stitches were uneven, and she pricked her finger twice. She tied off the end of the apron's hem and broke the thread with her teeth. "Why would you want to marry me anyway?"

Miloš sat next to her. She turned to meet his eyes and moved a few inches away, but at least she looked at him. "I want to marry you because I've seen how strong you are in adversity. You're never unkind to anyone, and you work hard. You know what's right, and you cling to it. You know what's wrong, and you reject it. I want to marry you because you're beautiful, and when you smile, you're more than beautiful."

Marija looked down. "And why should I want to marry you?"

"I would be a good husband, Marija. I would never hit you or insult you. I would work hard to make sure you had enough to eat, and I would protect you from anyone who wanted to harm you. I think I could make you smile more often and maybe even laugh. And I love you, Marija. When you do get married, you want it to be to someone who loves you, don't you?"

Marija didn't answer. She stood, even though she hadn't yet repaired the torn apron tie.

"Let me finish your mending." Miloš took the end of the apron and reached for the needle. She backed away, pulling the apron with her. "Please, Marija."

"Have you ever sewn before?"

"Phst. Lots of times." He didn't clarify that his sewing experience was with stitching torn skin rather than torn fabric. He stood and reached again for her needle. She let him take it and let him pull the apron from her hand. She walked away, but Miloš caught her glancing back at him.

* * *

Dearest Genevieve,

I wish I could see you smile again. Everyone here is focused on survival, but making it through one more day doesn't bring us much joy, just the knowledge that we're still here and the war still continues and the snow is still falling, trapping us in the mountains until springtime. I miss you so much it hurts. And I worry about you. I hate that I left when you said you needed me. I thought I'd be back in a few days, but now it's been months. I hope you'll forgive me and that when I get back, you'll love me as much as I love you.

Love,

Peter

* * *

Peter woke to the sound of something hitting the wood floor.

"Any luck?" Moretti asked.

"No," Krzysztof said. "Maybe if the plane wasn't so damaged."

Peter opened his eyes. Krzysztof sat at the table, working on the radio, but he paused long enough to retrieve a screw that had fallen to the floor. Krzysztof had a habit of taking the radio apart whenever he had a new part, whenever he was bored, and whenever anyone mentioned Iuliana or Anatolie. All the men were hoping for a lucky break—like a repaired radio. The news Brajović and his men had brought from Serbia wasn't good. Mihailovic and his Chetniks had been attacked by Partisan, German, and Soviet troops. The Chetnik survivors had fled west, leaving behind the airfields they'd used to evacuate Americans.

A month ago, Peter had told Moretti and Krzysztof they should go with Bogdan to one of the fields in Serbia, where, if the rumors were correct, American OSS men with radios could arrange a flight to Italy. But they'd refused to leave Peter and Jamie behind. Peter had suggested they carry Jamie with them, but they hadn't liked that plan either. Now those options were gone.

Sometimes Peter wondered if they'd be better off seeking out the Partisans. Peter didn't like Communist ideology, but the Partisans had more contacts with the British and Americans—perhaps they could arrange something the written-off Chetniks couldn't.

It was ungrateful of him to think like that. The little village was full of starving people, but they always made sure their foreign guests were fed. And yet, sometimes Peter wasn't sure what to think of the Chetniks. They were kind to him and his men but brutal when it came to their Yugoslav rivals. The day before, the Chetniks had executed their wounded Ustaše POW. It was difficult enough to feed everyone without an extra prisoner, but there had been no trial, no mercy, no remorse. The news had left Peter with a cold sense of foreboding.

He pushed himself into a sitting position. He was still weak but better than he'd been the past month. Jamie brought a map over and spread it next to Peter. He shifted his crutches into one hand and pointed to where Mihailovic's men were headed, into northwest Bosnia.

"We could try to go with them, but Bogdan said some of the men have typhus. Did you know seventy thousand people in Serbia died of typhus during the last big war?"

Peter hadn't known, but even if he got over his pneumonia, he doubted he'd survive typhus. "I think we better try for the Dalmatian Coast."

"You do realize it is winter and we would have to cross the Dinaric Alps to get there? Maybe we could get some skis. I might manage skiing, even with a busted leg."

"How is your leg?"

"How are your lungs?"

Peter studied the map. "Not up to mountain climbing."

"Nor is my leg."

"Well, if we can't go out on skis, that leaves us the sky." Peter glanced at the radio, wondering where they could get a new one or parts to fix the old one. He was starting to feel tired and depressed again when Miloš came through the door.

He walked over to Peter. "Feeling better?"

"A little."

He placed a hand on Peter's forehead. Peter tried not to scowl. He hated being sick, and he was beginning to hate this Serbian village in the mountains.

He knew Miloš was trying to help, but Peter always felt trapped while in hospitals. The little stone cottage wasn't a hospital, but he'd been there for three months. It felt like a prison.

"No fever." Miloš smiled. "The pukovnik and his men are drilling if any of you would like to watch. It would get you out of the house. Moretti and Krzysztof can even participate if they like."

Peter was embarrassed to admit he might not be able to walk by himself, but Moretti and Krzysztof practically carried him outside while Miloš gathered everyone's blankets and a rickety wooden chair. It was cold, but the fresh mountain air made Peter smile. He inhaled deeply, which sent him into a coughing fit.

"Maybe this wasn't such a good idea," Miloš said.

"No, let me stay out for a while. Please?"

Miloš hesitated before agreeing. "Twenty minutes." He called out to one of the Serbian soldiers, who disappeared into a cottage, then reappeared with a chair for Jamie.

Pukovnik Brajović came over to join them, letting Bogdan lead the training. "They are good men, no?"

Stoyan Brajović looked like an uneducated peasant, with a long beard and equally long hair—like many of the Chetniks, he'd vowed not to cut his hair until the king returned and the country was free. Brajović's uniform was old and patched in several places, and he wore a Cossack-style fur hat on his head. Peter wondered where he'd learned such competent English.

"Yes, they seem to have good morale, considering," Peter said.

"Imagine what they could do with a good stash of American supplies."

Peter wasn't sure what to say. The Allies were giving plenty of supplies to Tito's men, and Bari was full of Partisan liaison officers. But no such support came to the Chetniks, even though Peter had witnessed them fighting Nazis. "I remember the radio reports when I was in Africa and Sicily. They said General Mihailovic was a hero. Then they stopped talking about him."

Brajović nodded. "We began our war eagerly enough. But German reprisals made us think twice as we continued. I suppose we're fighting to get our territory back, rid of Nazis, but more than that, we're fighting for the people. If we had kept fighting the way we started, the Germans would have killed off the entire population. In October of '41, some guerrillas killed or wounded a few dozen German soldiers near Kragujevac. The Nazis lined up most of the Serb men from the town and shot them. The boys as well. And the population of Kragujevac wasn't big enough for them, so they brought in fifteen hundred people from Kraljevo and killed them too. They massacred thousands, plus one German soldier who refused to fire his weapon.

"So we waited until the time was right for a massive uprising, one that could be successful before reprisals were enacted. We became more sneaky, made our sabotage hard to detect. But that made it easy for the Partisans to take credit for everything we did. And the Partisans aren't fighting for the people; they're fighting for an ideology. If a village full of religious peasants is destroyed, what do they care?"

Out in the town square, Moretti took the lead for drills. Peter watched them, thinking of the pukovnik's words and of row upon row of innocent villagers being mowed down by machine guns.

"To be fair to the Germans, the Ustaše have been much worse," Brajović said. "In the area that became Fascist Croatia, the massacres were designed to convert a third of the Orthodox Serbs, drive a third of them away, and kill the remainder."

Brajović turned to Miloš and said something in Serbo-Croat. Miloš hesitated and said something back, seeming to disagree with him, but Brajović insisted, and Miloš left.

* * *

Miloš was used to the pukovnik's speeches. Brajović would talk of the five hundred years when the Serbs had been slaves under Ottoman rule. He would tell Jamie and Peter of how the Serbs had saved European Christianity from extinction and of how much they'd suffered during the last war.

Miloš agreed with Brajović, for the most part. He also admired him and would never disobey an order. Yet Brajović and men like him worried Miloš because they never forgave their enemies, never moved away from the past.

Miloš remembered frequent conversations with Croatian students while he attended Belgrade University. When he asked them why they didn't support the government, they answered that it was composed almost entirely of Serbs. Miloš would explain that, of course, it was made mostly of Serbs because the Croats had fought with the Austro-Hungarian Empire during the last war, so they couldn't be trusted in government until they proved their loyalty. His Croatian friends would explain they had little loyalty to a government that didn't include them. They might support a government that included more Croats. But the Serbs didn't trust the Croats. And so it would go, on and on until they had to head for class.

He'd understood some of the resentment his Croatian friends harbored. But he'd been shocked by the level of violence and hatred that had erupted when Ante Pavelić was made head of the Independent State of Croatia, with control over huge swaths of Bosnia and Herzegovina, including the village where Miloš and Marija had grown up. Hitler's Nazi troops had created a deadly war. Pavelić's Ustaše troops had created a terrifying hell.

Miloš had always believed Yugoslavia—a union of the southern Slavs— could exist as a free, peaceful kingdom. But the war was proving him wrong. Serbs like Pukovnik Brajović would never forgive or trust the Croatians. And Croatians like his classmates or the men who followed Pavelić would never see a Serbian king as *their* king and would always resent having to share power with the Serbs. Communism wouldn't change that. The return of King Peter wouldn't change that. The end of the war wouldn't change that. Miloš wasn't sure if anything ever *could* change mistrust and hatred into brotherhood.

Marija was in her aunt and uncle's cottage, cleaning the fireplace. "Your uncle would like to see you," Miloš said.

Marija finished the hearthstone. "Do you know why?"

"He wants to ask you a question." Miloš could even guess what Brajović would ask, and he owed Marija a warning. "He wants to ask about when the Ustaše came to our village, I think."

Her brush froze midair. Miloš didn't want to seem like a guard tasked with bringing a prisoner to trial, so he left. Marija could come if she wanted. She always obeyed her uncle, so he expected she'd soon join him, but he wanted it to be by choice, not by coercion. He walked slowly, hoping Brajovič would move to another subject by the time he returned, but as he approached and heard the pukovnik's deep, resonant voice, he could guess his friend was only getting started.

Brajović paused long enough to nod at Miloš when he returned. Jamie and Peter listened, but Miloš wasn't sure if it they were interested or just being polite. Marija came hesitantly only a minute behind him but hung back as if hoping her uncle wouldn't notice her.

"Marija, tell these men what happened to your village," Brajović said.

Marija closed her eyes for a few moments. Then she squared her shoulders and glanced at the men before staring beyond them, focusing on something in the distance—or perhaps on something in the past. "It was summer, three and a half years ago. A group of Ustaše came, maybe fifty of them. They brought all the Serbs to the town square, and the Catholic priest offered to baptize us so we could go to heaven when we were dead. Then they took the men away in groups and shot them. They took the women and children to a cliff and pushed them over the edge."

"They had no warning," Brajović said. "And even if they had, the Germans had sealed the border and cut off the escape route."

Everyone was quiet.

"Were you the only survivor?" Jamie asked.

"I'm the only Serb survivor. Our Croatian neighbors were never threatened. The Ustaše would have killed me with the rest of the women, but they had other uses for me first. I was beautiful then."

Miloš reached out and gently placed his hand on her arm. "You are still beautiful, Marija," he said as she slowly backed away.

"How did you escape?" Jamie asked.

Marija hesitated, so Miloš answered for her. "The men who ravished her left her for dead. Some Italian soldiers found her and cared for her."

"I wanted them to let me die, but they didn't speak Serbo-Croat." She fingered her apron's repaired hem for a few seconds, then abruptly dropped it. "I need to milk the goat."

"You see," Brajović said as Marija walked away. "The Croats in their village didn't lift a finger to save their neighbors. The Serbs have no friends, only enemies. And a few allies who look the other way while we suffer. We can't trust anyone else, not to free us, not to help us, and certainly not to rule us."

Miloš followed Marija with his eyes. "Peter, you should go back inside."

Peter didn't argue. When Jamie called the other foreigners over to help take Peter indoors, Miloš went after Marija.

He found her in the shed with the goat, her jaw clenched and her hands working furiously. Miloš should have known it was a bad idea, should have stood up to the pukovnik when Brajović asked him to fetch Marija. "I'm sorry, Marija, for bringing up such horrible memories. It wasn't my intention to open old wounds."

She was quiet for a few seconds, still milking. "I'll never forget what happened that day, Miloš. They needed to know, and I'm the only one who survived." She hesitated, then continued. "I didn't think you knew."

"Your uncle told me. A long time ago." Miloš rubbed the goat's ears as Marija worked. He was surprised when she spoke again.

"How you can still want to marry me, knowing what those men did to me?"

"You did nothing wrong."

Marija's hands paused. When she spoke, her voice shook with emotion. "I should have thrown myself off the cliff with the others or run into their knives."

"No, you did just what you should have done. You survived. And I'm glad you did. And if you ever agree to marry me, I swear I'll do everything in my power to protect you so nothing like that happens to you ever again. I wish I could have been there that day. I would have helped."

"If you'd been there, you'd have been shot with our fathers and our brothers and all the other men."

"Is that why you hate me, Marija? Because I wasn't there?"

Marija stood abruptly. "I don't hate you, Miloš."

"But you don't love me either?"

Marija stared at the milk bucket. "I'd like to be alone, Miloš."

"I'll finish the goat for you."

"Do you know how to milk a goat?" Her voice was more tense than usual.

"Phst. Of course."

Marija left, and though Miloš watched her go, she didn't look back.

CHAPTER SEVENTEEN
INTERNMENT

Monday, January 1, 1945
Bisevo, Liberated Yugoslavia

IULIANA IONESCU HAD BEEN IN captivity on the Adriatic island of Bisevo for one hundred nineteen days. It was a small island, and she supposed parts of it were beautiful—the olive trees and vineyards, the caves that cut into its limestone coast. Iuliana was more familiar with the dejected faces of her fellow captives and the cruel expressions of their Partisan guards.

A few kilometers from Bisevo was the larger island of Vis, a hub for British and American supplies on their way to the Partisans in Dalmatia and Croatia. She could see it from the camp where she was held and thought if she could somehow get to Vis, she might convince the British or American servicemen there to help her. She often saw fishing boats traveling between the islands, but armed guards and tall barbed-wire fences kept her from asking any of the fishermen for passage.

She'd met a few of the other prisoners and learned what she could from them about the island and the Partisans, but she'd formed no friendships. The other prisoners, like her, had done something to upset the Communists, and they'd been sent to Bisevo for trial and execution. Many of them were POWs from Germany or one of its allies. The ones who made it here were lucky—the Germans didn't consider the Partisans within the protection of the Geneva Conventions and usually slaughtered any who fell into their hands. The Partisans generally responded in kind, so the POWs who made it to Bisevo had already escaped death once. But death usually came for them anyway—by disease, overwork, or execution at the end of a hangman's noose.

Iuliana lit the gas stove in the camp's kitchen and moved a heavy pot of water over to heat up, then checked the oven to ensure the chicken was cooking properly. As she stood, she almost stepped on the gray cat that had crept behind her.

"Careful, Momma." Anatolie sat by the oven, warming up after playing outside most of the morning. Over the last few months, she'd gradually given him more freedom—as long as he stayed where she could see him through the field kitchen's windows. As he wandered around the camp, the guards seemed content to give him free range. After all, what harm could a three-year-old do?

Anatolie picked up the cat and scratched behind its ears. Iuliana didn't like cats, but she'd learned to appreciate this one. Her son loved it, and it kept the field kitchen rodent-free. The cat wasn't the only thing she'd gradually developed gratitude for over the last hundred nineteen days. She'd also come to see two tragedies from her past as blessings.

Iuliana's mother had died when Iuliana was fourteen after a long, lingering battle with cancer. Her mother had spent most of her last year teaching Iuliana how to cook. She'd lain on a sofa near the kitchen, instructing Iuliana how to make soups and sauces, her mother's specialty. At the time, Iuliana had thought it silly to spend so much time in the kitchen. There was more to life, after all, than food. But now she wondered if her mother had been acting under divine inspiration.

Over the next decade, Iuliana had been driven from her home in Bessarabia and settled in Bucharest. She'd married, been widowed, then been driven from yet another home when American bombers targeted the Romanian capital. She'd taken little Anatolie to the mountains, where she thought they'd be safe. It was there she'd learned to cook for large groups—all of the other refugees living on the estate owned by her late husband's cousin.

Iuliana peeled and chopped potatoes as rapidly as she could. *Cook for your life*, she repeated, just as she did every day. Her skills in the kitchen were the only reason she and her son were still alive. Iuliana was in charge of preparing eight meals a day: three for the officers in charge of the camp, three for the guards, and two for the prisoners. As long as she kept the camp commandant satiated with savory soups and fluffy bread, he continued to postpone her trial. Acquittal was rare, and she knew her trial would end with a guilty verdict. The commandant saved her life every week when he scheduled trials and left her name off the list.

Iuliana put the potatoes for the prisoners' soup in the simmering pot of water and sliced bread for the officers' midday meal. She handed a piece to her son, then gave him another when he requested it. Sometimes she felt guilty for taking more than her share of food, but most of the other prisoners would be dead in a matter of weeks anyway. Would death be any less final if they weighed a few pounds less when it came?

She was nervous about the upcoming meal. The pukovnik over the camp didn't hold his alcohol well, and he, like most of the guards, had rung in the new year with a seemingly endless supply of plum brandy. He hadn't been to breakfast that morning, so she suspected he had a hangover. When he came for his next meal, he would no doubt have a headache and be more hungry than usual. If the meal didn't meet his expectations, Iuliana predicted her trial would come by week's end.

"Momma?"

"Yes?"

"The oven is smoking."

Iuliana pushed her son out of the way and ran to the oven, pulling the chicken out with a towel and looking at it in despair. The unpredictable oven had burned the breast and the ends of the drumsticks and had no doubt left the rest of the meat overcooked. She set the pan on the counter and stared at it. The officers would complain if they had dry meat, and there wasn't time to cook anything else—not that she had much to work with in the larder. Would a burnt chicken really be what sent her to the camp gallows?

"What's wrong, Momma?"

Iuliana forced a smile. She didn't want her son to live in constant fear, so she lied. It was becoming habit. "Nothing, dear. The chicken's a little well-done, is all. Will you run outside and tell me if it's any warmer now?"

Anatolie scooped up the cat and left. He'd been making a tower with rocks earlier, and through the window, she saw him head back to his improvised blocks.

Iuliana glanced at an old watch with a broken armband. She had ten minutes. *Just enough time for a sauce.* She hoped it would be enough to disguise the tough meat. She'd give the commandant the best portion and hope it would be enough to postpone her trial yet again.

* * *

Iuliana had lived to see her hundred twenty-second day of captivity. She kept track in the larder with a pencil mark for each day. She'd been assigned to the kitchen her first week at the camp, so she was confident in her count's accuracy.

She was always exhausted by day's end, and this evening was no exception. She finished washing the pots, hung her apron, and went outside for her son. It was dark and cold, but Anatolie often left the kitchen when she started cleaning, not wanting to help dry pans. Sometimes she insisted. He was only three, but that didn't mean he couldn't help. Today, however, she'd let him wander.

Iuliana walked all around the field kitchen, went back inside to check the larder and the cupboards, then checked their tent. No Anatolie. She felt a horrible tightness in her chest. Cheating death would be pointless if she lost her son in the process.

She finally found him outside the camp's fence, watching the Partisans unload something from a truck. She wondered why they'd let him out of camp, then recognized the only guard she'd never seen beating a prisoner. Ivan spoke a little English, and he always thanked her when she gave him his meals. Whenever he was on duty, Anatolie seemed to gravitate to him, sensing he'd be safer beside him than near any of the other guards.

"Anatolie, come back."

He looked at her and pouted.

"Now."

She could see his frown, but he took a few steps toward her just as one of the German POWs attempted to run through the open gate. Iuliana heard shouts and gunshots and saw the prisoner fall. When she looked back at the truck, the crate Ivan and another guard had been unloading was on the ground, on its side. She couldn't see Anatolie, but she heard his cry, and she could tell from the sound that he was scared and in pain.

Iuliana ran toward him, closing half the distance before one of the guards grabbed her arm, jerked her around, and yelled at her in Serbo-Croat.

She looked past the guard to the overturned crate hiding her son. She understood why the guard had grabbed her—trying to run through the camp's entrance seconds after another prisoner's escape attempt was foolish, but Anatolie was hurt.

The guard shook her roughly before releasing her and ordering her to stay where she was. Her eyes teared up as she listened to Anatolie's sobs and watched the Partisan guards struggle to turn over the crate they'd dropped. One guard shot the wounded escapee in the head, then joined the other guards and helped them move the crate. Seconds later, Ivan bent down, and when he stood again, he was holding her son.

Ivan brought Anatolie to her, and she took him to the kitchen, praying her little boy would be okay. His right arm was covered in blood from the elbow down. She kissed his forehead and hugged him before wiping away the gore to reveal a bloody mass of skin, sinew, and shattered bone. Feeling lightheaded, she tightly wrapped his hand and forearm in a towel, then sat on the ground with him on her lap, trying to calm his hysterical breathing and slow his tears.

Iuliana felt helpless. What could she do for her son? She couldn't fix his arm; she couldn't even soften the pain. Nor could she seek help outside the camp. Inside the camp, the options were depressing. There was no camp infirmary, and she saw all the camp's inhabitants when she gave them their food, so she knew there were no German doctors among the prisoners. The most she could hope for was someone who knew a little first aid, but that wouldn't fix mangled bones.

Anatolie's cries had softened into whimpers when Ivan pushed hesitantly through the kitchen door, his face lined with worry. "Sorry about boy. I talk to commandant. He say Partisan doctor come tomorrow. But Partisan doctors, they see wound like that . . ." Ivan made a swift motion, acting like he was amputating his hand. "Commandant also say when shift ends, I can take boy to Vis. British doctors there. Maybe they can fix arm. But commandant say you can't leave."

Iuliana looked down at her son. She didn't want him to lose part of his arm, but she knew he'd be terrified if they were separated, especially while he was in so much pain. The crossing to Vis would be in darkness, but what about the return? Any boats in the open during daylight became inviting targets for the Luftwaffe. And what if Anatolie was mixed up with all the other refugees passing through Vis and she never saw him again?

"How long would he be gone?" she asked.

Ivan looked at the floor. "I can bring him back on next day off, in a week. If weather good. Sometimes they evacuate bad cases to Italy. Then who knows?"

She squeezed her eyes shut, praying for wisdom to do whatever would be best for her son. She opened her eyes and met Ivan's, surprised by what she saw there. Ivan's eyes were a lighter shade of blue, but she saw in them the same kindness she'd seen in Krzysztof. Knowing she had her answer, Iuliana nodded her agreement.

She spent the next few hours cradling her son, singing softly to him, telling him she loved him. When Ivan's shift ended, Anatolie had fallen into a fitful sleep. Hesitantly, she placed the most precious thing in her whole world into the arms of a near stranger and kissed her son good-bye.

* * *

Days at the camp were always long, but the next seven passed more slowly than usual. All Ivan had been able to tell Iuliana was that the British hospital had admitted her son. Whether they'd be able to save his arm or not was unknown, and Iuliana felt a twist of pain whenever she thought of how lonely and scared Anatolie must be.

On Iuliana's one hundred twenty-ninth day of captivity, she started the morning meals as usual, hoping for her son's return or at least news of him. It was hard to concentrate, and she had to remind herself several times what the consequence would be if she ruined the commandant's breakfast.

"Momma!"

Tears blurred her vision before she'd even turned around. Anatolie ran into her arms, and she pulled him into a tight embrace and covered his forehead with kisses. She blinked away her tears and gently handled the plaster cast covering his right hand and forearm. "Thank you," she whispered to Ivan, who stood in the kitchen door.

Ivan came into the kitchen again after his midday meal. Iuliana was preparing the prisoners' second meal, but she stopped and pulled a piece of cake from the larder. "I saved you something from the officers' dinner. Thank you for taking care of my son."

He glanced out the window, where Anatolie played with his cat in the sunshine. "I came to talk about boy." Ivan wouldn't meet her gaze when he turned back, looking instead at the floor. "I talk with lady in Komiža. She say she'll take care of boy if something happens to you."

Iuliana felt tears sting her eyes. Anatolie's future had been her biggest fear since leaving Bari. Surviving the camp on Bisevo was a battle she knew she'd eventually lose, and what would happen to her son when she was gone? In her mind, it wasn't *if* anything happened to her; it was *when*. "The woman, she's a good woman?"

"Recommended by priest. Goes to church every day. Her children, six of them, all grown now. She can read and has vegetable garden. A few goats. Her husband a fisherman. He die last year. She say cat can come too."

Iuliana blinked away her tears. She was touched by Ivan's inquiries— that he had not only taken the time to find somewhere safe for her boy but had even made sure Anatolie could take his pet. "Thank you. I worry about him all the time, about what will happen to him." Komiža was one of the two ports on Vis. Compared to the camp on Bisevo, it sounded like the promised land.

* * *

Ivan's gifts were a huge relief. Anatolie would have both his hands, and he wouldn't be abandoned when she was executed. Iuliana wished she could meet the woman who would raise her son but had to be content with Ivan's judgment. She began looking at each new day as another miracle, another day to enjoy her little boy and place herself in his memory.

The British doctor who'd fixed Anatolie's hand had requested the boy return for follow-up care, so Anatolie would have to go away again. Iuliana dreaded sending him to Vis again, but this time, she wasn't so distraught.

On the evening of her one hundred forty-third day of captivity, Iuliana put Anatolie to bed while they waited for Ivan's shift to end. When the kind Croatian guard was finished, he would take Anatolie back to the hospital.

As she waited, Iuliana paced the floor of their little tent. It was a private tent because she was the only female prisoner. She thought of Krzysztof and was surprised at how strong her feelings still were, bringing tears to her eyes. *Please let him be alive.* Could he have survived somehow, despite his injury and Kimby's sabotage? Was he waiting for her in England, thinking she'd forgotten him? She couldn't get to him, but maybe she could send a message.

She found a piece of paper and contemplated what to write. She wanted Krzysztof to know she'd loved him in the brief time they'd been together. And she wanted him to rescue her. She also wanted someone to rescue her son. The Croatian widow sounded nice, but Iuliana wanted Anatolie to grow up where he would be free. It seemed inevitable that Vis would be part of Yugoslavia after the war, and what kind of life would Anatolie have in Communist Yugoslavia?

She imagined what would happen if she told Krzysztof her location. He would do his best to come for her if he was alive. But what if, after surviving all the dangers Major Kimby had heaped upon him, Krzysztof died trying to help her? How many times could she ask him to risk his life for her? And what if she went to trial before he even received the letter?

Iuliana weighed her love for her son and her love for Krzysztof, pondering what was right and what was fair. She spent a long time thinking of Krzysztof, of how much he'd already done for her and of how he always did the right thing, the selfless thing. She finally made her decision and wrote her letter.

When she heard the guards changing shifts, she shook her son awake. "Anatolie, I want you to do something for me."

"Yes, Momma?" He yawned.

"Ask the doctor in Vis to mail this letter for you."

CHAPTER EIGHTEEN
CANES AND CANDLES

Friday, January 26
German-occupied Serbia

THE FIRST THING PETER NOTICED when Krzysztof came into the cottage was the slight smile on his lips. He was up to something, but he sat at the table and took the radio apart without saying anything.

Peter chucked a makeshift baseball at Moretti, who caught it easily before returning it. Peter loved baseball, but more than that, he loved not having pain shoot through his ribs when he moved his arms or having a cough that left him struggling for breath.

Jamie looked up from his book and glared at them. Over the winter, they'd all had their moments of crankiness—cabin fever, missed girlfriends, food that was low in quality and in quantity. Krzysztof was the only one who'd maintained an even temper all winter despite several months of being the lone healthy member of the team. He'd done more than his share of cooking, cleaning, and emptying bedpans.

Moretti took his frustration out by training with Krzysztof and any Chetniks who wandered through. Now that Peter was mobile and relatively healthy, he found the exercises good for his restlessness too. But today the weather had forced them indoors.

"What's the matter, Jamie?" Moretti asked.

Jamie didn't answer.

"That's what I thought," Moretti said as he caught Peter's next throw. Miloš had just checked Jamie's leg and told him to stay on crutches at least another week. Jamie had hoped to graduate to a cane. Moretti threw the ball at Jamie, who swatted it aside with his book. The ball ricocheted into the table, scattering pieces of the radio in every direction.

Krzysztof stared at the mess for a long moment, his right hand still holding a small screwdriver. Then he laughed. Before long, the rest of the men—even Jamie—joined in. It felt good to laugh again, although the effort left Peter out of breath. His lungs were still fragile.

"You won't fix it anyway, not without new parts," Jamie said as Krzysztof and Peter gathered the pieces.

"Maybe, maybe not." Krzysztof dumped the pieces back onto the table. "But you could show a little more gratitude. I have a present for you today."

Jamie raised one eyebrow. "I hope any present involves high-quality chocolate or a part that really will fix that radio."

"It ain't food or electronics." Moretti caught Peter's questioning look. "You had pneumonia when we started. We weren't trying to keep it from ya."

"Well, what is it?" Peter asked, since Jamie wouldn't.

Krzysztof went to the door and opened it far enough to stick a hand outside and bring back a wooden cane. He tossed it to Jamie, who caught it with one hand. "You won't be able to use it yet, but pull the top off."

Jamie glanced over the cane. It was made of smooth, light wood, and it had a handle. Jamie tugged the handle away from the shaft and grinned when he saw the narrow foot-long blade, complete with blood gutters.

It was the best smile anyone had gotten out of Jamie all year.

* * *

Dearest Genevieve,

There's a bird singing outside the window. I can't see it, but the sound reminds me of you. Almost everything reminds me of you somehow. I remember you singing in the kitchen the week we met. Your brother said he used to call you his little canary, but you hadn't sung like that in years. And I remember the first time I called you un beau canari. You said I was using the wrong adjective, but I'm still sure it's the right one. Yesterday Moretti was whistling a song, one you and I danced to when I was on leave in London. I thought of you then too. Like I said, everything reminds me of you, makes me wish I was with you. Some nights I dream about you. I still have nightmares too, but if I can get back to you, I don't think they'll matter so much because you'll be there when I wake up, and seeing you will make them fade.

I love you,
Peter

* * *

Miloš found Marija alone in her aunt and uncle's kitchen. "Hello, Marija."

She was getting her bread ready to bake, placing it in the fireplace on top of a plate and under an upside-down bowl, then piling hot ashes on top. "Hello, Miloš."

"I was thinking, Marija, that we should get married."

"We can't get married."

"Why not?" he asked, wondering what excuse she'd give today.

"We haven't known each other long enough."

"Phst. We grew up in the same village."

"But you're several years older than I am. We never spoke when we were children." She wiped her hands on a rag, cleaning the ash from her fingers. "It's like we only met here."

Miloš shook his head. "No, Marija, I've loved you since you were twelve."

"What?" He could see the smallest hint of surprise on her face.

"The schoolteacher called us all together. You were wearing a gray dress that was too big for you. And your hair was in two braids, with pink ribbons at the ends. He asked you what you wanted to do when you grew up, and you said you wanted to live in America because you had an uncle there, and he said it was wonderful. And you wanted to teach children to read so they could enjoy reading as much as you did."

She stared at him, mute.

"He asked others what they wanted to do too. I don't remember what anyone else said, but I remembered your response and tried to find out which books you liked. Do you know why I learned English?"

She shook her head.

"Because you said you loved Jane Austen, and I couldn't find any Serbo-Croat translations."

"You learned English so you could read Jane Austen just because I liked her books?"

Miloš nodded.

"Why?"

"So I'd have something to talk to you about if I ever worked up the courage to speak to you."

Marija stared at him as if she'd never seen him before. "But you were popular in school. You were smartest in your class, and you were the fastest runner in the village, and your parents owned more land than anyone else, and you had a new bicycle. Why would you be scared to talk to someone like me?"

Miloš smiled. "You remember all that about me, and you still think we haven't known each other long enough to get married?"

Marija shook her head. Miloš thought he saw a hint of color rising in her cheeks, but he couldn't be sure. "It doesn't matter," she said. "We still can't get married."

"Because you don't love me?"

"No, not yet," she whispered.

"Perhaps tomorrow you will love me." Miloš headed for the door, and as he stepped across the threshold she spoke again.

"Which Jane Austen books did you read?" Her voice was soft, hesitant.

Miloš turned around. "*Pride and Prejudice* and *Emma*."

"Did you like them?"

Miloš shrugged. "They were all right. I liked them for your sake, but I liked *Treasure Island* better. You said you liked that book once, didn't you?"

Marija nodded.

"I read a lot of Robert Louis Stevenson. Have you read *The Black Arrow?*"

Marija shook her head.

"You'd probably like it. It has adventure and romance. I'll try to find a copy for you."

"I don't have time to read anymore. There's work to be done all day long."

Miloš thought for a moment. Marija was busy from dawn until sunset, but she'd loved reading when she was younger, and Miloš thought a few good books might lift her spirits. "What if I found you some candles? You could read after sunset, when all the work is finished."

"I can't waste candles on leisure."

"You could if I got them for you."

Miloš could see her thinking, could tell she was tempted. Ever so slowly, she nodded her head. Miloš left before she changed her mind.

* * *

The creek near the village was mostly frozen, but the day was warmer than normal, and part of the creek had thawed. Miloš saw Marija sitting beside it and walked over to join her. "Hello, Marija."

She didn't look up when he approached. "Hello, Miloš."

"I was thinking, Marija, that we should get married."

"We can't get married."

"Why not?"

"Because you are still full of life, and I've been dead since the Ustaše destroyed our village."

Miloš hesitated, then sat next to her and watched the creek splash past as he thought of what he should say. "I read in the Bible about a man who suffered horrible things and died. But He rose again. And He promised His followers that He would heal them of their physical and spiritual ailments. And then He promised them that they would live again like Him."

Miloš waited for her normal response, waited for her to say she didn't love him. But she was silent. When he looked at her, there were tears running down her cheeks. He'd never seen her cry before, nor heard of anyone else who'd seen such a sight. He gently, hesitantly, reached out to touch her hand, and to his surprise, she didn't pull away. "Perhaps tomorrow, Marija, you will love your Savior and love yourself, and maybe then you can love me."

* * *

Marija sat at the creek for a long time after Miloš left. He'd stayed for a while, holding her hand, letting her think. Now he was gone, and the creek seemed colder. Her hands were cold. Her face was cold. But that wasn't the problem. She always spent most of the winter shivering. The problem was her heart was cold too.

It hadn't always been that way. She'd been a happy child. Her parents had been poor, but they'd loved their children, and family life had been harmonious. Her uncle Stoyan Brajović had visited regularly, usually bringing sweets and a bolt of soft fabric purchased in a fine Belgrade store. And her uncle Lazar Brajović had written regularly, often sending a parcel with a book or two, most of them in English, purchased at a secondhand bookstore in Pittsburgh, Pennsylvania.

She remembered the day Miloš had spoken of, when she was a schoolgirl. She didn't remember the gray dress. It had probably been a hand-me-down from one of her sisters, still too large for her. But she recalled the pink ribbons. And she remembered her old dream: to go to America and teach children how to read. But that was a long time ago—another life.

In her old life, she would have long ago agreed to marry Miloš. She'd liked him in the village when he was the bright, friendly boy who sometimes met her eyes but never spoke to her. She'd always been glad to see him return home between terms after he'd gone to study medicine in Belgrade.

In her old life, Marija had been full of dreams and laughter, so it would have been only natural to love and marry someone like Miloš. But the old Marija was a stranger now. The fire inside her had long ago burned out, and she had no idea how to relight it. Religion had been important to her as a child, and she pondered what Miloš had said at the creek. But her faith had vanished the day the Ustaše killed her family and neighbors and left her in the woods ravaged, beaten, and bleeding.

As she walked into her uncle's home and past the kitchen table, she noticed something lying there. It was a pair of candles tied with string. She turned the attached piece of paper over, recognizing Miloš's handwriting.

For Marija. Something to relight some of the happiness of your youth.

Marija pulled her hand back as if the paper were on fire. *How could he have known? How could he have known I was thinking about fires and lights and lost happiness?* She backed away from the table and took a few deep breaths. Even though the morning fire had burned out hours ago, the home suddenly felt stuffy, so she left, ignoring her chores, just wandering. She was surprised when she found herself outside the village church.

Chapter Nineteen
LIGHT

THE CHURCH WAS COLD, ALMOST as cold as the creek. The flickering light cast by dozens of candles illuminated the Byzantine-style paintings of Serb saints. Marija sat in the church, staring at them, wondering if they had any advice for her. But their stories all ended in martyrdom and sacrifice for one's people, and she was no martyr, no matter how many times she wished she could join her slain family.

She focused on the carving of Christ hanging wounded on a cross, and as she looked at Him, she felt not His pain but His love. Her eyes stung with tears, and she quickly blinked them away. After her village was destroyed, Marija had tried to suppress her emotions. They were all bad ones anyway: grief, terror, disappointment, pain. It was easier not to feel anything, and that's what she'd tried to do since her family was murdered. But sitting there, staring at the cross, she was reminded that there were other emotions too, ones she hadn't felt for years: faith, hope, and love.

The ancient priest came into the church, so she slipped out, not wanting anyone to see her crying. Her vision was blurry as she hurried away, and she nearly ran into Peter. He had a load of firewood in his arms and wore one of the scarves she'd knitted.

"I'm sorry, Peter."

"I should have been paying more attention. Are you all right?"

"Fine." But as she spoke, her voice cracked, and she knew the American was smart enough to catch it. She'd spent a lot of time in the foreigners' cabin, especially while Peter was battling pneumonia.

He didn't say anything for a few moments. "You look cold. Come on, I'll walk you home and build you a fire."

She nodded but kept her head down most of the way to her uncle's home. She sat numbly in a chair as Peter arranged the logs and lit them.

"I'm a horrible cook, but Krzysztof's not bad. I could have him send some food over. Seems only fair. You've brought us food for months."

She glanced from the flames to her guest, studying his face. If anyone in the village were to see her cry, she was glad it was Peter. She'd seen him delirious with fever and so weak from coughing she wasn't sure he'd make it another day. It didn't seem quite so horrible being vulnerable in front of someone she'd helped nurse back to health. She meant to thank him for the offer and decline further assistance, but instead, she found herself asking a question. "Do you believe the next life will be good if we suffer enough in this one?"

She could see Peter thinking before he answered. "I believe the next life will be good, and I believe this life is supposed to be good too. I think God wants us to be happy, now, even when life is hard."

Marija watched him adjust one of the logs. She felt the fire's warmth and was no longer cold for the first time that week. She had chores to complete, but all she wanted to do was sit by the fire and not shiver. "I think that's what Miloš believes."

"Miloš is a smart man."

"And a happy one."

Peter smiled. "He's a smart, happy man who wants to marry you."

Marija looked away. "I know." She thought for a few moments. "But I don't think he'd be happy married to me. I have a hard time remembering what it's like to be happy. If we were married, I'm afraid he'd stop smiling."

She heard Peter add another stick to the fire before he spoke. "You know, nothing makes me happier than seeing my girlfriend smile or laugh and knowing I'm responsible." He was quiet for a few moments, thinking about his girlfriend, Marija supposed. "And nothing haunts me more than knowing the last time I saw her, she was crying, and it was because of me," he said softly. "Maybe you should let Miloš love you. Let him make you smile and make you laugh. Let him make you happy, and then he'll be happy too."

"I'm not worth marrying."

"That's not true."

"Yes, it is," she insisted. "I'm ruined and not worth having."

Peter was silent for a time, and Marija stared out the window. She was convinced the words she'd spoken were true and assumed he was wise enough to agree with her. When he did speak, he surprised her. "Being the victim of a horrible crime doesn't decrease your value as a woman or as a child of God."

She looked at him. He met her gaze and held it, and she found herself believing he was sincere—sincere but wrong. "If your girlfriend had been raped, would you still want her?"

"Yes," he said immediately.

She studied him closely. He still seemed sincere, but how could he really mean that? "It wouldn't change your relationship at all?"

He stared at the fire, his face thoughtful. "It might affect our relationship a little because that kind of crime leaves scars—if not on the body, then on the soul. But it wouldn't diminish her value, and I wouldn't love her any less." He threw another stick into the fire before turning to face her. "And I would still want to marry her, just as Miloš still wants to marry you."

Marija sat and watched the fire for hours after Peter left. There were chores she should be doing, but she saw Peter and his friends walk past the window and knew they were doing her work for her. She meant to protest but couldn't find the willpower to leave the fire's warmth. She thought about Peter's words and about Miloš's words and about what she'd felt in the church. Tears trickled down her cheeks, and she thought about the past. And for the first time in years, she thought about a future.

* * *

Miloš knocked on the Brajovičs' door, and Marija told him to enter. "Hello, Marija."

She looked up from her knitting and held his gaze. "Hello, Miloš."

He handed her a candle. It was thicker than the ones he'd given her yesterday, so it would burn more slowly and hopefully provide light for just as long.

"Thank you." She seemed a little embarrassed: her eyes downcast, extra color in her cheeks. "I used up the ones you gave me last night. I stayed up too late, but I don't regret it."

Miloš smiled. "Did you find a good book to read?"

She nodded.

"What is it called?"

"Matthew. In the New Testament."

Marija had stayed up late reading the Bible? Well, that was a good book. Miloš tried to read from it every day, but he'd never yet gone through two candles in one night doing so. "I was thinking, Marija, that we should get married."

"We can't get married."

"Why not?"

"Because we have no appointment at the church."

"Phst. I can talk to the priest today. We could get married tomorrow."

Marija smiled, the edges of her lips turning up ever so slightly. "Not tomorrow."

Miloš sensed something was different, the pattern broken, because Marija was somehow changed. "When?"

"Thursday?" She looked at her knitting, but her small smile had turned into a giddy grin.

He watched her until she met his eyes. "Do you love me now, Marija?"

"I do love you, Miloš."

* * *

Beau Canari,

There's going to be a wedding tomorrow. I'm happy for the bride and groom. They deserve this bit of happiness. But I wish it was going to be a double wedding. I miss you.

Love,

Peter

* * *

According to Serb tradition, the brothers of the groom were to barter with the bride's father for the bride. Miloš's brothers were dead, and so was Marija's father, so Peter and his team went to Pukovnik Brajović to make an offer. Peter was sure Brajović would have agreed to marry off Marija for nothing, but knowing Marija's past, he didn't want her to think her value was so low. Peter and his men didn't have much—a few weapons with little ammunition, a cane, a broken radio, and clothes that needed patching, but they offered training for the Chetnik men, and Brajović accepted it with pleasure.

Peter sat next to Jamie during the ceremony so Jamie could translate what was said. The priest spoke of how Miloš and Marija both had weaknesses, but they would be compensated for by the other's strengths. He crowned them king and queen of their home and said the crown was also a symbol of martyrdom because both bride and groom would have to be self-sacrificing. The symbolism continued with a candle representing the light of Christ and reminding the couple to be a shining example of virtue. Then the priest tied the bride's and groom's hands together, making them one, and prayed for them before leading them around the altar as husband and wife.

Everyone in the village came to the wedding and sang in celebration. No one had any money, so instead of throwing the traditional coins as the couple left the chapel, the guests threw wood chips. Outside, they danced the kolo—a traditional group dance, where participants formed a circle and placed their arms on their neighbor's shoulders. Jamie stood to the side with his cane, a contented look on his face, and a few of the older, more feeble members of the village stood near him, watching.

During the entire ceremony and the celebration that followed, Miloš smiled, and Marija beamed. Peter watched their faces, happy for them, and found his thoughts turning to Genevieve. Did she think of him as often as he thought of her? Would she marry him if he found his way back to her? And would she look as happy as Marija did on her wedding day?

CHAPTER TWENTY
DANCING WITH DANGER

Thursday, February 22
Bari, Italy

GENEVIEVE DIDN'T WANT TO GO to the USO dance, but Dorothy wouldn't back down. "Come on, Genevieve, it's your patriotic duty to help the boys forget the war for a few minutes."

"I just finished my shift. I look awful." Genevieve was more interested in sleeping than dancing. She had no idea how Dorothy still had so much energy. She'd worked a shift just as long as Genevieve's that day.

"The ratio is about three hundred guys to every girl—trust me, you'll do."

Genevieve held up a hand in surrender. "All right, but give me five minutes?"

Dorothy smiled mischievously. "I'll give you ten. We'll make a better entrance if we're late."

"That many men, and you're worried about making an entrance?"

"Don't ruin my fun!"

Since Dorothy wasn't in a hurry, Genevieve washed her face, combed her hair, and put on fresh lipstick. She even wore her favorite dress.

When they arrived at the dance ten minutes late, the hall was comfortably full. A half hour into the dance, it was packed. There was no band, just someone with a pile of records, a record player, and a set of speakers. With such a large crowd, a band wouldn't have fit anyway.

Genevieve never had a chance to stand still—on most dances, different soldiers cut in three or four times. The men were upbeat, and Genevieve found herself laughing, really enjoying herself for the first time in months. She danced until her feet hurt, and even then, she didn't stop. There were too many airmen, and she knew a little of what they went through on their missions. If they could forget their bad memories for a few hours, she would help them.

Most of her dance partners were American airmen, and the hazel-eyed one she found herself dancing with at 2330 was no exception.

"I'm the ball-turret gunner on the *Lucky Lucille*," Sergeant Shelton said proudly.

Genevieve held back a shiver. They didn't see many ball-turret gunners in the hospital, but not because it wasn't a dangerous job. Someone had told Genevieve the average life expectancy of a ball-turret gunner in combat was measured in seconds.

"Our pilot named the plane for his wife. I don't know how lucky it is—if there's ack-ack going off within a mile, it always seems to hit us first."

"But it still gets you back? Maybe that's the lucky part," she suggested.

Shelton considered it. "Maybe. I would've liked to have named it *Hitler's Coffin* or *Death from the Sky*. This song is great, isn't it? Both the waist gunners on our plane are from New Orleans, and they've got us all hooked on jazz."

The noise on the dance floor hadn't let Genevieve concentrate on the music and her conversation at the same time, but as her partner pointed the lyrics out, Genevieve could hear "How High the Moon," a song about a woman longing for the man she loved. The words hit Genevieve like a brick wall, and she could barely breathe. She'd danced with Peter to a slower version of the same song.

"Would you like some fresh air, miss?" Shelton stopped moving and watched her with concern.

Genevieve nodded weakly. By some small miracle—or perhaps her face looked gray—no one tried to cut in as she took his arm and he led her outside into cooler, fresher air. "Thank you, Sergeant."

He nodded. "My pleasure, miss." Leaning against the building, he offered her a cigarette.

"No, thank you."

"Are you all right?" He put his cigarettes back in his pocket without lighting one for himself.

"I will be in a few minutes."

"Do you want to talk about it?" he asked.

Genevieve looked at him more carefully. She'd danced with so many men that most of their faces had blurred together. Sergeant Shelton was a few inches taller than her, with large arm muscles and sparkling green-brown eyes. His light brown hair reminded her of her brother's. Surprised, she realized she did want to talk to him.

"My boyfriend took me dancing in England. There was a live band playing jazz music. And a singer—she was beautiful. I think she was from New Orleans, like your waist gunners. She sang that song, 'How High the Moon,' and we danced to it. I'd never heard the song before, but Peter whispered part of the chorus in my ear while we danced." Genevieve lifted her hand and brushed her cheek with her fingers, the way Peter had brushed it with his lips. "It was our last dance."

"Where's your boyfriend now?" Shelton's question was hesitant. Like everyone in Europe, he knew what the answer could be.

"He's missing. Since September."

"Is he a Brit?"

Genevieve was grateful he'd said *is* instead of *was*. "No, he's American. From a little farming town in Idaho."

"In the Air Corp?"

"No, he's in the army, but . . ." Genevieve hesitated, not sure she could tell Shelton Peter was a spy.

Shelton raised one eyebrow as if to question her. "But?"

"But he was part of a commando group."

"Oh." There was less optimism in his response. He thought for a while, then smiled. "I grew up on a farm in Pennsylvania. Us American farm boys are tough—if anyone can make it back, I bet your Peter can."

"Thank you," Genevieve said. "Everyone else keeps telling me he's dead."

"Would you like me to walk you home? You're a little pale still."

"That would be lovely, Sergeant Shelton."

He offered her his arm. "You can call me Rick."

"That would be lovely, Rick."

As they passed the hospital on their way to Genevieve's section of the tent city, she paused when she saw a shadow move past the entrance.

"Is something wrong?"

Genevieve glanced from the shadow to Rick, then back again. "I thought I saw something over by the hospital."

Rick stared in the direction she pointed. The shadow moved again, walking away from them. "Yeah, you saw something. Something about six foot two and well over two hundred pounds. You recognize him?"

"Maybe." The man had been watching the hospital—perhaps innocuously, perhaps not. Genevieve slipped her arm away from Rick's. "I think I'll follow him and see. Thank you for taking me home."

She stepped away, and Rick stepped with her. "You aren't home yet. Why don't I come along?"

Genevieve hesitated. If it was Ercolani or one of his accomplices, having Rick along would be helpful for her but dangerous for the sergeant.

"Come on," Rick said. "I haven't done anything like this in years. It sounds kind of fun."

"All right, but I don't want our subject to know we're following him."

Rick nodded.

When they came to a main street, Genevieve took Rick's hand so they looked like a couple and drew closer to the man they tailed. A door opened a few meters in front of their quarry, and light spilled into the street, briefly illuminating a square face, a cleft chin, and dark hair mostly hidden under a hat. It was Ercolani. He was back and was watching the hospital.

"Someone you know?" Rick asked. "Peter?"

"That's not Peter. But yes, I recognize him." Genevieve let a few of the patrons exiting the bar get between Ercolani and her. She realized she'd been holding Rick's hand a little too tightly and relaxed her grip. "Sorry."

"It's fine. But who is he? And why are you following him?"

Genevieve looked at Rick for a moment. Ercolani had killed before, and she didn't doubt he'd kill her and anyone unfortunate enough to be beside her if given the chance. "You should go back, Rick," she said, releasing his hand.

"Not without a good explanation." Rick kept his voice down, matching her slight volume.

"He's a Fascist spy, and I need to find out where he's going. And he's dangerous, so you should leave."

Rick was silent. Ercolani turned a corner, and Genevieve hurried so she wouldn't lose him. Rick kept up with her. When they reached the corner, Ercolani was still in view.

"Please, Rick. Go before you get hurt."

Ercolani turned around. He was too far away to recognize Genevieve's face in the dark, but she and Rick were the only other people on the street. She felt Rick wrap his arms around her and pull her toward him, then felt his hand on her face, tilting her chin until her lips were a mere inch from his. She was motionless for a few seconds, startled, then she pulled away.

"Relax and play along." There was nothing mischievous or amorous in Rick's eyes; they were very serious. "We'll look like just another couple sharing a kiss on an empty street." He brought his lips next to her ear. From Ercolani's view, it would look like Rick was kissing her.

Genevieve tried to relax, keeping an eye on Ercolani, who slowly turned and crossed the street. "Are you armed, Rick?"

He released her and nodded. "Yeah."

She followed Ercolani, walking next to the wall, where she'd blend in with the building, and Rick followed her. She didn't want him to, but it was nice to have someone with a weapon along, and he had managed to throw off Ercolani's suspicion with his pantomimed kiss.

"So your boyfriend's an American commando, and you're a French spy. I can think of all sorts of crazy ways the two of you could have met."

Genevieve felt herself smiling. "I'd love to hear your theories sometime."

Ercolani turned another corner, and she hurried to catch up. Rick stayed right behind her. He wasn't as quiet as she was, but Ercolani didn't seem to hear him. They followed him for what Genevieve guessed was another fifteen minutes, until he walked into an apartment.

"What now?" Rick asked.

Genevieve wasn't sure. She didn't want to let Ercolani get away again. "Could you take a message back to Dr. Lombardelli for me? He's the doctor on duty at the hospital we passed. Tell him I've found Ercolani, and give him directions. And if it's not too much to ask, I'd like to borrow your pistol."

Rick pulled his pistol from his pocket. "You know how to use a .45?"

"Yes."

"Have you ever shot anyone?"

Genevieve looked down, remembering the Gestapo agent and the hole she'd left in the center of his forehead. "Yes."

"Genevieve, you are the most frightening woman I've ever met. No wonder you're dating a commando. No one else would be brave enough to stick around."

She could tell by his smile that he was teasing her. "May I borrow your pistol?"

"No, but I'll stay here and make sure he doesn't sneak away while you go talk to that doctor of yours. I suppose he's a spy too?"

"He's been a doctor for decades. A spy for only a few years."

Rick nodded. "Right. Off you go."

"Don't you have to fly somewhere tomorrow?"

Rick shrugged. "Maybe. Depends on the weather and if our ground crew gets the *Lucky Lucille* repaired from our last mission. One of the engines was acting up."

"Rick, please just give Dr. Lombardelli the message and go back to your base where you'll be safe."

He laughed silently at her. "Go back to my base so I can be safe? We've got another twenty missions before we've completed our tour. Do you have any idea what it's like to be in a ball-turret with an enemy fighter coming at you? It's like every shot is aimed at you personally. The last ball-turret gunner I saw, they didn't even have enough of him left to bag when the plane landed. They just hosed off a pool of gore and sent a green replacement up in his spot the next day. So don't talk to me about going back to my base and flying a nice, safe mission."

"I'm sorry, Rick. I didn't mean to—"

"It's all right," Rick interrupted, placing a hand on her shoulder. "I'm not angry, and I didn't mean to go off on what was left of Sergeant Wright's body. We all have a different battle to fight. Tonight, let me help you fight yours. You know Dr. Lombardelli, and I don't. So you go talk to him."

"That man is dangerous. He'll kill you if he needs to."

"Then you better come back with reinforcements."

CHAPTER TWENTY-ONE
THWARTED PLANS

LOMBARDELLI AGREED WITH RICK WHEN Genevieve arrived at the hospital and explained everything to him. She stifled a yawn after he took her to his office to call Bari's OSS headquarters for reinforcements. "Someone should be here soon," Lombardelli said.

Genevieve nodded, hoping Rick was safe. "Do you suppose Ercolani was looking for you?"

Lombardelli twirled a pen in his fingers for a few seconds before answering. "I don't suppose I'm off his list of people to eliminate."

"You'd better have OSS send a bodyguard for you, then."

The twirling stopped. "And one for you."

"For me?"

"He saw you in the alley, and he knows someone your height met Giacomo. It wouldn't be much of a stretch for him to assume you're the link between Giacomo and me."

Genevieve sank into a nearby chair. "Won't you arrest him?"

"It would be more useful if we could follow him for a while and arrest some of his friends along with him."

Genevieve nodded. She'd met a German officer who'd thought along the same lines, only she'd been the one followed in the hope that she'd lead him to other Resistance members. "So for now, we'll just keep an eye on him and try to discover what he's up to?"

"Yes. But I want that airman out of it as soon as possible. And I want you to keep your distance. By morning, headquarters will have a large pool of anonymous faces organized to keep track of him, but they can only send one man tonight, so I'll need your help till morning. I'll think of something to explain your absence at work tomorrow. Truth be told, Dr. Bolliger thinks very highly of you. I doubt one missed shift will change that."

A half hour later, an OSS man arrived in a jeep. Genevieve directed him to within a few blocks of Ercolani's apartment, but they walked the last bit, wanting to arrive silently. The man gave his name as Black and said he'd been a police officer in Los Angeles before the war. Genevieve guessed he was in his midforties, but he was sleepy and uninterested in conversation.

Rick was still there when they arrived.

"Did you see anything?" she asked.

Rick shook his head. "Nothing. I walked around a bit, and it looks like none of those apartments have more than one door, so I'll bet he's still in there."

"Thank you for your help, young man," Black said. "Someone will debrief you tomorrow. In the meantime, make sure you don't talk to anyone about any of this."

Rick nodded, then grinned. "If anyone in my tent is sober enough to notice how late I am, I'll say I walked a pretty brunette home and got distracted. They can draw their own conclusions from there. I guarantee they won't guess I was tracking down Fascist spies."

* * *

Genevieve had picked up a sweater at the hospital, but even with the extra layer, she spent most of the night shivering. Her dress had been made during the war, when scarcity of fabric dictated hemlines should be closer to the knees than the ankles. Nylon rationing meant she didn't have any stockings, so her bare legs were covered in goose bumps.

Morning came, but replacements from OSS headquarters didn't arise as early as Ercolani. He opened the door shortly after sunrise, leaving the apartment with a beautiful, fashionably dressed woman on his arm.

"I'll follow them," Black said. "Dr. Lombardelli says you pick locks?"

Genevieve nodded.

"See if you can find anything inside."

Black sneaked away behind them. Ercolani and the woman paused outside a bakery half a block away, and a third man joined them. After they turned a corner, Genevieve walked to the apartment, testing the knob before removing some of her hairpins. She wondered when she had crossed the line from a simple courier to a full-flung counterintelligence agent. She'd never wanted to be a spy, yet each time Lombardelli asked her to help, she found herself unable to refuse. Maybe someday she'd tell him no, but she did want to help end the war. She wanted it to be over so badly. *Not much longer now. We're winning. It's just a matter of time. And soon Ercolani will be under arrest, unable to harm anyone else.*

Genevieve bent her hairpins to the correct angles, smiling at the irony that the man who'd taught her to pick locks was also the man who'd introduced her to the gospel. She caught her breath, concentrating on the lock and hoping Peter was still alive somewhere.

The apartment's lock was a basic pin tumbler model, easy to pick. She entered and closed the door behind her. It was a cramped apartment: the front room merged into the dining room and kitchen, and the bedroom at the back of the apartment was small, as was the bathroom. She began her search in the bedroom. It contained two small closets. In Ercolani's closet, the clothes hung neatly, all the shirts and all the hangers facing the same direction. She found the boxes at the bottom of the closet more interesting than the civilian clothing hanging above. The first contained dynamite, detonators, and grenades. The second contained 9 mm ammunition—which would fit a Walther P38 pistol or the Beretta 1938 machine pistol leaning against the inside corner of the closet. *Who is he planning to assassinate now?*

The other closet was stuffed with clothes, half of them falling off the hangers. A multitude of hats cluttered the shelf above the hanger rod, and the floor was covered with shoes, stockings, and other items of clothing. Genevieve had expected as much. Several dresses were strewn across an armchair in the corner of the bedroom, and the small bathroom counter was covered with perfume bottles and hairpins.

Genevieve glanced at the clock in the hallway. She'd been in the apartment five minutes already and wanted to leave quickly in case the couple returned. Black wouldn't let Ercolani hurt her, but if she was discovered in the apartment, it would ruin the possibility of following Ercolani to his accomplices. She checked the remaining furniture in the bedroom and front room, hoping to find some hint of his plans, then searched the coat closet and the kitchen cabinets.

Were I in his position, where would I hide my plans? She spent another ten minutes searching for hiding spots behind picture frames, diaries hidden in the bookshelf, or compartments under floorboards. As she studied the floorboards under the table, she noticed the table's unconventional design. The tabletop was a single, flat piece of wood resting on an almost normal frame. But on the bottom of the frame was a second piece of wood, covering the frame like the bottom of a box, and she recognized two pins on one side that seemed to have no purpose. She removed the pins, lifted the top of the table, and gasped.

* * *

Basileo made sure Mario still guarded the far end of the hallway. He walked to Belina, put his arms around her waist from behind, and kissed her neck. "Did you disable the telephone?"

"Mm."

"That's a yes?"

She turned around in his arms. "You know I'm not very articulate when you're kissing me. But yes, I cut the lines."

"Then I'll go arm our little device." He kissed her again, letting his lips linger on hers before he left to complete the final part of his plan.

* * *

Genevieve knew Lombardelli would be off duty, so she rushed directly to his apartment. She sighed with relief when he opened the door for her.

"Did you find something?"

"Maps with OSS headquarters circled and diagrams of the building's interior," Genevieve said. "I think he's planning to destroy it."

Lombardelli looked surprised, then sickened. He glanced at his watch. "Just before you arrived, I received a phone call. Someone found Black's body midway between Ercolani's apartment and headquarters. There's a meeting scheduled to take place at HQ in fifteen minutes. All the top men will attend."

"He's going to destroy it today, during the meeting."

Lombardelli nodded. He reached for the phone and asked to be put through to the building. He hung up in frustration. "The operator can't put me through. Come on, we'll drive."

The next five minutes left Genevieve fearing for her life. She'd been in a high-speed chase before, but having Lombardelli behind the wheel of the ambulance he'd borrowed from the hospital bordered on suicide. She distracted herself by strapping on a shoulder harness with a pistol and hiding it under her sweater. Lombardelli slammed on the brakes near the building, and the vehicle skidded to a halt.

"I'll go find the MPs," he said.

Genevieve nodded. She already knew what she was going to do. On the diagram hidden under the tabletop in his apartment, Ercolani had marked exactly where he intended to plant his bomb. She jumped from the ambulance and ran.

The meeting had just begun. Were she in Ercolani's place, she'd have the bomb go off in ten minutes—allowing any stragglers to join the meeting before they were all killed. But she wasn't Ercolani. For all she knew, she might have only seconds.

The building itself was easy to enter. She remembered the layout from the diagrams and turned left down one long hallway, then right down another, nearly running into a military policeman patrolling the corridor. She apologized and was about to explain the situation when he spoke.

"What's your hurry, miss? This area is off-limits." His English was good, but he didn't sound American. There were recent immigrants serving in the US Army, but she suspected the man in front of her wasn't one of them. He looked a lot like the man who'd met Ercolani at the bakery that morning.

She hesitated for a moment, unsure of her next move. It would take several minutes to reach the bomb with an alternative route, and she guessed Ercolani or the woman would be guarding the other points of access.

Genevieve gazed beyond the guard to the empty hallway. "If it's off-limits, who's that?"

As the man turned to look behind him, she drew her pistol and slammed it into the back of his head, just below his helmet. He fell to the floor and didn't move as she ran past him.

The bomb was exactly where the plans had shown it would be, hidden in a dark storage room with a wall that bordered the meeting room. She knelt next to it and examined the simple, deadly device— she'd made similar ones for use against the Germans. After removing the detonator and disassembling the sticks of dynamite, Genevieve sat back on her heels and said a small prayer of gratitude. There would be no massacre at the OSS meeting that morning.

She heard one footstep directly behind her and felt a muscular arm wrap around her neck and yank her to her feet.

Her assailant released her for a second and slammed her into the wall. "Who are you?" Ercolani growled. He pinned her against the wall, his forearm pressed into her throat, then removed her pistol from its holster and tossed it across the room. His forearm constricted all airflow, and she couldn't breathe. She clawed at his hands, but he only pressed harder, lifting her so high her toes barely touched the floor and trapping both her wrists with his other hand. She tried to kick him, but he kicked her back, making the pressure on her neck even worse. Everything she tried failed—he was too strong, and he was going to strangle her.

"I suppose you're the link between Lombardelli and that traitor Giacomo. I'm going to kill you, and then I'm going to kill everyone in that meeting, and then I'm going to kill Lombardelli."

Genevieve's vision was fading when she heard a scream. At first she thought it was her imagination. She'd be screaming herself if she was capable of it, and the voice was feminine. Another cry followed and a gunshot.

Ercolani lost his focus, pulling a few inches away and looking the direction of the sound. "Belina?"

Genevieve gasped for air and slid to the floor. He reached after her, gripping her sweater, but she pulled away, losing a few buttons and scrambling across the floor to her handgun. She pointed it at him, holding it with both hands, praying he wouldn't recognize what a bad state she was in. She was as likely to faint as to pull the trigger.

He glared at her, his hand inches from his P38 pistol. Another gunshot sounded. He glanced in the direction of the sound, then back at Genevieve before barreling past her. She kept her weapon aimed in his direction as he bolted down the hallway, but her vision was so blurry she saw two of him, so she didn't pull the trigger.

When he was out of sight, she relaxed her arms, still gasping for breath. Her neck ached, and her hands shook. She was on the floor, fighting to stay conscious when a few MPs—real ones—found her a few minutes later. They helped her through several corridors, past the lifeless body of Ercolani's beautiful associate, and through a scorched hallway. Dr. Lombardelli was speaking with several high-ranking officers, but he halted his conversation when he saw her.

He swore in Italian and examined her neck. She winced under his touch. "I thought you were going to wait in the ambulance."

"Did you get him?" Genevieve asked. "He ran this direction."

Lombardelli looked at one of the officers for an answer.

"We captured one man and killed the female accomplice."

"Did you find the man I knocked unconscious? The one dressed as an MP?" Genevieve asked.

The muscles around the officer's eyes scrunched together. "The man we captured was dressed as an MP. He was shooting at us, so my men shot back. He's wounded, under arrest."

"But what about Ercolani? The tall man with dark hair and a P38?"

The officer looked past her to a broken window. "I guess he got away."

Chapter Twenty-Two
BY THE SEA

Saturday, February 24

Genevieve's neck was so sore the next morning that she wasn't sure she could manage a full shift. When she arrived at the hospital, Dr. Lombardelli met her at the door and motioned her back outside. "I need you to skip work today."

"Why?"

"You remember the man you knocked unconscious yesterday?"

Genevieve nodded.

"He's a patient here. Under guard, but I suspect he'd recognize you. I'll make sure he's gone by tomorrow, but for today, you need to disappear. I know you wanted Sunday off, but I'm switching your shifts. You'll have to work tomorrow instead."

"Sounds like you have reason."

Lombardelli glanced at her neck. "Nice scarf. Trying to hide a few bruises?"

Genevieve nodded, tugging at the flimsy fabric so it would cover more of her throat.

Lombardelli removed the scarf, studied her bruises, and retied the fabric. Genevieve checked her reflection in a window. Lombardelli had a better sense of fashion than she did, and he'd managed to hide all the discoloration.

"I think it's wise for you to get out of Bari for the day. With any luck, they'll have Ercolani rounded up by the time you get back."

"I don't have a car. If you'd like, I can stay in my tent or play the piano all day." There was a piano in the patient's lounge, and she'd played it a few times.

His smiled broadened. "Actually, I've got your ride arranged too. Dr. Bolliger is taking you to lunch at a little restaurant up north, along the coast."

"But I don't think he's had a day off all month. Why would he spend his holiday keeping me away from Bari?"

"He thinks I'm trying to be a matchmaker."

"Matchmaking? I'm still planning to marry Peter. And what if Ercolani comes after us? Don't you think you should warn Nathan that this isn't an innocent day at the beach?"

Lombardelli shook his head and hushed her protests.

Seconds later, Nathan was at her side, the tall, handsome man who was taking her on a date so no Fascist saboteurs would target her. "Good morning, Genevieve. Are you ready?"

Genevieve was too stunned to think for a few moments, then looked down at her uniform. "I guess so, as soon as I change."

"Oh, uh, happy birthday, Genevieve," Lombardelli said as he turned to go back into the hospital.

"But—"

Lombardelli gave her a look that silenced the rest of her reply.

* * *

Genevieve spent the morning pretending to enjoy the scenery. In reality, she was afraid every shadow hid an assassin, and it was a struggle not to obsessively look over her shoulder. Ercolani hadn't returned to his apartment the day before. He'd disappeared. She didn't know where he'd gone, but she suspected he still wanted to kill her. Yet by lunchtime, she was enjoying the day anyway. The weather was sunny and windy, but it was pleasant, and so was the company.

"Would you like to walk along the beach?" Nathan asked as they finished their meal.

She nodded, noticing a sparkle in his eyes as they left the restaurant. "Thank you for lunch. And for bringing me here. It's nice to get away."

He nodded and helped her down the slope to the beach. "You need a break. You're always working. You don't even take smoke breaks."

"I don't smoke. Why would I need a smoke break?"

"It's the break part that's important. Anyway, I'm glad Dr. Lombardelli came up with this plan for me to whisk you away on your birthday."

She broke eye contact. Her birthday was in November, and it didn't feel right to lie to Nathan.

"Is something wrong?"

"It's not really my birthday."

To her relief, Nathan laughed. "Dr. Lombardelli—that scoundrel. But no matter, I've been looking for an excuse to spend time with you outside the hospital for a while now."

"You have?"

Nathan smiled. "I've been altering the shifts for months so we could work together. On the surface, it makes sense. Dr. Lombardelli wants the night shift because he doesn't like surgeries, and there are more of those during the day. And you have a good bedside manner, so it's natural for you to work while the patients are awake. If that happens to be the same shifts I'm working, well, I suppose that's my good fortune."

Genevieve was taken aback. Lombardelli wanted her to work the opposite shift from him so one of them was always available for OSS work. That he'd managed to control the schedule and make Nathan think it was *his* idea was one more sign of Lombardelli's skill. But she was also concerned. She and Nathan spoke with each other often at work, but she hadn't known he was so fond of her.

They walked along the beach for an hour, Nathan with his hands in his pockets and Genevieve with one hand holding her sweater together so it wouldn't blow open. She needed to replace the missing buttons but hadn't found thread or a needle yet. Nathan told her about medical school, and she told him about the hospital in London where she'd briefly worked. When they returned to the beach below the restaurant, where Nathan's car was parked, he offered a hand to help her up the sandy slope. When they reached the top, he didn't let go.

She looked at his hand holding hers. She admired Nathan and all he'd accomplished with his hands. How many lives had those hands saved? But she didn't have any romantic feelings for him. Those were all reserved for Peter.

He noticed her gaze and dropped her hand. "I'm sorry. I forgot you were forced into this outing."

"No, I'm sorry, Nathan. I shouldn't have let Dr. Lombardelli play his games, not when you're involved." She'd been worried about Nathan being caught in an assassin's crossfire. She should have been less concerned with his physical safety and more concerned with his feelings.

"It's someone else, isn't it?"

She dared a glance at him. The smile that had been a permanent feature on his face all day was gone. She felt horrible but thought telling the truth now, even it if was painful, was better than lying. "Yes, there's someone else."

"One of the airmen you see every Sunday? Is that why you always want Sunday off?"

Genevieve was surprised he knew how she spent her Sundays. "No, I go to the base for worship. Some of the aircrews share my religion."

"That British major . . . Dr. Lombardelli's friend? Baker?"

"Not Major Baker. One of his men."

Nathan stared past her to the ocean. "And where is this man now?"

"I'm not sure."

"Is he alive?"

Genevieve closed her eyes. She wanted Peter to be alive so badly, but with each passing day, that possibility seemed more and more remote. "I hope so."

"Will you tell me about him?"

She studied Nathan's face, wondering if he really wanted to hear about Peter.

"Please?"

Genevieve nodded. "I met him last spring." She closed her eyes and pictured Peter with the mischievous grin that had first caught her eye and her heart. "He had to go on assignment at the end of the summer. He wrote me a letter before he left, telling me he wanted to marry me. Then he came back, but he had to go away again, and his unit disappeared."

"Is he French like you? Or British like Major Baker?"

"He's American, a lieutenant in the army."

"And what did you do together?"

Genevieve smiled, remembering Peter's kisses and his lock-picking tutorials. "We walked a lot. And he saved my life a few times."

Nathan was quiet, and the sounds of waves and gulls suddenly seemed loud and solemn. "And when was the last time anyone saw him alive?"

Genevieve didn't answer immediately, afraid her voice would catch. "September 3." Peter had been missing for almost six months.

They reached Nathan's car. He'd been so happy earlier, but now he looked depressed.

"I'm sorry, Nathan. I didn't mean to ruin your day."

He smiled, but it seemed forced. "Maybe I just need to be patient. Thank you for letting me take you away for a bit."

He was about to open the car door for her when she noticed the back tire was flat. She looked more closely and saw a nail embedded in the rubber. It really wasn't Nathan's day. "There's a nail in your tire."

Nathan studied it and exhaled deeply, shaking his head. He loosened his tie, took off his jacket, and opened the front passenger side door to lay his jacket on the seat so it wouldn't get dirty while he replaced the tire. Then he shut the door, and the car exploded.

The blast shattered the glass in all the windows and forced Nathan and Genevieve to the ground. A wave of heat enveloped them, making Genevieve's eyes sting and her throat burn. After the explosion, everything was strangely silent. Genevieve couldn't even hear the ocean, but she could feel slivers of glass sticking into her skin. Nathan's eyebrows were singed, and he had a bloody gash on his forehead. She looked more closely, and although Nathan's cut was long, the blood flowing from it was a trickle rather than a gush.

Nathan stared at the car, then at her, his mouth open in shock. Eventually, he pushed himself to his feet and brushed himself off with shaking hands. He reached down to help her to her feet, and as she reached up to take his hand, she realized her arm was trembling just as much as his was.

His lips moved, but she couldn't hear what he said until he brought his mouth to her ear. "Are you all right?"

She nodded despite an overwhelming feeling of nausea. "Yes, and you?"

Nathan nodded, but his face showed haggard worry. He was used to dealing with crisis, but this wasn't his usual emergency. Genevieve stared at the car. As car bombs went, it had been a relatively small one. The windows were blown out, and smoke billowed from the interior. A small fire still burned on what had been the passenger's seat.

It was then that it hit Genevieve. Nathan was supposed to have opened the car door for her. She would have sat down, and he would have shut the door and triggered the bomb. That nail had saved her life.

* * *

Basileo watched the Italian countryside blur past him from the window of a northbound train. *Recalled and widowed in the same day.* He fought to keep his emotions in check, remembering the last time he kissed Belina, almost feeling her lips again. She'd been mortally wounded when he found her the day before. She'd known it, and he'd known it, but he still hadn't wanted to leave. They'd held off the OSS men for a while, but when he ran out of bullets, she'd told him to escape and continue his work. Knowing she would die within minutes, he'd kissed her softly, distracted his pursuers with a grenade, and followed Belina's final wish.

He found a phone during one of the train's stops and put a call through to the restaurant. He'd followed Lombardelli's courier there that morning but hadn't been able to stay. He had an appointment with his superior at OVRA, and he had to follow his orders. The man who answered told him all about the car bomb and that there were no fatalities. Basileo hung up the phone and returned to the train. Disappointment and grief overwhelmed him as the train resumed its journey.

He had failed to destroy the OSS group, he'd failed to protect Belina, and he'd failed to kill the woman. He would be given a new assignment, a new chance to serve Il Duce, and he wouldn't fail again. *I will serve Mussolini to my last breath, and I will have my vengeance on Lombardelli and the little brunette.* He was going north for a while, but he would return, and then he would kill them both.

Chapter Twenty-Three
AN OLD CLASSMATE

Thursday, March 1
German-occupied Serbia

DEAREST GENEVIEVE,

I love you. Spring is finally here, and we've made our plans to leave Yugoslavia. I hope I'll be able to see you again soon so I can tell you I love you instead of writing it. Dreaming about you is a poor substitute for holding you. And I want to kiss you again. More than I miss square meals and hot showers and clean sheets, I miss your kisses. Sometimes I worry about what you'll say when I see you again. Will you be angry that I left? I hope you'll forgive me, but sometimes I wonder how many times you can overlook the problems I keep bringing into your life. I've long known you're more than I deserve, but I also know being near you makes me want to be better, so I have faith that someday I'll be what you need me to be. In the meantime, please don't give up on me. Every step I take will be one step closer to you, and when I see you again, I will do everything I can to make you happy.
    Love,
    Peter

* * *

Snow still covered the ground, but the days were growing longer, and the first hints of spring were beginning to show. Brajović and his men had long ago left the village, on their way to join other Chetnik survivors. Peter and his team planned to leave that night for the Adriatic Sea. He leaned on the cottage's stone wall and looked west through the trees. There were formidable geographic hurdles to cross and multiple enemies to avoid, but he was eager to leave.

The team had little to pack. Chesterfield's grenade blast had destroyed or damaged most of their gear. The food was long since consumed, and they didn't have anything to replace it with. The villagers had been generous all winter—sharing their goat cheese, turnips, and bread baked with hay to make it more filling—but the village was poor, so the team would have to live off the land or the kindness of other villages as they headed west.

Krzysztof insisted on bringing the wrecked radio along, and he would carry it. They wouldn't make Jamie carry anything but his pistol and his cane. Moretti and Peter would divide the remaining gear between them—rifles, ammunition, bedding. They'd parachuted in with enough explosives to destroy a bridge, but they'd given those to Brajović, along with the Bren gun and its ammunition.

The village had seemed like a prison over the past six months. *A prison, a sanctuary, and a gracious host.* Peter watched the women working and the children playing. Any one of them could have mentioned Peter's presence to the nearest German garrison and collected a reward. Then the whole village would have paid for their hospitality with their lives. Peter inhaled deeply. The village always smelled of fireplaces and wet hay. He wasn't going to miss the village, but he was grateful for it.

"Good morning, Peter."

He turned his head toward Marija. "Good morning."

She was like a different person now. She smiled, she laughed—sometimes she seemed to glow. Marija held out a loaf of bread. "Something for tomorrow."

Peter hesitated to take it but not because they wouldn't need food. "Don't you and Miloš need this?"

"We'll manage." She pressed the bread into his hands. "Thank you for your friendship."

Peter often felt guilty that he and his men had taken so much from the village and given so little in return. They'd chopped firewood and hunted when they were healthy, but the village had provided safety, shelter, and sustenance. Marija had told Peter he'd helped her decide to marry Miloš, so he'd take her bread because he knew it was a symbol of her gratitude. "Thank you."

Marija nodded, then looked past Peter, toward the edge of the village, and her face drained of color. Peter spun around to see what was wrong. Emerging silently from the woods were eight men in uniform, rifles slung across their shoulders, caps with red stars on their heads.

"Get inside." Peter dropped the bread and took Marija's arm to propel her toward the door, but she broke away.

"I've got to warn Miloš." She ran across the street to the cottage she shared with her husband.

Peter almost ran after her, worried one of the soldiers would shoot her, but they let her go. He noticed another group of soldiers approaching town from the other direction. He backed into the cottage as more appeared in the woods. "The Partisans are here."

Krzysztof, Jamie, and Moretti joined Peter outside as the Partisans began a house-by-house search, commandeering food and forcing the villagers onto the main road. Some of the soldiers were female, and none of them looked much older than twenty.

Miloš and Marija emerged from their home, and Marija slowly crossed the street to stand between Peter and Jamie. Her shoulder was next to Peter's, and he could feel her shaking. "Miloš said if you tell them you're British and American, you should be all right," she whispered.

The soldiers made everyone gather in the village square in front of the church. Peter didn't see a machine gun, but he remembered the destroyed village he'd seen in September, and he remembered what had happened to Marija's hometown. Her eyes were wide with fear, her face pale, and she was still trembling. Peter supposed she was thinking of her village too.

A pair of soldiers demanded Peter's pistol, but Jamie spoke up in Serbo-Croat, and one of the men called their kapetan over. He was a tall, thin man with brown hair and glasses.

"You are British?" the Partisan officer asked.

"I am," Jamie said. "My friends are American and Polish. This village sheltered us while we were recovering from injuries. I hope you will take their hospitality into consideration and leave them in peace."

The man seemed to consider it, looking at the assembled villagers—all of them other than Peter and his men very old, very young, or female. His eyes stopped on the other exception. "Miloš Colić."

"Hello, Tomislav." Miloš smiled but seemed more wary than pleased to be recognized.

"It's been awhile."

"Since the bombing of Belgrade. Almost four years."

Tomislav shook his head. "You and your stupid Serbian nationalism provoked that disaster and the hell that's followed. Anyone with half a brain would have known Hitler could crush us."

"'Rather war than the pact. Rather a grave than a slave,'" Miloš whispered.

"Still spouting off that same propaganda? Well, we've had war and slavery and plenty of graves. Are you still happy with your little coup? Your chance to spit in Hitler's eye?"

"No, Tomislav, I'm not happy about the war."

The Partisan leader frowned. "What are you doing here, Miloš?"

"Phst, practicing medicine."

Tomislav took out a cigarette and studied Miloš, then turned his glance to the other men. "And these men? How long have they been here?"

Jamie cleared his throat. "We have been here all winter, but we planned to leave today."

"Where are you going?" Tomislav asked.

"West. To the sea. From there, to our base in Italy."

Tomislav inhaled through his cigarette and thought for a few moments before exhaling smoke. "We can assist you. We are, after all, your allies."

Jamie glanced at Peter, neither of them sure they wanted Tomislav's help. "What will you do with the villagers?" Peter asked, stalling his decision.

Tomislav's soldiers had already removed all the food from the village. He issued a few orders in Serbo-Croat, and the soldiers dismissed most of the villagers—all the elderly couples and all the children. A few young mothers, Peter's team, Miloš, and Marija remained.

Tomislav finished his cigarette and dropped it to the ground. "We're searching for someone, Miloš. Perhaps if you help us, it will prove to me that you are no longer the dangerous Serbian nationalist you were in medical school."

"I've been nothing but a doctor since King Peter's speech," Miloš said.

Tomislav smiled. "The king? We don't need a king—especially not a Serbian one. He won't be invited back. I am interested not in former royalty but in former collaborators and Serbian nationalists. Do you know Stoyan Brajović?"

"Phst, yes. That's his cottage over there." Miloš pointed. "But he doesn't live there anymore."

"And what of his family?"

"They left with him."

"That's not what I heard. Brajović, his son, his wife, and his men were killed a few weeks ago." Marija inhaled sharply as Tomislav spoke. "But we were told his niece is still in the village." Tomislav examined the women in the group. "Which one is she?"

Miloš kept his eyes fixed on Tomislav. "Brajović's niece left two weeks ago to find her uncle."

"We were told you and the woman in question are close friends. If she left, why didn't you leave with her?"

"My first duty is to protect our allies," Miloš said.

"Then identify each of these women." Tomislav pointed to the women one by one, and Miloš gave Tomislav their names and verified where they lived. But when Tomislav pointed to Marija, Miloš said her name was Marija Molovich, and the house he pointed to was the one where Peter and his men slept.

Tomislav studied Marija and studied the men. Jamie figured it out before Peter and put his arm around Marija, pulling her toward him possessively. Jamie was, after all, the group's best actor. Tomislav didn't approve, but he didn't seem to suspect the lie.

"If this woman is providing companionship for our allies, why did she run to your cottage when we arrived?" Tomislav asked.

"I asked her to tell Miloš," Peter said. "The village has been quiet all winter. I'm sure you can understand our surprise when we saw your men."

Tomislav weighed Peter's fib before nodding. "How many of these women have children?" All of the village women did, except Marija. Their children stood on the edge of the village square, waiting for their mothers, who were dismissed as Miloš pointed out their children. Soon the village square was occupied solely by the Partisans, Peter's team, and the Colićs.

Tomislav turned to Peter. "Please come with us. We travel west, as do you. Miloš Colić, Marija Molovich, you are hereby conscripted into the People's Liberation Army of Yugoslavia."

Marija looked shocked but didn't say anything. Miloš glanced at her, then glanced at the two dozen men and women in caps with red stars. "I will shoot the Germans, I will shoot the Ustaše, and I will bandage anyone you bring to me. But I will not fight my brother Serbs."

Tomislav took out another cigarette and lit it. "You will follow your orders, or you will be shot."

CHAPTER TWENTY-FOUR
PROMISES

THE SENSE OF FOREBODING THAT began when Peter first spotted the Partisans hadn't left by evening.

"How long will we stay with them?" Krzysztof whispered as he marched next to Peter. Kapetan Tomislav had been polite to Peter and his team, but he'd made Krzysztof furious when he confiscated the team's broken radio.

"I don't know. If we run into the Nazis, it'll be nice to have the extra men. And the women too, I suppose."

Marija marched a few rows ahead of them, flanked by soldiers. The Partisans had given her a cap and rifle, and she looked like she was about to collapse.

Peter turned back to Krzysztof. "I'm going to talk to Miloš before I decide."

Tomislav hadn't trusted Miloš with a rifle and had assigned him a position near two of the largest Partisan troops. Peter pretended to adjust his boot and let a few lines of troops go by before he slipped in next to Miloš.

"Could you see her from where you were?" Miloš whispered.

Peter nodded.

"How is she?"

"She looks exhausted."

Miloš glanced at the men around them, keeping his voice down. "She can't stay in the army. They'll kill her. Take her with you, please. I don't care what you say to Tomislav—claim Jamie can't live without her if you need to. But do it soon."

"Will someone recognize her?"

Miloš seemed confused for a few seconds, then shook his head. "She can keep her identity secret. That's not the problem. But pregnancy comes with a death sentence in Tito's army."

Peter looked around to make sure no one was listening to their conversation. If Marija was expecting a baby, that explained why she'd seemed to glow the last few weeks and why the march was taking such a heavy toll on her. And it explained the urgency of Miloš's plea. It wouldn't take long for someone to suspect Marija's condition.

* * *

When they made camp and the Partisans lit their cooking fires, Tomislav assigned Marija the first shift of guard duty. She nodded her submission and went to her assigned post a quarter mile south of camp. She sat on the ground next to a tree and leaned against its trunk. She laid her rifle next to her and took off the horrible Communist cap. Her fingers found their way to her abdomen, something that had become a habit over the last two weeks. She'd have to watch herself. If one of the Partisans saw her doing that, they might suspect the truth. "Baby Colić, I hope you are growing well today because you are making your mother very tired," she whispered.

She didn't know how she was going to do it—keep up with the marches day after day. What would happen tomorrow morning when she couldn't keep her breakfast down? *Please help my little family*, she prayed. *We need a miracle.*

Marija hadn't meant to fall asleep, but some time later, she jerked awake. It had been twilight when she'd said her prayer; now it was completely black. She heard a noise behind her and reached for her rifle in case it was a Nazi. She also pushed herself to her feet in case it was her relief. She hated to think what the punishment would be if she was caught sleeping while on guard duty.

"Hello, Marija." She recognized her husband's voice before she saw him. In an instant, he had his arms around her, and for the first time since that morning, she felt safe. "I was thinking, Marija, that we should get out of here."

"I couldn't agree more, Miloš, but how?"

"Supper first." He helped her back to the ground and pulled some pancakes wrapped in a handkerchief from his pocket. "Eat what you can, then eat more in another hour. They're supposed to save you some back at camp too, and I want you to pretend you haven't eaten."

"Then whose is this?"

"The foreigners and I weren't very hungry tonight."

"I don't want to eat everyone else's food, Miloš."

Miloš found the sore spot on her back and rubbed it with his fingers. "This is where it hurts, isn't it?"

"Yes." Her lower back had started aching about the time she'd first suspected she was pregnant. Miloš had given her a back rub before bed every night since.

"Don't worry about the food. You're eating for two. And since half the time you don't feel like eating, you need to eat extra when you can. I don't want you to worry about me or the foreigners anymore. I just want you to worry about you and our baby."

"But Miloš—"

"Just worry about you and our baby."

She nodded and ate some of the food.

"Can you make it another day?" Miloš moved from her back to her feet. Her feet had never been so tired or so dirty, but Miloš didn't seem to care how filthy they were. His fingers were magic, working their way along the soles of her feet and up to her calves, massaging out the fatigue and the cold.

"I don't know. I'm worried about tomorrow. What will the soldiers think when I vomit up my breakfast? And the marching—I was afraid my feet wouldn't even carry me to my post. And I accidentally fell asleep."

Miloš smiled. "I know. I heard you snoring."

"I snore?"

"Only when you're really exhausted. Peter and the others thought Tomislav might be more at ease if we wait another day or two, but if you don't think you can make it, we'll leave tonight."

Marija forced herself to eat and weighed the risk of early escape against the risk of not making it through the next day's march. "I think it will have to be tonight."

"Then we'll go tonight. When your relief comes, walk back to camp with Jamie."

Marija glanced around. "Is Jamie here?"

"Nearby, keeping lookout. You're going to have to pretend you're in love with him because if Tomislav realizes we're married, he'll know your uncle was Pukovnik Brajović."

Marija nodded, still shocked that her aunt, uncle, and cousin were dead. She didn't want to be in the army, and she didn't want to pretend to be Jamie's consort, but she could do it for a few more hours.

"Someone will come for you when most of the camp is asleep. We'll march hard until we find somewhere to hide. After that, we'll take it easy again."

"Where will we go?" she asked.

"The coast. After that, we'll see. You always wanted to live in America, didn't you? Maybe that's where you'll end up."

"Me? What about *us*?"

"Phst, that's what I meant, that *we* might end up in America." Miloš finished rubbing her feet and replaced her flimsy canvas shoes. "Now, I want you to close your eyes and repeat what I say."

"But, Miloš—"

"Please, Marija?"

She nodded and closed her eyes.

"I, Marija Colić," Miloš began.

"I, Marija Colić."

"Will do everything in my power to survive this war."

"Will do everything in my power to survive this war."

"And I will be happy again for my husband and for my baby, no matter what happens."

"And I'll be happy again—" She heard her voice crack. "For my husband and for my baby, no matter what happens."

She knew he was going to kiss her before his lips touched hers. She could feel his warmth and smell his scent. The kiss was long and tender, and as it ended, she wondered how a kiss could be so sweet and so melancholy at the same time. She had to blink away tears at the bittersweet beauty of that moment. Miloš held her in his arms until Jamie came to warn them that her replacement was coming.

* * *

Peter ignored the hunger pains in his stomach, wondering why he wasn't used to them by now. When Jamie returned with Miloš and Marija, the camp had quieted. Marija looked numb, like she had the first few months he'd known her. She nodded a greeting, then went to lie down near the other female soldiers.

The situation wasn't that different from what they'd planned. Peter and his men would have the same supplies—minus the broken radio—and they'd still have to find food along the way and avoid the Nazis. But they'd also have to avoid the Partisans now, and the group would be six instead of four.

Moretti volunteered to stay awake and alert them when it was time to leave.

"'Where we are there's daggers in men's smiles,'" Jamie mumbled as the rest of them settled down for a few hours' sleep.

Peter had just gotten comfortable when Tomislav approached their fire.

"Please, my allies, come join me in my tent." Tomislav was the only one in camp with a tent. "We need to plan your trip."

Peter nudged Krzysztof awake, and the four of them followed Tomislav. Inside, a lantern lit a map and two radios—Krzysztof's and a second set that looked to be in perfect condition. Another Partisan soldier poured plum brandy for each of them. Peter politely declined.

"You are the leader?" Tomislav asked.

Peter shrugged. He outranked Krzysztof and Moretti, and Jamie was a civilian, but he couldn't remember the last time he'd given any of them an order.

Tomislav motioned Peter outside. "Come, please. I have a question for you while your men study the map." He turned to his aide. "Find something without alcohol for this man to drink."

Peter was sure any question Tomislav had could be asked in front of his teammates, but he didn't want Tomislav to suspect that Peter and his men didn't trust him and would, in fact, soon be leaving, so he cooperated. Tomislav began telling Peter the history of Tito's resistance to the Nazis. Peter didn't interrupt, hoping his patience would ease away any suspicion.

The aide returned with a tin of goat's milk. "From the village."

Peter was hungry, so he took a large swallow as he listened to Tomislav's rant, but he suddenly felt incredibly sleepy. His eyelids seemed heavy, and after every blink, it was an effort to open them again. He dropped the tin and mumbled an apology, but his vocal chords didn't seem to be working properly. Peter reached out to use a nearby tree for support, but he misjudged the distance and fell to the dirt. Getting back to his feet seemed like an impossible task, so he stopped fighting it and slipped into sleep.

* * *

Something near Peter's head pounded loudly. He opened his eyes and squinted in the dim light of Tomislav's tent. Jamie was next to him, asleep or unconscious. It took some effort, but Peter managed to lift his head to see Krzysztof and Moretti lying beyond Jamie, their eyes closed and their breathing slow. The four of them were bound with ropes, their wrists pulled over their heads and attached to tent stakes.

Peter turned the other direction and found Kapetan Tomislav watching him, a hammer in his hand. Peter assumed it had been Tomislav's hammer that had awakened him.

"I guess we didn't add enough sleeping potion to your milk. Pity you don't drink plum brandy. If you had, you wouldn't have to see this."

Tomislav's aide came into the tent dragging Miloš with him. Miloš was unconscious, his face swollen and trails of blood streaming from his ears, nose, and mouth.

"What's going on?" Peter asked, his voice barely cooperating.

"Miloš has proven himself a disobedient soldier."

"How?"

"He threatened me with a rifle while I was dragging you into the tent."

Peter swallowed. His throat was so dry he could barely speak. "Miloš has seen me through broken ribs and pneumonia, so he's a little protective. I'll talk to him. He won't disobey again. Surely you can forgive him?"

"Forgiveness doesn't come easily in the Balkans."

"What are you doing with us?"

Tomislav picked up his map and folded it. "A prisoner exchange. We're short on German prisoners, but for two British and two American commandos, seven Partisans will be released." Tomislav pointed to Krzysztof. "I know he's not really British, but I don't anticipate the Germans finding that out until after we've gotten our men back and have been given safe passage through the valley."

Peter didn't bother to express his disgust, trying instead to untie the knot in his ropes.

"That won't do you any good." Tomislav turned to his aide and said something in Serbo-Croat. The aide brought Miloš closer to Tomislav, who took out a knife.

"What are you doing?" Peter shouted. He kicked Jamie in his bad leg, hoping it would wake him, but Jamie didn't stir.

"I am executing a disobedient soldier and a dangerous Serbian nationalist."

"No—he's not a radical nationalist. He wants what's best for Yugoslavia— for the Croats and for the Serbs."

Tomislav looked at Miloš, then at his knife. "Tito is what's best for Yugoslavia. And that's not what Miloš wants, is it?"

"He's a doctor. You'll need men like him when the war is over." Peter strained against the ropes binding his hands and kicked Jamie again.

"No, an educated enemy is more difficult to control. Ignorant peasants are docile. It's the former university students you have to watch out for."

"Please let him live," Peter begged.

"That would ruin our army's discipline."

Peter looked at Jamie, who was still unconscious. Despite the shouting, the same was true for Krzysztof and Moretti. "Then exchange him with us. Let him pretend to be our medic."

Tomislav shook his head. "I have already contacted the German garrison. They expect four men. And they only have seven of my men still alive, so why would I give them anything more than what I have to?"

Peter hesitated but only for a second. "Then kill me instead and spare him."

Tomislav seemed surprised. "Kill you instead? We don't kill Americans. That would be biting the hand that feeds us, or at least the hand that supplies us with weapons."

"You're turning us over to the Nazis, and they'll kill us, so how is that any different?"

Tomislav ignored him. Peter tried to kick him, but Tomislav was too far away. He glanced from Peter to the knife to Miloš.

"Please!" Peter pleaded. But it did no good. Tomislav slid his knife across Miloš's throat. "No!" Peter shouted, but he knew it was too late. Miloš was dead. The Partisan commander walked over to Peter, grabbed his hair, pulled his head up, and knocked the hammer into the back of Peter's head hard enough to make him lose consciousness again.

CHAPTER TWENTY-FIVE
WHISPERED GOOD-BYES

MARIJA COULDN'T SLEEP. SHE WAS worried about the escape and expected someone to come for her any moment. She finally gave up, left her cap behind, and crept toward the spot where Miloš and the other men had camped. Their weapons were there, but the men were gone. She began to doubt herself, thinking she'd found the wrong dead campfire, but she recognized the rifles. The men wouldn't leave camp without them, and Miloš wouldn't leave without her. She wondered if she'd missed them somehow.

She went back to where she'd lain. Everything was still quiet, but she felt she should leave camp. She argued with herself until she saw Tomislav's aide coming toward her cold campfire. It wasn't time for her to have another shift as lookout, so any extra attention would be of the negative variety. As quietly as she could, she took her rifle and slipped away from camp to wait out the night.

The eastern sky grew light, and still, she waited. When the sun peeked over the nearby mountain ridge, she crept back to camp, finding it deserted. The Partisans had spent the night in a clearing, and she walked around its perimeter, making sure no one was hiding in the thicker trees. Everything seemed empty, except Tomislav's tent.

She paused beside it, listening through the canvas.

"Is he awake yet?"

It wasn't until she recognized Moretti's voice that she dared enter the tent. Moretti, Krzysztof, and Jamie looked up at her. Their hands were wrapped in ropes, lifted over their heads, then staked to the ground. Their legs were also bound. Peter was similarly tied, but he seemed to be sleeping.

"I'm so sorry, Marija," Krzysztof said.

She wasn't sure what he meant until she followed his gaze to the corner of the tent, where Miloš was crumpled in a heap. She'd felt weak all morning, but now she felt dizzy too. She dropped on the ground next to Miloš, knowing what she'd see. The front of his clothes and the ground underneath him were covered in blood. One eye was swollen shut, and the other stared lifelessly at the top of the tent. She reached out hesitantly and closed the open eyelid.

In life, Miloš had always been warm, but his skin no longer held heat. Her fingers lingered on his face, and as she looked down, she realized her hand was shaking and so was her arm. She didn't want to believe he was dead, but he'd somehow known what would happen. The promise he'd made her give, his kiss—both had told her good-bye the night before. Tears blurred her vision, and her breathing became erratic. Her Miloš was dead.

She hadn't sobbed since she was nineteen and her village had been destroyed, but she sobbed now. Of everyone she'd ever met, Miloš was the one with the most hope, the most life inside him. If someone like her husband could be slaughtered, then what would be left? Certainly nothing worthwhile—just misery and evil and pain.

She wept for a long time before remembering her promise to Miloš, that she would do her best to survive, no matter what. She didn't bother to dry her tears—they hadn't stopped—but she did her best to catch her breath and started untying the foreigners. But the knots were tight, and her fingers were still shaking.

"I keep a knife in my boot," Moretti said.

It wasn't there.

"Try my cane," Jamie said. None of the men had their weapons anymore, but the Partisans hadn't stolen the cane. "Take the handle off."

Marija struggled as she tried to remove the top of the cane. Her shoulders strained, and she finally succeeded in unsheathing the blade hidden inside. She sawed the ropes away from Jamie's hands, then let him undo the bindings on his legs and on his teammates.

"Have the Partisans left?" Krzysztof asked.

Marija nodded.

"And took all our equipment with them," Jamie said. He'd untied Krzysztof and Moretti and was working on Peter's legs.

Moretti patted his pocket. "Took my cigarettes too."

Krzysztof reached into the front pocket of his shirt. Marija could see his fingers handle the end of an unlit cigarette.

"Still there?" Jamie asked.

Krzysztof nodded.

She'd never seen Krzysztof smoke, so she wasn't sure why he and Jamie seemed so relieved that the single cigarette was still in Krzysztof's pocket.

Moretti picked up Marija's rifle and ejected the clip, checked it, and put the gun back together. "Down to one rifle," he said.

"What happened?" Marija asked.

Jamie looked up from untying Peter's wrists. "Tomislav drugged us. When we came to, Miloš was dead." Jamie turned Peter's head slightly. "I am not sure what happened to Peter because I doubt he had any plum brandy, but he does have a knot on the back of his head."

Jamie fingered the raised area on Peter's skull, eliciting a violent twitch and a groan of pain. Peter's eyelids squeezed together, and he groaned again before suddenly opening his eyes and jerking himself to a sitting position. He glanced around the tent before his eyes stopped on Marija.

"Marija . . . I'm sorry . . . I'm so sorry . . . It was Tomislav. I tried to stop him, Marija . . . but I couldn't." Peter's eyes looked haunted. He put his hand to his head and winced again. "We've got to leave."

"Can you travel?" Jamie asked.

"Doesn't matter." Peter pushed himself to his feet and swayed before righting himself on one of the tent's poles. "Tomislav left us as part of a prisoner exchange. The Nazis will be here to collect us before long."

"What time was this exchange to take place?" Jamie asked.

"I don't know," Peter said. "Jamie, make sure we're clear outside. Marija, come with me. Moretti, Krzysztof, grab Miloš."

Marija was dizzy and still overcome with grief as Peter helped her to her feet. She followed him out of the tent and made it two meters before a wave of nausea enveloped her. She hunched over and vomited and probably would have collapsed, but Peter held her, one hand around each of her arms. He let her catch her breath before encouraging her forward again.

She wasn't sure how long they walked before they stopped and the men prepared a grave. They didn't have shovels, only sticks and their bare hands, so it took some time. She walked to a stream not far from the grave and rinsed her mouth. The Partisans hadn't issued her a canteen, but the men had theirs still, so she filled them. When she came back, they'd stopped digging.

"Still got your book, sir?" Moretti asked Peter.

Peter checked his pocket and took out his little Book of Mormon. Marija had seen him read it before, up in the village. "Marija, would you like me to read a scripture?"

She nodded, knowing Miloš would have liked a scripture, and then she asked Peter to pray. He took a few moments to gather his thoughts, and when he prayed, his words made her cry again. He prayed for everyone on the team individually, mentioned a few names she didn't recognize, and then prayed for her and her baby. The words were poignant, fitting, and comforting.

When Peter finished, Marija knelt next to her dead husband's body, running her fingers through his hair and whispering her farewell. "I was thinking, Miloš, that I'm glad we got married. I'm sorry I made you wait so long and that our time together was so short. Most of all, I'm sorry you'll never meet the child I'm carrying. You would have made a good father, Miloš." She paused, blinking away tears. "Thank you for helping me find my faith again. I won't go back to the way I was before I married you because I know that's not what you'd want. I will cry, and I will miss you, but I will be strong. My Savior healed me before, and I know He will heal me again. I loved you, Miloš. I think you knew that before I did." She stopped, unable to speak as her tears choked her voice. "Good-bye, Miloš. I will always love you."

CHAPTER TWENTY-SIX
"BUSTED UP BEYOND REPAIR"

Sunday, March 4
Bari, Italy

IT WAS HER DAY OFF, but on her way home from church, Genevieve felt she should stop by the hospital. Bari was miles from the frontline, but it didn't seem that way today. The normally quiet ward looked like an overwhelmed field hospital on the edge of a combat zone.

"Genevieve!" Vittoria shouted from halfway across the room. "Can you help Dr. Bolliger?"

Genevieve nodded and ran across the hall to scrub, then rushed into the operating room to join Nathan and Dorothy.

"Genevieve, you're an angel," Nathan said. "You couldn't have picked a better day to stop in."

"What happened?"

"The Luftwaffe isn't as dead as we thought. It's just been waiting to protect targets in Germany—and that's where the mission was today. Dorothy, prepare anesthesia for the next patient. Genevieve, I want you to wrap."

"Yes, sir." Genevieve bandaged the end of the leg Nathan had just amputated while Dorothy prepared a syringe.

Three more patients lay in line, the nearest one with burns along the left half of his face and shoulders and a bloody bandage across his stomach. The poor man was just conscious enough to feel pain until Dorothy injected him with sodium pentothal. Nathan removed the dressing from the patient's abdomen, dug out a piece of shrapnel, and began repairing the man's intestines.

"Dorothy, get morphine for the next two patients and make sure Vittoria has room for this one in the burn ward." Nathan spoke without taking his eyes off his work. He had an amazing ability to focus on his current task while preparing for the next one. He was a perfect field doctor.

"Yes, sir," Dorothy said.

Nathan glanced at Genevieve. "They ran into flack and fighters. We've got fifteen burn victims, plus everyone who was shot up."

The next patient didn't have burns—one of the few—but an explosion had left his hand dangling from his wrist by a tendon, and his knee looked bad too. The hand was a lost cause, so Nathan clipped it off and stitched the remaining skin together. Genevieve disinfected the stub and bandaged it while Nathan tried to save the man's leg.

As Genevieve wrapped the stub in sterile gauze, she glanced at the airman's face. He was unconscious, and that was a blessing. For now, he was out of pain. But he would wake to life without a hand and possibly without a leg. He had light brown hair, and he seemed familiar, but it took her a few seconds to realize it was the ball-turret gunner from the *Lucky Lucille*, Sergeant Rick Shelton. Genevieve had often wondered if it was easier to treat patients who were strangers or patients who were friends. At that instant, she realized it was harder to treat friends.

Genevieve didn't let it affect her work. She couldn't; there was too much to do. She had to carry on, and she did, through Nathan's surgery on Rick's knee, through the next patient who had shrapnel in his ankle.

When the surgeries were completed, Genevieve went to assist Vittoria, cleaning and bandaging burns. The night staff came in early to help, but no one went home when evening fell. Some of the airmen had died before the planes landed, but not one of the patients who made it to the hospital died there.

* * *

After three hours of sleep, Genevieve arrived back at the hospital for the morning shift. Sergeant Shelton was her first patient. He sat in bed, staring out the window with a depressed look on his face.

"Rick?"

He met her eyes and smiled his recognition, but his smile seemed empty. She changed the bandages on the end of his arm, checking for signs of infection.

"I kind of hoped I'd run into you again. But not like this," he said.

Genevieve was quiet for a few seconds, concentrating on the new bandages. "Looks like the *Lucky Lucille* brought you back again."

"Hmm, but she'll never fly again. Busted up beyond repair." Rick stared at the stub on the end of his arm. "Just like me."

Dealing with amputation was difficult. It was hard enough for Genevieve, and she knew it was exponentially harder for the amputee, but it was her job to help. "Dr. Bolliger managed to save your leg, so you'll walk again."

"How long will it take?"

"That depends a lot on you." Genevieve knew the averages but thought his mental condition would be a greater factor in how long it took him to recover and adjust. "Two weeks ago, I would have labeled you an optimist. If you can find that optimism again, I think you'll do well."

He stared out the window as Genevieve changed the bandages on his leg. "Rick?" Genevieve asked when she was done. He looked at her again. "I know it's hard. But you can do it."

He put on a brave face. "Have you found any Fascist spies lately?"

"No, not recently."

"Maybe that's a good thing," he said. "Heard anything from your missing boyfriend?"

"No," Genevieve whispered.

"But you haven't given up?"

Genevieve wanted to cry because there was still no word of Peter, but she knew tears wouldn't help anyone. "No. It takes more than a Nazi prison . . . or loss of limb . . . to keep those tough American farm boys down. He'll make it," she said, and she almost believed it. "And so will you."

Rick smiled. He was facing an enormous challenge, but there was strength in his smile. Genevieve felt sure Rick was going to be all right in the end.

CHAPTER TWENTY-SEVEN
A MESSAGE

Independent State of Croatia

PETER REACHED FOR MARIJA'S ARM as she stumbled over a log, catching her before she fell. She looked dead tired. "Let's take a break," he said.

Jamie hobbled away from the group and motioned for Peter to join him. "We need to put some distance between us and that German garrison we just passed."

"I know." He glanced at Marija, who was staring off ahead of them, tears streaming down her cheeks. They'd taken a break not long before, but Peter didn't want to push Marija too hard and risk losing her baby. "How's your leg?"

"It is the worst it has been in two months."

"Sorry. I was trying to wake you that night we were drugged. I kicked you a few times."

Jamie frowned. "I am tempted to whack you with my cane in return, but that won't make my leg feel any better, so I shall refrain."

Moretti knelt on the ground next to Marija. "Would you let me carry you, Marija? We can't stop for long this close to those Nazis."

Marija seemed hesitant. She wiped away her tears, but her face was pale. "I'm feeling ill this morning. What if I get sick all over you?"

Moretti laughed. "It wouldn't be the worst thing I've had all over me." He helped her to her feet and passed the rifle to Peter. With Marija on Moretti's back, they set off again. Peter wondered how long Moretti would be able to carry her. Marija was skinny, but Moretti had lost some of his muscles over the winter, and they'd had little to eat the past few days.

"Did I ever tell you about the time I dropped into Salerno?" Moretti asked. "I was headed right for a farmhouse, so I tweaked my chute and just missed the roof. Landed in a pile of manure instead. It fouled up my pistol and got in my boots. I smelled like a barnyard for the next two weeks. And I picked up an interesting nickname, but it wouldn't be polite to repeat it around a lady."

"You need a nickname," Marija said. The story hadn't made her smile, but it had drawn her back to the present. "Why does everyone call you by your last name?"

"Because none of us know his first name. What is it, Moretti?" Krzysztof asked.

"I don't like my first name," Moretti said.

"'What's in a name? That which we call a rose by any other word would smell as sweet.'" Jamie limped along, leaning on his cane. "And he who we call Moretti would smell just as foul should he parachute into a pile of manure again."

Moretti smiled but refused to say his name.

"Come on, Moretti," Peter said. "If you don't tell us, we'll tackle you when you least expect it and pull out your dog tags."

Moretti grinned. "My dog tags just have my first initial on them."

"Did you parents name you Adolf?" Krzysztof asked. "Benito?"

"Almost that bad."

"I brought you fresh goat milk every day for months, and I'd like to know your full name." Marija raised her eyebrows, expecting an answer.

Moretti sighed and muttered something under his breath.

"That doesn't sound so awful," Marija said. "And I'm feeling well enough to walk again." Moretti stopped, and Marija slid off his back.

"What is it?" Krzysztof asked.

Moretti shook his head. "Galeazzo."

Jamie smiled. "Like the late Count Galeazzo Ciano?"

"Yeah." Moretti grimaced. "Count Ciano, Mussolini's foreign minister and son-in-law."

"It's better than Benito," Peter said. "We could call you Gale."

"I prefer Moretti."

Peter had never seen Moretti so insistent. He was usually laid back about everything that wasn't a matter of life or death, but as Peter glanced around, he could tell everyone was in slightly better spirits. Everyone except, perhaps, Sergeant Galeazzo Moretti.

* * *

They marched west for nearly two weeks. It was usually cold, they had no food, and their only weapon was Marija's rifle with a single clip of ammunition. The rivers and streams they passed were swift with the spring snow melt, and the inhabitants of the region lived in desperate poverty. Yet, once again, the mountain villagers kept them alive by sheltering them from the cold and giving them food. Two villages provided guides. Both guides led them farther north than they would have planned but also helped them avoid enemy troops. And one of the guides helped them hitch an overnight ride on a freight train headed west.

All the villages seemed the same: stone cottages with thatched roofs, gray like the March sky. The village they studied from its outskirts while Jamie inquired to see if they could stay the night was much like the one where they'd spent the winter: a narrow dirt road with homes on either side, surrounded by a mountain forest. Their last guide had suggested they stop here. Peter hoped to stay a few days—Marija needed a day off, and no one else would complain about a break.

Jamie returned with an elderly villager. The man's shoulders were stooped and his hat patched, but his smile was welcoming. "He says we are welcome to stay as long as we like. He is married to the village midwife and has offered to host Marija. The rest of us can stay with his neighbor."

The man fed them standard fare for mountain villages: goat cheese, bread, root vegetables, and plum brandy. After eating and ensuring Marija was safe at the midwife's home, the men gathered around their host's kitchen table and pored over his map. The village was too small to appear on paper, but the villager pointed out the large German garrison in nearby Bihac and the ring of smaller garrisons surrounding it. After their map study, their host brought out a surprise left behind by a team of British commandos: a Type 3 MK II suitcase radio.

The radio was broken, but Krzysztof repaired it in under an hour. "Who should we call?" Krzysztof looked up from his work. Like the rest of the men, he was grinning.

"Not Major Kimby," Jamie said.

"Cairo?" Peter asked. During their mission the previous fall, they'd directed their radio traffic to an SOE station in Egypt. "Or would they get word back to Kimby?"

Jamie started pacing. "Do you remember the codes for Cairo?"

"I remember the call signs and a few phrases." Krzysztof adjusted one of the radio's knobs. "Everything else would have to be sent openly."

"So Cairo would hear us and inform Bari—including Kimby. And the Gestapo would hear us as well." Jamie paused in his pacing. Peter had seen him pace before, but his dependence on the cane seemed to hamper him. "What we need is to get a message directly to someone we trust. Wesley."

"How many Major Bakers do you suppose there are in the British Army?" Peter asked.

"If we specified Major Wesley W. Baker, SOE, Hertfordshire, I think it would get to the right man." Jamie shook his head. "But it would be easy for Kimby or the Gestapo to listen in."

Krzysztof cleared his throat. Peter, Jamie, and Moretti looked from him to the cigarette he held in his hand. "What if we sent a message in code, directed to Major Baker, care of someone who can decode it for him?"

"You gonna smoke that?" Moretti asked.

Krzysztof smiled and pulled the cigarette apart. It wasn't a cigarette after all. It was a hollow container with a cipher pad inside. "My father has the same cipher. He can read it, and I doubt anyone else can."

They spent the next hour deciding what to say. They sent the first part in plain text so it would be delivered to the right person—Krzysztof's father at the Government Code & Cipher School at Bletchley Park:

Attention Marek Zielinski, GCCS, BP, England.

The next part was written in code.

K. Zielinski, J. Nelson, P. Eddy, G. Moretti, and one civilian seek evacuation from Yugoslavia. Contact Major Wesley Baker, SOE, to arrange transport. Do not, repeat, do not inform Major Phillip Kimby, SOE. Will await reply noon and midnight British War Time.

The message closed with the proper frequencies. Krzysztof encoded the message, first with the cipher groups, then with a secondary encoding method, as was custom when he communicated with his father. "Send it every hour for the night? Someone ought to intercept it."

Peter nodded.

Krzysztof smiled as he tapped out the message. "My father could be reading this by tomorrow, which means I could see Iuliana again within the week."

* * *

The group rested the next day, helping the villagers chop wood and clear gardens for planting, accepting food in exchange. It was late afternoon when Peter finished chopping wood and looked behind him to see Jamie, a frown on his tense face. "What is it, Jamie?"

Jamie gazed around. No one else was nearby. "I overheard some of the villagers. The Germans know we are here, and they have given the village an ultimatum: give up the Americans, or be shelled into dust."

How did they find us so fast? "Do they know how many of us are here?"

Jamie was one step ahead of him. "You want to ask the villagers if half of us can sneak away and hope the other half satisfies the ultimatum?"

"Yeah."

"That won't happen." Jamie said.

Peter nodded, thinking that if his entire town was faced with destruction, he too might be unwilling to risk anything other than full compliance. "Maybe we should send Marija away before the villagers arrest us."

"The villagers do not plan to arrest us. They'll transfer us to another village tomorrow morning and take their shelling. The German guns should be in position within two days."

"What?" Peter asked.

"They don't plan to turn us over to the Germans," Jamie said.

"Are you sure?"

"Certain."

"Keep everything quiet for now," Peter ordered.

Jamie nodded.

The evening went on, just as it had for centuries in the small Serb village. It was an idyllic scene, but Peter wasn't thinking about goats and melting snow. He was thinking about mortar shells and execution squads.

CHAPTER TWENTY-EIGHT
A SACRIFICE

THERE WAS NO ONE ON the other end of the radio that night, which wasn't surprising. They hoped the British Navy in the Adriatic or Mediterranean would pick up their signal, but it would take time for the message to be passed on and decoded.

Peter waited until everyone was asleep, then crept outside and prayed more fervently than he had ever prayed before. He knew what he needed to do, but he didn't want to do it. Twenty minutes into the prayer, the irony hit him. *If it be possible, let this cup pass from me.* The Savior's words from Gethsemane crossed Peter's mind, and he knew what he had to do wasn't difficult, not in comparison.

The problem was, Peter knew too much about Nazi executions. They didn't crucify people but were fond of several other brutal techniques: slow, torturous hangings by piano wire or meat hook, making death agonizing, undignified, and horrifying. Peter ended his prayer with a strange request. He prayed that if he was to be hanged, it would be with rope rather than piano wire or a meat hook and that when it happened, his neck would snap quickly.

Peter went back inside. By the light of the dying fire, he scribbled a final entry in his letter to Genevieve:

> *Beau Canari,*
> *I don't think I'll be making it back to you after all. I'm sorry. Please know it wasn't for lack of love. I'll be gone soon, but I'll always be yours.*
> *Love,*
> *Peter*

He folded and tucked the papers in his Book of Mormon and left it on his blanket, where his friends would find it. If they survived, they could eventually deliver it to Genevieve. Then Peter grabbed the radio. Krzysztof was asleep, but when Peter touched his shoulder he sat upright immediately.

"Quiet," Peter cautioned him. "I need your help."

Krzysztof nodded and followed Peter outside. It was a cold night with a stiff wind, and it was dark because the moon had already set.

When he thought they were far enough away from the village, Peter held the radio out to Krzysztof. "I need to speak with the commander at the nearest German garrison."

Krzysztof crossed his arms, refusing to take the radio. "Why?"

"To arrange terms."

"Who's surrendering? The Fascists?" Krzysztof asked suspiciously.

"No, just me."

Krzysztof took a step back. "I won't help you do that, sir."

"If you don't, in two days' time, the village that's hosting us will be shelled by German artillery."

"Why would they waste their artillery on an obscure village?"

"To make an example," Peter said. "The Germans know they're harboring Americans."

"So you think by giving yourself up, you can spare the village."

"Yeah." Peter tried to keep his voice even.

Krzysztof set up the radio and tapped out the same signal over and over again, waiting for a response and making minor adjustments. Nearly an hour passed. "I've got someone. From a unit between here and Bihac."

"Ask for the officer in charge."

Krzysztof sent the request and waited. "They say 'Major Hegel does not like his sleep disturbed in the middle of the night.'"

"Ask if he'll make an exception for an American field agent wishing to surrender."

Peter and Krzysztof waited for what seemed like a long time, listening to the static rise and fall. "He says the commander is there now and wants us to identify ourselves."

Peter nodded. "Tell them it's the American hiding in a village south of Bihac."

"'What are your terms?'"

"I surrender; they leave the village in peace. Remind them the only people in the village are harmless, defenseless civilians. But they might damage their artillery pieces if they pull them up the mountainside, and they'd waste their ammunition."

Krzysztof sent the message and received the reply. "Now he's asking how many of us to expect."

"Tell him one."

Krzysztof hesitated, so Peter repeated himself.

"Here's the response," Krzysztof said. "'You lie. My source said there was more than one of you.'"

Peter blew out a breath of frustration. "Tell him my last associate died yesterday. Typhus. That should be believable; it's been going around."

"Now he wants your name."

"Send it," Peter said.

"Your real name?"

Peter nodded.

The next response came quickly. Krzysztof switched the set off before repeating it. "He wants you by dawn. If you're lying, he'll level the village. I think I'd better go with you, Peter."

"No."

"Yes." Krzysztof's eyes met his, intense and unyielding. "He won't be satisfied that you're the only one hiding here."

"The villagers found a pair of dead Chetniks last week. They buried them on the edge of the village."

"Why would he believe those bodies are Allied soldiers?"

Peter pulled a dog tag from his pocket, the one Krzysztof and Miloš had found while searching a plane wreck for radio parts. They were from Air Corp Second Lieutenant Vincenzo Romano's body. "I still have this," Peter said, showing the metal plate to Krzysztof.

Krzysztof took it, studied it, then handed it back to Peter. "It won't be enough, sir. I'm coming too."

"Krzysztof, we're commandos. The garrison's commander will be under orders to execute us. There's no reason for you to die too."

"What about your girl, sir?"

Peter had thought about Genevieve a lot that night. Leaving her behind was the worst thing about the whole situation, worse even than the fear of meat hooks, but Genevieve would do the same thing if she'd been given Peter's choice. He didn't want to die, but he couldn't let innocent women and children be slaughtered in his place. "Yes, I'm leaving a girl behind, and it kills me to do it. But I've been thinking a lot about Marija's baby and how it will have to grow up without a father. I couldn't save Miloš, but maybe I can help his family." Peter's mind had replayed Miloš's murder over and over again. He knew it would never stop haunting him. "I've also thought about Iuliana's son. I doubt he even remembers his father. But Anatolie might get a stepfather who would be just as good as a real dad."

"Iuliana and I never talked about anything like that."

"But you've thought about it," Peter said. "I can tell when you're thinking about her. You get this faraway look in your eyes, and then you spend hours taking apart a broken radio that everyone—especially you—knows will never function again."

Krzysztof glanced away for a few seconds. "I have my duty, sir. Iuliana understands duty, and Anatolie wouldn't want a father who shirks it. I'm going with you."

"To execution?"

"Yes, to execution."

"No," Peter said. "If you go, who will answer Major Baker when he responds to your code? You have to be here to get the rest of the team home."

"We have two days. We can evacuate the village."

Peter sighed. He'd already prayed about all of Krzysztof's suggestions, and none of them would work. "Whoever told the Germans that Americans are in the village will also tell them if the entire village up and leaves. It might take a few days to haul their field guns up the mountain, but a patrol could get up here a lot sooner—and be just as deadly."

Krzysztof looked down in frustration. "Let's at least talk to Jamie and Moretti before you sacrifice yourself."

The last thing Peter wanted was another conversation like the one he was having, only with Jamie and Moretti included, but he nodded, grabbed the radio, and started back toward the village.

When the first house came into view, Peter stopped and held his hand out. "What was that?" he whispered.

Krzysztof looked around. As soon as his back was turned, Peter knocked the side of his hand into the back of Krzysztof's neck like he'd been taught to do in training. Krzysztof slumped to the ground, unconscious. It was a risky move—Krzysztof had suffered multiple concussions over the last year—but it would be far more dangerous to allow Krzysztof or one of his other teammates to follow him to the German garrison. Peter hoped Krzysztof wouldn't do anything stupid when he woke and that one day he would forgive Peter for trying to save his life by knocking him unconscious.

Peter took his jacket off—he wouldn't need it much longer anyway—and spread it over Krzysztof's limp form. "Have a good life, Krzysztof. Get the others home. Then take good care of Iuliana and Anatolie."

Peter walked downhill to surrender, his mood mirroring the black sky. He didn't want to die. According to radio reports and rumors in the villages they passed, the war in Europe was almost over. What a shame to survive so much of it only to die without a fight in what was probably the final months. Peter thought about his family. He would have liked to see them all and been given a chance to see his dad again without any hard feelings between them. He wished he could set foot on American soil just one more time. And he would have liked to see Genevieve again. That was the hardest thing to walk away from—the girl who had almost been his.

He'd walked about a quarter mile when he heard something and stopped. He heard the noise again: footsteps. If it was the Germans, Peter could surrender, but if it was someone from the village, he preferred to remain unseen. He waited for a while, then he saw who it was and cursed—he knew swearing wasn't the wisest thing to do when preparing one's soul for death, but it came out anyway. Jamie and Moretti stepped out from the trees.

"You're supposed to be sleeping," Peter said.

"Where you going, sir?" Moretti asked. "You weren't planning on walking into that German garrison now, were you?"

Peter glanced at Jamie, who quickly explained. "You told me to keep it quiet, but you never said you planned to sacrifice yourself. It won't work, Peter. They expect more than one person."

"I have a plan for that. Go back to the village."

"Where's Krzysztof?" Moretti asked.

"I had to knock some sense into him. I expect him to be back in the village by dawn—where you will both be waiting for him."

"Actually, Peter, we have discussed the situation, and we have each decided that we will accompany you," Jamie said casually, as if they were escorting Peter to a local pub.

"As your senior officer, I order both of you to return to the village." Peter had never before pulled rank, but they were being ridiculous. "If the Germans are still suspicious, the villagers will need your help to evacuate."

"They have nowhere to go. And I am tired of obeying orders from a Yankee farm boy. I am a civilian, so you don't really outrank me."

"Go back to the village anyway. The Germans didn't ask for any Englishmen." Peter shook his head in frustration when Jamie didn't respond, and then he turned to Moretti. "I do outrank you. Moretti, I order you to return to the village. On your way back, pick up Krzysztof. It's cold outside, and I don't want him freezing to death." Moretti didn't move. "You'd better not disobey a direct order, sergeant."

Moretti shrugged. "What are ya gonna do, sir, court martial me? Or hit me over the head? That might be entertaining to watch; you're getting kinda scrawny."

Peter's hands, currently in his pockets, balled up in frustration. He felt the dog tag and had an idea. "I won't fight you because you'd win. But take this." He threw the dog tag at Moretti, who caught it. "You are not to mention anything about OSS. You are now Lieutenant Romano of the Army Air Corp. Your parents are still from Italy, and you're still from New York. You were the bombardier on a B-24 Liberator that was shot up over Romania and crashed somewhere in Bosnia. You hooked up with us by accident."

"Why?" Moretti asked, fingering the dead airman's dog tag.

Jamie answered. "Because downed airmen are usually sent to prisons administered by the Luftwaffe. It is still a POW camp, but conditions there tend to be vastly better than in camps run by the army."

Peter nodded his agreement. He preferred Moretti stay with Krzysztof and Marija. But if he insisted on coming, he would rather have Moretti shipped off to a Luftwaffe-run POW camp than executed as a commando.

"I'd rather stay in prison with you, sir," Moretti said.

Peter didn't expect to be in prison long. He expected to be dead. "Don't fight me on this, Moretti. Just trust me."

Peter could tell Moretti didn't like it, but he nodded, signaling his willingness to compromise.

"Jamie, can I speak with you privately?" Jamie followed Peter when he walked out of earshot. "Moretti would be better off staying here. You know that, right?" Peter whispered.

"Yes, but neither of us will change his mind. I tried, and so did you. He woke up and noticed you and Krzysztof were gone. I guessed what you were up to, though I was surprised you took Krzysztof."

"I needed his help with the radio."

"And you hit him over the head when he wouldn't let you leave by yourself?" Jamie asked.

Peter nodded. "Which is what you should have done to Moretti. And that's what I should do to you now. They'll execute us."

"I know. I remember Hitler's commando order," Jamie said.

"Then stay. Help the villagers."

"Why don't you?" Jamie asked.

"I already gave them my name."

"Then give me your dog tags."

Jamie's offer was tempting. But Peter couldn't let his friends die in his place. That, and Peter was certain the Gestapo already had a file on him. If it didn't contain a picture, it would certainly contain a physical description. Jamie was a few inches taller than Peter, with lighter hair and blue eyes instead of brown. "Major Hegel only needs to make one phone call and he'll have my description. We don't look enough alike for it to work. Go back to the village. If anyone can find a place for the villagers to evacuate to, it's you." Jamie spoke more languages than he had fingers, and the Balkan languages were decidedly difficult for the rest of the team.

"Peter, I am going to the German garrison, with or without you. I have rarely been more certain of anything."

CHAPTER TWENTY-NINE
THE GARRISON

Monday, March 19

THE GERMAN ARMY HAD TAKEN over a town in the valley, driven its residents away, and dug in, expecting a fight with the Partisans. The small garrison was part of a ring surrounding Bihac and the larger garrison there. Some of the men who manned the pillboxes and defensive trenches were German, some Croatian Ustaše.

When Peter, Jamie, and Moretti arrived, they were immediately apprehended and searched. Then they were taken to the commander's headquarters, the local school, and locked in an office. The men didn't try to escape—doing so would result in the village's destruction, and even if they'd wanted to run away, the stone and mortar walls were thick, and the schoolyard outside was surrounded by a high block fence topped with razor wire. From the barred window, they could see guards patrolling the grounds and manning machine guns on the wall's corners.

At midday, they were taken to an abandoned classroom guarded by an Ustaše soldier. A German major walked into the room and sat behind the desk. He clasped his hands together and laid them on the polished surface, scrutinizing each of his prisoners in turn. "Which of you is First Lieutenant Eddy?"

"Me, sir," Peter said.

He stared at Peter with cold eyes. "I am Major Hegel. I see you decided to stop lying about your numbers. Good. I can skip shelling ze village now." He turned to the guard and told him in German to send Raditch. "I prefer to aim my guns at ze Partisans. You are commando?"

Peter nodded.

Hegel pointed to Jamie.

"James Nelson, SOE."

Hegel turned to Moretti. "And you?"

Moretti swallowed, looking from Peter to the German major as he decided what to say. "Lieutenant Romano, Army Air Corp."

Peter held back a sigh of relief. He hadn't been sure Moretti would follow orders and lie about his identity.

"Lieutenant, why are you not in uniform?"

"I crashed in August, and my uniform fell apart by about February."

Hegel kept his hazel eyes fixed on Moretti, one booted foot beating rhythmically on the bottom of the desk. "Your unit?"

Moretti didn't hesitate. "Fifteenth Air Force, Forty-Seventh Bomb Wing, Three-Hundred Seventy-Sixth Bomb Group."

"Target on your last mission?"

"Ploieşti."

Hegel seemed satisfied, glancing at an Ustaše officer who came into the room. "When?"

"August 18," Moretti said. Peter didn't know if Moretti was right about the bomb wing and bomb group, but there had been an American air raid targeting Ploieşti on August eighteenth. Peter had watched it from the ground, then reported what he'd seen to Moretti and the rest of the team the next day.

"You have been in Yugoslavia a long time."

Moretti looked at the floor. "Yeah."

"And you are with zese commandos. Why?"

"Thought they'd get me home."

Hegel stared at Peter and Jamie. "Your mission?"

Peter and Jamie had already discussed what they'd say, so Peter let Jamie do the talking. "We were ordered to destroy a rail line last fall. We spent the winter recovering from wounds received in a skirmish shortly after we landed."

"Where?"

"Given your record for reprisals, we won't be revealing that information," Jamie said.

Hegel leaned back in his chair and motioned to the Ustaše officer. "Raditch, bind zeir hands," he ordered.

The Ustaše man tied their hands with rope and left the three of them standing before the desk, Jamie a little unsteady without the support of his cane. Hegel stood and strode around the desk, his hands clenched behind his back. He faced Raditch. "Take zis airman to Bihac. Zey can arrange shipment to a POW camp."

As Raditch grabbed Moretti's arm, Moretti shrugged free of his grip. "What about them?" Moretti asked.

Hegel eyed Jamie and Peter. "Zey are commandos. I shall have to execute zem. Tomorrow, I suppose."

"What?" Moretti's question was a mere whisper. He looked from Hegel to Peter in shock. "You knew this would happen?"

Peter nodded.

"Oh no, I ain't getting shipped off to a cozy Luftwaffe camp while the two of you get executed. Forget that dog tag. My name's—"

"You promised," Peter said, cutting Moretti off. At the same time, Jamie questioned Hegel about the POW camp in German. Peter hoped the distraction would work.

Moretti was quiet for a few seconds, his mouth opening and closing a few times before he spoke again. "I didn't know what I was promising."

"I know."

"Sir, this ain't right."

Peter nodded his agreement. "It never is during war, is it?"

Moretti was one of the toughest men Peter had ever met, but he looked suddenly vulnerable as Raditch grabbed his arm again. "I guess you wouldn't of left your book if you planned on being around much longer."

"Raditch." Hegel finished talking with Jamie and walked back to his chair. "When you get back, organize a patrol. After ze execution tomorrow, I want you to take care of ze village."

"You said you'd leave the village alone if I surrendered," Peter said.

Hegel smiled. "No, I said I wouldn't shell ze village, and I shan't. But zey will still be punished for harboring commandos."

"You can't do that. They have no defenses. It's just women and old men and little kids—"

"I have my orders," Hegel cut Peter off. "And zey include consistent reprisals. You should have zought of zat before you surrendered."

Peter was shocked, remembering the deserted village he'd seen the day Chesterfield turned on them, with its mass grave and piles of spent machine-gun casings. Was that what would happen to the villagers who'd sheltered him? And to Krzysztof and Marija, despite Peter's sacrifice to save them? Peter glanced at Jamie and saw the same bewilderment and anger he felt reflected in Jamie's eyes.

Peter figured he had less than a day to live anyway—only a few hours to lose. His hands were tied, but he barreled into Raditch and, with Moretti's help, pushed him to the floor. He turned to see Jamie slide across the desk, knocking Hegel's arm and the pistol it held so the bullet hit the wall instead of Peter, where it had been aimed.

Perhaps if their hands weren't bound or if they'd had adequate food throughout the winter, the three prisoners would have had better luck. Instead, Hegel overpowered Jamie, and Moretti and Peter were unable to come to his aid, struggling instead to keep Raditch down. When four guards, alerted by the gunshot, ran down the hallway and into the classroom, Moretti and Peter were quickly forced to the floor and Raditch freed.

Flat on the ground, Peter could feel the end of a rifle shoved into his temple. Moretti was getting the same treatment, and a quick glance revealed Jamie, blood streaming from his nose, pressed against the wall by the two other guards.

Hegel straightened his uniform and stood erect over the two Americans on the floor. "If you are finished with your futile display . . ."

Peter met Moretti's eyes. He wanted to say something, but *Good-bye* seemed inadequate. Saying *At least we tried* wasn't right either. *Too bad about that village, huh?* was callous, and *Good luck in the POW camp*, well, it would take more than luck. And their attack on Raditch might have canceled out Moretti's shot at surviving the war.

"Your orders stand, Raditch," Hegel said.

Raditch said something in Serbo-Croat, and another guard hauled Moretti to his feet and marched him away. Peter felt a mix of emotions as his friend left. He was glad Moretti would have a chance to live, but for what? So the villagers, Krzysztof, and Marija could be killed by a .3-inch bullet from a machine gun instead of by shrapnel from an 88 or some other type of field cannon?

At Hegel's order, the guards yanked Peter to his feet. As they escorted Peter and Jamie from Hegel's office, Peter saw a bird cage in the corner of the room. He hadn't noticed it before. Inside was a canary—a quiet one. Peter's eyes locked onto it, wondering why the canary wasn't singing.

As the guards marched him down the hall and locked Jamie and him in the office prison, Peter thought of Genevieve. After her sister-in-law's death in 1941, Genevieve had stopped singing, and it had taken her three years to start again. Peter wondered if his *beau canari* would stop singing again when he didn't return and how long that silence would last.

CHAPTER THIRTY
THE FIRING SQUAD

Tuesday, March 20

PETER DIDN'T SLEEP THAT NIGHT. Nor did Jamie. If the villagers were going to be slaughtered anyway, they had every reason to escape. The guards had left their hands untied. They used the metal on their belts in an attempt to wear away some of the mortar but made scarcely a scratch. When their belts broke, they used their fingernails.

When the first hint of morning showed through the window, a black sky turning gray, Peter stopped trying. He'd filed his fingernails down past the ends of his fingers, and most of them were bleeding. With their current methods, it would take years to break free of their block prison, and they had only minutes.

Jamie's mouth curled into a half smile as he too gave up clawing their way out. "I thought you would be praying by now."

"I prayed before we left. I don't know what else to say now . . ." Peter trailed off. "It's strange. Do you plan to pray?"

Jamie sighed and stared at his own bloody fingers. "A deathbed repentance would be cheating, wouldn't it?"

They sat in silence for a few minutes. Peter shivered. The cell was cold, and spring seemed to be late this year. Jamie stood and walked around the room—a mix of limping and pacing. "If you could have one hour to do anything at all, what would it be?"

Genevieve's face appeared in Peter's mind, and he smiled.

Jamie paused in his pacing, glancing at Peter. "Oh, you would spend it with that French tart of yours, wouldn't you?"

"I wish you wouldn't call her a *tart*. I met her in a respectable farmhouse, not in a brothel."

"Sorry," Jamie said, laughing. "The rest of my life, I will never refer to her as a *French tart* again. We have perhaps ten minutes left, so I know I can keep a promise that long. You would want to see her again, wouldn't you?"

Peter sighed. "Yeah, if I had an hour to do anything, I would spend it with Genevieve. But I'm not sure what I would tell her. *Hello, beautiful. I love you. I wish I could marry you, but I'm going to be shot by a firing squad instead. I don't want you to be sad and lonely the rest of your life, but the thought of you finding someone else makes me want to die. But I'm going to die anyway very soon.*" Peter thought about what he'd just said, wondering if those were the words he'd really pick if given the chance to tell Genevieve good-bye. "I don't know, Jamie, it would seem a little unfair to tell her good-bye like that, but I do wish I could see her one last time." Peter glanced at his fingers, wondering if Genevieve would ever know what had happened to him. "What would you do?"

Jamie smiled. "Maybe some revenge. I would love to fight Hitler himself without any weapons."

"He'd probably last about five seconds."

"Good. At that rate, I could take out half the Nazi high command in an hour."

"Why did you come, Jamie? You didn't need to die."

"You know, Peter, I could be described as a lot of things: brilliant, brave, handsome, charming, clever, and, of course, completely modest." He paused, a bittersweet smile on his face. "But I have never done anything noble before, not until now. Perhaps a noble death will make up for some of my past shortcomings."

It wasn't long after that they heard footsteps outside the cell. When the door was unlocked, Peter glanced at what he assumed would be the last new faces he'd see during his lifetime: a German feldwebel with an angular, somber face and a young gefreiter with a thick shock of blond hair and an equally serious expression. They tied the prisoners' arms behind their backs and led them outside to the school's courtyard.

The sun was up but hadn't risen high enough to peer over the garrison wall. That made Peter angry. He wanted to see the sun one more time before he died. There were a lot of other things he'd like to see again as well, mostly people, but the sun seemed like such a small thing to ask for. Their guards placed them against the wall and blindfolded them just as Hegel walked into the courtyard. That also made Peter angry. His last sight on earth was an ugly Nazi who kept unhappy canaries in cages.

Peter's German was only fair, but he could hear orders for the firing squad to assemble. He also heard the sharp strike of boots running through the courtyard and wondered if one of the squad's members had overslept. Several moments of quiet conversation followed. Peter couldn't pick out any meaning.

"What's going on, Jamie?"

Jamie answered in a whisper. "Rumors of a Partisan offensive. If, in the confusion, they decide to shoot us in the back of the head instead of from across the courtyard, turn your head to the side when they give the order to fire. I know someone who survived execution that way."

"Really? Or is that a final practical joke?"

"I haven't played a practical joke on you since August of last year, old boy. Why would I start again now?"

Old boy. The phrase sounded in Peter's head. It was just an expression, but it reminded him that he was only twenty-two years old.

Before he had a chance to answer, he heard the crack of a rifle. His first thought was surprise. He'd expected Hegel to say something before he executed them. Why hadn't there been a drum roll or at least a *Ready, aim, fire!* to warn them? His second thought was the sound had come from farther away than the other side of the courtyard. His third thought was it couldn't have been the firing squad because if it had been a rifle aimed at him, he would have felt it by now.

A shrill whine followed by a nearby boom gave Peter another suspicion: the small arms fire and the bursting artillery shell weren't coming from the fort; they were aimed *at* the fort. Maybe the rumor of a Partisan advance was true after all.

Over the sound of another exploding artillery shell, Peter recognized Hegel's voice barking out orders for his men.

"Jamie?"

"Get down," Jamie's voice said from below.

Peter followed Jamie's advice, sitting on the ground with his back against the wall. "Do you think you can get my blindfold off?"

He heard Jamie turning on the ground and pushed his face into Jamie's hands. When Jamie ripped the blindfold off, he could see that the firing squad had dissipated and one of the garrison's walls was burning. He'd suspected as much, even before he could see again, because the air was heavy with smoke. German soldiers ran across the courtyard in all directions, most with rifles, some with buckets spilling water as they ran toward the fire. Peter maneuvered so he could take Jamie's blindfold off, then worked on the ties around Jamie's wrists. The rope had been tied tightly, and Peter counted six mortar bursts while he wrestled with the knot, but eventually, he managed to free Jamie's hands.

"I see Raditch," Jamie said. "Time to leave."

Peter struggled to his feet and followed the hobbling Jamie toward a recessed doorway. In the shadow, Jamie untied Peter's hands and the two of them watched Raditch scan the courtyard, pistol in hand, searching for his prisoners.

A tank bursting through the garrison wall and plowing into the courtyard distracted the Ustaše officer. It was an Italian Ansaldo-FIAT M13/40 tank, but a red star was painted on its turret. The Yugoslav Partisans had arrived. A German soldier aimed a panzerfaust at the tank, and the tip of the Yugoslav spearhead was engulfed in flames. The soldier who'd destroyed the tank was quickly shot down by Partisan infantrymen riding on the next Yugoslav tank that pushed past the flaming wreck and took out a machine-gun position just above Peter and Jamie's hiding spot.

They stayed where they were. They were unarmed, and the door behind them was blocked off. The German and Ustaše troops launched a counterattack, but they were outnumbered, and it broke apart in minutes. More Yugoslav troops poured into the courtyard and advanced into the garrison's buildings.

When a squad of Partisans suddenly appeared in front of them, Peter and Jamie raised their hands. It still looked like the soldiers would shoot them, but Jamie blurted out something in Serbo-Croat, and the men took them prisoner instead.

"What did you tell them?" Peter whispered.

"That we are British prisoners. I don't think they take German prisoners."

Jamie's suspicion proved true as the Yugoslav soldiers mopped up the remaining defenders and secured the schoolyard. Peter saw a group of desperate Ustaše men throw their hands up in surrender, only to be cut in two by Partisan submachine-gun fire. When the last of the Fascist defenders were defeated, the Partisan squad pushed Peter and Jamie back into the courtyard.

"Did they believe you when you told them we aren't Nazis?" Peter asked as one of the guards gave him a rough shove forward.

"We are still alive, aren't we?"

Peter and Jamie stood in the center of the courtyard for what Peter guessed was an hour. Two of the Partisans kept their weapons pointed at them. The rest of the Yugoslav troops were busy salvaging German weapons, gathering the garrison's papers, and casting suspicious looks at the prisoners in the courtyard whenever they spoke to each other. *At least we aren't blindfolded.*

Finally, a high-ranking officer entered the garrison. Some of the Partisans approached him and pointed toward Peter and Jamie. The man nodded, and as he walked toward them, two motorcycles drove through the breached wall into the courtyard. A tall, lean man stepped off the second one and removed his helmet to reveal dark hair and a narrow face. The man's blue eyes locked onto Peter and Jamie immediately and started for them, but the man on the first motorcycle caught his arm and motioned for him to stop. Krzysztof shoved the man's hand away and ignored the protests that followed in heavily accented English.

"You must wait for permission to approach them!"

Krzysztof didn't let the order slow his stride. He stopped a few feet away from them, beside the Yugoslav pukovnik, who was watching his approach with one eyebrow raised. "Where's Moretti?"

"He was sent to a POW camp yesterday," Jamie said.

Krzysztof's face relaxed. "When I didn't see him, I assumed . . ."

"No, the execution was to take place this morning, thirty seconds after the offensive began." Jamie smiled. "Your timing is impeccable."

"Why were you separated?" Krzysztof glanced at the other motorcyclist as the man joined the pukovnik and spoke to him in whispers.

"We convinced Major Hegel—the late commander here—that he was a shot-down airman. Peter and I had to admit we were commandos. How is the village? Hegel planned to machine-gun its inhabitants this morning."

Krzysztof frowned. "It's under Partisan control as of yesterday evening. They only machine-gunned a few of its inhabitants—including the men who hosted us."

"Marija?" Peter asked.

"She sneaked away with the newly widowed midwife, who has family in Rijeka. They headed there yesterday while I made an alliance with the Communists." Krzysztof managed to utter his last word without contempt in his voice, but Peter knew Krzysztof hated the Communists. It couldn't have been easy for him to join people he considered his enemy.

"Last I heard, our air forces were bombing Rijeka." Jamie said.

Krzysztof's frown deepened. "They didn't have anywhere else to go."

The Yugoslav pukovnik finished speaking with Krzysztof's escort and turned to Peter, Jamie, and Krzysztof. "It is with great honor that I welcome you as liaisons to the Yugoslav Fourth Army. We are always delighted to have representatives of the British government with us."

Peter clenched his teeth. He didn't mind being mistaken for a British commando, but something about the way the pukovnik welcomed them seemed to hint that they wouldn't be leaving anytime soon.

* * *

That night, the three of them were left alone in a tent.

"I owe you a headache, Peter," Krzysztof said.

Peter wasn't sure if he should apologize or not, so he changed the subject. "I think we're ready to be filled in. What happened after we left?" Peter and Jamie had asked questions earlier, but Krzysztof hadn't wanted to speak until they were alone.

"By the time I came to, word had spread around the village that the Germans knew about the Americans, and the Americans had disappeared. I told Marija good-bye and left for the garrison, hoping I could help. I ran into a Partisan scout who spoke German and tried to get him to move their attack up half a day, but his superior wouldn't budge. And they wouldn't let me out of their sight, not once I knew the plans for their offensive. They took over the village, executed the leaders, and conscripted most everyone else."

"And today?" Peter asked.

"Today they kept me with their headquarters staff. They *borrowed* our rifle to inspect it, then somehow lost it. I kept asking for updates about the attack and volunteering to help. They kept coming up with excuses. They think I'm British, and I haven't corrected them. I think they're hoping to use us for propaganda purposes."

"And the radio?" Jamie fingered his cane, which they'd found after the battle.

"Nothing yesterday at noon. They've had the radio since then and won't give it back."

Jamie cocked his head to the side and held up his hand. After a few seconds, he lowered it. "Someone stopped to listen to us, but they moved on."

Peter wasn't surprised the Partisans were spying on them. "So where to now? Rijeka?" Peter had promised Miloš he'd help Marija. If Tomislav had orders to kill Pukovnik Brajović's niece, Peter feared the other Partisans would as well. He wasn't sure how long Marija could keep her identity a secret, and she was technically a deserter—if the Partisans found out, she'd be executed for that, regardless of her family.

"I'll ask my escort if he'll let us leave," Krzysztof said. "He's strict with his orders, but seems to like the British."

Krzysztof left and returned a few minutes later with a young soldier. "This is Andro Pavlović."

Andro nodded his greeting. He was the man who'd had a motorcycle at the garrison.

"Do you speak English?" Peter asked.

Andro nodded again.

"We've been stranded here for months, and we're anxious to return to our base in Italy," Peter said. "Can you assist us?"

"I will speak with the pukovnik. Perhaps he can arrange something for tomorrow or the next day. He is very busy today."

The next day, there was no news, no permission, just excuses. The day after brought the same.

When they were alone again, Krzysztof shook his head in frustration at Andro's most recent response. He spoke quietly in case someone was spying on them again. "When I ran into that scout, I thought it was divine intervention—help exactly when I needed it. But I feel like a prisoner now."

"Have you heard their plans?" Peter asked.

"Isolate and take the German positions here. Gain control of the roads and move north."

"North," Jamie whispered. "That will take them to the Ingrid Line and to Rijeka."

Krzysztof nodded.

Peter glanced around and waited for a Partisan soldier to pass. "So if we are to be prisoners, at least we will be moving in the right direction."

CHAPTER THIRTY-ONE
BENDING THE RULES

Friday, March 23
Bletchley Park, England

MAREK ZIELINSKI WALKED INTO THE Nissen hut, where he normally worked twelve- to twenty-hour days breaking German codes. It was half past seven in the morning—a late start for him. Now that the German armies had been pushed back into Germany, they were using their telephones more and their Enigma encoding machines less. There was still plenty to do, but Marek had actually slept six hours the night before. It was an improvement over his normal nocturnal allowance from the previous five and a half years. In comparison, the sleep he'd received during the first year of his twin daughters' lives seemed a holiday.

The war was wearing on him. Since 1939 when he'd left Poland with his wife, son, and one of his three daughters, his black hair had turned gray and then white. His face was lined with new wrinkles, and even with the wartime rationing, he'd put on weight. Being stuck at a desk did that sort of thing to one's waistline.

The code-breaking center at Bletchley Park, about fifty miles north of London, was already full of workers. Some, like Marek, were university professors. Many were with the military. And there were the assorted chess players, linguists, and other men and women with a knack for breaking codes.

"Morning, Marek," Neville Farnsworth said.

"Good morning, Neville."

The young British Army captain standing in front of Farnsworth's desk tapped his foot as Farnsworth sipped his tea. "Sir, I believe we should forward this information to OSS."

Farnsworth shook his head. Marek watched, sympathetic. Farnsworth's job involved analyzing the decrypted information and determining where it should go. Occasionally, his job was easy: send the important information to Churchill or Eisenhower, file away the more obscure bits of information, such as weather reports for the eastern front. But usually his job was more complex, and not everyone agreed with his decisions.

"Marek," Farnsworth said, "would you mind explaining to this young man why I can't allow him to compromise our entire operation for the sake of men we can't do anything for anyway? He wants to inform the families of two executed field operatives that they've been killed."

Marek took the paper Farnsworth held out to him but didn't read it. "We must have the information from a source other than Enigma decrypts if we want to inform the families. Suppose the Germans found out what we'd told them? They'd know the only way we could know was by breaking their encryption, and then they'd change it, and we'd have to start over again. We'd be sure to miss out on something more vital than updating a few men's status from *missing* to *killed*."

"Thank you, Marek."

Marek handed the paper back to Farnsworth, glancing at it more closely. As Farnsworth's fingers grasped the edge of the page, Marek read the names: Lt. P. Eddy, OSS, and J. Nelson, SOE. Marek's son, Krzysztof, had trained with a Lieutenant Peter Eddy of OSS and with a James Nelson of SOE. It could be a coincidence, of course; Nelson was a common name, and Eddy didn't seem too unusual. Marek read the rest of the decrypted dispatch, and the note stating where it had come from: a German garrison in Croatia. The message had been sent four days ago on the evening of March nineteenth.

"Marek?"

Marek released the paper. "Sorry, Neville."

Marek went to his station, but his mind wasn't on his work. What had Eddy and Nelson been doing in Croatia in the first place? And where was Krzysztof? Marek had lost track of three of his four children: his oldest daughters had stayed in Poland with their husbands, and Krzysztof had been missing since September. Was he dead, shot with Eddy and Nelson? But if Krzysztof had been with them, why wasn't his name included in the dispatch?

Marek was staring at the wall instead of his work when a Royal Navy commander stepped in front of his desk. "Marek Zielinski?"

Marek nodded, wondering why a naval officer wanted to see him. He'd been working on Luftwaffe codes for years and had never been involved with the Kriegsmarine's encryption system.

"A word in private?"

Marek followed the commander to one of Bletchley Park's quiet areas.

"One of our ships in the Adriatic picked this up last Sunday. It landed on my desk yesterday."

Marek took the offered paper. Across the top it read:

Attention Marek Zielinski, GCCS, BP, England

The rest of the message was a series of seemingly random numbers and letters.

"I assume you are the only Marek Zielinski who works here?"

Marek nodded.

"Who would send a message directly to you?"

Marek didn't know many soldiers. He knew people in Poland—but he hadn't seen or heard from them in more than five years, and while some of them might suspect he'd gone into code-breaking work, none of them would know for sure. *And they wouldn't know about the government code and cypher school.* Would Krzysztof send him a message? He would know better than to use a header like that, wouldn't he? But what if he had no other option? "My son is with SOE. He's been missing since September."

"And the code?"

"I think I can break it if you'll let me try."

* * *

Marek only worked nine hours that day. He didn't own a car, so he took the train to Croxley Green and had a long walk to a small cottage on the edge of town. As he knocked on the door, the thought crossed his mind that he probably should have called first.

A young woman with blonde hair and a protruding abdomen answered the door. Marek glanced at her and guessed she would have her baby within the month.

"Can I help you?" she asked.

"I'm looking for Major Baker. Is he home?"

The woman nodded and turned from the door. "Wesley?" She turned back to Marek. "Would you like to come in?"

While Marek hesitated, a tall man appeared behind the woman. He dried his hands on a towel as his green eyes studied Marek, who extended his hand. "Major Baker? I'm Marek Zielinski. Could I have a few minutes of your time?"

"Perhaps a stroll down the lane?" Baker smiled at his wife and left her in the house as the two men set out. "You're Krzysztof's father, I presume? You have the same face."

Marek nodded. "When was the last time you saw my son?"

Baker didn't say anything.

"Please, Major, I need to know. The British government trusts me with some of their most important secrets. I think you can trust me as well."

Baker's hand reached up to his chin. "September 3. We'd just completed our mission and landed in Bari. After the debriefing, I escorted two of my wounded men home to England and left your son in a Bari hospital."

"Krzysztof was injured?"

"He'd been shot in the shoulder. Nothing to cause permanent damage if he received the right care."

Marek looked at the ground. "And since then?"

"I'm sorry, sir. Your son and several of my other men disappeared. I was back in Bari within a week, but there was no trace of them. Between new assignments, I've been investigating the man I think is behind their disappearance, but I still haven't discovered what happened to them."

"Your men, did they include an Eddy, a Nelson, and a Moretti?"

Baker's eyes widened. "How would you know that?"

Marek shrugged. "Were they with my son?"

"Yes."

Marek walked farther along the lane. "The man you suspect is responsible for their disappearance. A Major Kimby?"

Marek turned when he received no answer. Major Baker stood unmoving, his face pale. "Yes," he whispered. "How do you know?"

Marek considered Baker's question. Hadn't he just that morning explained to a young officer why information like that shouldn't be passed on?

"Please, sir." Baker's eyes pleaded with Marek. "I still feel responsible for the men. Jamie Nelson is a close friend and my wife's cousin."

Marek studied Baker's face. He'd brought a handwritten copy of a document from Bletchley Park. Taking it was illegal, but Marek wanted to know what had happened to his son. He'd already come to accept the possibility that he'd never see his twin daughters again or any of his siblings and their families, all the loved ones who'd stayed in Poland. Last month his youngest daughter's boyfriend, a Royal Air Force navigator, had been killed in action over Germany. Hadn't his family lost enough in this war? Couldn't he bend a few rules if it would help him find his son? Slowly, Marek pulled a paper from his pocket and handed it to Baker. It was the decoded message from the Royal Navy:

K. Zielinski, J. Nelson, P. Eddy, G. Moretti, and one civilian seek evacuation from Yugoslavia. Contact Major Wesley Baker, SOE, to arrange transport. Do not, repeat, do not inform Major Phillip Kimby, SOE. Will await reply noon and midnight British War Time.

Baker read the paper and glanced up, a hopeful look in his eyes. "When was this sent?"

"Sunday."

"Less than a week ago . . ." Baker's voice trailed off as he read the sheet again. "Has anyone tried to contact them?"

"No. I received the message this morning, and it was encrypted."

"So Kimby doesn't know?" Baker asked.

"No one knows except you and me. It's from Krzysztof. He and I are the only ones who have the key to this code. I told the navy I couldn't read it. I lied, but I want my son back."

"I'll get a radio. We can talk to him at midnight." Baker smiled. "And get a plane to them within a few days, I imagine."

Marek frowned. "It might not be so simple. I also received less hopeful news this morning. Eddy and Nelson were executed a few days ago at a German garrison in Croatia."

Baker's face grew white. "You're sure?" His inquiry was soft, barely audible.

Marek nodded. "Lieutenant P. Eddy, OSS, and J. Nelson, SOE. The message was sent Monday night. The execution was scheduled for Tuesday morning."

Baker was quiet for a few moments, staring past Marek. "Poor Jamie. And poor Peter." Baker shook his head again. "And no news on your son or Sergeant Moretti or the civilian?"

"No."

Baker nodded. "Well, perhaps they are still alive, then. But I wonder why they only mentioned one civilian. I evacuated two after our last mission, and they've both disappeared, the same day as the others. The Ionescus. I suppose one of them must have died."

"Iuliana Ionescu?" Marek asked.

"Yes."

"She's not with them."

Baker seemed surprised. "How do you know her name? And how do you know her location?"

Marek removed an envelope from his pocket. "I am not in the habit of reading my son's mail, but I made an exception when I received this last month. Perhaps you can explain it. The letter was for my son but delivered to me."

Marek listened as Baker read it out loud:

Dearest Krzysztof,

I hope you'll receive this letter because if you do, it will mean you've returned and you're safe. I'm sorry I couldn't meet you in England. I wanted to, but Major Kimby broke his promises. Anatolie and I are being held in a camp for people undesirable to the ruling authority. I thought long and hard about whether I should tell you where I am, but I'm afraid if I did, you'd try to come for me, and you might get killed. It's not that I don't want to be rescued. Especially when I consider Anatolie's future, I'm tempted to beg for your help. But I can't ask you to do any more than you already have for me.

I've been in love before, so I know what it feels like, and I know I'm in love with you. And because I love you, I hope you'll soon forget me. Maybe the Communists will honor their promises and allow free elections in Poland, and you'll be able to return to your homeland. But I doubt that will happen. And maybe I'll find a way to make it to England someday, when the war is over. But I doubt that too.

I'll think about you every day and pray that you won't do the same.

Iuliana

"Who is she?" Marek asked.

"She's a Romanian widow. She helped us on our last mission, then disappeared once we reached Bari. I've tried to track her down without success."

"What went on between her and my son?"

Baker's mouth pulled into a smile. "The letter explained that, didn't it?"

"The letter says she loves him. Does he love her?"

"Mr. Zielinski, I am not sure how your son acts at home, but at work, he is extremely quiet. I've not heard him say anything about his heart, but yes, I think he loves her."

Marek took the letter back, wondering if his son would have the chance to read it. "So you are missing four men and two civilians. Eddy and Nelson are dead." Marek held the letter up. "Iuliana and her son were alive in January but not with the others. Moretti and my son were alive as recently as Sunday, as was a third civilian. Somewhere in Yugoslavia."

Baker stared at his cottage. "Mr. Zielinski, I need to tell my wife I'll be away for a few days. Then I'm heading to Bari as quickly as I can. Would you like to come with me?"

Chapter Thirty-Two
LEARNING TO SING AGAIN

Monday, March 26
Bari, Italy

GENEVIEVE WALKED PAST THE REC room on her way home from work and heard the slightly out-of-tune piano. It was a simple song, but the artist was not only hitting the notes correctly but also infusing the piece with extra emotion. She stepped in to see who was playing and was pleasantly surprised to see Rick in front of the upright Feurich, his crutch leaning against the piano's side. She walked behind him and glanced at the music. It wasn't a simple piece after all, but he was limited to playing only the right-hand portion.

"That's nice, Rick. I didn't know you played."

He smiled when he saw her. "I used to play better. I haven't had much of a chance to practice the last few years." He motioned toward the bench, and she sat next to him.

"I used to play a little, but my brother sold our piano to pay taxes when my father died. I was so angry with him." She wished she could go back and apologize for being so short-sighted. She'd been only thirteen, but she should have understood. She missed her brother. She shook her head, trying to overcome the sudden pang of emotion as she remembered how hard he'd worked to keep a roof over her head. "There was a piano in a place I lived last summer. I thought I'd start playing again, but I didn't stay long enough to practice more than a couple of times."

Rick played a few notes. "Too busy spying?"

"Something like that."

"My mom always wanted me to keep playing. After I enlisted, she started sending sheet music with her letters. I've got a huge packet of it now.

Hauled it all across the US during training, then over here." He leafed through a pile of songs, a little clumsily with his one hand, then smiled as he pulled a sheet out. "You ever heard this one?"

He played the top hand of "Over There."

"Something about the Yanks coming and not leaving until the war's over. Appropriate. Do you know how long you'll be here?" Genevieve asked. Hospital patients who wouldn't return to active duty were usually shipped home once they were stabilized.

"Did you know Dr. Bolliger used to specialize in amputations?"

Genevieve shook her head. "No."

"I'll probably stick around longer than usual. Don't know that I'll find a better doctor to work with back in the States—and I don't want to go home until I can walk and get dressed by myself." As he spoke, the upbeat song he played somehow shifted into a more haunting version.

"May I look through your music?" she asked, trying to distract him.

"Sure."

She leafed through the choices, surprised at the variety. She paused when she reached a portion of Bizet's *Carmen*, arranged for the piano. "This one always gets stuck in my head."

Rick took it from her and arranged it in front of him. "Sing along."

"I'm not really in the mood for singing."

"I'll let you in on a little secret, Genevieve. Some mornings when I wake up, I'm not really in the mood for living."

Genevieve stared at him and felt her eyes tearing up. "I'm sorry, Rick." She thought about all he was going through—about how many friends had died when his plane was damaged and how difficult it must be for him to lose a limb and suddenly be dependent on others for simple things like cutting his food and buttoning his shirt—but that didn't mean things wouldn't get better. "It must be so hard, Rick, but you have a lot to live for. Your family loves you, and you're smart and brave and self-disciplined and funny—"

"And permanently crippled." He played a few mournful notes. They weren't from the piece in front of him; they were from his head.

She reached out and put her hand on the stub of his left arm. He let his playing taper off. "So you're just putting on a brave face when I see you in the hospital?" she asked.

Rick played a few random notes, staring at his hand. "That's the trick, I guess. Some days you don't feel much like living, so you pretend you feel differently. And sometimes, by the end of the day, living doesn't seem so hard."

"Then I suppose I should sing, even if I'm not in the mood for singing."

Rick ran his hand along the keys. "I don't want to make you sing."

"No, Rick, you're right." She thought of how she'd been all autumn, all winter: competent but sad, busy on the outside but hurting on the inside. "I need to learn how to be happy again. Singing might be a good place to start."

Rick forced a wan smile. "All right, we'll give it our best shot, the two of us, pretending everything is just fine."

Rick played the treble half of the music, and Genevieve sang along, softly at first, then with more confidence. She knew the words wouldn't spontaneously spring from her lips over the next week like lyrics had when she was younger or when she was with Peter, but as she finished, she did feel better.

"Are you sure you want to be a nurse? You could probably make it as an opera singer."

Genevieve recognized Nathan's voice and looked up to see him leaning against the piano.

"Naw, not unless she gains a few hundred pounds. Don't most operas involve fat ladies?" Rick asked as he dragged his fingers across the keyboard, causing a quick descent in the notes.

"You might be right, Rick. I haven't seen many scrawny opera stars."

"Gentlemen, I don't think it's proper for either of you to discuss my weight in front of me."

Nathan smiled. "Would it be proper for me to take you to supper tonight?" He glanced at Rick as if he was just as concerned about getting Rick's permission as he was about getting Genevieve's.

"She's all yours. I've been playing for a couple hours, and my hand's tired. And if she is going to sing in the opera someday, you should fatten her up a bit." Rick gathered his music and slid it into a bag. "Remember, Genevieve, sometimes you have to sing again before you're ready." Rick pushed himself to his feet, slung his bag over his left arm, and gripped his crutch with his right hand. "Have fun, you two."

Rick smiled at them and left. He still had an obvious limp, but the accident had been only two weeks prior. He'd get better with time; she hoped that would be true not just for his physical abilities but also for his spirit and his emotions.

Genevieve turned to Nathan, and he helped her to her feet. "I hope you're hungry," he said. "I discovered a little restaurant last week. Doesn't look like much when you walk in, but the food's wonderful."

"I am hungry, actually, now that I think about it."

Nathan chuckled as he held the rec room's door open for her. "You do that a lot."

"Do what?"

"Get so involved in what you're doing that you don't stop to take care of yourself."

Genevieve turned toward him. "So do you and Dr. Lombardelli and Vittoria."

"Sometimes I think it's a wonder we don't all work ourselves sick. Especially in the field hospitals."

"I always thought you'd be good in a field hospital."

Nathan looked away.

"What?"

He shrugged. "I was right behind the frontlines for almost a year. And I did all right, except when I was asked to operate on German POWs. I know I should see them as patients, not enemies, but it was hard. I have a younger brother who's been in a German POW camp a few years now. I would start thinking about him, and I'd find myself pulling stitches a little too tight and being rough with the bandages. I didn't kill anyone or anything, and I didn't quit. But when the chance to come to Bari came along, I thought I'd take it. The airmen don't bring home many German prisoners."

"And the workload? I imagine it was exhausting?"

Nathan rubbed his eyes at the memory. "When the army was on the offensive, I would go days on only a couple hours' sleep. How do you tell a man who's bleeding to death that he needs to wait until your next shift?"

They entered the restaurant, a dark, smoky room filled with mismatched tables and chairs, American officers occupying half of them. Genevieve ordered the same thing as Nathan but declined the offered wine. Before long, the waiter placed a steaming plate of pasta in front of her.

"Do you hear much from your brother?" she asked. She and Nathan talked frequently at work but rarely about personal subjects.

Nathan shook his head. "Just the Red Cross postcards. He can't say much on those, and we've only received three since his plane crashed. But I think the war will be over soon, and then he'll be back. Speaking of the war ending, what are your plans?"

"I'll try to get into nursing school."

"Where?"

"I'm not sure yet."

"Genevieve, the army crossed the Rhine two and half weeks ago. It's probably time to decide."

She twisted noodles around her fork as she wondered what she would do. She wanted to marry Peter, but what if he didn't return? Would she go to the US or back to France? She thought of Rick, of how he'd lost friends and colleagues, then his hand and his independence. Yet he was soldiering on, and that was what she'd have to do if the war took Peter from her just as it had taken her brother and sister-in-law. But where?

"The University of Michigan has a good nursing program. Have you heard of it?"

Genevieve shook her head.

"I worked at a hospital in Ann Arbor before the war. It was just for a year, after I finished school and before the US got involved in the war, but I think I'll go back. Have you thought about going to the US? My father has a friend in Congress, so if you need help with immigration, I can pull some strings for you."

"That's a kind offer. Thank you." She considered telling him she had a visa, but he might ask how she'd received it. She wasn't supposed to disclose the details of her Marseilles assignment or that a US visa had been part of her compensation.

"You'll be a good nurse." Nathan smiled at her over the top of his wine glass. "You're doing a good job with Rick."

Genevieve looked at her plate, still half full of food. "I think he's helping me more than I'm helping him."

"Amputations are hard."

"Rick said that was your specialty before the war."

Nathan nodded. "I'm sure there will be plenty of work in that area after the war as well." He shook his head. "That sounds callous. I am grateful to have an abundance of prospective work, but it's more than that. Men like Rick need help adjusting, and that's something I can do. And something you can do. Maybe Rick needs to help someone more than he needs to be helped. Feel like he's still of use to someone."

"Of course he's of use to someone. Just because he's missing a hand doesn't mean he's not good for anything—"

Nathan held his hand out. "I know that, and you know that. But like any man recovering from severe, permanent wounds, Rick will have his doubts from time to time. So I'm glad he has you for a friend. Although if it were to go beyond friendship, I might be jealous."

Genevieve's cheeks grew hot, and she tried to stop blushing but didn't think she had much success. "Surely a doctor like you wouldn't be jealous of an injured ball-turret gunner?"

Nathan smiled, his teeth perfect, his blue eyes reflecting candlelight. "Maybe, maybe not."

* * *

Rick was in the rec room again the next day when Genevieve finished her shift. She listened to him play a few lines, then went and sat beside him. "How are you, Rick?"

He smiled slightly, playing "Over the Rainbow" with his right hand. "I'm all right. I got this from my mom today." He motioned with his head toward the music. "Guess she sent it before she heard about my hand."

She listened to him play through the piece a few times, getting better with each repetition.

"How was the food last night?"

The mischief in Rick's grin reminded Genevieve of Peter and his smile. But Rick's mouth didn't leave her breathless, just curious. "Your smile makes me think you're up to something. I'd be eager to hear if you had any part in yesterday's supper date."

Rick shrugged. "When he was fitting me for a prosthesis, he mentioned he had his eye on you."

Genevieve studied Rick's face, not sure if he was serious or if he was teasing her.

"I didn't tell him you're a spy. I figured it's not my place to share your secrets, and that OSS man who debriefed me made some pretty serious threats. I know you've got that boyfriend, but it's been awhile since you heard from him, hasn't it?"

She nodded.

"I'm not trying to push you or anything, but, well, what if he doesn't come back? You don't want to be alone for the rest of your life, do you?"

Genevieve blinked away a few tears. With her family dead and Peter missing, there were days when she did indeed feel completely alone.

"I'm sorry, I didn't mean to make you cry. I've just been thinking about that a lot lately—going home and getting on with life." Rick played a few more notes, then gave up. "Who am I going to date back in the States? This war has chewed me up and spat me back out, mangled and wretched. The girls back home might feel sorry for me, but they won't understand me. Maybe I'd feel more comfortable with someone who needs a little fixing just like I do. Does that make sense? Someone who's seen the type of things I've seen so she understands where I've been. And I figure someone like that will need me as much as I need her."

"You're not broken, Rick, and I'm sure there's someone out there for you."

"I hope so. Do you remember that night you were chasing your Fascist spy, and I pretended to kiss you?"

She nodded.

"I realized your eyes remind me of my little sister, and I had absolutely no desire to kiss you for real."

Genevieve laughed.

"Well, I'm glad I haven't hurt your feelings. But I was thinking about that. Maybe what I need is someone who's a little like you but not you. And I'll teach her how to sing again, and she won't mind that I can only use one hand to help her."

Genevieve ran her fingers lightly over the piano keys. "I'm supposed to be cheering you up, but you keep cheering me up instead."

Rick began playing *Carmen*. "What happened to that spy you were chasing?"

"He was planning to blow up a building. We helped stop him and saved about twenty lives, so thank you for your help that night. But he got away."

Rick hit the wrong note and quickly looked at his hand. "Well, if he hasn't been caught yet, I'm sure he'll get rounded up eventually."

She hoped Rick was right. Ercolani scared her more than most of the men she'd worked against, and the reasoning behind it bothered her. She'd seen ruthlessness in his eyes but also a hint of tenderness when they'd heard the woman scream. Ruthless but with a few soft spots, just like her brother, only Ercolani was fighting against the Allies, not for them. She hoped he wasn't as good as Jacques, because if he was, she didn't think she could win.

"Are you in the mood to sing today?" Rick asked, tilting his head toward the music.

"I'm closer than I was yesterday, so play away, and I'll sing along."

As she finished the song, Lombardelli walked into the room. "When you have a minute, will you come see me?" He had a serious expression on his face, making Genevieve worry that Ercolani was back and that he'd succeeded in sabotaging something.

She nodded.

"He doesn't look very happy," Rick said when Lombardelli left.

"No, he doesn't."

Rick gave her a sideways glance. "If he wants you to be a spy again, be careful, all right?"

"I will. You'll be here again tomorrow?"

Rick smiled. "Not shipping off anytime soon."

"Thank you for the music, Rick. I'll see you later."

Genevieve found Lombardelli in his office with an older man in civilian clothing, an American army captain, and Major Baker. They all had gloomy expressions on their faces. Rather than introducing her to everyone, Lombardelli nodded to Baker, who took Genevieve's arm and led her back into the hallway.

"Miss Olivier, I'm sorry to be the one to tell you this." He hesitated for a moment. "Last week, Lieutenant Eddy was executed at a German garrison."

It took a minute for Baker's words to hit her. "Peter's dead?" Genevieve was too shocked to do anything other than stare at Baker, understanding what he'd said but having trouble comprehending it. Then tears stung her eyes, and emotion choked her throat. "I need to be alone," she whispered.

"I understand," Baker said, his voice compassionate.

Her vision was blurry as she left the hospital. By the time she reached the spot where Peter had told her good-bye, she could barely breathe. Somehow, she made it to her tent and fell onto her cot as sobs shook her body. How could anyone kill Peter? Didn't they understand how wonderful he was . . . and how much she loved him? Would she never feel his touch again, never hear his laugh or see his smile? Peter meant everything to her. What would she do without him?

CHAPTER THIRTY-THREE
DESPERATE DECISIONS

Wednesday, March 28

GENEVIEVE HAD A HEADACHE THE next day. Crying did that to her. But the ache in her head was dwarfed by the ache in her heart. She walked to the hospital through a chilly morning breeze, feeling completely alone.

She'd lived through difficult things before: the death of her parents, her sister-in-law's murder, attempted rape by a German soldier. Her brother had been there to grieve with her, and then when her brother died, it was Peter who had held her until she'd run out of tears, combing his gentle fingers through her hair as he tried to comfort her. Peter had been so kind, so patient despite his own injuries. He had been exactly what she'd needed.

She thought back to the last time she'd sobbed uncontrollably, when she'd killed Rottenführer Weiss. Peter had been away on assignment, but she'd received a letter from him the day after, reminding her she wasn't alone and that her dear friend Peter still had faith in her.

There would be no letter from Peter to cheer her up this time and no reunion, and that made this heartache worse than the others. She knew exactly what Rick meant: living hardly seemed worth it anymore.

She completed her shift, moving mechanically from patient to patient. She tried to lose herself in her work, but the hospital contained too many young Americans. They all reminded her of Peter.

As she was leaving, Lombardelli called her into his office. He shut the door when she stepped in and pulled her into an embrace. "I'm so sorry. Are you all right?"

The tears started before she could open her mouth to answer, and she sobbed into his shoulder. He didn't say anything for a few minutes, letting her cry.

"I got your shirt all wet," she said when she calmed down enough to speak. "I'm sorry."

"You don't have to apologize for being human or for being in love." He helped her into a chair. "But I'm worried about you. You've been on the melancholy side since I met you, but you'd finally started to come out of it. What will happen to you now?"

"I don't know. I can't think of anything right now except Peter and that he's gone. I—" She broke off, emotion choking her voice again. "Peter's friends, are they dead as well?"

Lombardelli sat behind his desk. "One was executed with him. The two civilians were alive in January, but their current status and location are unknown. The last two were alive a week and a half ago and sent out a radio message. The other men in my office yesterday are trying to contact them, and believe me, they're motivated to succeed. One of the men is a code expert, and his son is among the missing. The other is from the Fifteenth Air Force. Major Baker pulled him in because he doesn't work anywhere near Kimby. But they haven't received an answer."

"And Major Baker?"

"He's discouraged. I told him to go home. His wife is expecting a baby soon, and Mr. Zielinski and Captain Anderson can take care of everything here if they contact any survivors."

Despite the sharp pain she felt at Peter's death, she found some sympathy for Mr. Zielinski's hoping to hear from his son and hearing only silence. "Who was executed with Peter?"

"James Nelson," Lombardelli said.

"Corporal Nelson?"

One side of Lombardelli's face lifted into a slight smile. "He was a civilian, but I've heard of him posing as military—from corporal to colonel, and not just in the British Army."

"You knew Nelson?"

Lombardelli nodded. "I was in Venice before I came here. Wesley Baker and James Nelson were there too, running a large spy ring. I was with OSS, so we interacted from time to time. Last summer I heard they were about to be arrested, and I warned them, and the three of us left."

"How did you find out?"

Lombardelli glanced at the photos on his desk. "An acquaintance, one of my son-in-law's friends, let the information slip. OVRA knew there were British spies in Venice, and someone pinpointed one of their duped sources, so OVRA—Ercolani, to be precise—was going to question their source and arrest the agents using her."

"Who named the source?"

Lombardelli shook his head. "I don't know. I'd have to ask my son-in-law's friend, but he's still behind the frontlines. He was scheduled for transfer back to Trieste." Lombardelli grew quiet, tapping a pen on his desk.

Genevieve recognized that look. "You've thought of something?"

Lombardelli nodded. "An OSS man is looking for someone to send to Trieste. He wants information for the military, and I was considering the assignment before Major Baker returned."

"You were?" Genevieve was surprised. Trieste remained in Nazi hands, and Lombardelli still had work in Bari. "Why?"

"Because my daughter married a man from Trieste. His family's there, and that's where she plans to settle when the war ends and her husband is released. I don't want my grandchildren raised in a Communist city, so it's tempting to do what I can to help the British get there before the Yugoslav Partisans do."

"She's all the family you have now, isn't she?" Lombardelli's wife had died before the war. Genevieve studied the picture of Vittoria and Lombardelli's son, wondering how Vittoria had gotten over Lorenzo's death. But she hadn't really recovered. Vittoria still bore the scars of heartache, just as Genevieve feared she would even when Peter had been dead for decades.

"Just her and her children," Lombardelli said. "And now I might have a new reason to go to Trieste—to find out who put Ercolani on Nelson and Baker's trail."

"Will it matter now?"

Lombardelli set his pen on the desk. "Maybe. Depends on the answer I receive. Major Kimby—Captain Kimby at the time—worked with an SOE group focused on northern Italy that summer."

"You think it was Kimby?" Genevieve hated Kimby for sending Peter away, but she doubted a British officer would purposely give away his fellow agents.

Lombardelli shrugged. "He knew who they were and who most of their sources were. Even if I found proof, it wouldn't bring back Nelson or your Peter. But it could prevent Kimby from causing the same type of mischief again."

"Can I go with you?" Genevieve couldn't stand the thought of staying in Bari, walking by the places Peter had kissed her, seeing all the other

Americans in the same uniform, trying to force a happy face when her heart was in constant pain.

Lombardelli hesitated. "You'd be useful. The work would consist of gathering information for the military. And tracking down my son-in-law's old classmate."

"Then I'll come."

"No, I don't want you to jump into this without thinking it through. Trieste will be dangerous, more dangerous than Bari. And there's no guarantee of success. We could end up stuck in the Communist zone or in the middle of a battle."

"Could you manage without me?"

Lombardelli leaned forward, putting a hand over hers. "I'd do my best. And if I fail, few people will mourn me. I'm getting old and don't have many years left anyway. I'm not much of a surgeon anymore. My hands shake; that's why I've been assigning surgeries to Dr. Bolliger. You, on the other hand, are only twenty years old. You have your whole life ahead of you."

"No one will mourn me, Dr. Lombardelli. Almost everyone I know is dead."

"I think you are mistaken, Genevieve. I know this isn't the best time to bring it up, but I've come to see you almost like a daughter. Professionally, I want you to come with me. But as your friend and mentor, I don't want you to risk it. Maybe it's time for you to retire from espionage. The war's almost over, and you've fought valiantly to end it. At least talk to Nathan before you decide what you want to do."

"No, let's not drag poor Nathan into any of this." Genevieve shook her head. "Don't you remember the car bomb?"

Lombardelli squeezed her hand. "I'm not trying to recruit Nathan. But I want you to talk to him because I think he can give you a reason to stay."

* * *

Genevieve didn't sleep well that night. She spent much of it praying and more of it crying. As the night progressed, she felt increasingly sure she should go to Trieste with Lombardelli. She packed away Peter's letters, his Purple Heart, the Book of Mormon he'd given her, and her few family photos, knowing she couldn't take any of them with her—if discovered, they'd blow her cover. She fingered the necklace her sister-in-law had given her when she was thirteen and decided to leave it around her neck. It wouldn't connect her to anyone still living.

She hadn't gone to see Nathan or Rick the night before, but Nathan found her as she was leaving Lombardelli's office the next afternoon.

"I'll get the car ready, Genevieve," Lombardelli said. He'd made all the preparations through OSS that morning.

Nathan glanced at Genevieve's bag. "What's going on? You looked like you were about to cry all day yesterday, and you missed your shift this morning. You've got me worried sick."

She looked at his shoulder, not wanting to meet his eyes. "Dr. Lombardelli is leaving, and I'm going with him."

"You're what?" He hooked a finger under her chin and pulled her face up to meet his gaze. "Look, Genevieve, I'm probably not supposed to say this, but I think Dr. Lombardelli's a spy. He's on our side, but whatever he's up to is dangerous."

"Yes, Dr. Lombardelli works for American intelligence. As do I."

Nathan's jaw dropped. "You're a spy?" His words were barely audible.

"Rick can verify it if you doubt me."

Nathan shook his head slightly, surprised. "I don't care. It's time for you to quit. I can tell you love medicine. Stay here where you'll be safe."

Genevieve shook her head. She didn't think Nathan would understand the consistent urge she felt to leave Bari, and she was too tired to explain it to him. Even she questioned if it was a spiritual prompting or just something her mind had made up. Why did she want to go to Trieste? She didn't have a simple answer. She wanted to help Lombardelli, and she wanted to save the city from Communist rule. But most of all, she wanted closure. If Kimby was behind Peter's death and Baker and Nelson's betrayal, she didn't want him to get away with it. Trieste might offer only straws to grasp at, but grasping at straws was better than staying in Bari and being suffocated by grief. "If it's dangerous, there will be people who need me."

Nathan stepped closer and put his hands on her shoulders. "Genevieve, there are people who need you here too."

"I think the rest of the staff can manage without me. Casualties have been tapering for months."

"I can't manage without you," he said. She looked into his blue eyes. They were striking, enchanting, the color of the sky on a clear day. "Please stay, Genevieve."

She pulled away. "I need to go."

His lips turned downward, and his eyelids tensed in pain. "Why won't you stay with me?" Genevieve looked away, thinking of Peter. Nathan read her mind. "He's dead, Genevieve. You have to let him go. Chasing his memory all across Europe won't bring him back. But I'm here, and I'm alive, and I love you. I will do everything I can to keep you safe and make you happy for the rest of your life. Don't go with Dr. Lombardelli. Stay here and marry me."

Genevieve stared at him. *Marriage?* They talked all the time, but their friendship wasn't nearly that serious. Nathan was handsome. He was smart. He was good. At that moment, a significant part of her wanted to believe she could be happy with him. But could she settle for an ordinary marriage when she'd been so close to one that would have been extraordinary?

Nathan saw her thinking, pulled her to him, and kissed her. It had been such a long time since Peter had held her—it felt good to be cradled in strong, adoring arms again. She'd missed it. Nathan's kiss was skillful and sincere, his offer tempting. A marriage to Nathan could be almost happy. She could almost love him. And maybe they could almost overcome their religious and cultural differences. She gently pushed him away, breathing rapidly and still tasting the tobacco on his breath.

Her mind cleared. Even with Peter dead, she couldn't marry Nathan. She didn't love him. And with Peter and her family gone, religion was the most important thing in Genevieve's life. She doubted a marriage to anyone who didn't share her religious convictions could turn out to be anything but miserable. "I'm sorry, Nathan." She hated how much she was hurting him. "I can't marry you. I'm going with Dr. Lombardelli." She blinked away her tears and turned to grab her things.

"Please reconsider, Genevieve. You can take as much time as you need. I'd be a good husband to you."

She looked at his eyes begging her to stay. Over his shoulder, she saw several of the nurses. Genevieve could tell from their expressions that they thought she was crazy to refuse his proposal. She grabbed her bag and fought back sobs as she stepped toward the door. "Good-bye, Nathan. I'm sorry I hurt you." She turned and walked away.

She heard his footsteps following her. "I know he saved your life, Genevieve, and that naturally created a strong emotional bond. But eventually that bond will fade and life will become ordinary again. You should not confuse gratitude with love."

Genevieve paused and thought about Nathan's words. She'd fallen in love with Peter before he'd rescued her, during ordinary tasks: laundry, weeding, milking the cows. She was grateful he'd saved her life, but more than that, she'd loved him through days that were in turn mundane, horrifying, and thrilling. She could have loved Peter through anything. She began walking again because Nathan was wrong.

"Your American hero is not coming back, Genevieve. Stop deluding yourself."

She didn't look back. "That doesn't change my decision."

"Are you going with Dr. Lombardelli so you can join him in the afterlife?"

"I don't plan to die there, Nathan," Genevieve said quietly. "Nor do I plan to stay here and marry someone I don't love."

His voice was softer when he spoke again from only a few feet away. "Please, Genevieve, you would come to love me."

She hadn't thought leaving would be so difficult. She did care for Nathan but not enough. Still, she was in anguish as she left him. Afraid to say anything longer than a syllable, she gave him her final answer. "No."

Genevieve walked out the door, and to her relief, Nathan didn't follow.

* * *

Five minutes later, Rick Shelton found her. She heard the rhythm of his cane—at a quicker pace than usual—and turned as he called her name.

"Dr. Bolliger told me you're leaving. He wants me to stop you."

"No, Rick, not you too, please." Genevieve bit her lip.

Rick dropped his cane and placed his good hand on her shoulder, looking directly into her eyes. "I don't want to fight with you. Just tell me you're doing this for the right reasons, 'cause if you aren't, the doc's right, you shouldn't go."

Genevieve looked away from Rick's hazel eyes while she considered his question—the same question she'd pondered the night before and all morning. "Dr. Lombardelli needs my help. I know a thing or two about the Communists, and if Dr. Lombardelli thinks he can spare a quarter million people from Communist tyranny, I'm eager to help him."

"Promise me it's not a suicide mission."

"Dr. Lombardelli has his grandchildren to live for. And I'm not planning to throw my life away."

Rick nodded slowly. "You be careful. Remember, you've got a lot to live for."

Genevieve noted the smile on Rick's face. "That advice seems a little familiar."

Rick's smile turned to a grin. "I figured you have to listen to your own advice. Come on, I'll walk you to Dr. Lombardelli's car. But promise you'll take care of yourself. And when the war's over, you've got to learn to sing again."

"I promise, Rick."

* * *

Genevieve felt her stomach lurch as the small Lysander took off from the OSS airstrip in Brindisi. *Flying can't be any worse than Lombardelli's driving*, she told herself. But it took her stomach several minutes to agree.

It was a British plane, with a British pilot. Small and slow, Lysanders had proven too vulnerable for use in normal combat. But they were ideal for sneaking behind enemy lines and landing on small airstrips.

She and Lombardelli were assigned to travel overland through Venezia Giulia province toward Trieste, locate key military installations, minefields, and barracks, and report their locations to the British Eighth Army via their portable radio. When they reached Trieste, they'd report on local defenses, and then they'd find the man from Venice who'd told Lombardelli of Baker and Nelson's impending arrest.

Lombardelli raised his voice over the sound of the plane's single engine. "When we land, the pilot doesn't want to stay on the ground long. You exit first, and I'll hand you the gear."

Genevieve nodded and squeezed her eyes shut as the plane descended, hoping she wasn't about to lose the meal she'd eaten before takeoff. When the plane hit the grass runway and slowed to a stop, she jumped to the ground and reached for the first bag of equipment, then the second. Lombardelli joined her on the ground, and they ran to the shelter of some nearby trees as the Lysander taxied to the end of the runway and turned for takeoff, leaving Genevieve and Lombardelli alone in the quiet countryside twenty kilometers west of Trieste.

As the noise from the Lysander's engine faded, the weight of what she'd volunteered to do hit Genevieve with full force: she was back in Nazi territory, where she would have to lie and might have to kill. She took a few deep breaths. *Give the military the right information, and you'll save a few lives. Find out who blew Baker's cover, and prevent the same man from hurting anyone else.*

CHAPTER THIRTY-FOUR
NO ESCAPE FROM THE PAST

Monday, April 9
Independent State of Croatia

MARIJA SANK ONTO A FALLEN log when Nada, the midwife from the village near Bihac, halted their trek. Marija hated being the slowest in the group of four refugees from the village, but she hated the thought of losing her baby even more. Miloš and Nada had both advised her not to push herself. She felt a stab of pain as she thought of Miloš. It seemed so wrong that he was dead. Rather than letting herself cry, she remembered the way he'd always brushed aside her excuses on why they couldn't get married. Why had it taken her so long to realize he'd always been right?

Nada sat next to her. "How are you?"

"Tired."

"Are you hungry?"

"If there is food to eat, I won't turn it down. If there is no food to eat, I won't miss it." Marija still felt sick most mornings, but she'd eat for her baby.

Nada handed her a piece of bread. "We're almost to Rijeka. My sister's house is near the harbor. I expect we'll spend the night there tomorrow."

Marija nodded. Nada had already told her all about her sister's home, more than once. She'd also told Krzysztof its location before he'd left to save the others. Marija wondered if he'd succeeded or if the foreigners were dead, despite all the sacrifices she and Miloš had made for them.

A snapping twig drew both their heads around. Marija caught her breath as twelve Partisan soldiers approached their group.

Nada explained how they'd been forced to abandon their village when threatened by a Nazi reprisal. She wisely omitted the Partisans' role in her husband's death and their flight from the village. "We're joining family in Rijeka."

The group's leader asked Nada questions about German soldiers in the area, then motioned for them to be on their way. Nada nodded, and Marija got to her feet—tired or not, she was leaving before the Partisans changed their minds. As she stepped away from the log, one of the soldiers reached out and grabbed her arm.

"Marija Brajović?"

Marija held back a gasp. That wasn't her name anymore; she was Marija Colić, but that didn't matter. She'd been identified. She recognized the soldier from the village where she'd grown up. She didn't remember his name—he was several years younger than her, a Croatian Catholic boy with older sisters. She'd last seen him the day the Ustaše came, peeking from behind the curtains of his home as the Serb villagers were herded to the town square. Knowing it was pointless to lie and hoping this group of Partisans wasn't seeking her the way Tomislav's unit had been, she nodded.

"You survived the massacre?" the boy asked.

"Yes."

"None of the Serbs survived."

Marija tried to explain. "They thought I was dead."

He shook his head. "No, I saw them checking corpses. One of my friends—" He broke off, his face tight. "The machine gun only hit his shoulder, so they finished him with a bayonet."

Marija had always thought the Serbs in her village were the only victims that day. But as she studied the soldier's face, she realized that he, at least, was still haunted by what the Ustaše had done to his neighbors.

"If you survived, you must have collaborated with them," he said.

"No. I was left for dead. I made no deals with the Nazis."

The boy from her village frowned; he didn't seem convinced.

The patrol's leader had been listening to their conversation. "We'll take her with us, see what the kapetan has to say."

Marija knew what that meant. She wasn't a Nazi collaborator— only one of their victims—but in the twisted Communist mind, might surviving rape be so close to collaboration as to merit the same penalty? Even if they overlooked her survival, there was her uncle's work as a Chetnik and her desertion from Tomislav's unit. She'd promised Miloš she'd do everything in her power to survive, but the Partisans had three reasons to kill her. How could she survive that?

* * *

Two days later, Marija's fate was decided. They hadn't labeled her a deserter or a collaborator, but being Pukovnik Stoyan Brajović's niece was all the reason they needed to send her to a prison camp. She'd receive a trial there, but its outcome was obvious. She was related to a Chetnik leader, and under Tito's rule, that was a crime. That she'd survived her village's destruction, married a Chetnik doctor, and deserted the army were aggravating circumstances.

I know you exist, Holy Father. And I know you can hear my prayer. I'm not scared of death, but I told Miloš I'd do my best to survive. Please help me keep my promise. As she finished her prayer, Marija felt a hand on her shoulder, reaching through the barbed-wire fence that held her and several other prisoners. "Nada?"

The old woman nodded. "Will they release you now?"

Marija shook her head. "No, they're sending me to Bisevo for trial."

It was dark, but Marija could see the sadness in Nada's face. "I'm sorry, Marija."

"When I see your husband, I'll be sure to tell him hello for you."

Marija hadn't meant to make Nada cry, but she saw the old woman's tears. "You're too good for Bisevo, Marija. I'm so sorry."

* * *

Nada's warning haunted Marija for days. What was so horrible about Bisevo? She was certain the Communists would kill her eventually. Was death on an island any worse than death on the mainland? Maybe it was one death too many for Nada—first her husband and their neighbor, now the frail pregnant widow she'd so quickly befriended. Nada's compassion gave Marija hope: there were wicked people all around her, but there were also good people, like Nada, and maybe some of them would survive the war.

One of the guards shook her and the five male prisoners awake when the ship taking them from the mainland pulled next to the Bisevo dock. They were marched off the ship in the dark and loaded into the back of a military vehicle. It drove over a bumpy road for perhaps fifteen minutes before it came to a halt.

The camp was surrounded by a double barbed-wire fence with razor-wire looped along the top. A Partisan guard and the driver ordered them out of the truck and into the camp's barren interior. The sky was growing light as they marched past the guard barracks and a justice building. There was a water tank in the center of the gulag, a long tent to the left, and a kitchen and small tent to the right. Armed guards patrolled the perimeter.

They were led toward the long tent, but one of the camp's guards stopped Marija before she went inside, and he guided her in the opposite direction. Marija said a quick prayer of gratitude. During the truck ride, one of her fellow prisoners had stared at her in a way that had made her uncomfortable because she was experienced enough to fear the lust in his eyes. Whatever the Communists' other failings, Tito's followers were strict in outlawing intimacy between unmarried men and women. Their reasoning was mostly practical—the army was no place for pregnant women and babies—but Marija hoped the guards would also shield her from rape.

The guard led her to the other tent and pointed inside. Not sure what to expect, she pushed aside the flap and entered. In the dim light, she could make out two beds, one occupied by a woman, the other by a little boy and a cat. The woman sat up in bed and said something. It sounded like a question, but it wasn't in Serbo-Croat.

"Who's there?" the woman asked again, this time in English.

"I'm a prisoner . . . The guard told me to come in." Marija answered in the same language.

The woman eyed her curiously as she stood and walked toward her. She seemed about Marija's age and had the hourglass figure and sculpture-perfect lips Marija had always envied in other women.

"I'm sorry, I shouldn't stare at you. It's just I haven't seen another woman in months."

"Months?" Based on the rumors Marija had heard, people rarely survived longer than a week or two on Bisevo. "How long have you been here?"

"Two hundred twenty-two days."

"Is that normal?"

The other woman shook her head. "No. Each day is a miracle. I'm the cook. The only reason I'm still alive is that the camp commandant likes my soup. Actually, it's time for me to get to the kitchen." She turned her back to Marija and slipped out of her nightshirt and into a well-worn dress. "You can rest for a few hours." She pointed to her own bed, then twisted her hair back and used a pin to hold it in place. "Please, make yourself comfortable."

Marija glanced at the bed. It looked warm, and she was cold and exhausted.

The woman washed her face with water from a dented bucket. "You're from Yugoslavia?"

"Yes."

"And what's your name?"

"Marija."

"Well, Marija from Yugoslavia, I won't say I'm glad you're here, because this isn't a pleasant place. But it's nice to meet you. I'm Iuliana, from Romania. That's my son, Anatolie." She pointed to the sleeping boy. "He speaks a little English and a little Serbo-Croat. When he wakes up, have him bring you to breakfast."

"Why are you here?"

One corner of Iuliana's beautiful lips turned up into a sad half smile. "It's a long story. Ask me again later." Then she slipped out of the tent.

Marija stared at the tent's exit for a few moments, then glanced around. The tent was largely bare—just the two cots with a blanket on each of them, a mismatched pair of wooden crates turned on their ends to form tables, and a rope strung across the tent to hold Iuliana's nightshirt and clothing for the little boy. The bucket rested on one table, and a candle balanced in a tin can sat on the other. Marija took off her shoes and slipped into Iuliana's bed.

* * *

Marija had been on the move for so long that it felt strange to sit still. She managed to keep her breakfast down and had a healthy appetite as the second meal approached. She walked to the kitchen to see if she could help and caught the scent of something strong. Marija was sure it wasn't a bad smell—some type of fish cooking—but it made her stomach lurch, and she vomited into the garbage outside the kitchen. Feeling weak and shaky, she went back to the tent.

She was surprised when she woke a few hours later. The light coming through the tent hinted that sunset was approaching. The last time she'd taken a nap was back in the village, in the cottage she'd shared with Miloš.

"Baby Colić, I miss your father." More than anything, she continued to regret waiting so long to marry Miloš. They'd had weeks together, and it could have been months if she hadn't let her past dictate her life for so long. She sighed, letting her hands wander to her abdomen. Miloš hadn't left her alone. And he hadn't left her the same as he'd found her. He'd helped restore her confidence and her faith and had given her the first taste of happiness she'd had in years. Marija squeezed her eyes shut, refusing to cry. She'd promised Miloš she'd be happy, and she was determined to see the joy in life, even if her life was to end on Bisevo.

Think of something good, she told herself. She had the baby, so the nausea was for a worthwhile cause. And in the camp, she wouldn't have to march; she'd be able to rest. Iuliana seemed nice; Anatolie was adorable.

Marija still had her eyes shut, trying to think of the positive things in her life, when she heard the tent flap move and opened her eyes to see Iuliana and Anatolie. Marija smiled at her new friends. It wasn't until she saw Iuliana staring at her stomach that Marija realized she was still holding her imperceptible bump. No one would know she was pregnant by looking at her, but she wondered if the caress had given her away. She moved her hands and straightened her skirt as she sat up.

She followed Iuliana and Anatolie to the water tank to fill the tent's bucket and wash, then observed Anatolie's bedtime routine. Though Iuliana seemed exhausted, Marija could tell she loved her son. Marija had noticed that the boy's right hand seemed stiff and uncoordinated, and Iuliana massaged it and gently stretched all the fingers.

Marija didn't catch much of Anatolie's bedtime prayer because it was in Romanian, but she heard him mention a Krzysztof, and it made her think of the foreigners. She missed them—Krzysztof's kindness, Jamie's wit, Moretti's loyalty, and Peter's faith. Had Krzysztof saved the others? Had their friend, Major Baker, sent them a plane?

Iuliana tucked her son into bed and moved the water from the crate so she could sit on it. "You can have that bed. I'll move the cat and crawl in with Anatolie when I go to sleep."

"You'll have enough room?" Marija asked.

Iuliana nodded. "We'll be fine. Will you tell me why you're here?"

"My uncle fought against the Partisans. My husband too. They were Chetniks."

"Chetniks?"

"They were opposed to the Nazis and Communists, loyal to the king."

"Were?"

Marija swallowed to hold back her emotions. "They were killed recently."

"I'm sorry. I know what it's like to lose a husband. Mine was killed by the Nazis."

"Does it get easier?"

Iuliana nodded. "Not for a while, and some days I still miss him. I'm sad when he's not here to see Anatolie accomplish something new, but we had some complications in our marriage. Now I'm just glad to have closure over his death."

"Did your husband die before or after your son was born?"

"After, but Anatolie doesn't remember him." Iuliana forced a small smile. "He does remember the man who I thought might take his place, but that was before we were sent here."

"Why are you here?" Marija asked.

"I angered the NKVD."

"That's not a very long story."

Iuliana smiled, then she told Marija about the commando team that had come to Romania and how she'd been tricked into marking their drop zone. She described how the team's radio operator had been arrested, then had escaped and sought her help. She'd been drawn into their fight against the Nazis, and the subsequent conflict with the Communists. "I don't know what happened to Krzysztof—the radio man. He and some of his teammates were given another assignment, even though Krzysztof was still wounded. The man who sent them away sent me here."

"Krzysztof?" Marija repeated softly. It was the first time Iuliana had mentioned the man's name. It could be coincidence, but how many radio operators by the name of Krzysztof had been sent on missions while wounded? And if it was the same man, that would explain the foreigners' reluctance to seek help from the Red Army. "Krzysztof Zielinski?"

Iuliana had been watching the candle, but her head whipped around. "How do you know that?"

"He and his friends were wounded, so they spent the winter in the same village as me. My husband was a doctor, and he cared for them."

Iuliana's tears glistened in the candlelight. "Krzysztof's alive?"

Marija nodded.

"And his friends?"

"Peter, Jamie, and Sergeant Moretti. They were all alive three weeks ago, but . . ." Marija let her voice trail off.

"But what?"

"The Germans discovered where we were hiding and threatened to destroy the village. Peter, Jamie, and Moretti turned themselves in. Krzysztof sent me away with a group of refugees and went to help them. I don't know what happened after that."

Iuliana stared at the flickering candle, tears of worry replacing her earlier tears of joy. "Of course he'd try to help his friends. He always does the right thing, even if it involves single-handedly storming a German garrison."

"Was Anatolie praying for him?"

"Yes. He always prays for Krzysztof and his friends. For some reason, he remembers them. I had hoped . . . I had hoped Krzysztof and I would end up in England together. Now it looks like neither of us will survive the war. Krzysztof dead trying to save his friends. Me dead when the commandant is transferred or when I run out of paprika." Iuliana stood and changed into her nightshirt. "I'm sorry. I shouldn't be so pessimistic. Sometimes it's hard to imagine any future at all, let alone a happy one. But now you know my secret—I'm in love with Krzysztof, even though I barely know him. Do you have a secret you'd like to share with me?"

Marija wasn't sure what Iuliana was asking.

"Marija, when I was expecting Anatolie, the smell of anchovies made me sick, and given the chance, I'd sleep away the afternoon. And my fingers always found their way to where Anatolie was growing inside me. I know what I was cooking when you walked by the kitchen and became ill, and I saw you when I came into the tent tonight."

Marija looked away. Maybe it didn't matter if Iuliana knew she was expecting a baby. Iuliana wasn't going to execute her; the Partisans were, but for a different reason.

Iuliana lifted the cat out of Anatolie's arms and placed it on the floor. "I'm not trying to be nosy, but I think you're going to need help, and I can help you."

Marija studied her new tent mate. If Krzysztof trusted her, couldn't Marija trust her as well? "Yes, I'm expecting. And yes, I'll accept any help you can give me."

Chapter Thirty-Five
SKIRMISH IN THE RIVER

Monday, April 23
Independent State of Croatia

PETER, JAMIE, AND KRZYSZTOF HAD been *guests* of the Partisans for over a month. With the exception of one week when they'd been afflicted with dysentery, each day they asked Andro Pavlović and his superiors for permission to leave. Andro dutifully made his inquiries and unfailingly passed on the excuses his officers made. They always said they'd consider it, that they'd no doubt work something out in a few days or after they'd achieved a specific military objective. But days had stretched into weeks. The Partisans didn't trust their guests and didn't want to let them go, either because Peter and his men knew their plans or because they hoped to gain something from working with British and American agents.

Peter had volunteered to fight alongside the Partisans, as had Jamie and Krzysztof, preferring combat to incarceration. But they'd been kept in the rear instead. They'd contemplated escape, but the Partisans controlled the countryside. The only places they could escape to were the German garrisons the Partisans were taking one by one, siege by siege, brutal battle by brutal battle.

They were told to wait and observe. Peter had thought the Partisans would give them their radio so Krzysztof could report their battlefield successes to the British and Americans who supplied them, but whenever Krzysztof asked to use the radio, the answer was no.

Today, when Andro made his daily round, he had a friend with him. They seemed in high spirits, which Peter assumed was the result of another battlefield win. He let Jamie ask the usual questions: Could they please have their radio back? Could they please set out for the coast? If not today, when?

After the Partisans walked off, Jamie motioned Peter closer. Over the last month, they'd figured out which Partisan guards spoke which languages other than Serbo-Croat. Jamie and Krzysztof could speak Polish whenever they wanted without fear of anyone else understanding. Peter and Jamie switched between French and English, depending on which guards were nearby.

"They were joking about taking Rijeka," Jamie said in English. That wasn't anything new. Rijeka lay on the other side of the heavily defended Ingrid Line, and the Partisans had begun their assault on the line a few days before. The Germans were dug in, but Peter figured it was just a matter of time before the Partisans breached the massive fortifications. "Then they joked about taking Trieste."

"Do they really plan to make it all the way to Trieste?"

Jamie nodded. "That may be why they won't let us leave. They plan to race the Allied army for as much territory as possible. They don't want us to report their progress; they would rather sneak as far west as they can without anyone but the Germans knowing it."

"We've got to get out of here," Peter said.

"You say that every day," Krzysztof whispered as a pair of Partisan soldiers passed by.

"I know." Peter thought about Rijeka. They hoped to find Marija there, and then they planned to slip away into Italy. Peter had made a promise to Miloš, and he intended to keep it. And Peter wondered what had happened to Moretti. He was unlikely to find much information about POWs in Yugoslavia, but maybe more information would be available in Italy.

Telling the Partisans their true plans wouldn't gain their cooperation, but what if Peter's getting past the Ingrid Line could somehow benefit the Partisans? Then would they let them go? "We need to make a deal with them."

"What type of deal?" Jamie asked.

"Intelligence on the Ingrid Line in exchange for our freedom."

Jamie smiled. "Gathering intelligence on the Ingrid Line is likely to result in our collective deaths."

"Can't be much worse than being a Partisan prisoner." If Peter had to stay where he was much longer, he was going to do something crazy—or was that what this idea was?

"I'll find Andro," Krzysztof said. "I'm ready to get back to England, even if I have to take a dangerous route."

Peter was shocked when a Partisan pukovnik called on them a few hours later. "You offer us intelligence?"

Peter nodded. "Let us sneak behind the Ingrid Line. Arm us and give us our radio. We'll report what we see: locations of German guns, minefields, which units you face."

The pukovnik tapped his foot as he considered the offer. "We have no weapons to spare, and we can't return your radio. But I can release you and provide passes. We have an agent in Rijeka. You can give her the information, and she'll report back to us."

Peter glanced at Jamie and Krzysztof. They weren't being offered much of a deal, but it gave them the opportunity for freedom. Krzysztof nodded ever so slightly, and so did Jamie. "We accept."

* * *

The first day back in the field with the type of mission he'd been trained for left Peter feeling alive and hopeful again, even though he and his men were unarmed, heading into tremendously strong German defenses, and working for an army they didn't trust.

By day three, Peter's optimism had faded. They were in poor physical shape, and as their supply of food disappeared, so did their energy. Before their first mission together, they'd been able to run ten miles in full gear, then repeat the exercise the next day without difficulty. Now they could barely walk a mile without feeling drained.

Peter was exhausted, but he smiled as the Rječina River came into view. On a map, the Ingrid Line ran along the river, but in reality, the definition wasn't that simple. The men approached the river slowly, trying to remain unseen.

"Up for a swim, Jamie?" Peter asked.

"As long as it gives me a break from climbing." The area around the river consisted of steep hills—challenging for Peter and Krzysztof, more daunting for Jamie, who was still using his cane.

The rocky riverbed was lined with tall trees stretching into the hills. Even in the dark, Peter could tell the water was swollen and white with movement. The Partisans had given them little food and no weapons, but they had provided rope for rappelling, and Peter had been carrying it over his shoulder.

He unlooped the rope. "I'll swim across with this. If I get into trouble with the current, you can haul me back in. If I make it, you'll have something to hold on the way across."

Krzysztof tied one end of the rope to a tree and took Peter's boots. Going across with the rope, maybe he'd be able to keep them dry.

Peter tied the other end of the rope to his belt and inhaled sharply as he waded into the icy water. The daytime temperature was pleasant, but the snow melt was a different story. He used a few rocks for balance until the water grew deeper, then plunged in. By the time he pulled himself onto the opposite bank, his muscles ached and his breathing was labored. Looking back across the river, he realized the current had carried him farther downstream than he'd expected. He rolled the rope along his arm as he walked back upstream, then tied it to a tree opposite where Jamie and Krzysztof waited.

The area seemed quiet, so Peter waved them over, shivering in his wet clothes until they arrived. "I thought we were better swimmers," Peter said, his teeth chattering.

The sky was more gray than black now, and Peter could see Jamie's smile. "A year ago, we could have made it to Rijeka in a day." Jamie yawned and closed his eyes.

Peter took his shirt off and wrung it out, then did the same with his pants before getting dressed again. Krzysztof had kept his boots mostly dry, so Peter put them back on. He was lacing his second boot when Krzysztof tensed and raised a hand in warning. Peter looked around, not seeing anything, not at first. Then a pair of Ustaše soldiers emerged from behind the trees, yards from Jamie, who still had his eyes closed.

"Jamie!" Krzysztof shouted.

Jamie reached for his cane and tried to get to his feet, but one of the Ustaše patrolmen, a tall man with thick muscles, knocked him unconscious with a rifle blow to the back of his head. Jamie dropped to the ground, and his cane flew into the riverbank.

Peter would have given just about anything for a weapon as he ran toward the man who'd attacked Jamie. The Ustaše had his rifle, but he clenched his fists and held them up like a boxer. He was taller and heavier than Peter, but Peter managed to block the man's first three jabs and land a pair of solid punches in the man's ribs. Peter's OSS training in hand-to-hand combat came back to him quickly as he dodged another hit and pummeled the man's chin. But the man easily shook off Peter's punches and resumed his attack.

Peter stepped away from the Ustaše man's hook, and then the man's fist connected with Peter's jaw in a forceful uppercut. The blow sent Peter sprawling backward, his hands landing in the river, lights flashing in front of his eyes. He turned away from the next punch but couldn't escape the man's boot swinging toward the side of his head. He tumbled into the water, and his opponent followed, picking Peter up by his shirt collar and smashing his forehead into Peter's nose.

Everything turned gray, then black, but as the cold river washed over him, Peter's mind suddenly focused. His hands grabbed at the river bottom, slowing his drift until he could get his feet under him again. His legs were wobbly, but he managed to push himself to his knees and balance. He gasped for air as his head broke the surface.

The Ustaše soldier who'd nearly knocked Peter unconscious was wading back to shore with his back to Peter, who'd drifted a dozen yards downstream. Jamie lay on the bank, not moving. Krzysztof wrestled with the other soldier, but Peter couldn't tell who was winning.

As the taller Ustaše reached Jamie, the soldier drew out a small knife. Peter had only seconds to prevent the man from slitting Jamie's throat, but his legs weren't working. "Hey!" he yelled. The Ustaše soldier glanced over his shoulder at Peter, then turned back to Jamie, refusing to be distracted.

Peter's hands felt in the water for a rock, hoping to find one small enough to throw in his weakened state and large enough to slow down the Ustaše soldier. Instead of a stone, Peter felt something bump into him—Jamie's cane. The Ustaše man must have knocked it into the swifter current while wading ashore. Peter wasted a full second staring at it in disbelief before ripping off the top. He brought his hand back and hurled the dagger at the Ustaše man, praying it would strike home. It hit the man in the center of his back, and his own knife, inches from Jamie's neck, fell to the ground, as did the soldier.

Peter crawled toward shore, planning to finish the man off and help Krzysztof. But Krzysztof didn't need help anymore. He jabbed his fist into the Ustaše's face, and the man tumbled away, limp. Krzysztof struggled to his knees and pushed his unconscious opponent's face into the river. He stumbled to his feet and staggered toward the other fallen Ustaše. "He's dead," Krzysztof said.

Peter nodded, dragging himself from the water at the shore's edge and using a tree to pull himself up. His right ankle felt sprained, so he tried to keep his weight off of it. Jamie was still unconscious, and Krzysztof had a cut on his forehead and blood streaming from his lips. Peter wondered how two poorly trained Croatian soldiers had caused so much damage to members of what had been an elite commando unit. "How's your head?"

Krzysztof felt his forehead and stared at the blood that stuck to his fingers. "It hurts."

Peter sat beside Jamie, stretching his ankle and trying to wiggle the pain away. *Haven't I had enough problems with my ankles this war?*

Krzysztof checked Jamie's vital signs, then sat next to Peter, his breathing heavy.

"How many pairs of Ustaše soldiers do you suppose are patrolling this river?" Peter asked.

Krzysztof used his sleeve to wipe at the cut on his forehead. "I don't suppose it will take more than a few more of them to finish us off."

Jamie stirred and groaned as his eyes opened. "'The wills above be done, but I would fain die a dry death.'" He stared at Peter and Krzysztof, then at the man who'd almost killed him. Peter was relieved. If Jamie was quoting Shakespeare, he couldn't be too badly injured.

Jamie focused on the top of his cane sticking from the man's back, then grasped it and yanked it free.

"That was an impressive throw," Krzysztof said.

Peter checked the dead Ustaše for extra ammunition. "I missed once about a year ago, so I practiced."

"How many German and Ustaše men did the Partisans estimate were behind the Ingrid Line?" Jamie sat up and rubbed the back of his head.

Krzysztof glanced at the dead men lying on the rocky ground beside the river. "Twenty-five thousand plus."

Peter wondered what he and his friends had gotten themselves into. Peter and Krzysztof wouldn't be able to pass themselves off as Croatian, so the next time they were spotted, they were likely to get the same reception they'd just received. *We need to blend in.* He glanced at the man Krzysztof had killed. "Krzysztof, grab that Ustaše before he washes away. We need his uniform."

They stripped the two soldiers and dumped their naked bodies in the river. Dressing as Ustaše soldiers was risky. Jamie was the only one who spoke Serbo-Croat, and they had two sets of uniforms to divide among three people. Jamie would pretend to be their leader, but Peter wasn't sure how many Ustaše patrol leaders used canes. At least it was spring, so no one would think it odd that Krzysztof didn't have a jacket and that Peter kept his buttoned to hide his civilian shirt.

If they ran into German soldiers, Peter and Krzysztof's limited, accented German would be expected. Peter prayed they wouldn't run into very many

Ustaše troops because the pistol, rifle, and two knives they'd taken from the dead men wouldn't save them for long.

CHAPTER THIRTY-SIX
OUT OF LUCK

Saturday, April 28
Trieste, German Operational Zone of the Adriatic Littoral

GENEVIEVE'S VIEW FROM THE ROOF was spectacular, with all of Trieste stretching out below. She admired the green hills gently ending in the ocean, the red roofs, the Vienna-influenced architecture. For the past week, she'd been combing the city for pillboxes and antiaircraft guns, but today she let herself enjoy Trieste's beauty.

She was grateful for the mission. It had given her something to do other than grieve and had kept her too busy to dwell on her nightmares. Weiss hadn't left her dreams, but the dreams had changed. She still shot Weiss, still saw him fall, but when she looked at the corpse, his hair and face were different, and he was wearing a blindfold. When she bent to remove the blindfold, it was Peter. She usually woke then with the feeling that somehow she'd been responsible for Peter's death. Was her mind playing tricks on her, or was it something more? Genevieve shivered in the breeze, the panoramic view less appealing as she remembered the image.

Lombardelli joined her on the roof. "The last report is in. They'll pick us up tomorrow night or early Monday morning either by boat or by plane. They'll confirm tomorrow."

Genevieve nodded, hoping a return to Bari wouldn't be too painful. She wondered if Rick would still be there and what type of greeting she'd get from Nathan.

"We just have one more thing to do."

"Find your son-in-law's friend and ask who his source was?"

"Yes. Antonio Girabaldi. I don't know him well. My son-in-law thought highly of him, but that was before the war. He's a member of OVRA, but I'm hoping with the war lost, he won't care so much about politics."

"He's with OVRA?" Genevieve shivered. Lombardelli hadn't told her that his son-in-law's friend was a member of Mussolini's secret police.

"He was last summer."

Genevieve put on a brave face. "Better OVRA than the Gestapo."

* * *

Lombardelli didn't trust Girabaldi, so he told Genevieve to wait outside while he asked about the OVRA agent's location. Genevieve had offered to help with the questioning, but she spoke little Italian and almost no Slovenian. Over the last month, she'd pretended to speak only Italian when she ran into Slovenes and only Slovenian when she interacted with Italians. If the staff at Trieste's police station was bilingual, she'd be in trouble.

After a half hour, Lombardelli emerged with a smile on his face. He took her arm and led her back toward the harbor as he reported. "Girabaldi was on duty, and he remembered the incident. He received an anonymous letter, promising him two British spies if he boarded a certain gondola at a certain time. Girabaldi went, and the gondolier picked up another man at the next stop."

"The man he met on the gondola, what did he look like?" Genevieve whispered, not wanting anyone to overhear her English as they walked past the market.

"It was dark, and the man wore a long coat and a hat pulled down over his forehead. Caucasian, medium height, dark hair, brown eyes, square face. He spoke Italian, but Girabaldi thought he was a foreigner."

Genevieve frowned. "Could Kimby fit that description?" She'd never seen him.

"Yes, but so could a lot of other people."

"So we still don't know who it was?"

Lombardelli smiled again. "No, I think we do. Girabaldi also remembered how the man identified himself: an SOE agent, newly arrived, who had personal differences with one of the agents. That was their deal: the man would tell Girabaldi where to find the two agents—one of their sources at least—and Girabaldi agreed not to tail him. Girabaldi promised to stay on the gondola for another ten minutes after the man got off, but he bribed the gondolier to let him off sooner. He still wasn't able to find the man with the tip. On his way back to headquarters, he stopped for supper, ran into me, and mentioned the big intelligence coup. He was hoping for a promotion. Girabaldi reported to Ercolani, who rounded up a team. And I went to warn Nelson and Baker."

Genevieve glanced over her shoulder. "Does Girabaldi suspect your role?"

"Not that I know of."

"I think someone's following us. No, don't look now. Wait."

Lombardelli kept his eyes forward. "How many?"

"I only saw one, but there could be more."

"We'll split up—meet back at the safe house in a few hours."

Genevieve nodded. At the next intersection, Lombardelli turned right, and she turned left.

* * *

Genevieve figured she'd walked five miles that afternoon, losing the short, stocky man who'd followed her after she'd left Lombardelli's side. She'd had no lunch and was hungry as she neared the apartment where she'd hid with Lombardelli the past week. She circled it, searching for anything that seemed out of place and not seeing anyone loitering or watching the entrances. She waited a few minutes, then approached the ground-floor flat. The door was unlocked. She pushed it open and held her breath. Someone had searched the apartment—the radio was smashed, clothing was strewn about the room, and the contents of the cupboards were tipped onto the floor. She walked through the mess, checking the two bedrooms. They were empty, but a brown-red spot stained one of the walls in Lombardelli's room. Blood.

Something made a sound near the apartment's entrance. Genevieve opened the window and descended into the alley below.

CHAPTER THIRTY-SEVEN
THE GOLDEN SWASTIKA

Rijeka, German Operational Zone of the Adriatic Littoral

AFTER THEIR SKIRMISH IN THE river, it took Peter, Krzysztof, and Jamie another two days to sneak into Rijeka. They noted enemy encampments and visited a few of them for meals, searched out concrete bunkers and recorded their locations, and counted troops and marked which units manned which positions. They would have done a more thorough job had it been American, British, or Polish troops attacking the Ingrid Line, but they were in a hurry to find Marija and leave Yugoslavia.

The details of their reconnaissance were in a plain-text report. Peter could tell that made Krzysztof uneasy. He wanted to encrypt it somehow, but their goal was speed, and Peter hoped they could drop off the information and leave within minutes.

Their Partisan contact lived in an apartment overlooking Rijeka harbor. Peter stationed himself across the street in the shadow of another building while Krzysztof and Jamie approached the contact's flat. Peter's injury at the river hadn't impeded his mobility, but his ankle was still sore, so he let Krzysztof and Jamie tackle the stairs to the third story. Walking was still a challenge for Jamie, but his language skills were needed.

A few people went in and out of the building's main entrance as Peter waited impatiently. He flexed his ankle and grunted in frustration. He'd wrapped it but not as well as Moretti had last fall. Not for the first time, Peter wished things had been different at the Nazi garrison near Bihac. His thoughts were interrupted when four men left the apartment building: Krzysztof with both hands on his head, Jamie with one hand raised and the other on his cane, and two German soldiers.

Peter felt sick to his stomach as he checked the clip in his pistol and raced toward them, staying in the shadows and stepping carefully so he wouldn't be heard. It was twilight, Saturday evening, well before curfew, so shooting the German soldiers in the street would involve more witnesses than Peter wanted. But breaking Jamie and Krzysztof out of the Rijeka prison was a task beyond Peter's abilities, so he followed, wondering what had happened, hoping the Germans would turn into a deserted alley, wishing it were darker.

As he stalked the four men, Peter prayed for help. Jamie and Krzysztof, in their partial Ustaše uniforms, wouldn't be sent to a POW camp. They would be interrogated and executed.

A door opened between Peter and his arrested friends, and a large group of middle-aged men left a café, still arguing passionately about something. Peter dropped his Ustaše jacket and cap and slipped into the group of roughly a dozen men. He covered his mouth and let out a soft bird call—one he and his friends had used on previous assignments. He saw Krzysztof's head turn a few inches to the side. Krzysztof, at least, knew Peter was nearby and would be waiting for the right moment.

The group Peter followed walked more quickly than the soldiers and their prisoners because Jamie was using his cane as an excuse to slow the Germans. Peter fell to the back of the crowd, glanced around, and saw no one behind him. They neared an alley, and Peter planned his ambush. The group passed the soldiers before the side street, walking around them, staring at the prisoners but for the most part continuing their heated discussion. They were close enough to drown out the sound of Peter's feet as he moved behind the last soldier, the one with a rifle pressed into Krzysztof's back. Peter grabbed him and slid a knife across his throat, pulling him into the alley, out of sight. When the rifle's pressure disappeared from his back, Krzysztof glanced back briefly before he attacked the guard in front of him, clamping one hand over the man's mouth and using the other to knock his rifle from his hands. Jamie spun around, took the knife from his cane, and stabbed the second soldier.

Someone in the crowd noticed what had happened and yelled. Krzysztof grabbed one of Jamie's arms to help him into the alley, and Peter stayed behind them, firing into the air to warn away civilians.

The Croatian civilians and the gunshots would soon alert patrols, and Peter, Krzysztof, and Jamie wouldn't be able to outrun them for long. They ran across a main road and into another alley. Halfway down, out of sight, Krzysztof kicked in a wooden door. The three slipped inside the back of a bakery. The smell of something sweet filled the air and made Peter's stomach growl, but they didn't linger. The back door's latch was damaged, so Peter moved a sack of flour in front of it, hoping the door would look normal from the outside.

It was a two-story building, so they sneaked up the stairs and onto the red roof. They slithered in the shadows of the low wall on the alley side of the roof, listening to the sounds of the manhunt they'd inspired. It sounded like dozens of men were looking for them, shouting orders and searching the buildings along the alley.

How long until they discover the broken door at the back of the bakery?

Jamie broke into another building from the roof, and as they reached the ground floor, Peter realized their good fortune. They were in a used clothing store. As with the bakery, the workers had all gone home for the night.

Peter had never shoplifted before, but this was a matter of life and death. The three of them changed clothes and emerged through the front door, where they blended into the sparse civilian foot traffic as the search for them continued. There were patrols in the bakery and on the roof of the shop they'd just left, but no one stopped them as they headed for the harbor.

"What happened?" Peter asked.

"Our Partisan contact offered to let us use the radio," Jamie said. "And while Krzysztof was adjusting frequencies, she signaled a Nazi patrol waiting in a room across the hall."

"It's my fault," Krzysztof said. "I should have known something was wrong when she left the room."

"We all want to get word to Bari." Jamie nodded toward the harbor. "But perhaps we should give up on a plane and take a ship instead."

They split up, Jamie going to the docks to see if anyone could smuggle them to Italy, Peter and Krzysztof to find Marija. When they drew near the address, they scouted the area thoroughly to make sure nothing seemed suspicious. Peter waited across the street from the entrance while Krzysztof went inside. He came out alone.

"Where's Marija?" Peter asked.

"Someone recognized her as Brajović's niece. She was arrested almost three weeks ago."

Peter could almost taste the disappointment, sudden and bitter. "Is she dead?"

Krzysztof frowned. "They sent her to Bisevo."

"Where's that?"

"It's an island; been in Partisan hands most of the war. It's to the south, halfway between here and Bari." Krzysztof paused, his voice subdued when he continued. "Nada said the Partisans have probably executed her by now."

"Could we get to Bisevo?" Peter asked. He wanted to keep his promise to Miloš. If there was any chance Marija was alive, he owed it to both Coličs to find her.

* * *

Jamie's teeth flashed into a grin as he approached Krzysztof and Peter, but his smile disappeared when he saw they were alone. "Where is Marija?"

"Bisevo," Peter said. "The big question is if she's still a Partisan prisoner or if she's a corpse."

Jamie swore.

Peter wondered about Jamie's earlier smile. "Did you find a way out?"

"Yes. First-class tickets."

"On what?" Peter asked.

"A yacht. A freshly stocked, fully fueled, beautifully decorated 1929 Elco 50."

Jamie had a taste for luxurious transport, but he didn't have any money with him, so Peter assumed Jamie planned to steal the yacht. "I don't suppose the ship's been freshly stocked and fully fueled for our benefit."

Jamie shook his head. "No. My guess is it belongs to rich Dalmatian Fascists trying to make their escape before the Ingrid Line is breached."

"So you propose we take their escape option for our own?" Peter tried to ignore the trace of guilt he felt for the shoplifted clothing he wore. Now he was going to steal a ship?

Jamie smiled. "Yes, and you won't feel guilty about it."

"I won't?" Peter asked.

Jamie shook his head. "The name of the ship is the *Golden Swastika*, and the saloon is decorated with portraits of Ante Pavelič, Adolf Hitler, and Benito Mussolini. It is, beyond a doubt, Nazi owned, and I plan on feasting on that Nazi food within the hour. And we are going to sail it to Bisevo to rescue Marija if she is still alive—quite an honorable quest. You will join me, won't you, Peter?"

Peter was worried about Marija, but he felt his mouth pull into a grin. "Food? I can't remember the last time I wasn't at least a little hungry."

* * *

An armed Ustaše soldier paced the dark pier in front of the *Golden Swastika*. "How did you get on board?" Peter whispered to Jamie.

"I pretended to be the owner's cousin, sent to inspect the preparations."

"And how do you propose the rest of us get on board?" Peter asked.

"I shall go speak with the guard again and knock him unconscious with my cane."

Peter took out the pistol he'd stolen from the dead Ustaše at the river. "Would you like to borrow this?"

Jamie took it with a nod and slipped it into his pocket. He spoke with the guard and, as planned, knocked him unconscious before waving Peter and Krzysztof out of the shadows, where they hid. They untied the boat and boarded it, and Jamie and Krzysztof went into the wheelhouse while Peter watched the pier to make sure no one followed them.

After the ship pulled out, Peter joined the others. "How fast does this thing go?"

"Ten knots." Jamie didn't even glance up from the instruments. "For Yankee landlubbers such as yourself, that is about eleven and a half miles per hour."

Peter found a large map of the Adriatic and tried to calculate the distance from Rijeka to Bisevo. There were islands to navigate around and probably marine mine fields to avoid, but it looked to be about one hundred seventy-five miles away. He knew nautical miles weren't the exact same as land miles, but they could make it in a day if things went smoothly. "We have enough fuel?"

Jamie nodded. "There are extra fuel drums on the aft deck. I am not sure of the intended destination, but I would guess Spain. So as long as we aren't attacked, we should make it to Bisevo and Bari with a surplus. I don't expect much trouble from the Luftwaffe or the Kriegsmarine, but we might be targeted by our own side."

"All this way to get shot by friendly fire. That's a happy thought," Peter said.

Krzysztof tested the radio as Jamie steered the ship out of harbor. Whoever owned the *Golden Swastika* had a connection with the German Navy—a map showed the safest route through the mine fields from Rijeka to the end of the Istria peninsula. There wasn't anything for Peter to do, so he wandered into the galley and helped himself to the amply stocked supplies. Never before had stuffing himself with food until it hurt sounded so appealing. Tinned meat, preserved fruit, crackers—none of it was gourmet, but actually having enough of it to make a satisfying meal was a wonder. He dug into the *Golden Swastika*'s supply of cheese and canned plums and brought plates full of food to Jamie and Krzysztof.

A half hour later, Peter found himself leaning over the rails losing everything he'd just eaten. He swished some water around to rinse the worst of the foul taste from his mouth. His stomach was rebelling from the sudden surfeit of food, but he still felt hungry.

Peter waited until his stomach settled, then stepped into the wheelhouse. Jamie and Krzysztof were just as he'd left them.

"In case you were wondering, gorging on food after starving for eight months isn't such a good idea," Peter said.

"And I thought your green complexion was a symptom of seasickness." Jamie smiled his sympathy.

Peter slumped into a chair. "I'm still hungry. I didn't know it was possible to be ravenous and nauseated at the same time."

Jamie laughed but stopped when Krzysztof held his hand up for silence, listening intently to the radio. He printed a series of letters and numbers. Peter glanced at his watch. It was just after midnight, British war time, but surely no one was still trying to contact them six weeks after their initial transmission.

Krzysztof took out his fake cigarette and decoded the short message. After a few minutes, he sat back in his chair, a bewildered look on his face. "The operator just asked me what my sisters' names are."

Jamie considered it for a few moments. "Trying to verify your identity."

Krzysztof wrote three names on the paper: Cecylia, Ania, Kasia. He encoded them and sent them over the radio waves. The next questions asked for his address in Krakow, then his parents' address in England, the name of his childhood English tutor, and the location of his 1943 bullet wound.

"Finally." Krzysztof finished decoding the most recent response. "I suppose they know it's really me and that I'm not under duress. Asking our location now and your names."

Krzysztof frowned at the next response. "They want me to repeat who else is on board. I don't know why it matters. They just need to tell any allied fighters in the area not to strafe us."

"Who do you suppose is on the other end?" Peter asked.

Krzysztof's face softened as he stared at the code. "I suppose . . . I suppose it could be my father. Or someone he gave the code to."

"I would guess your father," Jamie said.

"Why?" Krzysztof asked.

Jamie picked up a cracker. "Anyone else would have written us off as dead."

The corners of Krzysztof's lips lifted into a smile. He tapped out the same series he'd sent earlier, and the three waited for the next response.

They didn't have to wait long. "They must have had it ready," Krzysztof said as he went to work decoding it.

Do not enter Adriatic in daylight until instructed. Check back every two hours.

Jamie flipped through the pile of charts. "There are enough small islands and peninsulas around that we can find a place to hide before dawn. In the meantime, I am quite capable of navigating on my own if the two of you wish to sleep or eat something. I suggest something light."

Peter skipped the galley. The ship's head was spotless, and stocked with sweet-smelling soap and shaving cream that worked into a rich lather. Peter washed up and shaved, enjoying the sensation of being clean again, then slid into one of the lower berths in the stateroom. For the first time since leaving England nine months before, Peter slept on a soft mattress with clean sheets and a feather pillow.

* * *

Before dawn, Jamie anchored in a cove until they received further instructions, and then they waited, hoping no one would notice the boat if it wasn't leaving a telltale streak of white behind it. There weren't many enemy planes over the Adriatic, but the friendly planes were just as dangerous. Anyone who flew close enough to read the ship's name would be justified if they came to the wrong conclusion about which side of the war the passengers were on. In the meantime, they had food, running water, and comfortable beds.

It was early afternoon when Krzysztof detected a message coming through. Peter went to wake Jamie, and when the two of them returned, Krzysztof handed Peter a piece of paper.

Requested to inquire on your mission readiness. If able to operate, change course for Trieste to assist in evacuation of OSS personnel. Meet contacts at north end of harbor 0200 hours tomorrow.

Peter handed the paper to Jamie. "If we wait until dark, can we get to Trieste by then?"

Jamie looked at his charts and made a few calculations. "No, but we can make it if we leave now."

Peter clenched his teeth. He had no desire to go to Trieste. If it weren't for his promise to Miloš and his sincere concern for Marija, he wouldn't even want to go to Bisevo. Trieste was one of the Partisans' targets. According to the BBC, they weren't there yet, but what if Peter and his men were delayed in Trieste and ran into the Partisans again? They didn't know if their contact in Rijeka had betrayed them on Partisan orders or on Nazi orders. So even though the Partisans had saved Peter from the firing squad, he preferred never to see any of them again. "Can they give us any more information?"

"I am sure they can. That doesn't mean they will." Jamie shook his head. "I am ready to be done."

"Yeah." Peter handed the paper back to Krzysztof. "Will you ask for more details?"

Krzysztof sent the request and waited for the reply. Peter read over his shoulder as Krzysztof decoded it.

"*Two evacuees headed by agent Lombardelli.* Not the most useful information, is it?" Peter asked.

"Dr. Lombardelli?"

Peter looked up from the paper and noticed Jamie's suddenly white face. "You know him?"

"He saved my life last June, and Wesley's when we were in Venice."

Peter bit back a curse. He didn't want to go to Trieste, but if Lombardelli had saved Jamie's life, how could they refuse?

"There's more." Krzysztof handed Peter the paper with the rest of the deciphered message.

Mission provided military intelligence for Allied armies advancing to Trieste and sought to gather evidence of treason committed by Major Phillip Kimby. Will alert Allied air patrols of your anticipated course.

Jamie folded his arms across his chest. "I would be willing to help anyone giving the Allied Armies the information they need to beat the Partisans to Trieste. I also owe Dr. Lombardelli my life. And I would love to see Phillip Kimby court-martialed. 'Vengeance is in my heart, death in my hand, blood and revenge are hammering in my head.'"

"Major Kimby robbed me of eight months with Iuliana. I vote for Trieste," Krzysztof said.

Peter nodded. He still wasn't sure what he wanted to do—play it safe or strike back at Kimby. Eight months was a long time. What was one extra day spent picking up evidence against Kimby? "I guess we sail for Trieste."

CHAPTER THIRTY-EIGHT
PERSUASION

Sunday, April 29
Trieste, German Operational Zone of the Adriatic Littoral

GENEVIEVE HAD SPENT THE PREVIOUS night in a warehouse near the harbor, but she'd been too frightened to sleep. There were people sympathetic to the Allies in Trieste, but she and Lombardelli had worked alone, so she didn't know whom she could ask for help.

Whoever had arrested Lombardelli knew he had an accomplice. They'd tailed her, and if Lombardelli was alive, they might have forced him to reveal her description and her aliases. Knowing OVRA or the Gestapo might be looking for her with a realistic sketch, she'd braved the streets that morning and afternoon, finding a few civilians who spoke French or German and asking them where OVRA kept its prisoners. Someone told her the location, and perhaps of even greater value, someone told her that the man in charge of the building Sunday evenings was less evil than most of his OVRA associates.

Staring at the harbor as the sun sank in the sky, Genevieve made a decision. She'd left Marseilles alone, and she didn't want to leave Trieste alone. Maybe death wasn't so bad after all. She believed death wasn't the end, and the thought of seeing her dead parents, brother, sister-in-law, and fiancé was appealing. Remembering her last conversation with Rick, she hesitated. *I'm not throwing my life away, and this isn't a suicide mission.* She said a prayer asking for courage.

She had a weapon, but she left it behind. She was going to see the OVRA officer on duty at the prison, and she assumed there would be enough guards that she wouldn't convince anyone to do anything by force. She'd have to rely on persuasion.

Genevieve's legs trembled as she climbed the stairs to the OVRA building, but she forced them to continue upward. She couldn't communicate with the Italian guard very effectively, but he nodded when she asked to speak with his commanding officer. He picked up a nearby phone and spoke with someone on the other line before disconnecting and telling her to wait. A few minutes later, a second guard searched her and escorted her upstairs.

The man in the office she was led to was middle-aged and had gray hair, a prominent nose, and dark-rimmed spectacles. The glasses made him look like a professor, but his immaculate uniform clearly stated his current occupation.

"Do you speak English, sir?" Genevieve asked.

"Yes." His reply was crisp and businesslike as he sat at his desk and examined the Slovenian identity papers she'd turned over to the guard. "Dominika Horvat." He read the name from her papers, then looked up. "Alias, Carmela Zoccarato." That was the name from her Italian papers. They'd been in the apartment when Lombardelli had disappeared. "And your real name is something else, I suppose."

Genevieve didn't answer.

"Come to turn yourself in?" he asked.

"No. I'm here to petition you for Dr. Lombardelli's release."

The man snorted. "I don't often release prisoners. What makes you think I'd make an exception?"

"Because you have an army from New Zealand approaching you from the west and an army of Yugoslav Communists approaching you from the east. Your German allies may hold out a few days or even a few weeks, but they will fall. Hitler's regime is dying, and your enemies will soon control Trieste."

He held her gaze as she spoke, and when she paused, he looked beyond her. When he replied, his words were quiet. "Yes, Mussolini was hanged yesterday."

She hadn't heard the news. It took effort to hide her satisfaction.

The officer's head snapped back toward her. "You have yet to justify Lombardelli's release."

"Dr. Lombardelli has information that can help the Allied army arrive before the Partisans do." That was partially a bluff. Lombardelli did have useful information for the Allied armies, but he'd already reported it. "Who do you prefer as a conqueror? The British and their allies or the Communists? And I am unfamiliar with your record, but should you cooperate,

I can report your kindness to my colleagues. Are you in need of mitigating evidence should you be tried for war crimes?"

He stood, his nostrils flaring, his face suddenly red. "I've committed no war crimes."

Genevieve hadn't meant to anger him. She felt her hope disappear, certain she would soon be in a prison cell next to Lombardelli. If she was honest with herself, that had always been the most likely outcome of this visit.

Staring at the ground, she heard the officer pace. It seemed like hours before he broke the silence. "You know I could arrest you?"

"Yes," she whispered.

"And you knew that when you came to see me?"

Genevieve nodded.

"I should arrest you." His pacing paused. "I should arrest you," he repeated, his voice so soft it barely reached her ears.

She met his gaze. He studied her fiercely, his eyes seeming to see her entire soul. Did he know how terrified she was? How alone? How close to collapsing with fear and exhaustion and hopelessness?

Slowly, his movements precise, he walked to the door and called his guard. His instructions were in whispered Italian, so Genevieve didn't hear them. She braced herself for arrest, but the guard never entered the room. The OVRA officer walked to his window and faced the darkening street, ignoring her. He stood there for fifteen minutes, according to the grandfather clock opposite his desk. It seemed much longer, the silence so complete Genevieve could hear each tick of the clock and each car that drove past on the road outside.

When the guard returned, the man with gray hair and glasses turned and nodded at Genevieve. "Follow him."

She was surprised when the guard led her not to the prison but to the building's back exit. As her eyes adjusted to the dim lighting, she noticed a man slumped against the wall as if drunk or asleep. It took her a moment to recognize him. His eyelids and lips were swollen, his posture stooped, his skin bloody.

"Dr. Lombardelli?"

He groaned and winced as she knelt next to him. "Genevieve?" She caught the smallest of smiles. "Well, that makes sense now."

"What makes sense?"

"Just before releasing me, they asked me about you again, wanting to know how valuable you'd be to them. I downplayed your role, saying you knew nothing that hadn't already been reported to headquarters and nothing they couldn't learn from me. I hope I haven't bruised your ego."

Genevieve helped Lombardelli to his feet and gently arranged his right arm around her shoulders. "No, you haven't hurt my feelings. Peter tried to do the same thing once. It didn't work, but I loved him for it." She took a few steps with Lombardelli and nearly tumbled. He was heavy. She didn't know how she could possibly take him somewhere safe all by herself. His breathing was labored and his face pinched with pain. He reminded her of the way Peter had looked after an interrogation by the Gestapo, but Peter had been forty years younger than Lombardelli. "What did they do to you in prison?"

Lombardelli shook his head. "Never mind; it's all over now."

They took a few more steps, then Lombardelli stumbled. It was all Genevieve could do to slow his fall. "I'm going to find some help," she said.

She left the alley and stopped a burly, balding civilian. She asked for his assistance in pathetic Italian and offered money in exchange. It wasn't much—enough to buy food for a week—but it was all she had. The man helped her carry Lombardelli to a nearby home, damaged and abandoned sometime during the war, and guided him inside.

Lombardelli moaned. "What about the harbor, Genevieve?"

She'd missed the radio appointment to finalize their evacuation—the radio was smashed. If OSS sent help by air, she doubted anyone would land without verification. But help by sea might still come, even without confirmation. "I don't think you'll make it to the harbor."

Lombardelli used Italian to speak with the man she'd paid. When he finished, he switched to English and turned to Genevieve. "Will you check my pockets? He says he'll go to the pier and give directions if we pay him enough."

Lombardelli's pockets contained a nearly empty pack of cigarettes, a pen, and nothing else, not even a match. Genevieve checked her pockets, but they were empty. Then she remembered her necklace. It was gold, with real gemstones, and it was valuable. She took it off and asked if it would be enough.

The man took the jewelry and examined it closely before placing it in his pocket and speaking with Lombardelli. Genevieve watched him leave with her necklace, the one her sister-in-law had given her, the one she'd worn next to her skin every day for close to seven years. She squeezed her eyes shut, feeling hints of regret, but if it could get them the help they needed, Genevieve knew her sister-in-law would have approved the trade.

Lombardelli was quiet, then said, "He agreed to help, but I'm not sure he will. If you want to leave, I won't blame you."

"I'm not going to leave you. If no one comes, we'll figure something else out."

"See if there's a basement or a cellar, will you?"

Genevieve explored the house. All the windows on the main level were broken. The furniture showed signs of weather damage, and the kitchen was mostly empty. There were half a dozen cans of food, a few pots, and a pile of broken plates. There was no basement, but there was a cellar outside. She pulled back the heavy doors and brought her hands to her mouth to stop a scream when a rat ran out. She returned to the home without exploring the cellar.

The upper floor of the home was roofless. Two bedrooms had once existed, but the bed frames were broken and the bedding moldy. She took the least-damaged bedding and returned to Lombardelli. She propped a pillow under his head, covered his body with a blanket, and described what she'd found.

"I want you to take all the food and blankets into the cellar and stay there," he said.

"I'd rather stay with you, and I don't think I can move you by myself. Besides, the cellar's wet and infested with rats."

Lombardelli found her hand and gripped it. "Genevieve, I'm not going to be around much longer."

"Don't say that. Someone might come for us."

He shook his head. "No, I'm bleeding internally. I don't even think Nathan could save me now. That's the real reason OVRA released me— they knew I was dying, and they believed they wouldn't get any additional information from you. With the war almost over, they chose mercy.

"I want you to promise me something, Genevieve. Don't mourn for me. I'll die trying to give my grandchildren a better world. Perhaps my work will even succeed. And I know you loved that American of yours, but promise me you won't mourn for him anymore either? You've seen a great deal of tragedy, but that doesn't mean you have to shun happiness. When it comes, take it. And think a little more about Nathan. He loves you."

Genevieve nodded through her tears.

"If anyone comes for you, get out quickly. If not, hide in the cellar. I was in prison with a CLN member. You remember who they are?"

"Yes." The CLN was the *Comitato di Liberazione Nazionale,* a resistance group opposed to the Nazis and Communists.

Lombardelli continued. "They begin their uprising in a few hours. I want you in the cellar when the firing starts. You might have to wait a few days, but don't leave until it's quiet. I don't care how hungry you get or how many rats there are. That cellar's the safest place for you. If the New Zealanders get here first, you'll be fine as soon as they arrive. If the Partisans get here first, you'll have to sneak out. Hide that pretty hair of yours, smear soot on your face, and head west. But first, get your hiding place ready."

Genevieve numbly followed the doctor's orders. She moved the food and bedding and even found a candle and a match to make the cellar not quite so spooky. When she was finished, she checked on Lombardelli again. He was dead.

CHAPTER THIRTY-NINE
A LIGHT IN THE CELLAR

PETER, STANDING ON A TRIESTE pier, watched Jamie speak to the man who'd been waiting for them.

"He described Dr. Lombardelli correctly," Jamie said.

"You think we should try it?"

Jamie hesitated. He asked the man another question, then explained. "I am not sure I trust him. And he isn't willing to take us there without additional payment. But he will give us directions."

"Well, I haven't seen any money in months." Currency was one of the few luxuries they hadn't found on the yacht.

"Nor have I," Jamie said.

While they spoke, the man shifted something shiny from one hand to the other, and it slipped partially from his grip. The pendant of a necklace swung into the moonlight, a gold cross embedded with gemstones. "Will you ask him if I can see that necklace?" Peter asked. Something about it looked familiar.

Jamie raised an eyebrow. "Since when are you interested in women's jewelry?"

Peter held his hand out, and after Jamie explained, the man reluctantly gave it to Peter. He stared at it, sure he had seen one like it before. "Do you think this is real, Jamie?"

Jamie handled it, studying each stone. "Probably."

"How many necklaces do you suppose there are exactly like this?"

Jamie looked at it again. "Not many. I would guess it is a few hundred years old. Why?"

"Genevieve had one just like it."

"I doubt this is hers, then. How would a cheesemaker's daughter have a necklace worth almost as much as our stolen yacht?"

Peter wished it were that simple. "It was a family heirloom from her sister-in-law. And her sister-in-law was an aristocrat."

"But Genevieve promised she would stay in Bari, didn't she?"

"Yeah," Peter said. But if Genevieve was in Bari, how did her necklace get to Trieste?

The man motioned that he wanted the necklace back. Peter surrendered it, concluding it was just similar to the one Genevieve owned. He had seen it only a few times, and that had been months ago.

"Peter, I asked him a little more about the woman with Dr. Lombardelli. He describes her as a scrawny brunette. The necklace was hers. She is foreign—French, he thinks."

"You'd better get directions from him." Peter walked back to the yacht to give Krzysztof an update. When he returned, the man with Genevieve's necklace was gone.

It was after curfew, so Peter and Jamie kept to the shadows and walked quietly. Jamie had even put a sock from the yacht's wardrobe around the end of his cane to keep it silent. Krzysztof had volunteered to go with Peter so Jamie wouldn't have to limp, but Jamie wanted to find Lombardelli, he spoke the local languages, and he'd visited Trieste before the war.

The home their contact described was within an hour's stealthy walk from the harbor. When they entered and no one greeted them, Jamie turned to Peter. "I suppose she is not here. Sorry, old boy."

"I don't want her to be here." The sudden sound of machine-gun fire in the distance was reason enough for that. Until then, the night had been quiet. Peter glanced at his watch. It was 0400 hours. They'd arrived in Trieste later than planned. He walked across the room and stared at a long form lying under an old blanket. "A body?" Peter stood fixed to the floor. It wasn't until he realized the body was too large to be Genevieve's that he relaxed.

Jamie knelt over the form and pulled the blanket back. The man underneath was old. His eyes were closed, and he looked like he'd been mauled by either a wild animal or a Gestapo agent. "Dr. Lombardelli," Jamie whispered.

The house seemed otherwise deserted. Someone had to have pulled the blanket over the doctor's head, but that could have been hours ago.

"Did he leave any paperwork?"

Jamie checked the body and shook his head.

Peter searched the home. The furniture was old and rotting but still capable of concealing something if Lombardelli had left behind evidence about Kimby.

"I will check upstairs," Jamie said.

Peter searched the kitchen that no longer had food and the bathroom that no longer had running water. The small-arms fire outside picked up, but Peter didn't want Lombardelli's work to be in vain. Still, after slitting open the cushions of the moldy sofa and finding nothing useful, Peter was about to call Jamie and head back to the pier. He glanced out the broken kitchen window and saw a sliver of faint light. He walked outside and discovered the source: a cellar door. Peter drew his pistol and pulled back one of the doors, hoping he wasn't making himself a target. Anyone looking his direction would see his silhouette against the light from below.

He stepped into the old cellar. A wax taper in a candlestick burned in the middle of the floor, but it wasn't until he'd stepped past the candle that he noticed the person sleeping on a pile of blankets along the back wall.

He wasn't sure at first, but as he stepped closer, the form's identity became unmistakable. Genevieve was sleeping on her side, facing the candle, and her thin blanket had fallen to her waist. She was every bit as beautiful as he remembered. He stared at her for a long time, wondering how in the world she'd ended up in Trieste with Lombardelli.

Kneeling beside her, Peter brushed his fingers along her exposed forearm until they rested on her hand. The movement woke her. Her free hand slipped under her pillow, but when her eyes met his, she paused and stared. He felt her other hand turn and grasp his. She looked from it to his face and back again, holding his hand as if she wasn't sure it was real. Eventually, she smiled.

"*Bonjour, mon beau canari*," he whispered.

Her smile deepened, but still, she said nothing.

"He couldn't read her expression, but she didn't seem surprised to see him, which Peter found odd—it wasn't as if he'd been able to tell her he was coming. "Are you all right? We found Lombardelli's body. The man with your necklace said the doctor was wounded. Are you hurt too?" He searched the part of her he could see for bandages, but nothing stood out. She raised her eyebrows ever so slightly but still kept her mouth shut. "Why won't you talk to me?" he finally asked.

"I don't talk in my sleep," she whispered.

"You think you're dreaming?"

"I always am. You come, and everything is just as I want it for a little while. You kiss me, and then I wake up."

Peter knew they needed to leave while they still had darkness to mask their movements, but he couldn't resist kissing her softly on the corner of her mouth. "There, I've kissed you, and I'm still here. You're not dreaming."

"Yes, I am," she insisted. "This dream's just a little longer than most."

"Am I in your dreams often?"

"Yes," she whispered.

"Do you usually dream in English?" Everything since his initial greeting had been in English.

"Sometimes."

"And am I usually scruffy and underweight in your dreams?"

She looked at him more carefully. "You do look awfully skinny. And your hair is so long." Her face crinkled in confusion, and she sat up in her bed. "That's so strange. I don't remember dying."

"Now you think you're dead?"

She nodded. "Well, I have to be, don't I? Because you look different than how I remember you in my dreams, so I'm not dreaming. But you're here, and you're dead, so I must be dead too."

Peter took both her hands in his. "Genevieve, we're both awake, alive, and in Trieste." When she didn't respond, he motioned with his head toward a half-empty water bucket. "I'd rather not pour the contents of that bucket down your back to convince you, but I will if I have to."

She still seemed unsure. She freed one of her hands and brushed it through Peter's hair. His last haircut had been the previous July, and his hair was longer than it had ever been before—completely covering his neck and falling into his eyes. Then she ran her fingers along his cheeks. "Oh, Peter, everyone told me you were dead. I didn't want to believe them, but I hadn't heard from you in so long. Everyone said I was crazy to keep hoping. And then Major Baker said you were executed by the Nazis—"

"How did you hear about that?"

"It happened?"

"Almost," Peter said. "We had a close call, but—" Peter shook his head. He'd explain later. He grinned at her as he stood up, and a second later, she was in his arms.

"You really are alive, then, aren't you? You have no idea how many of my prayers have just been answered."

Peter thought he had a reasonable idea of how many prayers she might have said because he'd been praying for the same thing for a very, very long time. He held her tightly and kissed her forehead, afraid *he* was the one dreaming.

Chapter Forty
SHOTS IN THE DARK

"Peter." Jamie's voice called from above. "It is time for us to be on our way."

As he turned, Peter noticed a helmet and a pair of boots in the corner. He dug around, but there were no weapons. He had his pistol, and Jamie had his cane and a Luger he'd found on the yacht. "Are you armed?" he asked Genevieve, wondering if, like her brother, she kept a weapon under her pillow.

She shook her head. "My pistol's in a warehouse at the harbor, and Dr. Lombardelli's was taken when they arrested him."

Peter picked up the German helmet—it was dusty but otherwise clean—and placed it on her head. He stopped her when she tried to fasten the chin strap. "Leave it undone. If a shell goes off nearby the strap could snap your neck." He brushed his hand along her cheek and down her neck. He wanted to kiss her, but a burst of rifle fire reminded him this wasn't the place or the time. "It's getting closer?" he asked Jamie.

Jamie nodded as he helped Genevieve from the cellar. "Pleasure to see you again, mademoiselle."

Peter blew out the candle and joined the others, taking Genevieve's hand. The helmet was too big for her, but it would protect her head from flying shrapnel. "Back the way we came?"

Jamie nodded and led the way along a dark road. They could hear explosions and gunfire, but the action was a few streets away. They paused at an intersection, and Jamie looked to Peter for directions. Peter knew what he was asking. If someone was covering the streets, the first person across was the least likely to be shot. But they had no way of knowing if the other side of the street was safe. They could all go at once, but while one person might draw rifle fire, three might draw a mortar shell. Peter wasn't sure who was fighting or what their weaponry included. And he didn't know how likely they were to verify their target before pulling the trigger.

"You go first, Jamie."

Jamie nodded before hobbling across the road as rapidly as he could.

"Genevieve, you're next. Run, because if someone saw Jamie, they'll still be aiming this direction."

"What about you?"

"I'll come after you."

Genevieve's lips tightened in what Peter recognized as worry. "But if someone's watching, they'll be homed in for sure by the time you cross."

"I'll run fast." When her concern didn't ease, he kept talking. "I can do fast dashes. For a couple years, I had more stolen bases than the rest of my baseball team combined." He didn't clarify that his baseball prowess was before two serious ankle injuries and one minor one, but she didn't know much about baseball anyway—or at least she hadn't last summer.

When Jamie waved all clear, Peter nodded at Genevieve, and she sprinted across the road. No one shot at her; no one yelled. No one seemed to have noticed. *Thank you*, Peter prayed. His turn was equally uneventful.

After they'd repeated the process another two times, Peter realized their intended path was through what seemed to be the center of the firefight. "Is there another way to the harbor?" he asked.

"We can go around," Jamie said.

Peter looked at Genevieve, and she nodded her agreement. It would take longer, but if it avoided the thickest combat, it would be worth it. She was standing right next to him, so close. Peter almost kissed her again, but Jamie was only feet away, and they were in a hurry. *Wait till we get to the yacht. There will be plenty of time for kissing on the way to Bisevo.*

They continued for what Peter guessed was an hour, cold, silent, and tense as small arms sounded all around them. They knew each crossroad might be monitored by a sniper, that each turn might lead them into a roadblock.

They turned a corner, and another stretch of moonlit road lay ahead of them, waiting to be crossed. Jamie limped to the other side, and Genevieve followed. Peter was halfway across when a shot sounded, and a bullet hit the cobblestones inches in front of him. He swerved and dove for the shadows near one of the buildings lining the street, wishing the moon would hurry and set.

They'd moved only a few yards into the side street when they saw a dead rat floating at the edge of a dirty puddle. Peter glanced at Genevieve, who stared at the lifeless rodent. "Do you hate rats as much as you hate mice?" he asked.

She nodded.

The street was filled with refuse, the stench was stomach-churning, and Peter could make out other rodents scurrying away from them. "We could go back and try a different route."

"So you can get shot at again?" Genevieve shook her head and led the way.

Peter held his hand out to help her over a mound of garbage. "I'll make it up to you. Dinner and dancing? I promise not to step on your feet this time."

Genevieve took his hand, her face softening into a smile. "I don't remember you stepping on my feet the last time you took me dancing. I just remember you staring at them."

Jamie's cane crunched into the garbage. "Peter, she might be more interested in promises of tidy brick homes with white picket fences and miniature versions of yourself running around the yard."

"Do you like brick houses?" Peter asked Genevieve. He still wanted to marry her, but he wasn't going to propose in a smelly alley or in front of Jamie.

"Right now, I'd settle for anything with a warm shower and plenty of soap." She shuddered as they passed a heap of trash with a pair of rats on top. "And no more rats."

"All right," Peter said. "No more rats."

They left the alley and grew quiet as the sound of gunfire increased. A set of headlights turned the corner and began speeding down the road. Not sure who was driving, Peter grabbed his pistol and pulled Genevieve down—right into a puddle. He could feel her shivers and her breath on his left ear as the car passed. He kept his handgun aimed at the car, as did Jamie, who was also crouched in the puddle, until the vehicle was out of sight.

Jamie glanced at one of the nearby structure. "We're almost there."

As they passed the building, Peter could see the harbor, but they were still a block from the pier where Krzysztof and the *Golden Swastika* waited for them. They crawled into the darkness bordering a warehouse, then crept around the building to their next obstacle: an open yard illuminated by moonlight.

"I'll see if I can find a way around it," Peter said as he slipped away. *Almost there, almost safe,* he told himself. *And you've found Genevieve.*

Peter's reconnaissance trip lasted ten minutes. The alternate way would take three times as long and involve an equally wide stretch of moonlit ground that went through another rat-infested alley.

"I think this is our best route," Peter said when he returned to Jamie and Genevieve.

Jaime nodded his agreement. "I am disappointed in our Nazi friend who stocked the yacht for us. He should have mounted a machine gun on the deck."

Peter smiled. They hadn't left Krzysztof completely unarmed—there were knives from the galley and a few heavy tools but nothing he could use to cover the pier as they approached.

Jamie went first, following the pattern they'd set at earlier intersections. His quick limp was surprisingly quiet, and he crossed the open area without incident.

Genevieve followed, her wet clothes clinging to her. With the German helmet, she'd be easy to mistake for a German soldier. Peter almost ran after her, but no one had shot at Jamie, and Genevieve was moving more quickly than he had. Peter began to relax as she neared Jamie's hiding place.

Then a single shot rang out, and Genevieve tumbled to the ground. Peter ran after her, not caring that whoever had shot her could shoot him too. Jamie reached her first and dragged her away as a hail of bullets hit the ground around Peter. He reached Genevieve in time to help carry her the last few yards to a wall that would shelter them from the machine gun.

Genevieve gasped in pain as Jamie sat her against the wall. Fighting back the horror filling his chest, Peter examined the bullet hole in her right shoulder. He tried to be gentle, but she winced under his touch.

"It's not that bad," she said, "but I never expected it to hurt so much."

A hundred emotions ran through Peter's mind, panic at the top of the list. He forced himself to take a few deep breaths. Panic would not help anything. Genevieve was shot, but she wasn't dead, nor was she likely to die from her wound. Her eyes teared up as Peter tied a handkerchief around her shoulder. He brushed a few strands of hair away from her forehead, uncertain what to say.

"I will scout ahead," Jamie said before disappearing.

Peter turned his attention back to Genevieve. "I'm sorry," he said, thinking of the German helmet he'd given her. Why hadn't he chosen a different route to the pier or gone across with her? *Couldn't they have shot me instead?*

"It's not your fault," Genevieve said. He'd never heard so much pain in her voice.

"We're clear." Jamie's voice came from the other side of the building.

Peter picked her up. "We'll get you back to Bari. Everything will be all right." Peter wasn't sure which one of them he was trying to reassure.

She nodded. "I know. You're alive, and you're here, and everything will be fine."

Following Jamie's lead, Peter carried Genevieve the rest of the way to the pier. No one else tried to shoot them, and whoever had shot Genevieve didn't try to track them down.

She was unconscious when they reached the yacht, and Peter felt like a part of him was dying with every drop of her blood that soaked through the handkerchief and trickled down her arm.

* * *

The first thing Genevieve became aware of was pain. The next thing was the hum of an engine and the up and down motion of a ship. She opened her eyes and saw Peter in a chair not far from where she lay, his head leaning against the wall, his eyes closed. She watched him sleep, tempted to wake him, but he looked like he needed the rest.

The next thing she remembered was waking to whispering male voices. She moaned without meaning to as she forced her eyes open. Peter and another man were in the cabin with her, and Peter broke off his conversation and moved to her side.

"How are you?" he asked.

She tried to force a smile, but the yacht's motion made her afraid she'd vomit. "Seasick."

Peter ran his fingers through her hair. "I'm sorry. Krzysztof's arranged for a plane to take us from Vis to Bari, and we're halfway there. I don't know if you get airsick too, but at least it will be over quicker. We'll sail to Vis first, then we need to make a quick trip to Bisevo."

She glanced at Krzysztof. "You look like your father."

"You've met him?" Krzysztof's blue eyes lit up with hope.

"He came to Bari with Major Baker." Genevieve closed her eyes again as the yacht lurched up and down, her stomach moving the opposite directions.

She felt Peter's hand on hers. "You can tell us about it later, when we're on solid ground and someone's stitched up your shoulder."

She opened her eyes to see Peter studying her face. He looked so serious, like he had the weight of the world on his shoulders. "One thing more. Kimby betrayed Nelson and Baker when they were in Venice."

"You found proof?" Krzysztof asked.

Genevieve nodded, then squeezed her eyes shut again. She wasn't sure which was worse, the motion sickness or the agony emanating from her shoulder. "We found Kimby's source. He's a Nazi, and if he survives the uprising in Trieste, he can prove Kimby committed treason."

CHAPTER FORTY-ONE
THE HANGMAN'S NOOSE

Tuesday, May 1
Bisevo, Liberated Yugoslavia

Iuliana's two hundred thirty-ninth day of captivity began like most of the others had, but a shroud of depression hung about her as she left her tent to prepare breakfast. Marija and Iuliana had formed a strong friendship, but Marija's trial was set for May 2. They knew she'd be found guilty. She'd be charged with being her uncle's relative, and neither of them knew how to disprove the truth.

Iuliana and Marija had spent night after night brainstorming ways to escape, but they'd witnessed other prisoners try plans similar to their best options and witnessed the swift executions that followed each failed attempt. Anatolie had left for medical care back in January, but that was because Ivan had taken him, not because he'd outsmarted their captors or found a secret exit.

"Momma?" Anatolie stood outside the kitchen door as Iuliana finished serving the guards—except Ivan, who was standing next to Anatolie.

"Yes?"

"Marija threw up again."

Iuliana smiled, not because she was glad for Marija's discomfort but because her son reported it so casually. Poor Marija began most mornings nauseated. Iuliana was grateful she'd found a second bucket so they could have one for washing and one for catching vomit.

Anatolie followed his cat toward the fence, leaving Ivan and Iuliana alone. "Are you going to eat breakfast?" she asked.

Ivan nodded. "Yes, but I want to warn you first. Commandant upset today. Horsewhipped two guards when they arrive five minutes late. Beat prisoner when he didn't move out of way quick enough."

Iuliana nodded, worried, but grateful she'd been warned. She could make the commandant's favorite meal. That should at least keep him from lashing out at her or her son. "Thank you for the warning."

He nodded.

"Ivan?" He paused in the doorway as she spoke. "I know I shouldn't ask, but Marija goes on trial tomorrow. Her uncle was a Chetnik leader, but she can't help who she's related to. She never took up arms against the Partisans. Is there anything you can do for her?"

He hesitated. She saw the compassion in his eyes but knew what she was asking—any help he gave a prisoner would put his own life at risk. And she didn't know if he could do anything anyway. "I am willing to help," he whispered. "But I am not sure I am able." He turned away before she could respond and didn't come for his breakfast.

After she'd cleaned enough of the morning's mess that she'd be able to start on the next meal immediately, she took out the bread and cheese she'd hidden from the officers' supper the night before.

Camp rules prohibited prisoners from hoarding food or removing it from the mess hall. The rations were so scanty that no one would have leftovers anyway, but it was still tempting because having a bit of food in one's pocket made it easier to hope there was another day ahead. Despite the rules, Iuliana regularly brought food to Marija in their tent.

The male prisoners were often given work assignments, and Iuliana had her kitchen work. Marija was officially assigned to the kitchen too, but Iuliana didn't really need the help, especially when the smells made Marija ill, so Marija spent most of her days in the tent. Anatolie, also without an assignment, usually joined her for part of the day. Iuliana was amazed at all Marija had taught him. His English and his Serbo-Croat were improving, and he could recognize all of his letters, count to sixty, and sing dozens of new songs. And with Marija's help, his right hand had regained some of its flexibility.

Iuliana often felt guilty that she hadn't taught her son more. She'd been so focused on preserving his life that she'd given little thought to preparing him for an existence outside the camp. A life, she supposed, with a deeply religious Croatian widow on Vis. *Don't be too hard on yourself. He's only three, and keeping him alive has taken all your energy.*

Iuliana saw the commandant strutting around camp. She waited until his attention was focused elsewhere before she went to her tent. "How are you this morning?" she asked as she pulled the tent flap closed behind her.

Marija managed a weak smile as she gestured to the bucket on the floor. "About the same."

As Iuliana pulled the food from her apron pocket, she heard the tent flap being ripped open. A guard stood there, holding the fabric, the commandant visible behind him, the incriminating food still in Iuliana's hand.

The commandant's eyes seethed with rage, but his voice was perfectly calm. "Chain them up next to the gallows."

The guard called one of his associates to assist him and marched the two women from the tent to the area behind the justice building, where prisoners were executed. Since the day she'd entered the camp, Iuliana had known she wouldn't leave again, not alive. And yet, even knowing she was going to die for the past eight months, having death be suddenly imminent left her terrified. The guards handcuffed the women and forced them to sit in the dirt where they could stare at the hangman's noose.

Iuliana felt tears forming in her eyes. She would be just one more victim of the war. One more death that few people would know about and that even fewer would remember. How long would Anatolie remember her? Through the fence, she could make out the one thing that gave her hope. Ivan and Anatolie were walking away from the camp. Ivan had kept his promise, and Anatolie was going to live.

Marija, sitting next to her, handled everything stoically, but that too made Iuliana sad. Marija was going to die. Iuliana blinked away her tears when she felt something brush against her knee: Anatolie's cat. Iuliana almost laughed. She had never liked the cat. She only put up with it because it found its own food and kept her son happy. It had never come to her before. *Stupid cat*, she thought. *Why didn't you follow Anatolie?*

* * *

Marija's back ached. *That will be over soon*, she thought. *I'm sorry, Miloš. I did my best to stay alive. And I tried to be happy—as happy as one can be in a prison.* What Marija really regretted was dragging Iuliana into her affairs. If the Partisans had just executed Marija a little earlier, Iuliana wouldn't be chained next to her, and Anatolie wouldn't be so close to becoming an orphan.

The noon sun beat down on them. The end of Iuliana's nose was pink, marring her otherwise perfect complexion. "I'm sorry, Iuliana," Marija said.

Iuliana shook her head, her eyes red from weeping. "You already apologized, and it's not your fault."

Marija stared at the gallows, wondering how painful death by hanging would be. She wasn't ready to die. For years, she'd regretted the circumstances that had kept her alive after her family and her village were destroyed, and she missed her husband. But she wanted to keep the promise she'd made to Miloš, and she wanted her baby to live. *I finally have a reason to survive, now that I'm about to die.*

A disturbance near the gate made both women twist their necks to try to see what was going on. Marija didn't understand the shouts, but she recognized the sounds that followed. Someone was in pain.

Iuliana shuddered with the man's cries. "Ivan said the commandant was upset today. He'd already beaten two guards and a prisoner before breakfast. And I smelled what my replacement is cooking. I don't think his next meal will put him in a better mood."

"Maybe he'll change his mind about executing his cook." Marija hoped that would be the case. It wouldn't save her or her baby, but if Iuliana survived, Marija could meet death with a lighter conscience.

Iuliana shook her head. "I've watched him for eight months, and I've never seen him change an order. At least my son is safe."

Marija was worried about Anatolie, but she didn't express her fears out loud. Vis wasn't big enough for him to disappear, and any of the camp guards would recognize him if they saw him. Anatolie's only hope was that none of the guards would *want* to find him and that the commandant wouldn't care.

Two guards dragged a beaten, bloody man around to the scaffolding and threw him to the ground. The man was in uniform—the commandant had ordered another guard beaten.

"Ivan!" Iuliana gasped.

The guard turned his head toward them. Part of his fair hair was matted with blood, and his boyish face was red and swollen. He opened his mouth, and several of his teeth were missing. "They saw me take boy away. But he is safe. Fisherman take him to Komiža."

"I'm so sorry, Ivan," Iuliana sobbed.

He forced a brave smile. "They say revolutionaries are all dead men on leave, but I never thought my own side would kill me."

The commandant marched into view. His face seemed made of stone. He showed no sympathy, no compassion. His job was to rid his country of internal enemies, and how could he have fulfilled such an assignment if his own conscience hadn't been his first victim?

The commandant pointed to Ivan, then Iuliana, then Marija. There was only one noose—the commandant had just decreed the order of execution.

Two guards grabbed Ivan's arms and led him up the platform. He stared at the ground as they tied his hands behind his back and slipped the noose over his head. Marija looked away when another guard stepped forward and placed a hand on the lever that would make the floor fall out from under Ivan's feet. She heard the scrape of wood and squeezed her eyes shut.

Iuliana leaned her head on Marija's shoulder and sobbed. "It's my fault."

"You never meant Ivan any harm. And there is a God, Iuliana. He'll welcome Ivan home."

After they'd removed Ivan's body and reset the trap door, one of the guards adjusted the rope's length while another one unlocked Iuliana's chains and forced her to her feet. She was deathly pale, other than her sunburned nose, and tears still streamed from her eyes. Her legs shook as she was marched up the scaffolding. Yet there was a calm dignity to the beautiful Romanian widow as one of the guards bound her hands and tightened the noose around her neck.

Marija heard a vehicle screech to a stop at the prison's entrance. *Please don't let it be Anatolie. And if he is captured, don't let Iuliana know. Let her die thinking he's safe.*

When three Partisan soldiers walked into view, she realized with relief that they weren't men from the prison, and they carried no three-year-old child. Two of them were enlisted men. Staring at them made Marija look into the sun, so she couldn't see them well, but she saw their jaws drop as they stared at the hangman's platform.

The other man was a general-potpukovnik, a few ranks above the commandant's pukovnik rank. His hair was gray and his face wrinkled, his posture a strange mix of feebleness and energy. The general ordered the commandant and his men at ease as he looked over the prisoners with a coldness equal to the commandant's. "What are their crimes?" He gestured to Iuliana, then to Marija.

"They were caught stealing food. And though they haven't yet been tried, they are suspected counter-revolutionaries."

"Are they dangerous?"

The commandant scoffed. "No. Not physically."

"Our glorious leader, Josip Tito, has nearly succeeded in driving out the evil Nazi Army. Those who would challenge his authority have been crushed. Now he wishes us to look forward to the peace that will come to our Communist paradise." The general spoke eloquent Serbo-Croat. "But there is much rebuilding to be done. Our struggle for liberation has left villages destroyed, farmland uncultivated, and factories understaffed." The general used his cane to point at the women. "Traitors like this will not be allowed to sully our victory. But Tito's new policy is to use our prisoners for labor. If they fail to survive the strain, it will be of little significance."

"Sir, I have orders to execute the prisoners sent to me."

The general turned sharply. "Now you have new orders." Both his hands rested on his cane.

It was Jamie's cane, and Marija supposed the man holding it was Jamie, but he looked so much older. A cloud passed in front of the sun, and she stared at the other men wearing Partisan uniforms—Peter and Krzysztof. "We will take the women with us now," Jamie said. "The vineyards on Vis need work, and if these women are not dangerous, they can work themselves to death in the fields. Hanging them would be a waste of labor."

The commandant nodded and motioned for one of his guards to release Iuliana. Krzysztof went instead, loosening the noose and removing it from Iuliana's neck. Marija held her breath, knowing how easy it was to read her friend's emotions, hoping Iuliana wouldn't blow everything when she recognized Krzysztof. Peter's finger was on his rifle's trigger, but Iuliana didn't give the men away. She looked at Krzysztof, stared, and fainted. He caught her as she slunk toward the ground, and he motioned for the prison guard to cut the rope from her hands.

The commandant ordered another of his guards to unlock Marija's handcuffs.

"I shall return when I have found positions for the male prisoners," Jamie said. "Death to Fascism."

"Freedom to the people," the commandant replied.

Marija followed Jamie while Peter and Krzysztof carried Iuliana to a waiting car.

"Marija, what happened to Iuliana's son?" Peter whispered.

"He was sent to Komiža, on Vis."

"We happen to be headed back to Vis anyway." Peter climbed into the driver's seat, next to Jamie. Marija sat with Iuliana—still unconscious—and Krzysztof in the back. As they drove away, Peter turned back briefly. "Is she all right?"

"In shock, I think." Krzysztof placed his fingers on Iuliana's neck to make sure she still had a pulse.

"Are you okay, Marija?" Peter was skinnier than she remembered, and he seemed uneasy.

Marija smiled. "Yes." She knew she shouldn't be happy. Ivan was dead, and so was Miloš and her entire village and all her relatives from Yugoslavia. But she was free, and for the first time in weeks, she thought she'd be able to keep her promise to Miloš. *Baby Colić, it looks like you'll have a chance at life after all. And I'm going to do everything I can to make sure it's a good life.*

CHAPTER FORTY-TWO
"THE BOTTOM OF THE ADRIATIC"

Vis, Liberated Yugoslavia

GENEVIEVE WAS GLAD TO BE on solid ground again. She waited for Peter and the others in the dining room of an SOE home near a gravel runway, the only airfield on Vis Island. American, British, and Partisan servicemen came through the home, but she sat and rested, exhausted after disguising Jamie. She was grateful she remembered the techniques her brother had used so often. Jamie was recognizable, perhaps, but only slightly after she'd added twenty years to his face, making him a believable Partisan general. The men had rushed off before she could disguise Peter or Krzysztof—Peter had felt they needed to leave at once, and she'd learned to trust his feelings.

They'd anchored at Vis that morning, doubting they could find disguises on Bisevo because it was such a tiny island, and the men had planned to take a boat with a less suspicious name to Bisevo and back. She hoped Peter and the others would return soon. She was nervous about their trip to the camp, but the Partisans were technically their allies, so she hoped everything would be all right, even though they were wearing stolen uniforms.

Genevieve tried to ignore the throbbing from her injury. She couldn't remember ever being in so much pain before. *Just a while longer, then you'll be in Bari, and the staff there will take care of you.*

"Excuse me, miss?"

She looked up at the British major who addressed her, assuming he was one of the commandos stationed on Vis. "Yes?"

"I need a passenger list for your flight to Bari."

"Peter Eddy, James Nelson, Krzysztof Zielinski, myself—Genevieve Olivier—and possibly one civilian. I don't know her name."

All the blood seemed to drain from the major's face. "Where do you travel from?"

Genevieve supposed that was a legitimate question for the man's records. "Trieste."

"You came by boat?"

She nodded.

"And what are the other members of your party doing at present? I see they borrowed one of our jeeps."

The man had brown hair brushed away from his face and brown eyes. Genevieve's shoulder still stabbed with pain, but now her stomach knotted too. The British major was asking too many questions and seemed far too interested in her answers.

* * *

Peter parked outside one of Komiža's Catholic churches. Iuliana held on to Krzysztof's arm as she stepped from the jeep, not trusting herself to stand without support. Krzysztof had always been thin, and it was more dramatic now, but Iuliana could still feel strength in his arms as he supported her. She hoped this was the parish Ivan had come to and that the priest would tell her where her son was. She met Krzysztof's eyes. His hair was longer, but his eyes were the same shade of blue she remembered, the same color she'd dreamed about so many nights. When she'd woken on the rickety fishing boat taking them to Vis, he'd been holding her hand.

"I suggest you escort the women inside," Jamie said to Krzysztof. "Marija can translate. The priest might find three Partisan soldiers a bit threatening."

Krzysztof nodded and led the way, but when they saw the priest, he let Marija walk ahead of them.

"How did you find me?" Iuliana asked.

Krzysztof looked to Marija, who spoke with the priest in reverent tones. "I would have gone anywhere to find you, but we actually came for her. She told you how we met?"

Iuliana nodded.

"How is Anatolie?" he asked.

"He's growing. He got hurt—his hand—but it's improving. I wish I wouldn't have sent him away. What if we can't find him?" The fear of losing Anatolie overwhelmed her again. "It seems you always have to help me find my son."

Krzysztof held her shoulders and peered into her face, probably checking for tears because her voice had cracked. "I think it was wise to send him away. It wouldn't have been good for him to see that noose around your neck. When I saw it . . . I . . . It was hard for me to play my role." He ran a gentle finger along her neck, where the rope had been. "I would have never forgiven myself if we'd arrived too late to save you."

Iuliana slid into his embrace. She was crying again. Why did she always do that? "I was so worried about you. From what Kimby said, there was little chance of any of you surviving."

"We're all going to make it home now," he whispered as he pulled her closer. "Or find a new home—one that's safe and free from tyranny."

* * *

Peter tried not to fidget as he waited outside the church. He felt strangely anxious. *It's all over now; you can relax.* Krzysztof's father had sent a plane, just as promised, and it was already waiting at the airstrip for them. And Genevieve would recover. She'd been in pain when they'd anchored that morning, but after watching her concentrate on making Jamie a Partisan general, Peter thought she would get better, especially without the motion sickness to deal with.

Peter felt his first rush of relief when he saw Krzysztof's smile as he emerged from the church with Iuliana and Marija.

"He's at a fisherman's house just a few minutes down the road."

Peter nodded, glad the priest had believed Iuliana was Anatolie's mother. Once they found the little boy, they could go home. Peter drove the jeep they'd borrowed from some British commandos to the fisherman's home, following directions the priest had given Marija.

When they arrived, the widow's home was empty. Peter picked the front door's lock to make sure the woman wasn't inside trying to hide Anatolie from a squad of Partisan soldiers.

"Mama!"

Peter turned at the shout, seeing the small boy run up a path from the ocean, an old woman trailing behind him. Peter smiled as he watched the reunion between mother and son, trying not to think of all the mothers whose sons wouldn't be coming home or of all the children who'd lost their parents. *You can't change everything,* he told himself, *so enjoy the good things when you see them.*

Anatolie remembered Peter, but he was scared of him, probably because he associated Peter with a bad memory. He ignored Jamie, let Krzysztof lift

him into the car, and chattered away on his mother's lap during the drive to
the airstrip. According to Marija's translation, he was telling the two women
all about his boat ride and walk along the beach. No one told the boy that
the blond-haired guard who'd started him on his adventure had been hanged
for his efforts.

When they reached the airstrip, Peter parked near the plane, then
walked back to the SOE house to get Genevieve. As soon as she was better,
Peter would take her dancing. And then he would kiss her for a long, long
time.

Peter went inside, but the house was empty, except for part of the American
C-47 crew that would fly them to Bari.

"Do you know where the brunette with a shoulder injury went?" he asked.

The pilot nodded. "Yeah, she forgot something on the boat. Went
back to get it. One of the SOE guys went with her."

Peter wondered what Genevieve could have forgotten on the yacht.
They'd left Trieste with nothing but their clothing, and Genevieve didn't
normally collect souvenirs. "When did she leave?"

"'Bout an hour ago."

That was enough time for her to have walked there and back, except
she was wounded. "Who went with her?"

"Some British major working with the Partisans." The pilot turned to
one of his crew members. "What was his name?"

"Kimby."

Peter ran out the door and sprinted for the jeep.

"Whoa, Peter, what's going on?" Krzysztof asked.

"Kimby's got Genevieve."

"What?"

Peter started the jeep instead of answering.

Jamie climbed in as Peter shoved it into gear. "Where are we going?"
Jamie asked after they'd left Krzysztof, Anatolie, and the women behind in
the dust.

"The ship. The pilot said she went back to the yacht with Kimby to get
something." Peter didn't know if that was really where Kimby had taken
her, but it was a place to start.

Jamie checked the clip in his pistol.

"Thanks for jumping in," Peter said.

In his peripheral vision, Peter saw Jamie grin. "Don't get me wrong,
Peter. I am happy to do my part to see that you and Krzysztof have happy

reunions. Those women, after all, are the reason for our eight-month stay in Yugoslavia. But I am also eager to find Kimby. If he knows we are alive, he will be making plans to change that fact. 'I'll never pause again, never stand still, till either death hath closed these eyes of mine or fortune given me measure of revenge.'"

"He'll be expecting us. How good is he?"

Jamie let out a frustrated breath. "I have never trained with him. At Cambridge, he was an effeminate pansy, but I suppose he has been through the normal SOE training. He has time on his side. And he has never lacked brains."

"So we're walking into a trap?"

"Most likely."

"I shouldn't have left her alone." Peter had thought she'd be safe surrounded by American airmen and British commandos.

"You were trying to avoid dragging her on another sea voyage and into a possible shootout with Partisan guards. How were we to know Kimby was visiting Vis?" Jamie's words were meant to comfort, but they didn't mitigate Peter's guilt.

The men hadn't wanted to sail a ship called the *Golden Swastika* into either of the main harbors on Communist-controlled Vis, so they'd abandoned it on the south shore in a picturesque cove. Kimby would be waiting for them, but he couldn't know exactly when they'd arrive.

Peter didn't want Kimby to hear or see the jeep, so he parked on the side of the road before they reached the shore. He wished it was dark, but the midafternoon sun shone brightly. Kimby would only have to pick up one of the high-quality binoculars the yacht's owners had left on board to see Peter and Jamie coming along the narrow beach.

Peter concentrated on his memory of the shore. The sand was shaped like a wedge, widening as it moved farther from the concave cove. They'd left the yacht partially covered by the cove's overhanging rocks. The easiest way to reach the yacht was to walk or drive along the beach, but that was where Kimby would look for them.

They could also swim around the rocks and approach the yacht from the opposite side. Or approach it from above. Peter untied the gear strapped to the jeep's hood, leaving the shovels and first-aid kits and winding up the rope that had held them there. "Jamie, would you rather rappel or swim?"

Jamie reached for the rope. "You board first; try the starboard stern. I will drop in on the port bow."

Peter nodded and ran off, moving his holster from his waist to his neck so his pistol wouldn't be submerged as long. When he reached the water's edge on the back side of the cove, he kicked his shoes off and threw his Partisan jacket, shirt, and cap to the ground. The water was shallow enough that Peter could wade most of the way around the massive rock blocking his view of the yacht. In chest-deep water, he inched his way around the cliff and saw the yacht. He spotted Kimby on the deck, searching the area with a pair of binoculars. Peter hid behind the rock and waited while Kimby finished his scan. When Peter checked again, Kimby was facing the narrow strip of beach, his back to Peter. The yacht's original owners had kept a collection of Wagner records, and over the sound of the waves hitting the rocks, Peter could make out the notes of a march.

Peter swam the remaining thirty yards to the yacht, keeping his head above water and using a modified breaststroke instead of a crawl stroke, hoping it would make less noise. He lost sight of Kimby as he drew closer and was breathing hard as he made it to the starboard hull.

He pulled himself from the water by the anchor rope, making more noise than he would have preferred. The wet rope was slippery, but Peter had climbed plenty of ropes in training. His hands hurt and his muscles ached by the time he reached the deck and used both hands to pull himself aboard.

Genevieve saw him first. She sat on the deck with her back against the wheelhouse, the skin around her eyes pinched with pain and worry. Her right cheek was swollen, and Peter guessed Kimby had struck her. Kimby stood nearby. He turned, released the binoculars, and grabbed his pistol as Peter reached for his. Peter pointed his weapon at Kimby, and Kimby aimed his at Genevieve.

"Lieutenant Eddy, you were willing to parachute into Yugoslavia so I wouldn't send her to Germany. What are you willing to do so I don't send her to the bottom of the Adriatic with a bullet hole in her head?"

"You don't keep your promises anyway. Why should I believe you'll let her go if I cooperate?" Peter was taking a risk, but maybe if he kept Kimby talking, Kimby wouldn't hear Jamie on the cliff above the yacht.

Kimby's lips twitched into a smile. "Believe this, Lieutenant: if you don't put your pistol down in the next two seconds, I will shoot her now."

"He'll shoot me anyway, Peter," Genevieve said. "He plans to kill all of us here, where there won't be any witnesses."

Kimby gripped his pistol with both hands. Genevieve glared up at him.

"Wait!" Peter dropped his pistol into the water.

"Tsk tsk. So predictable."

"It's over, Kimby." Peter kept his eyes on his foe, willing himself not to look at the cliff jutting out over the yacht. "Krzysztof already sent our report. Your career is finished. No one will forgive you for sacrificing four agents on an unnecessary mission, sabotaging their parachutes, and ordering them killed. Chesterfield told us everything before he died."

Kimby laughed. "Don't be so dramatic, Lieutenant. Chesterfield couldn't have told you everything because he knew very little. All my actions were for the benefit of the British Empire and its vital alliance with Soviet Russia. I have friends in high positions who will defend me, especially when all the witnesses are dead."

"And Venice? How did turning two SOE agents over to OVRA benefit the British Empire?"

Kimby frowned. "James Nelson hates the Communists almost as much as he hates the Fascists. His talents are a threat to the greater good, and his death was meant to benefit the entire Soviet Union."

Jamie slid silently down the rope behind Kimby, his pistol in one hand and his cane hooked in his belt, but Kimby seemed to sense his presence. While Jamie was still ten feet from the deck, Kimby spun and fired. Jamie dropped from the rope, his pistol fell overboard, and his cane clattered to the deck beside him.

Peter took a quick step toward his friend, but Kimby pivoted his pistol back to Peter.

"I'll give you credit for being clever, but you won't win. Nor will you be around to assist Zielinski should he climb on deck next." Kimby smiled, and his finger tightened on the trigger.

Genevieve had stood when Jamie fell, and as Kimby fired at Peter, she yanked the binocular strap around Kimby's neck, sending his shot wild.

Kimby swore, bringing the pistol around and landing a vicious blow on Genevieve's injured arm. She cried out in pain and crumpled to the deck. Peter rushed Kimby, gripping the wrist that held the pistol with his right hand and thrusting his left into Kimby's neck. Kimby gasped for breath, but he kept hold of his pistol and stomped on the insole of Peter's shoeless left foot.

Peter swayed to the side, right into Kimby's punch. In the wave of dizziness that followed, Peter felt himself falling and focused all his willpower on bringing Kimby down with him. He plowed his shoulders into Kimby's abdomen and felt the British major tumble. Genevieve reached for Kimby's pistol. He seemed to realize he was about to lose it, so he threw it overboard.

Peter landed on top of Kimby, which should have given him an edge, but the advantage didn't last long. The broken ribs, pneumonia, lack of food—even the swim to the yacht—were wearing on him. In prolonged hand-to-hand combat, Kimby was going to win. They grappled with each other, punching and blocking, kneeing and kicking. Each of Kimby's strikes left Peter reeling in pain, but Kimby seemed to recover instantly whenever Peter made headway against him. As Kimby flipped Peter to his back and pinned him to the deck, they met each other's eyes, and Kimby too seemed to know his victory was inevitable.

Genevieve tried to grab the binocular strap again, but Kimby threw her off as though she weighed no more than a child. She landed on her bad arm and winced.

Kimby turned his attention back to Peter, swinging his fist toward the side of Peter's head. Peter blocked it, but Kimby's other hand clamped around Peter's throat. *How did Kimby get hands like vises?* Peter saw Genevieve behind Kimby. "Run," he croaked. If she left now, she might make it to safety before Kimby was finished with Peter.

Jamie's whisper in French barely reached his ears. "Genevieve, my cane."

Peter didn't hear the rest of the instructions, but he held out a hand instead of blocking Kimby's next punch. His vision blurred when Kimby's fist connected, but he felt the handle of Jamie's cane in his hand. When he gripped it, Genevieve held the bottom, pulling it away from the knife.

Kimby didn't see it coming—the knife in his ribs. It wasn't a fatal blow, but it made Kimby release Peter's neck. Gasping for breath, Peter gripped the knife's handle again and twisted, eliciting a howl of pain. Peter slid out from under Kimby and kicked him in the head.

While Kimby moaned in pain, Genevieve helped Peter to his feet.

"Do you surrender?" Peter's voice sounded strange in his ears.

Kimby crawled to the side of the ship so he could use the rail for support. He stood, his eyes darting from Jamie to Peter to Genevieve. He hesitated for an instant, then dove into the water below.

Peter ran to the railing. The sun shone into the clear water, and Peter could see the trail of bubbles from Kimby's descent straight to the bottom. He kept his eyes on the water, but Kimby wasn't trying to escape death; he was trying to escape justice.

When Peter was certain Kimby was no longer a threat, he knelt next to Genevieve, who was examining the bullet hole in Jamie's ribs.

"How bad is it?" Peter asked.

"It must have missed his lungs, or he'd already be dead," Genevieve said.

Peter went down to the stateroom and grabbed the first-aid kit they'd used on Genevieve. It wasn't fancy—no sulfa powder, no painkillers, just iodine and bandages.

Jamie moved his head and inhaled as if preparing for a speech.

"No, keep your mouth shut," Peter said. "Knowing you, you're planning to say something dramatic and then die. And I don't want you to die."

Jamie looked indignant. "I have five perfectly lovely Shakespeare quotations about death."

"And I don't want to hear any of them."

"After all we have been through together, you won't even listen to my quotes? How many times have I saved your life?"

Peter felt his lips pull into a smile. "I haven't been counting, but I guess the number's a little higher today than it was yesterday. Once we're in Bari, I'll listen to as many scenes as you care to recite. But none until then."

Genevieve finished dressing Jamie's wound. "Peter, I don't think Jamie should walk, and my shoulder's making me dizzy. Maybe you could pull the car around?"

Peter checked his pants pocket. The key to the jeep was still inside.

CHAPTER FORTY-THREE
SHARPENING THE KNIFE

THE REST OF THE TRIP to Bari was uneventful. Peter moved Jamie and Genevieve from the yacht to the jeep without dropping them in the water, and the plane took off ten minutes after they arrived at the airstrip. Peter sat next to Genevieve on the flight, but she was quiet. He hoped it was just a symptom of her motion sickness and her injury, but in the back of his mind, he worried it was something more. He had left last fall, even though Genevieve had asked him to stay. And when he'd rescued her in Trieste, she'd been shot, and then Kimby had used her for bait. Did she harbor any resentment? Was that why she was being so quiet?

There were stretchers waiting in Bari when they landed. Peter followed the wounded to the hospital only to be told he couldn't stay.

"It's all right, Peter. You can go," Genevieve said when Peter clenched his jaw, tempted to argue with the tall American doctor trying to send him away. "Come visit me later."

Peter, Krzysztof, Iuliana, Anatolie, and Marija were debriefed, deloused, and given a thorough medical examination. By the time he was released to visit the mess hall, Peter was hungry. But this time, he knew to start with something simple.

* * *

The smooth sound of the blade running along the whetstone filled Basileo's ears and mind with satisfaction. When he finished the knife, he loaded the clip for his Walther P38 and placed the pistol in his jacket pocket with an overwhelming feeling of serenity.

The war was almost over, and his side was losing. Mussolini was dead. Hitler was dead. For months, Basileo had planned to join his Fascist brothers at the national redoubt in the Bavarian Alps, where they would hold out until the Western Allies sued for peace. But rumors of the national redoubt had proved fantasy. With Belina dead and the war lost, Basileo had sunk into despair.

But his depression had fled a few hours before when he'd walked along an airstrip and recognized two people from his past: the blue-eyed British agent who'd broken Belina's heart and Lombardelli's brunette assistant. To have them appear together—both wounded and weak—was an opportunity he felt fate itself had bestowed upon him. He knew little about security procedures in the hospital, but if he couldn't get them there, he would wait. He had nothing else to do, no reason to live other than revenge. He would wait as long as necessary because nothing else mattered.

* * *

The doctor in charge hadn't allowed anyone to visit Genevieve or Jamie the night they were admitted. The next morning, after a shower, a shave, a haircut, and a new uniform, Peter returned to the hospital. Genevieve was sleeping. A doctor, the same man from the night before, was making notes on her chart when Peter arrived.

"How is she?"

The doctor looked up from his writing and eyed Peter as he sat in a chair next to Genevieve's bed. "I expect her to make a full recovery."

Peter nodded, glancing at the bandages on Genevieve's left shoulder. Her face was still pale, and the bruise from Kimby had turned purple, but she looked peaceful in her sleep. He was glad the pained look she'd had on the ship was gone. Peter brought his hand up to take hers but stopped when the doctor cleared his throat loudly.

"She needs her sleep."

Peter hadn't planned to wake her, but one look at the doctor convinced him to keep his hands to himself. "Sorry, sir."

"That's all right, Captain."

Peter's head jerked slightly at his new title. Baker had pushed Peter's promotion through last October, but he'd just learned of his advancement. The doctor turned and left. Peter watched him go, wondering why the man had seemed so pleased to call him captain.

* * *

It was a few days before Genevieve felt the fog of pain and pain medications ease. She woke from a nap to find Peter sitting in a chair beside her. It wasn't the first time she'd woken to find him nearby, but it was the first time Nathan hadn't also been hovering.

Peter had bruises on his face and swollen skin on his neck. "How are you?" she asked.

"I'm fine. The more important question is how are you?"

"Better than yesterday." She looked around the long hospital room. All the other patients seemed far away. "How's Jamie?"

"Improving."

"Did he recite his quotes on death yet?"

Peter laughed softly. "No, I asked him about them yesterday, and he told me to go away and let him sleep. He's kind of cranky when he's injured, but all the nurses seem to find him endearing."

"Hmm, I can think of someone else who's a cranky hospital patient."

Peter smiled and took her hand. "Guilty. But the nurses find me irritating, not endearing."

"There's something I've been wondering, Peter."

"Yeah?"

"When we were on the boat, what did Kimby mean when he said you'd gone to Yugoslavia to keep me out of Germany?"

Peter looked beyond her for a few moments. "Back in September, the day I left, he pulled me aside after the debriefing and asked me to leave on another mission. I was going to turn him down. I didn't want to go, and I thought you needed me. But he threatened to send you on a mission to Germany if I refused."

Genevieve squeezed her eyes shut, feeling tears run down the side of her face. "You didn't have to do that for me, Peter."

His finger followed the path her tears had made. "I'd do it again if it would keep you safe."

"He tried to send me to Germany anyway. Major Baker and Dr. Lombardelli stopped him."

"Maybe I wouldn't do it again," Peter said. "I'd kill Kimby instead. But if Baker and Lombardelli were helping you, how did you end up in Trieste?" He kept his eyes locked on her face, his expression full of concern.

"It actually started in Marseilles." She told him then, briefly, about the work she'd done in Marseilles, about her time in Bari, and about her decision to go to Trieste.

"I wish I'd been around to protect you," Peter said when she finished.

"You had to obey your orders. I've always known you're part soldier, part spy. I never wanted to be a spy, Peter. But everyone in my family stepped forward when they were needed, and so did you, so how could I sit on the sidelines when they needed my help?"

Peter brushed his thumb along the top of her hand. "Now that the war's almost done, will you retire from OSS?"

She nodded, and Peter seemed relieved.

"But there's more, Peter." She could feel new tears forming, but she pushed on, despite the emotion. "I killed a man."

Peter's hand froze, and he seemed surprised. But then he reached his other hand up to gently caress her face. "Do you want to tell me about it? You don't have to, but you can."

She leaned into his hand and closed her eyes, working up the courage to speak. "It was Rottenführer Weiss. He found me in Marseilles, and he was going to kill me. You remember what he did to you, and the things he did in Marseilles were even worse. I still didn't want to kill him, but he wasn't going to just shoot me; he was going to kill me a piece at a time. So I shot him. I see it happening all over again every time I go to sleep."

Peter was quiet. She'd wondered for months what he would think of her when she confessed to murder. He'd left a sweet, innocent girl behind, but she wasn't so innocent now. "Sometimes we have to do things we'd rather not do, but I think your heart is in the right place, so I think you should let it go."

"How can I let something like that go?"

"It was self-defense, Genevieve."

"You don't think I was wrong, then?"

Peter shook his head and wiped a tear from her cheek. "No, I think you did what you had to do. And I'm glad you did it."

"You don't think less of me now that I have his blood on my hands?"

"No, of course not. You're still an angel." Peter let his gaze fall from her face for a few seconds. "I've killed more men than I want to think about. I still see most of their faces in my nightmares. Some of them were bad men, but a lot of them were just doing their duty, obeying orders. I know the Lord doesn't like war, but I feel He's forgiven me for what I've done during it, and I'm sure He's forgiven you too. So leave it in the past."

He brushed his fingers through her hair, and she remembered the first time he'd done that. It was still comforting, just as it had been then, but it seemed like the memory was far in the past. "Sometimes I feel like I'm a different person now—like I'm not the same girl you met in Calais."

Peter's mouth pulled into a smile. "No, I don't suppose you'd give your brother a hard time for ruining a cake like you did the morning I met you.

But I imagine you'd still do something nice to make an orphan feel special on her birthday. And if you can find anything to regret in ending Weiss's life, I think that means you're still looking for the good in others like you did back then. War changes us all, but you're still a good person." He leaned over and kissed her softly on the forehead.

"Visiting hours are over."

Genevieve looked beyond Peter to where Nathan stood, his arms crossed and his face stern.

Peter turned around and brought his hand away from her face, but he didn't let go of her hand.

"Could we have a few more minutes, Nathan?" she asked.

Nathan nodded reluctantly but stayed close enough to overhear anything Peter and Genevieve said to one another.

Peter squeezed her hand. "Don't let what happened in Marseilles bother you, all right? Let it go, and keep getting better. I've got somewhere I have to be tomorrow morning, but I'll come see you in the afternoon."

"You're not getting another assignment, are you?"

"No, I'm not going anywhere until you're completely healed, even if I have to go AWOL. And by then, I'm hoping the war will be over and there won't be any more assignments." Peter glanced at Nathan, then he squeezed Genevieve's hand again and said good-bye.

She watched him walk away, wishing he could stay. Nathan sat in the chair Peter had just vacated.

"Are you all right?" he asked. "He made you cry, didn't he?"

"I'm doing better than I was, Nathan. And yes, I've been crying, but for me, that's part of the healing process."

"Who is he?"

Genevieve wasn't sure how to answer. She'd long thought of Peter as her fiancé, but they hadn't talked about marriage since September. "A ghost, Nathan. Someone I thought was dead."

CHAPTER FORTY-FOUR
"WHAT'S BEST FOR HER"

Tuesday, May 8, 1945

PETER SPENT THE MORNING OF V-E Day asking about POWs. None of the officers he spoke with had a comprehensive list of liberated Allied military personnel, but one of them suggested Peter try to contact Moretti's family. If Moretti was safe, he'd probably send them a telegram. Peter didn't have Moretti's address but resigned himself to shuffling through old OSS files in search of it as soon as he finished a few other tasks. First he had a package to deliver and a few hospital visits to make.

He found Marija in the hospital rec room. She sat on the piano bench, playing the left-hand notes of a song while Rick Shelton played the right-hand notes. She wasn't very good at the piano, and after a few errors, she laughed. Peter was glad. When he'd first seen her, she'd seemed so melancholy, so lifeless. She'd been briefly happy with Miloš, but grief had engulfed her so soon after her wedding. She deserved happiness again.

Peter walked to the piano and nodded at Rick. He'd met the airman a few days before at Genevieve's bedside. "Happy V-E Day," Peter said, grateful the war in Europe was officially over.

Rick and Marija both smiled and replied in unison. "Happy V-E Day."

Peter picked a book up from the top of the piano: *The Black Arrow* by Robert Louis Stevenson. "Is this yours, Marija?"

"Yes."

Rick glanced at the two of them and stood. "I'm going to find some soda. Would you like anything, Captain Eddy?"

Peter shook his head. "No, thanks. I won't be here long."

After Rick left, Peter opened Marija's book and placed a forged US passport and 500 British pounds between the cover and the front page.

Rumor was, all Yugoslav citizens would be forced home regardless of their wishes. The Communists would be in power there and would no doubt still be seeking the death penalty in the case of Marija Brajović Colić.

"Do you still want to go to the United States?" Peter asked.

She nodded. "I think my uncle will sponsor me. He lives in Pennsylvania. There's just all the paperwork and the waiting. I'm not the only refugee trying to get there."

Peter handed her the book. "A little something to expedite your journey. The money's from Jamie. Krzysztof and I pitched in for the other item."

Marija flipped through her novel, then opened the small booklet inside and gasped.

"It's not official, but no one will notice unless they dig through records at the State Department. You can go through the normal process if you want. But if there's a delay or if some other roadblock turns up, you can use this. We want you to be all settled in before the baby comes."

Marija nodded, tears in her eyes. "Thank you," she whispered.

Rick returned with two bottles of Coca-Cola. His eyes were focused on Marija, and Peter suspected the limping sergeant was falling hard for her.

"Better keep practicing that piano," Peter said, then walked to the main wing of the hospital.

When Peter arrived at Jamie's hospital bed, Jamie was preoccupied, kissing the beautiful nurse who was sitting on his lap. Doubting Jamie could have really fallen in love, Peter cleared his throat.

The nurse pulled away, startled. Her face turned red as she caught her breath. "I was just leaving," she whispered. She looked back at Jamie with a bewildered look on her face. Jamie gave her his classic charming smile.

"Come see me again?" he asked as she got to her feet.

The nurse nodded and rushed away.

"Jamie, you shouldn't do that. The poor nurse is going to fall head over heels for you, and you won't even remember her name."

"Her name," Jamie said, "is Vittoria, and she is the head nurse here. Her boyfriend since she was fourteen—Dr. Lombardelli's son—was in the navy. The Germans killed him on their way out. They suspected him of helping to orchestrate the Italian Navy's surrender to the Allies. Vittoria thinks he probably did but, of course, considers it heroism, not treason. She hasn't kissed anyone since he died, and I think she rather missed it."

Peter looked at Jamie with a hint of surprise: he knew something beyond hair color and dress size about the woman he'd kissed. Peter sat in a seat next to the bed. He'd been worried about Jamie's injury but assumed he was on the mend if he was wooing nurses. "I'm glad you're feeling better."

"So am I, and the nurse turned out to be a good source."

Peter laughed. "Oh? What does she know of interest to Allied Intelligence?"

"Not a source for them, actually. A source for you."

Peter cocked his head to the side. "A source for me?"

"Vittoria worked with your French girl."

"And?"

"There was a huge scene right before Genevieve left for Trieste. One of the doctors here, Bolliger by name, tried to stop her. They were in the hall, and Vittoria and several other nurses heard him begging her to stay and marry him. He kissed her in front of the entire hospital staff."

"Then what happened?" Peter asked.

"Genevieve left in tears. And Bolliger has been sad ever since, until Genevieve's return. Now he seems to be back to his normal, cheerful self."

Peter was silent with worry, thinking about what Jamie had told him. "And you're sure Vittoria is a reliable source?"

"Yes. And Bolliger is the one who repaired Genevieve's shoulder when we arrived."

Peter wondered if that explained why he'd been told to leave during her admission. And was that why she'd been so quiet on the flight from Vis? Had she been trying to sort out her feelings before she returned to Bari? He'd once been able to read her so easily, but now her emotions were more hidden. She'd said she felt like a different person from who she was when they met. Did that mean her preferences were different too? They'd been apart for eight months. Peter had thought if he still loved her, she would still love him. Now he realized just how groundless that assumption was.

A doctor. A doctor was a noble profession, and Genevieve was interested in medicine. She'd seen Peter be less than noble—lying, killing, stabbing Kimby in the ribs and kicking him in the face. All in the line of duty, but in the back of his mind, Peter had always thought she deserved someone better than him. "What type of man is Dr. Bolliger? Did Vittoria say?"

"He is trying to steal your girl, Peter; he might as well be Mussolini. Other than that, most of the hospital staff thinks rather highly of him. Competent. Good family. Treats the staff well. Everyone thought Genevieve was crazy to leave."

Peter's mood grew darker with each sentence Jamie pronounced.

"You really love her, don't you?" Jamie asked.

Peter nodded.

"Look, Peter, I brought all this up so you would know you have a rival. I meant to spur you to action, not discourage you. Vittoria seemed to think Bolliger initiated their kiss, and if Genevieve refused to marry him then—when you were dead—I think you still have a fighting chance now." Jamie lowered his voice. "And if you want to make sure he won't get in your way, I could pull a few strings for you, get him packed off to the Pacific."

"That would be cheating, wouldn't it?"

Jamie shrugged. "All is fair in love and war, old boy. This is both."

Peter stood, hoping it wouldn't come to that.

"Where are you going, Peter?"

"I'm going to look for Genevieve."

He needed answers. He walked through the hospital wing, but Genevieve wasn't there, so he went to look for her outside. As he left the hospital, he came face-to-face with Dr. Bolliger. He was taller than Peter and had fair hair and blue eyes. Peter froze, not sure what, if anything, he should say. He was tempted to punch the man for falling in love with *his* girlfriend. But Peter knew Genevieve didn't belong to him. Part of Peter was ready to fight for Genevieve, no matter the casualties. Part of him knew that having to fight for her love would only be proof that he hadn't earned it.

Bolliger spoke first. "May I have a word with you, Captain Eddy?"

Peter nodded cautiously. He followed Bolliger into the hospital, to an office, and sat when Bolliger motioned to a chair.

"I understand you've known Genevieve Olivier longer than a few weeks," Bolliger began.

"Almost a year."

Bolliger stared out the window. "I'd been expecting a dead lieutenant." Peter wondered if that was why Bolliger had been so pleased to call him captain a few days before. "I don't know everything about your relationship with Genevieve, but I understand you've been through some precarious events together."

Peter nodded.

"I love Genevieve," Bolliger continued. "I love her, and I would make her happy if she married me. But right now, she feels obligated to you, and until you release her from whatever it is you're holding over her, she won't be happy. You may have saved her life, but that doesn't grant you license to control it."

"I'm not trying to control her—"

"I am sick of seeing Genevieve manipulated," Bolliger cut him off. "She's been forced into espionage repeatedly, and it's not what she wants. She may be good at it, but she has other talents too, talents that would be put to better use in a safer career choice. As long as she's connected to you, she'll be pulled toward danger, and she won't be happy."

"I don't plan on staying with OSS or the army now that the war is over," Peter said. "I want her to be safe just as much as you do."

"Then why has her life been in constant danger since you met her?"

"Genevieve's life has been in constant danger since Adolf Hitler invaded France."

Bolliger's eyes narrowed. "And have you made it any safer? Any richer? Any happier? Think about it, Captain. I believe if you think about it long enough, you'll realize she's better off without you."

Peter was stunned into silence. Perhaps Bolliger didn't know it, but he'd hit on Peter's biggest fear. Genevieve's life had become more complicated since she met him. Peter's mistakes had led to her brother's death, and without her brother to protect her, she'd been talked into a mission in Marseilles, and Marseilles had led to Trieste. And what of the German helmet Peter had put on her head and the rifle shot it had attracted? Or the way Kimby had used her for bait and blackmail?

The truth was, her life *had* been in greater peril since Peter walked into her farmhouse last May. He'd never meant to endanger her or cause her pain, but he had, and he couldn't blame her if she decided to hold it against him. Yet Peter wasn't ready to give up. "Does she love you in return, Dr. Bolliger?"

Bolliger turned to gaze out the window. "If you are asking that question, then I think it means you don't know if she loves you. And if she doesn't love you, I think she'll come around to me before too long. If you really love her, Captain Eddy, you'll do what's best for her."

CHAPTER FORTY-FIVE
OCEANS AND ALLEYS

IULIANA STOOD ON THE BEACH, watching Anatolie and Krzysztof toss rocks into the ocean. Krzysztof had gotten a few of his to skip, and Anatolie was trying to mimic him. After a while, Krzysztof straightened and turned toward Iuliana with a smile.

"I have a gift for you, Iuliana."

"You do?"

She saw a sparkle in his eyes as he nodded and pulled something from his pocket. He hid it behind his back when she approached for a closer look. "You know how much I love Poland?"

Iuliana nodded.

"And you know how little I trust Stalin's promise that we'll have free elections?"

She nodded again. The same thing was happening in Romania—broken promises and what looked like a future scarcely better than the years of war.

"Peter and I went to visit one of our old teammates, Private Quill. He specializes in forged documents. We convinced him to do a little work for us."

He held out two British passports, and her hands trembled with disbelief as she took them. The first she opened had a picture of Anatolie with his correct date of birth. But it said he'd been born in Liverpool, and the name listed was Anton Johnson. The other book was hers. She was Juliana Johnson, also from Liverpool.

"I think my father's connections can keep my family in Britain for the time being. Will you come with me?"

Iuliana nodded.

"And let me visit you?"

"If a single day goes by and I don't see you, I'll be very cross."

"You'll want to see me every day?" Krzysztof smiled. "You know, seeing you every day would be easier if we shared a residence. Maybe my next gift should be an engagement ring."

"Does your father approve?" Marek Zielinski had been waiting when their flight arrived from Vis. Like his son, Marek was quiet and hard to read. She'd spent most of her time in Bari with the pair of them, until Marek had flown back to England. She still wasn't sure what Marek thought of her but knew Krzysztof respected his father's opinion.

"Before he left, my father mentioned that he and my mother have been waiting a long time for a grandchild and that it would be exceedingly convenient if I were to marry someone who already had a son."

Iuliana glanced at Anatolie, who was building a mound of sand. *It would be nice for him to have grandparents.*

Krzysztof put his hands on either side of Iuliana's waist, and she turned back to face him as he said, "But I made my mind up long before my father said anything. I never want to be away from you again." He was so close she could feel his breath and see the conviction in his eyes. "If you'll take me, that is."

"Of course I'll take you," she whispered. Their lips met, and like the other kisses they'd shared the past week, it was sweet and satisfying, sending shivers of pleasure all the way down to her toes.

* * *

Genevieve recognized Nathan's voice calling to her as she walked past the hospital, but she ignored it.

"Genevieve," he called again.

She turned and let him catch up to her.

"Don't you think it's time you came back inside?"

It had taken Genevieve what seemed like an hour to convince Nathan to let her leave the hospital that morning. Her primary motivation to escape was wanting to talk to Peter without Nathan hovering nearby, but she hadn't found Peter yet. "No, Nathan, I need more time."

"But it's getting chilly, and you need to rest your shoulder."

Genevieve looked at the ground, glad Nathan didn't know how much her shoulder hurt, or he'd force her back inside. "There are a few things I need to do before I return."

Nathan sighed. "That American captain?"

"Yes."

"Genevieve, he's made a career of violence and deceit. Do you think Germany's surrender will change that? Those are poor qualities for a long-term relationship. When you run into difficulties, he'll fall back on solving his problems with his fists and telling falsehoods to cover up his mistakes, and I don't want you on the receiving end of his bad habits. He's trouble, Genevieve."

"Don't be ridiculous. Peter would never hit me or lie to me." Genevieve turned to walk away, but Nathan's hand held her healthy shoulder.

"Are you sure? Even if you were certain of it last fall, a lot could have changed since then. Don't be foolish."

Genevieve eyed Nathan's hand until he released her. "I'm sure." She turned away, but his words made her pause.

"And how long will you wait for him? The army needs more junior-level officers with combat experience. Do you really think he'll survive the invasion of Japan? Even if he doesn't hit you or lie to you, loving him will only lead to heartbreak, so cut your losses now."

Genevieve had a sudden image of Peter leading a company of soldiers into a hail of Japanese machine-gun fire, and it terrified her. But she loved Peter, so no matter what his future held, she would fight for every day she could spend with him. "I love him, Nathan, more than anything. And I always will."

She rushed away from the hospital, but as soon as Nathan was out of sight, she slowed her pace. As much as she hated to admit it, Nathan was right; she should be in the hospital. She was in pain and exhausted and thought about going back, but she wanted to see Peter without an audience. They'd managed only one private conversation her entire time in the hospital. She wanted another one.

She found him several minutes later when she turned a corner and almost bumped into him.

He smiled when he saw her, but it wasn't the mischievous smile she loved. It was his serious smile, the one he used when he was worried about something, the one that made her nervous. "Hey, I've been looking for you," he said. "What are you doing out of the hospital?"

"I was trying to find you."

He seemed to hesitate, then he reached up and softly brushed his fingers along her cheek. She'd almost forgotten what Peter's simple touch could do to her heart rate. "I guess you found me," he said. She leaned into his hand, then shivered as the breeze picked up. "Are you cold?"

"A little."

Peter took his jacket off and helped her into it, being cautious with her injured shoulder. The jacket was warm, and it smelled like Peter, her favorite smell. "Come on, I'll walk you back. Find you something that isn't so big on you."

"It's too big on you too."

"I must have given them my old sizes. I'll grow back into it. Besides, I like it a little baggy. Makes it easier to hide things in the pockets."

Genevieve reached for the pockets, wondering if there was something currently hidden there. She hoped it was an engagement ring, but Peter took her hand in his before she could check.

He was quiet as they walked, and as they neared the hospital, Genevieve slowed her pace. "I don't think I'm ready to go back yet."

"How's your shoulder?"

"Fine." It was throbbing, but she didn't want to go back to Nathan's hovering.

"Genevieve, there's something I need to ask you, and I need you to be completely open with me. More frank than you're being about your arm. It's still pretty bad, isn't it?"

She stopped walking and stared at him. "How can you tell?"

"You get these little lines right here and here." Peter caressed the skin on either side of her lips. "I've noticed it before when you've been worried about something. Or when you're in pain. I should take you back. We can talk later."

Genevieve was flustered, surprised he could read her face so completely. But she could do the same with him, which was one more reason they were perfect for each other. Instead of heading toward the hospital, she led Peter into a nearby alley. "If we go back, it might be a week before we can really talk again. Nathan's being horrible. I suppose he has his reasons, but it's wrong of him to be so rude."

"He's in love with you. That's reason enough to keep me away from you, isn't it?"

Genevieve felt her face go hot. Was that was what bothering Peter? Had he heard what happened?

"I'm sorry," Peter said. "I didn't mean to make you uncomfortable."

Genevieve shook her head. "No, I owe you an apology. I let him kiss me before I went to Trieste. I didn't ask for it, and I wasn't expecting it, but I could have stopped it, and I didn't. I . . . . I was vulnerable. I'd been told you were dead, and there Nathan was, saying he loved me. He's a good man, and he's been a good friend, but I never meant for anything romantic to happen."

"Genevieve . . ." Peter looked away and swallowed a few times. "I'm sure he is a good man. He talked to me, and I believe him when he says he loves you." Peter glanced at her face before staring at the ground. "But before you choose him, I want you to know that I love you too. I don't think it's possible that anyone else could love you as much as I do. I still want to spend the rest of my life with you. But more than that, I want you to be happy, and I want you to be sure you've made the right choice. If you need time, I'll wait." Peter swallowed again and then, after a long pause, continued in a whisper. "And if you love Dr. Bolliger, I'll leave you alone and wish you nothing but joy."

It took Genevieve a few seconds to comprehend what Peter was saying. Did he really think she could be in love with someone else? She gently held Peter's chin and forced him to meet her eyes. "I think you've severely underestimated your hold on my heart, Peter." She stepped closer so that only inches separated them and stood on her toes, hoping a kiss would convince him of her love. But his glance shifted from her to something behind her, and he turned sharply and threw her into the brick wall of the alley.

Genevieve was shocked. Peter had never hurt her before, but she was sure her collision with the wall would leave bruises. She stared at him, her mouth open, too surprised to be angry. Had Nathan been right after all?

Peter stared past her into the alley, groaned softly, and fell to the ground. Only then did she see the knife protruding from his torso.

Chapter Forty-Six
"WORTH SAVING"

Genevieve gasped and knelt beside Peter. The closer she got, the worse it looked.

"Your boyfriend has quick reflexes."

Genevieve turned to see Basilco Ercolani approach from deeper in the alley. Peter must have seen Ercolani throw his knife and pushed her out of the way to protect her. Ercolani was still armed, and his P38 was pointed at her. She looked from the pistol back to Peter. He was conscious, and his lips moved, but she couldn't hear his words.

"Go ahead, watch him die. Just like I had to watch my Belina die."

Genevieve moved the torn shirt away from Peter's wound. Ercolani was right. Peter would die within minutes if nothing was done immediately. She met Peter's eyes and could tell he knew. "No, Peter, don't give up!" she sobbed. "I'll get you to a doctor, and he'll patch you up."

Ercolani chuckled as he walked past her, blocking the alley's exit. "There are no doctors in his future, just gravediggers, and the same is in store for you."

Genevieve grabbed Peter's handkerchief from his shirt pocket and pressed it into the worst of the bleeding. His hand pushed hers away. She put the handkerchief back on the wound and glanced at Peter's face. All the muscles along his jaw were tense with pain, his skin was pale, and his breathing was ragged and labored. But his eyes held hers.

This time when he pushed her hand away, she let him guide it to the pocket of the jacket she wore. She felt the outline of a handgun there and risked a glance at Ercolani. He still didn't seem to have noticed the significance of Peter's action. Genevieve slowly slipped her hand into the pocket, the movement hidden from Ercolani by Peter's body. Peter's breathing was weak, and the pool of blood on his shirt was growing larger.

"Let me get him some help." She gripped the pistol inside the pocket and pivoted it to face Ercolani.

"No. You can watch him die, and then you can join him."

Genevieve didn't want to shoot Ercolani, didn't want his face to visit her every night as a nightmare. She'd never wanted to kill anyone, not Weiss, not Ercolani. With the war in Europe over, she'd thought she'd never have to make a decision like this again. But as Peter struggled to breathe, she knew what she had to do, so she squeezed the trigger and shot Ercolani in the heart.

She leaned over Peter. "Hold on just a little longer . . ."

But Peter couldn't hear her. He was no longer conscious.

"Someone help me, please!" Genevieve shouted. She took off Peter's jacket and used it to staunch the blood flow. But the knife had struck through his ribs. The worst of the bleeding would be inside. *Don't let him die*, she prayed. *Not after everything he's been through, not before he knows how much I love him, not when the knife was aimed at me, and not when we're less than a block from the hospital!*

As if in answer to her prayer, she heard footsteps, and Krzysztof ran into the alley. He had his weapon out and paused to examine Ercolani, Genevieve assumed to make sure he was no longer a threat. "Iuliana!" he called as he bent over Peter. He grasped Genevieve's good shoulder. "Iuliana and I will bring him. Run to the hospital and tell them to get ready."

Genevieve nodded as Iuliana and Anatolie came into the alley, then she ran ahead of them. She burst into the hospital wing and saw Nathan and Vittoria.

"Peter's been stabbed. He needs your help." Her voice and hands were shaky, her breathing hard, but Nathan and Vittoria were used to emergencies.

They immediately started prepping the operating room. When they brought Peter in, Krzysztof carrying his shoulders and Iuliana lifting his feet, everything was ready. Vittoria gently tugged on Peter's dog tags to check his blood type, then went to prepare a transfusion. Nathan examined Peter's wound and glanced at Peter's face.

"In triage, I'd write him off as a hopeless case."

"Please, Nathan," Genevieve pleaded. "You don't have any other emergencies. Peter's strong; he'll pull through."

Nathan shook his head as he cut away Peter's shirt. "No, he and his men are young, but they've had poor nutrition for months now and several rounds of dysentery. He had pneumonia, a sprained ankle, broken ribs. He won't be as resilient as you remember. I'll do my best, but don't expect much."

Peter hadn't told her about his injuries or his illnesses. Nathan looked up at her, his eyes boring into hers, his voice hinting that he was upset. "And if he does survive, maybe it's time you stayed away from him. Like I said before, he seems to be a magnet for danger."

Genevieve felt her anger flare. "That knife was aimed at me. It was thrown by the same man who blew your car apart on the beach last March. I was the target then, and I was the target today."

Nathan's hands stopped their work but only for a second.

"You can save him, Nathan; you have to try," Genevieve begged as Vittoria returned.

"You had better save him," a voice behind her said. "Because if I think you let Peter die because you are trying to steal his girl, I will blow your head off." Genevieve turned to see Jamie in the doorway. Even without a weapon, he looked deadly serious.

* * *

Genevieve put another blanket over Peter's chest and ran her hands along the fabric until the wrinkles were gone. The hospital had a few private rooms reserved for officers of high rank. In the nearly empty hospital, the rank of captain had been sufficient for Peter to get one. Nathan had finished the surgery hours ago. Peter's face was gray, and he hadn't regained consciousness. Genevieve found his wrist under the blanket and felt his faint pulse. She studied his face and could tell by the way his muscles were set that somewhere in his comatose mind pain was registering despite the morphine Vittoria had given him.

"Don't die, Peter," she whispered, squeezing her eyes shut in a vain attempt to stop the tears. Peter hadn't mentioned pneumonia or dysentery or broken ribs. Could he recover from a wound this serious after all of that?

It wasn't until she heard a sound behind her that she opened her eyes again. Jamie limped into the room. He looked at Peter and then at her and reached for her hand. She didn't know Jamie well, but she did know that he too loved Peter. Enough to kill for him. So when Jamie pulled her to her feet and wrapped his arms around her, she leaned into his shoulder and sobbed.

* * *

Peter tried to open his eyes, but for some reason, he couldn't. His side burned with pain. He couldn't remember why—but it was bad. He tried to feel the source of his agony, but it was as if his fingers weren't connected to his brain. *Is my hand gone?* He couldn't remember being wounded, but he couldn't remember anything else either. He tried his other hand next, then his eyes again, but nothing worked like it was supposed to, so he gave up and slipped back into an uneasy sleep.

The next time consciousness returned, his eyes obeyed his brain when he told them to open. The first thing he saw was Genevieve. Her lustrous brown hair was pulled into a braid that lay across her shoulder. She'd missed a few hairs, but Peter thought the stray strands made her more attractive. She read through some papers attached to a clipboard, then looked up, met his eyes, and smiled. She found his hand and kissed him softly on the forehead. "Hello, Peter."

"Hi," he croaked. His brain seemed to switch on: the war was over, at least in Europe, and he was in Bari. He even recognized the hospital, though he still couldn't remember why he was a patient.

Genevieve helped him get a drink of water, then reached for his hand again. "I'm glad you finally woke up. You've been out for almost two days."

"What happened?"

"You don't remember?" A few worry lines appeared around her mouth.

Peter thought about it. "The last thing I remember is coming to see Jamie. I think he was kissing a nurse." Peter thought a little longer. "Everything after that is kind of fuzzy."

"Do you remember being stabbed?"

Peter shook his head. "No, but that explains why my side hurts."

"It was because of me. I'm sorry, Peter. I was so afraid you'd die and that it would be my fault again." He hadn't noticed before, but her eyes were red, like she'd been crying.

"Who was trying to kill us?"

"An Italian Fascist out for revenge."

Peter had a new memory float into his head, but he wasn't sure it was real. It was of him guiding Genevieve's hand to the pistol in his pocket, which he kept even on V-E day because Bari was full of Partisan liaison officers he didn't trust.

"Did you use my pistol to shoot him, the Italian Fascist?"

Genevieve nodded.

"I'm sorry you had to do that." He knew how she felt about killing, remembered her describing the nightmares she'd had after shooting Weiss. "He's dead?"

"Yes," she whispered.

"Are you all right?"

She forced a smile. "I've been worried sick about you, and my shoulder hurts, but it's getting better."

"And about having to shoot him?"

She looked away, blinking back a few tears. Then she turned to meet his eyes. "You were worth saving, Peter."

Peter was relieved the Fascist was dead. He was fed up with people trying to kill his girlfriend. *She is my girlfriend, isn't she?* Then he remembered Bolliger and the conversation in his office. That seemed real. So did another memory—worry that Genevieve was in love with someone else. Peter didn't realize he was frowning until he felt Genevieve's fingers on his cheek. He met her eyes, wondering why she wasn't with her doctor. "Why are you here?"

"Because I love you, Peter."

"You do?"

She smiled. "It might not have been love at first sight, but I think the second time I saw you, I could hardly breathe. And whatever that feeling was, it long ago grew into the strongest type of love. Even when you were dead, I never stopped loving you."

"Are you sure? You're not in love with someone else?"

Genevieve shook her head.

"You're not worried that I'll somehow get you killed?"

"That's a silly question to ask after saving my life yet again. But I am worried something will come up and you'll go off to the other side of the world and get yourself killed instead of staying here with me." She played with his hair, and he closed his eyes, savoring her touch. "Will you promise not to volunteer for anything else, not without my consent?"

"You want me to stay?"

"Yes."

"Then I'll stay. For as long as you want me."

Her lips curved into a smile. "I'll want you for a very, very long time."

It was good to see her smile again and to know he was the reason. "I remember an old attic in Rouen, France," Peter said as the memory came vividly to his mind. "You were scared of the mice, and I was teaching you how to pick locks. You were concentrating so hard, and I wanted to kiss you so badly, but I was afraid if I did, I wouldn't be able to stop. That's when I knew I wanted to marry you."

"Way back then?"

"Yeah, way back then." There were many things Peter wanted to say, but what came out was very simple. "I love you, Genevieve. Will you marry me?"

"Yes. There's nothing I want more than to be your wife." Genevieve leaned over the bed and kissed him, letting her lips linger on his. Then she trailed her fingers through his hair and brushed his ear with her mouth. "I should probably keep my kisses gentle, since you're recovering from a nearly fatal stab wound, but I'll make it up to you later."

"Hmm, I was just thinking your lips were a good distraction."

She smiled and kissed him again. She began slowly, softly, letting him feel again the shape of her mouth, the taste of her skin. As the kiss progressed, it became more passionate, and any remaining doubts about Genevieve's affections for him vanished. He pulled her closer, feeling a longing to begin their life together and relief that she would be his forever. If he ever caught his breath again, Peter knew marriage to Genevieve was going to be paradise.

CHAPTER FORTY-SEVEN
"WE HAPPY FEW"

Friday, May 11

PETER HAD A ROUGH NIGHT. The pain in his side interrupted his sleep whenever he dozed off, and it grew worse as the hours passed. Genevieve slept in a chair next to his hospital bed, and he didn't think it was the first night she'd slept there, but it was the first night he was conscious to notice.

"The pain's worse this morning, isn't it?" she asked when she woke up.

"Yeah." Bolliger had changed the bandages on Peter's side about an hour before, and he'd been a little rough. Peter suspected Bolliger had seen part of Genevieve's kiss the night before.

"Did you sleep all right?" She fingered some of his hair, putting it back into place.

"Like a baby." He closed his eyes and focused on Genevieve's fingers as the pain in his side flared again. "A colicky baby."

Genevieve kissed his forehead, then checked his chart. "No morphine, no codeine. Did Nathan give you something and forget to write it down? You're past due."

"Not that I remember."

She kissed him again, on the cheek. "I'll be back in a few minutes."

Peter heard part of the tongue lashing she gave Dr. Bolliger when she found him. Whether it was an honest mistake or an act of revenge, Peter wasn't sure, but he was grateful when Vittoria brought him some painkillers.

He slept for a few hours. When he woke, he let Genevieve assist him to a sitting position and managed to eat most of his soup. Then Genevieve brought him a toothbrush, a washcloth, and a clean shirt.

"Better?" Genevieve asked when he was finished.

"Yeah, better."

"I'm glad."

A knock on the doorframe pulled Peter's attention from his fiancée to Rick and Marija standing in the doorway. "Can we come in?" Rick asked.

Peter nodded.

"I'm sailing home tomorrow," Rick said. "Dr. Bolliger is headed back with some wounded men, and I thought I'd go with him. Anyway, I just wanted to say good-bye. And tell Genevieve thanks for all her help with this." Rick held up the stub at the end of his left arm.

"Are you ready to go home, Rick?" Genevieve asked.

"Yeah, I think I am. And it turns out Marija's uncle doesn't live too far from my parents' house. Small world, huh?"

Marija smiled. It was good to see her smile. "I bought a ticket, Peter. I leave tonight." She walked forward and sat in the chair next to Peter's bed. Genevieve and Rick walked into the hallway to give them a moment alone. "I don't think Yugoslavia will be safe for me."

Peter shook his head. "No, probably not."

"Do you remember the officer who questioned us when we arrived?"

Peter did. He'd been British, and they'd convinced him to investigate Kimby.

"He interviewed all the SOE officers Kimby debriefed and compared their reports. Kimby had skewed them and given credit to the Partisans for Chetnik sabotage. When field agents reported collaboration between the Partisans and Ustaše, he omitted it. When they reported collaboration between the Chetniks and the Serbian puppet government, he exaggerated it. The people making decisions about supplies read Kimby's summaries," Marija said. "It's hard to know how much damage he caused. I suppose it's sorted out now, but the man investigating wasn't sure they'd make it public. No one wants a scandal, and Tito's in power now. They have to work with him if they want to avoid war over Trieste."

Peter had heard bits about Trieste. The Partisans had arrived first, barely, but the German forces had held out so they could surrender to the New Zealand Army that arrived the next day. The Germans were gone now, but Partisan and New Zealand troops were still there in an uneasy truce.

"Of course, Tito might have won anyway, even without Kimby."

"I'm sorry, Marija."

She stared past him. "At least we know why everything happened the way it did." She was quiet, then her hands moved to her abdomen. "I went to visit the new doctor. My baby seems healthy. He even let me listen to the heartbeat. If it's a boy, I'm going to name him Miloš Peter."

Peter smiled. "After his father and his king. It's a good name."

Marija shook her head. "No, thanks to you, my child will be born in freedom. He'll have no dictator and no king."

"After the Apostle, then?"

"No. After you, Peter."

Peter was flattered but also surprised.

"You were a good friend to Miloš. You tried to save his life, and you managed to save mine. Thank you." She held up the passport. "And thank you for this."

"Will you be all right? Your uncle's in Pittsburgh?"

Marija nodded. "An uncle, an aunt, and five cousins. Rick's parents are only a half hour away, and he said he'd come visit."

"Rick seems like a good guy. An optimist, kind of like Miloš. You know, you've both come out of this war a little scarred, but I saw you playing the piano with him. You were smiling, Marija. And laughing."

Marija blushed. "It's too soon to draw any conclusions. But he's nice. And he helps me look on the bright side."

"If things do work out, maybe you should cut him some slack. Don't make him propose to you every day for a year before you agree to marry him."

Marija's blush deepened. "No, I won't do that again. If things work out." She was quiet, then said, "Do you think Miloš would mind . . . if I did get married again?"

Peter considered her question, thinking about Miloš. "Your husband loved you more than anything. He would want you to be happy. So if the opportunity for a good marriage presents itself, I think he'd want you to take it."

Marija's eyes teared up. "I miss him. But I promised him I'd be happy. Some days I have to remind myself of that promise every five minutes." She ran her fingers along the edge of the passport. "Sorry, I didn't mean to come in and cry. I need to get to the ship, but I wanted to say thank you. And tell you good-bye."

"You'll write to me? Let me know how everything goes with the move and the baby?"

"I will." She stood to leave. "Good-bye, Peter. Thank you. For everything."

* * *

Peter slept most of the afternoon. When he woke again, Genevieve was gone, but someone else was sitting in her place, someone Peter had mentioned in his prayers every day for the past eight weeks.

"How ya feeling, sir?" The deep voice was more familiar than the face, which was thinned and haggard.

"Moretti? What are you doing here?"

Moretti smiled his easy smile. "Bari seemed like a good place to start searching for answers. Thought I'd see if Krzysztof and Marija made it out, see if Iuliana was still around, find your girl and give her this." Moretti pulled Peter's Book of Mormon from his pocket and handed it to him. The letters were still inside. "I didn't expect to find you and Jamie here."

"Did Jamie explain what happened?" Peter asked.

"Yeah."

"What about you? The POW camp?"

Moretti stared at the floor. "They sent me to Stalag VII-A near Moosburg, in Bavaria. They stopped separating airmen from the other prisoners awhile ago, so I was with a hundred thousand other POWs. All in there together, behind double fences, getting a little skinnier each day. The guards were starving too, but I guess I never gave 'em much sympathy."

"I'm sorry—"

"Ah, you don't have to apologize, sir. I know you were trying to save my life." Moretti took a cigarette out and played with it but didn't light it. "There was a bet going around camp, everyone guessing who'd come first—the Americans, the Red Army, or the vultures. I bet on the vultures, but it ended up being our army. April 29, while you and Jamie and Krzysztof were floating in a yacht. I didn't believe it was really happening at first. The SS put a panzerfaust through the guards' barracks 'cause they weren't gonna fight, and the camp went crazy with rumors. I didn't wanna get my hopes up, ya know? But when they ran the flag up the flagpole, I knew it was true." Moretti glanced at his hands. "And I'll confess to you, sir. When I saw the flag, I cried—for the first time in twenty years." Moretti sounded like he might cry again.

"I'm glad you made it. I was afraid I'd blown your chance when I attacked Raditch."

"Some army officer asked me about him. Hegel too. Wrote up a report about it, but I don't suppose the Partisans left 'em alive to face trial?"

Peter shook his head. "No, they were killed."

"I saw Marija when I arrived, just before she left. She looked good."

"Yeah, she's going to Pittsburgh. And you? Are you headed home?"

Moretti nodded. "I've got extended leave, then I'm gonna train paratroopers at Ft. Benning so they can drop into Tokyo, I guess. Better them than me. I wanna be done."

"Yeah." Peter knew exactly how Moretti felt. The United States was still at war, but he never wanted to fire another weapon as long as he lived.

"I didn't read your letters. But I read a bit of your book. There wasn't much else to do in Moosburg."

Peter glanced at his Book of Mormon, then pulled out the letters he'd written to Genevieve. "Do you want to finish it?"

Moretti shrugged.

"Genevieve has a copy, so I can borrow hers." Peter held the book out, and Moretti stuck it back in his pocket.

"Well, it was good seeing ya again, sir, but I better get going. I ran into an old acquaintance and talked him into flying me home instead of shipping me home. Don't wanna miss my flight. And a couple Mother's Days ago I wrote my mom and told her I'd take her to Yellowstone when I got back. She's always wanted to see the geysers. The thing is, when I wrote it, I didn't think I'd live that long. But I'm still here, so I'll let ya know when we head out west."

Genevieve peeked around the doorframe and smiled when she met Peter's eyes.

Moretti stood and reached into another pocket. "This is for you, sir." He placed a nearly empty package of cigarettes and the unlit one from his hand on the table next to Peter's bed. "I know you don't smoke, but back in camp, we used those things like currency, so I ain't willing to throw 'em away. But I don't really wanna smoke 'em either. It was kind of a joke up in Moosburg: my lieutenant who didn't smoke 'cause it ain't healthy. I figure smoking's the safest thing I've done since enlisting, but I'm gonna give it up."

"You are?"

"Yeah, but I still ain't sure why." Moretti turned to Genevieve. "Pleasure to meet you, miss. Take good care of him, huh?"

Moretti saluted, and then, with half a smile, he turned to leave.

"Wait, Moretti," Peter said. He wanted to apologize again for sending him to a hellish POW camp, wanted to express gratitude for Moretti's loyalty and strength and friendship, but he couldn't find the right words. "Thanks."

Moretti ran a quick hand across his eyes. When he spoke, his voice was raspy. "Don't make me cry, sir. I'll see ya at Old Faithful." Then Moretti was gone.

Peter had to blink a few times to prevent tears from forming. Genevieve put her hand on his. "I gave him your parents' address while you were sleeping. He said he'd write."

Peter nodded. "Thanks." Peter's eyes fell to the papers lying on his blanket. "These are for you."

He watched Genevieve read her letters. She smiled, then she cried, and then she reached for his hand. "It looks like you came back to me after all."

She kissed him, and he kissed her back, wrapping his arms around her and gently holding her next to the uninjured side of his body, savoring each second.

"I missed you," he mumbled between kisses.

"Not as much as I missed you," she said, her hands in his hair. He kissed her again, not as gently as before.

A few minutes later, Peter heard someone clearing his throat. "And I thought you disapproved of patients kissing their nurses."

"Go away, Jamie," Peter said without bothering to look at the doorway. "Come back in five to ten minutes."

"Eww." Peter recognized Anatolie's voice.

Peter relaxed his hold on Genevieve and turned to the doorway. Jamie, Anatolie, Iuliana, and Krzysztof were all there.

"Someday you will understand, Anatolie," Jamie said. "But until then, you had best get used to it. I am sure you will catch your mother and soon-to-be stepfather doing the same thing."

Krzysztof glanced at Iuliana and smiled, then turned to Peter. "We're sorry to intrude, Peter. It's just that we're leaving first thing tomorrow, and we wanted to say good-bye."

"We came to see you yesterday and the day before, but you weren't conscious," Iuliana said.

Peter met Jamie's eyes. "You as well?"

Jamie nodded. "I have interviewed the new doctor. He is a good chap, and he will make sure you recover."

"Interviewed, or interrogated?" Peter asked.

Jamie shrugged.

"And Vittoria?"

"I scared her away when I threatened Dr. Bolliger. But don't worry, she thinks too highly of Genevieve to let it affect your care." Jamie grinned. "No huge loss. I still have phone numbers for a few dozen women in England. Some of them will no doubt find it possible to overlook my cane if I am taking them to the fanciest clubs in London."

Peter laughed.

Iuliana stepped forward and kissed Peter on the forehead. "Good-bye, Peter. Thank you for rescuing me, even if it was an accident. And thank you for keeping Krzysztof alive." She was crying. Peter knew Iuliana cried easily, but that knowledge didn't make it any easier for him to keep his own tears from forming. Iuliana gave Genevieve a hug next. "Cherish him. He's a good man, and he loves you."

Anatolie stepped forward and gave Peter a parade-ground-perfect salute.

Peter returned the gesture. "Good-bye, Anatolie. And good-bye, Iuliana. Good luck in England."

Iuliana smiled, then took Anatolie's hand and led him into the hall, leaving Jamie and Krzysztof.

Peter stared at the faces he'd come to know so well. *What do you say to someone when you've saved their life and they've saved yours and you've been through the worst life has to offer together? What do you say to the men you've starved with, to the man you've faced the firing squad with? How do you say good-bye, knowing it might be for the rest of your life?*

"The British postal system is both efficient and reliable," Jamie began. "And you Yanks have managed to corrupt most of the things you inherited from us, chiefly the language, but I hear good things about the US postal service."

Peter nodded dumbly.

Krzysztof seemed equally tongue-tied.

Jamie lifted one eyebrow. "'From this day to the ending of the world but we in it shall be rememberèd, we few, we happy few, we band of brothers.' I don't have a brother, Peter. But even if I did, I am sure fraternal bonds would seem weak in comparison to how highly I esteem you. Take good care of him, Genevieve." Jamie gave her a hug and slapped Peter on the shoulder.

"Thank you for the blow to the back of the head back in that unpronounceable Serb village." Krzysztof rubbed his neck as he spoke. "And for the other times you saved my life."

"Thanks for rescuing me from the firing squad. And for everything else." Peter hesitated, then repeated what he'd said the last time he thought he was saying a permanent farewell. "Have a good life, Krzysztof."

"The same to you, Peter. The same to you."

And then Jamie and Krzysztof were gone. Genevieve stood next to Peter's bed and slipped her hand into his. Peter looked up at her and was grateful when she understood what he needed and wrapped her arms around him so he could hold her. He was letting go of everyone else, it seemed, but not Genevieve. He could hold on to her for eternity.

Epilogue
GOOD FOR EACH OTHER

September 1945
Shelley, Idaho, USA

PETER CHECKED HIS WATCH AND smiled. He was getting married in less than six hours. It had been a long recovery, but runs along the beach in Bari and days working on his father's farm had brought him back to his normal weight and strength. He stood in the early-morning light and packed his things quietly, trying not to wake his cousin—his roommate since returning to Shelley, Idaho.

Yesterday, Genevieve and Peter had gone to the newly dedicated Idaho Falls Temple for the first time. Peter was amazed at the blessings promised and was comforted by how he felt at the day's end—like he'd been washed clean and healed of everything that had happened the last four years. Regardless of what he and his generation had been through, regardless of the nightmares that still haunted his sleep, and regardless of what might happen in the future, he was whole. Somehow, everything was going to be all right.

He paused as he picked up a handful of letters.

Rick Shelton had written, telling Peter and Genevieve about his acceptance to the University of Pittsburgh and reporting that Marija was settled into an apartment with a cousin. She lived near the school, so Rick stopped by often. He and Marija didn't have any announcements yet, but Peter suspected their relationship was growing into more than just friendship.

The next letter was from Krzysztof, postmarked from Cheltanham, where he and Iuliana had moved after their wedding.

Dear Peter,

You asked how Anatolie was adjusting to England. He's doing well. His English is improving, and he's learning Polish as quickly as he picked up Serbo-Croat. My parents are happy to have a grandchild nearby—they're spoiling him mercilessly. We still hope we'll hear from my older sisters, but the news from Poland is infrequent and outdated. For now, Anatolie is the only grandchild around, but that will change come spring and perhaps earlier if we have good news from Poland.

My father and I work together. I see Jamie on occasion. He's working with S5 and seems to have a new woman hanging about him whenever I see him outside the office. He often passes on his condolences that I'm chained to just one woman and asked me to send a similar condolence to you. Perhaps one day Jamie will settle down with one nice girl, but I don't expect it to happen soon. His loss, I suppose.

We spent last weekend with Jamie and his grandfather, who is in good health again. They acted out the sword fight from Macbeth *using their canes as swords and entertaining all of us, especially Anatolie. Jamie swears he'll pack the cane away before Christmas, and I think he's right. His limp has almost disappeared.*

Jamie is guilty of spoiling Anatolie almost as much as my parents are. Over the weekend, he decided Anatolie's hand would benefit from piano lessons, so yesterday a piano was delivered to our flat. Jamie must have forgotten how small our apartment is, but we made room for it. Iuliana said she prefers the piano to another cat, which Jamie has also threatened to purchase.

I'm not sure if this will arrive before or after your wedding. In any case, congratulations. Iuliana and I wish you every happiness.

All the best,

Krzysztof

Peter put the letter back in its envelope. If Krzysztof was working with his father, that meant he was cracking foreign codes for the British government. And Jamie working with S5 would mean Section 5, or MI5, counterintelligence with the British Security Service. Before the war, Jamie had been with MI6—foreign intelligence. The change made sense to Peter. Jamie was skilled at gathering information, playing a role, or recruiting a new source. But he was also proficient at tracking double agents. It was as if Jamie had an extra sense that could smell a Communist from across the room at a cocktail party. Peter suspected Jamie's talent would be put to good use and wondered if his thirst for adventure would ever be satisfied.

Peter felt his own craving for action was completely satiated. He planned to attend college and find a career that didn't involve risking his life on a daily basis. As he put the letters from Rick and Krzysztof next to a wedding card from Moretti, he smiled, thinking he should retract his earlier thought. Becoming a husband was, after all, an adventure of sorts, wasn't it?

* * *

Genevieve bit her lip to keep from singing. She'd roused Peter several mornings already with her songs and didn't think it was fair to interrupt his sleep just because he made her so happy.

Knowing she'd grown up near the sea, Peter had taken her to the Oregon coast for their honeymoon. The water was too cold for swimming, but they'd found plenty of other things to do. They would check out of the hotel in a few hours and were planning to stop at the temple on the way back to Shelley to do the temple work for her brother, sister-in-law, and parents. She was glad to keep a promise to her brother, to give him an eternity with his wife, but Genevieve didn't want to leave. Their honeymoon had been the best week of her life.

She studied the man she'd married seven days ago. Her husband, the man with a slightly crooked nose, mischievous brown eyes, a grin that still made her giddy, and twenty-nine scars—or was it thirty?—received while fighting the Fascists and the Communists. She'd counted them all a few nights ago but couldn't remember the total. She supposed she'd have to count them again but not while he was sleeping.

He lay on his side with his face toward hers. She was glad he was still asleep and that the muscles in his face were relaxed. He'd had a nightmare earlier that morning. It was the first of the week, which Peter said was an improvement, but it had been a bad one. Peter's thrashing had woken her, and by the time she'd shaken him awake, his face was covered in sweat and his whole body was trembling.

Her own nightmares had stopped back in May. She wasn't sure why—because she'd killed again, or because Peter had told her to let it go? Whatever the reason, she was glad they were gone and hoped Peter's would soon disappear as well.

He hadn't wanted to talk about what he'd seen in his dream. Genevieve thought some things were best left in the past, so rather than pushing him for more information, she'd distracted him. Peter's war demons might have followed him across the Atlantic, but she would be his angel and force them to retreat.

Peter's eyes cracked open, and a grin stretched across his face. He wrapped his arms around her and pulled her to him until his lips touched hers. "Have I told you how much I love you yet today?" he whispered.

"Not for a few hours."

"I love you."

Genevieve smiled and returned Peter's kiss. The scars in his memory, like the scars on his body, would never completely go away. But they would fade. And the same was true for her scars. Peter was going to be good for her, and she was going to be good for him, and it would be that way forever.

Author's Notes

I BEGAN RESEARCH FOR THIS book in 2006. At the time, I had a basic idea of what had gone on in Yugoslavia during WWII. In addition to the German conquest and occupation, I knew there was a vicious civil war between the Communists (Partisans) and the Royalists (Chetniks). When I started my research, my sympathies were with the Partisans. They were, after all, always the good guys in Alistair MacLean novels.

During my research, my feelings about the Yugoslav civil war changed. I learned of the horrible massacres of Serbs by both Ustaše Fascists and the German Army, and those victims gained my sympathy. I read accounts of OSS agents and shot-down US airmen who interacted with Chetniks and other Serb peasants who were willing to sacrifice their food, beds, and lives to keep the Americans alive and out of German hands.

Declassified documents have shown how Communist moles manipulated intelligence to make the Chetniks look bad and the Partisans look good. In the end, the Allies backed the Partisans because they wanted to be on good terms with whoever ended up in power when the war ended. The Partisans were easier to supply, and intercepted German communications led the Allies to believe they were the larger threat to the German Army. It was a self-fulfilling prophecy. As the Partisans were given more and more support, they did end up being the more powerful side of the civil war, and when the war ended, they had defeated their rivals.

Though the Chetniks earned my sympathy, none of the factions involved in the war were completely innocent. I could have changed the groups the Yugoslav characters in this novel belonged to and the book would still have been historically accurate. The Yugoslav civil war was a messy, horrible affair—just as previous and subsequent Balkan wars were and have been. The divisions run deep in that part of the world, yet I hope things will improve and the people there can be governed fairly and learn to love their neighbors, even when their neighbors' grandfathers mercilessly slaughtered their grandfathers and vice versa, depending on which war and which generation one is dealing with.

Estimates of civilian casualties in Belgrade during the April 1941 bombing campaign ranged from 5,000 to 24,000. Though fewer than 3,000 civilian deaths were registered during the action, Miloš's 17,000 killed was an oft-cited estimate. Miloš's recollection of the coup is also accurate. Brajović's description of the October 1941 massacre of Serbs from Kragujevac and Kraljevo is fact, though the number of victims is still disputed.

Along with other stretches of rail, Chetnik forces did target the line between Višegrad and Sarajevo in early September 1944, but the bridge over a ravine is a detail from my imagination. As shown in this novel, there were women in the Partisan Army, and pregnancy was outlawed. Partisan and German forces did exchange prisoners on occasion, though my research did not turn up examples of prisoners being left tied in a tent.

There were groups other than the Partisans, Chetniks, and Ustaše in Yugoslavia during WWII, but for the purposes of this novel, I've chosen to simplify rather than create characters from the Slovenian Domobrans, Bosnian Muslim groups, Montenegrin separatists, or other, smaller factions.

Phillip Kimby is loosely based on the infamous British spy Kim Philby and the lesser-known Communist sympathizer (and suspected Soviet spy) James Klugmann, who was an SOE officer in Cairo and then Bari and worked with the Yugoslav section. Klugmann's skewed reports were key in pushing Allied support away from Mihailovich toward Tito.

The prison camp on Bisevo did exist, but it wasn't well documented (at least not in English), so I filled in details based on Soviet gulags. Information about the Moosburg POW camp and its liberation are historical. So are the dangers Chetniks faced after the war. In May and June of 1945, thousands of Chetniks, Ustaše troops, and other Anti-Communist Yugoslav refugees were forcibly repatriated from Austria to Yugoslavia. Most of them were killed by the Partisans. The number of people killed in the Bleiburg repatriations is disputed, but most historians suggest the number reached or exceeded 20,000.

Even after the Allied liberation of southern Italy, Bari remained a hotbed of espionage, but Genevieve's work is fictional, as is Ercolani's. Details of the

Bari hospital are based on WWII medical facilities but are adjusted to fit the story. The situation in Trieste and the timing of the CLN uprising are fact, as are the timing and progress of the Yugoslav 4th Army from the area near Bihac to the Ingrid Line and on to Trieste.

Jamie's Shakespeare quotes are from the following plays: *Macbeth* 4.1, 61–62; *Twelfth Night* 3.1, 32–34; *Troilus and Cressida* 5.1, 86–87; *Titus Andronicus* 2.1, 58–59; *Cymbeline* 3.4, 85–86; *Macbeth* 2.3, 138–139; *Romeo and Juliet* 2.1, 85–86; *The Tempest* 1.1, 63–64; *Titus Andronicus* 2.3, 38–39; *3 Henry VI* 2.3, 30–32; and *Henry V* 4.3, 58–60.